PRAISE

Prickly Company

"*Prickly Company* has it all: romance, suspense, intrigue, and a community of quirky characters all learning to help each other. As a bonus, there are lots of lovable, prickly hedgehogs that will have you rethinking your landscaping situation. I loved every page of this book!"
   —Maddie Dawson, bestselling author of *Matchmaking for Beginners*

"Bursting with witty dialogue and plenty of hilarious moments, *Prickly Company* will enchant readers from the first page. I adored every quirky character and felt like part of the neighborhood by the end of this smart, funny, and charming novel."
   —Kerry Lonsdale, *Wall Street Journal* bestselling author

"*Prickly Company* is such an absorbing read, featuring a tangle of fascinating characters and a hedgehog's-eye view of the multitudes of things that can go very wrong—and very right—when they begin to cross each other's paths. Johnson's writing is warm and earthy, and the inhabitants of Hilltop Place—human and hedgehog—will stay with me for quite some time."
   —Suzy Krause, author of *Sorry I Missed You*

Five Winters

"This book is such a tonic. Entertaining characters, a heartwarming storyline, and an ending guaranteed to make you smile."
   —Imogen Clark, bestselling author of *Impossible to Forget*

CLOSEST
KEPT

OTHER TITLES BY KITTY JOHNSON

Prickly Company

Five Winters

CLOSEST KEPT

KEPT

a novel

KITTY JOHNSON

LAKE UNION
PUBLISHING

Published by Lake Union Publishing, Seattle

www.apub.com

Amazon, the Amazon logo, and Lake Union Publishing are trademarks of Amazon.com, Inc., or its affiliates.

EU product safety contact:
Amazon Media EU S. à r.l.
38, avenue John F. Kennedy, L-1855 Luxembourg
amazonpublishing-gpsr@amazon.com

ISBN-13: 9781662518102 (paperback)
ISBN-13: 9781662518096 (digital)

Cover design and illustration by Philip Pascuzzo

Printed in the United States of America

For Ann Warner, with thanks for her clarity and insight

Fire that's closest kept burns most of all.

—*William Shakespeare, The Two Gentlemen of Verona*

1

"I bet you're glad I forced you out this evening, huh? Those guys are gorgeous."

Inga was touching up her sparkly eyeshadow in front of the mirror in the ladies' toilets, trying not to dislodge her Christmas reindeer antlers as she did so. Even with the door closed, I could still hear the festive music pumping from behind the bar. With two days to go before Christmas, the city was exactly how I'd imagined it would be, packed with girls in shiny dresses and guys with mistletoe and smooth chat-up lines.

Hideous. My worst nightmare.

Which was exactly why I hadn't wanted to come out tonight. All that glittery exuberance. The compulsion to be jolly. The complete lack of acknowledgement that, for some people, the festive season was the pits.

I'd much prefer to be at home trying to drive old memories away with a gripping book. But Inga was like a kid about Christmas, and Inga was my best friend, so here I was.

And it wasn't as if I hadn't got through plenty of nights like this before; I could do it again. Besides, Inga would be on her way to see her mother in Denmark tomorrow, so I'd have all the time in the world to hide out until the festivities were over. And I had to admit she was right; the guys were gorgeous, so maybe it had been worth letting Inga drag me out, after all.

Matt, the dark-haired one, was a big bear of a man you could imagine hugging. Alex was slimmer, with blond hair, blue eyes, and a body to die for, tapering from broad shoulders. We weren't the only appreciative women in the bar—I'd seen every female eye in the place checking them out when they walked in. Which probably meant it wasn't a good idea to spend too much time in the ladies' cloakroom.

"So, what are we going to be tonight? Air hostesses? Chefs? Company directors?" Inga asked.

Inga and I were both artists, but she rarely wanted to tell people that because it inevitably led to lame jokes about modern art.

"Can't we just be ourselves for once?"

"I do more waitressing than creating these days," she said, putting her eyeshadow back in her bag, her expression momentarily bleak.

"Oh, Inga," I started to say, but she pushed my sympathy aside.

"Look, it's Friday night, it's Christmas, and by some miracle I've got the night off. I don't want to spend my precious time debating whether a pile of bricks or an unmade bed count as art. Or to pretend to die laughing when some dimwit who thinks he's God's gift to witticism makes some crack about us being piss artists, not artists."

She hitched her bag onto her shoulder and headed for the cloakroom door. "Come on, babes," she said, "this is just a bit of Friday night fun, okay? The blond guy—is he Alex or Matt?"

"Alex."

"Alex is not going to get down on one knee and ask you to marry him at the end of the evening."

I got the message straightaway. Inga liked Matt. Which was a shame, because so did I. It was predictable that Inga would like him, though. She always went for guys with brown eyes if there was a choice. With her Scandinavian heritage, she said she'd had enough blue eyes and blond hair to last her a lifetime.

"I take it you fancy Matt, then?"

She glanced back, giving me puppy-dog eyes. "D'you mind?"

I smiled, as usual unable to deny her anything. Which was the whole reason I was here, drowning in pre-Christmas celebrations instead of at home in my pyjamas in the first place wasn't it? "No, that's fine. Alex seems really nice." Less complicated than Matt too. Less likely to ask me lots of questions I didn't want to answer. Someone perfect for a casual relationship. "Though there's no guarantee he's into me."

"Trust me, he's into you. The guy could barely tear his eyes away, you amazing marine biologist, you."

I raised my voice as we headed out of the ladies' cloakroom into the buzz of the bar. "Oh, no, I'm not being a marine biologist again. Or a firefighter, or a trapeze artist."

Inga smiled, pressing on through the crowd. I could see Alex and Matt waiting for us, pressed in on all sides by preening, giggling women.

"You were amazing as a trapeze artist."

"Yeah, except for my terminal fear of heights."

"Well, you didn't exactly have to actually dangle upside down and swing across a big top, did you?" Inga pointed out.

"No, but I had to talk about doing it. That was enough to give me vertigo."

We were almost back at our spot at the bar. As normal, Inga would make the decisions about how the conversation would go. I didn't really mind. It was usually fun being in Inga's riptide. Having to improvise and think on my feet. And it was an effective distraction from the depressing tackiness of Christmas in the city.

We'd started inventing professions for ourselves years ago after we'd met at art college, as a way of avoiding having to justify or explain what we did to people who would never understand in a million years. Somehow, it had carried on.

"There you are," said Alex, his eyes smiling at us both, but lingering on me. "We thought something had happened to you."

"Well, the hand dryer did look a bit threatening, didn't it, Lily?" Inga said. "Like it might suck us right into some sort of vortex or something if we used it."

I shivered dramatically, playing along. "Yes. We decided to drip-dry to be on the safe side."

Matt laughed, the skin next to his eyes crinkling. I decided his eyes weren't a straightforward brown. That, if you were going to paint them, you'd need to add some honey gold to the raw umber; maybe with a touch of burnt sienna, too, if you wanted to get the shade exactly right.

"Listen," said Alex. "We were wondering whether you'd mind getting out of here? Going someplace quieter?"

Inga and I exchanged glances.

"Not somewhere like a dark alleyway or a deserted park," Matt said quickly.

I saw the way Inga was looking at him and suspected she wouldn't say no to going to either venue with him after she'd had a few more drinks.

"Where, then?" I asked.

"To a restaurant? To get a bite to eat?"

"Yeah," Alex said. "Our parents have gone to a party together, and every bit of food in our houses is earmarked for Christmas."

"You guys both still live with your parents?" Inga said disbelievingly, at the same time as I saw the boys exchanging glances—Matt's saying, *What did you say that for?* And Alex's, *Whoops, sorry.* It was quite sweet.

"Like I said," Matt said, "we've been away travelling. Now we're back, we're going to get a flat together."

"How long were you away?"

"Six months," Matt said.

"We went all over," Alex added. "Working as we went to pay our way. It's been a blast."

I bet it had. World travel was what me and Inga had always said we'd do. But so far we'd managed only a couple of package holidays. I was jealous as hell. And eager to hear more. Somewhere quieter where we didn't have to shout to be heard sounded fantastic. Even though Inga and I had scarfed a giant pizza before we'd set off tonight and I wasn't in the least bit hungry.

"Well," said Inga, taking Matt's arm, "let's go, then. And by the way, I predict you'll find an amazing flat somewhere high up, with city views."

"Oh, you can predict the future, then, can you?"

Inga nodded. "Didn't I tell you? We're both fortune tellers."

Oh, wow. This was going to be fun. And at least it would be a distraction from the relentless festive cheer.

Ten minutes later, after a brisk walk along frostbite-inducing streets, we were in an Italian restaurant waiting for Alex's and Matt's pasta and mine and Inga's strawberry ice cream to arrive. Inga had hold of Matt's hand across the table and was pretending to read his palm. She'd gone all trance-like—a spookily accurate re-creation of Madame Rosa, a fortune teller who we'd both consulted on a weekend break to the seaside in the summer.

I hadn't wanted my fortune told at all, because if there was the smallest chance of finding out that your future was going to be as bleak as your past, why would you? But Inga wouldn't go in unless I did, and suddenly a consultation with Madame Rosa seemed to have become the whole reason she'd wanted to go to Brighton. So, not wanting our weekend to be soured, I'd reluctantly agreed.

Inga went first, while I sat cynically at the back of the booth, listening to Madame Rosa as she told Inga she would find hidden jewels in her life. That something would happen that would feel like a disaster, but which would actually turn out to be a miracle. For months afterwards, I asked her whether her disaster had happened yet.

If Madame Rosa had told me I'd find hidden jewels, I'd have questioned her further, cynical about her talents or not. *Do you see me ever finding my family?* I might have asked. But she didn't say anything like that to me. She said I'd have to work hard to get what I wanted from life—something I could have told her myself. My life had never been easy: living in hostels, working several different jobs to fund my higher education. Why should things be any different in the future?

Especially as I was set on being an artist. Artists always had to work hard to get anywhere.

In the restaurant, Inga was throwing everything into her fortune-telling role. I hoped she wouldn't go as far as doing the eyelid-fluttering thing Madame Rosa had done. It had been a bit scary, and definitely unpleasant, to keep seeing the whites of her eyes.

Matt was smiling, enjoying being the focus of Inga's attention. It wasn't difficult to predict his immediate future. The waitress who'd taken our order could probably do it. Matt was going to eat his pasta, drink his wine, laugh at Inga's jokes, then take her home to make passionate love to her. All while getting his head round the fact that his fortune teller slept in a room that was a shrine to surrealist art and there was a doll's head pierced by a thorny stick looking at him from Inga's dressing table.

I sensed that he wouldn't care about such eccentricities, though, because he seemed pretty smitten. I wondered whether Inga could tell that, whether she minded. Whether she was, for once, contemplating more than just a one-night encounter. I'd never known Inga to have a serious relationship since we'd first met.

"D'you want to read my palm?" Alex asked me, holding out his hand, palm upwards.

"I don't read hands," I said. "I'm a tarot card kind of girl."

I wasn't, not really. I didn't believe in fortune telling at all, or any other kind of fairy tale. But I did at least like the illustrations on tarot cards, and I liked to try to keep an element of truth in my story when Inga and I invented our professions.

"Tarot cards, eh?" said Alex, not withdrawing his hand, his eyes devouring mine. They really were very blue.

"Yes. And I only use a pack I designed myself."

"You designed a pack of tarot cards?"

I did. As part of an art project. I used them in a giant mixed-media painting about fates that was currently taking up space behind my sofa, along with eight or nine other paintings.

"You must be an artist as well as a fortune teller, then," Alex said, and I felt Inga looking at me and knew she'd be frowning. *Don't give the game away!*

I kept my tone casual. "I guess so."

Alex picked up his beer. "Matt and I had our fortunes told when we were in China. Not with tarot cards, though. She used these sticks. What were they called, Matt?"

"*Kau chim* sticks."

"What did she tell you?" I asked, but Inga said something to Matt, reclaiming his attention, so it was just Alex who answered.

"That one day I would meet a dark-haired girl with green eyes who would change my life."

I couldn't help laughing. "Was the fortune teller really as corny as that?"

He smiled, a cute lopsided smile, like a little boy. "How can it be corny if it's true?"

The waitress brought our order, effectively ending the fortune-telling chat. For around thirty seconds there was only the sound of the grating pepper mill and the boys' deep appreciation of their food. Then a family came into the restaurant—a family, at nine o'clock on a Friday night. The little boy was wearing a Santa hat and a giant badge that proclaimed he was four today, so perhaps it was a birthday treat. Either that, or the parents were at their wits' end, searching for a distraction, because the boy's little sister was crying her head off in her buggy.

The sound went straight to my gut the way it always did when I heard a distressed child, making me think of my sister crying helplessly in the middle of the night.

Inga was glaring in their direction. "Great. I predict an end to our peaceful meal," she said under her breath.

"They'll settle down when they get pizza," Matt said easily. Then, "So, what do you girls really do for a living?"

Distracted by the crying, I let Inga answer. Saw her look mock offended. "Are you accusing us of lying to you about being fortune tellers?"

Matt grinned. "Er, yeah."

Inga put a hand to her chest. "I'm wounded to the heart. No, to the soul."

Alex laughed.

I found my voice again. "We're artists. That is, when we're not waitressing, serving in shops, cleaning, or doing practically anything except childminding."

"Lily and I have taken a vow never to have babies," Inga said.

It was true, we had, and every time I encountered a child like the distraught kid at the neighbouring table and it plunged me straight back into bleak memories, it was a decision that was reaffirmed for me. But what was Inga doing bringing it up when we'd only just met these guys?

"How did you guess we weren't fortune tellers?" I asked Matt to change the subject.

He shrugged. "Call it a hunch."

"Tell us about the real you," urged Alex. "What do you paint?"

Inga was attacking her ice cream. "I don't paint; I construct. Lily's the painter. She will only paint seals at the moment, though."

"Seals?" asked Alex, smiling.

"Yeah," said Inga. "You know, big eyes, swim in the sea, look a bit like Labrador dogs? She's totally obsessed with them. Seals swimming in the sea. Seals basking. Seals rolling on the sand. Cute seals. Scary seals. Seals, seals, seals."

It was true; or at least it was for the moment. I didn't expect to be painting pictures of seals forever.

"Why seals?" Matt asked.

I shook my head, unsure whether I'd be able to adequately put my fascination into words.

"Well, they live in the sea, and I've always loved paintings of the sea. There's this one artist in particular I like—Joan Eardley. One of her sea paintings was in an exhibition here once, and I just stared at it for hours."

It had been years ago now, but I could still remember the way I'd connected with that painting. Maybe the crashing, pulverising waves had felt like the storms I'd weathered in my own life, I don't know. But as I stared at the painting, I imagined the life which might be living beneath the surface—creatures swimming effortlessly, in their element, safe from the storm.

"Anyway, I went to the North Norfolk coast for a walk a few months back, and there were hundreds of seals on the beach with their babies. Literally hundreds of them, and swarms of people coming to visit them, to go ooh and ah and take photos. Some had no clue. They thought they'd be able to go right down on the beach to get close to the poor things. That it would be okay to put their children on the seals' backs to get a snap for their Instagram. There were these volunteer seal wardens there to stop them and to educate them about the seals. I volunteered myself the very next day. And when we had to take some injured pups to a rescue centre, I started to go and help out there too."

"And you dragged me to that amusement park that time," Inga added. "I thought we were there for the roller coasters, but no, it was the performing seals."

"That was just sad," I said, remembering. "Seals belong in the wild. Out in the ocean, not performing tricks for an audience. I love the way the ocean transforms them. I could watch them for hours."

"We went swimming with fur seals when we were in New Zealand, didn't we, Matt?" said Alex, and proceeded to transfix me by telling me all about it.

By the time he'd finished I was envious and filled with so many thoughts and feelings I could have gone straight home to paint. But judging by the way Alex was looking at me, I knew that wasn't what he had in mind at all, and I decided that was fine by me. It had been a long time since anyone had looked at me like that. A long time since I'd felt like responding. Painting could wait.

Across the restaurant, the little girl was still crying. My head was starting to ache, and it was getting harder to keep bad thoughts at bay.

I glanced over. Saw the parents tiredly shovelling down their plates of pasta. The little boy with tomato paste from his pizza smeared all over his face and up his arms. The dad had given up trying to get his daughter interested in her food. If anyone knew what it was like to be powerless in the face of a child's crying, it was me. But with the past crowding in on me, I was totally incapable of summoning a sympathetic smile.

It was time to go.

Alex and Matt had just about finished their meals. "Listen, does anyone fancy a walk by the river?" I asked, suddenly wanting to put as much distance between me and that very unhappy little girl as possible.

"It's on the way to our flat," added Inga. "We've got coffee. At least, I think we have, haven't we, Lil?"

"Yes," I said, managing a smile. "We've got coffee."

"Come on, then," she said. "Let's go."

Half an hour later we were back home drinking coffee and looking at my latest seal painting.

"It's beautiful, Lily," Matt said, and I got a glow because I could tell he meant it. "Exactly what it was like when we were swimming with those seals in New Zealand. Isn't it, Alex?"

Inga spoke quickly to Matt, before Alex could reply. "I've got a heap of etchings next door you can take a look at if you feel like it."

"Sure," Matt said with a grin, and they sloped off to her room, hand in hand.

Alex smiled at me. There was a pause. And when he asked, "What is it you like about seals?" I wondered if he was shy.

"You mean apart from their cute faces?"

"Yeah, apart from them being Labrador-puppy look-alikes."

"Puppies with flippers."

"And a strong liking for fish."

We smiled at each other. I stroked my hand down the velvety nap of the sofa arm while I thought about how to put it into words.

"I love the ballet of their movement when they're underwater. Their effortlessness and grace as they twist and turn. The contrast between that and the way they lollop along on the ground like giant slugs."

"Giant slugs?"

"Yes. They have to bunch their bodies up and push themselves forwards. It looks so difficult to get along like that, and yet they still do it. That gives me hope, I think."

He wrinkled his brow. "Hope about what?"

I shrugged. "About life, I suppose. Being an artist can feel like being a seal bunching itself along in the sand sometimes. You have to do work you hate, just to pay the bills. Walk to places because you can't afford a car. Half the time all of that makes you so tired you haven't got the energy to make art. But then there are times when everything comes together, and you've lost yourself in your art, and you're like a seal who's finally reached the waves and can suddenly really be itself. Twirl and spin and dive. Be fluid and free. It's magical."

That was what I'd been thinking about as I stared at the Joan Eardley seascape—about the freedom of swimming beneath those stormy waves. Of having the whole glorious unseen ocean to do what I liked with.

Alex looked at me, nodding, thinking about what I'd said. I wasn't usually this open with people; certainly not when I'd only just met them, anyway. But Alex wasn't smiling as if I were some dumbass idiot. He didn't try to make a joke of it, and he wasn't running out the door because I was this crazy, overly intense woman talking about seals and slugs and twirling in water instead of making out with him. So maybe it was okay to have opened up a bit.

I liked the pale blue of his eyes, like Wedgwood china. The way the overhead light picked out the shine of his hair, accentuating his cheekbones. Matt had dazzled me when we'd first met, but now that it was just me and Alex, I could see how attractive he was. And it really was nice to have someone so interested in what I had to say.

"D'you think you're only really you when you're creating? Is that what you're saying?"

"No, but that's when I'm the most me."

"What about with friends or with lovers? When you're not pretending to be someone you're not?"

I shifted slightly away from him, returning the conversation to safer ground. "Hey, you liked me being a fortune teller."

"I never believed you were a fortune teller."

"Come on, you so did."

"Oh, all right, maybe for just a little while. But I'm glad you're not. It must be so hard if you're able to predict the future if you're looking for love. You'd take hold of someone's hand, and you'd know straightaway if it wasn't going to last."

"But I guess you'd also know straightaway if they were the one."

"True, you might. Do you believe that, then? That there's one person on the planet who's right for you? Your other half?"

I shook my head. "Not really. People would never get together, would they? Mathematically speaking, it's just not possible."

"Well, if we're talking about mathematics, what's the probability of two guys going out to celebrate getting back from a trip round the world and meeting the girls of their dreams in the very first bar they go into?"

"Did your parents try to stop you from travelling?"

He put out a hand, laid it on the space between us on the sofa. "No. They weren't very happy about it, but they didn't try to stop me. They trusted Matt would look after me, I guess. They've always liked Matt."

"Who was looking after Matt?"

"Matt doesn't need looking after."

I didn't know Matt, but even so, I could sense it was true.

"Do you need looking after?" I asked him.

"No, not really. Not any more than anyone else, anyway. What about your parents? Did they support your decision to be an artist?"

It was a logical question. My fault for bringing up the subject of parents, I supposed. But certainly not a conversation for a first meeting. Or a second, or a third.

Maybe it was time to stop talking.

"I had the freedom to do what I wanted to do."

Alex nodded, looking at me. I guessed he probably sensed there was more to my answer than I was prepared to share just then. He looked away from me, back at the seal painting. I looked, too, remembering the joy I'd felt painting it.

"So, I don't suppose seal seduction techniques are very pretty?" he said, drawing me back, making me snort with laughter.

"Er . . . no. The poor females are on the beach with their pups, and the bull seals want to mate before the pups are even weaned. They lollop towards them, fighting any rivals as they go, not caring about any babies that get in their way." I shuddered. "It's horrible."

"A bit different to meeting in a bar, then?"

"Oh, I don't know. Me and Inga have come across some pretty bullish guys in our time. Guys who think they own a space, standing there with their chests puffed out, looking around for a girl to target. Squashed up next to you with their manspread thighs and their arm around the back of your chair. *'Where've you been all my life, darlin'?'* One look at them and you know they'd be splashers in the water. Dive-bombers, not twirlers."

Alex was grinning. "What's your prediction about my swimming skills, then?"

I slid my hand across the space to entwine with his. "I'm not a fortune teller, remember? So, it's more of a theory than a prediction."

"Oh, yes?"

I nodded. "Mm-hmm. But I think someone who's prepared to talk to me, to try to find out about the real me, is more likely to twirl than to lollop."

He moved towards me, looking at my mouth. "Want to see if you're right?"

"Okay, then," I said, moving to kiss him.

2

"Where did you say you were spending Christmas?" Alex asked me much later, after a very satisfying demonstration of his twirling techniques.

"I didn't," I said, running a hand down his smooth, suntanned chest. "But I'm going to see my great-aunt. In Hampshire."

He propped himself up on one elbow to look down at me. "Will there be many other family members there? As in, such a crowd of you that you won't be missed if you don't show up?"

I shook my head, listening to myself trot out my usual answer. Alex and I may have just slept together, but we were still strangers, really, so lying to him didn't feel so bad. "No, it will be just the two of us, as in, my aunt's depending on me."

"Pity. I was going to suggest you cancel and spend Christmas with me and my family."

"I'm sure your mother would love that."

"Listen, Mum was so terrified me and Matt wouldn't be back from our travels in time for Christmas she wouldn't complain if I'd invited everyone from the pub to join us for dinner." He reached out suddenly to grab me, pulling me in for a kiss. "Please, Lily," he begged when we surfaced again. "Please phone your aunt. Tell her there's been a rail strike. Tell her you've got an allergy to Christmas. She'll understand. She's a very understanding person."

"You know nothing about her," I pointed out.

"True, but she's related to you, isn't she? And you're perfect in every way."

"Sorry," I said. "No can do."

He sighed and flopped down onto his back. "I'll really miss you."

"Alex, you've only known me for five minutes."

"Five hours and five minutes actually," he corrected me, stroking a hand down my thigh, making me tingle with desire all over again.

But there was no way I would change my plans, so Alex had to make do with sizzling sex and a promise that we'd meet up as soon as Christmas was over.

The next morning, Inga and I called to each other through our open bedroom doors as we packed our suitcases.

"What a night. I really, really like Matt."

"Yes, you said already. About fifty times."

The boys had left earlier, and ever since then, Inga had been mooning about, doing nothing very constructive, checking her phone every five minutes for messages.

"You do like Alex, don't you?" she asked me now.

"Yes, I like Alex," I said. I knew it was what she wanted me to say. And it was true; I did like Alex. I just had no idea whether or not it was going to lead to something. Whether I even wanted it to. And now wasn't the time to speculate about it. We'd see how things were after the whole wretched business of Christmas was done with.

"Well, then!"

I wasn't sure exactly what point Inga felt she'd proved. I just wished she'd hurry up with her packing. At this rate she wouldn't be finished by the time her taxi arrived, and if it drove off without her, she'd miss her train. And if she missed her train, she'd also miss her flight. Inga is half Danish, and her mum lives in Copenhagen.

"Your mother will never forgive you if you aren't on that flight."

"Ha! Nothing I do is right for her, anyway. If I miss my flight, I can just come to Hampshire with you."

My brain whizzed into overdrive, conjuring up unpleasant images to put her off. "You won't enjoy it. Auntie Alice isn't exactly a great conversationalist. And her house is like an ice box. You think this place is cold—believe me, it's a positive sauna compared to Auntie Alice's house. Oh, and she has three cats." Inga loathed cats. "The whole house stinks of cat wee."

Inga appeared at my bedroom door, suitcase in hand. "Why d'you bother going there year after year, then? I hate that I miss your birthday every year."

I avoided her gaze, managing to quip, "My fault for being born on Christmas Day."

"Sweetie, I'm not sure that was entirely your fault." She looked at her watch. "God, I really had better get going. I wish you could have at least caught an earlier train. We could have travelled part of the way together."

I zipped my suitcase up and joined her as she went downstairs. "I told you; the connections work out better if I travel in the afternoon."

Lie after lie after lie. But I'd been telling them to her for years, so I really ought to be used to it by now.

As we reached the front room, I saw a car pull up outside. "Look, here's your taxi. Come here and give me a hug."

She bundled herself into my arms, and I closed my eyes, inhaling the scent of her strawberry shampoo as I held her.

"Have a great Christmas and birthday, kiddo. Ply your aunt with whisky, and you'll soon have her playing charades and pulling wishbones like a pro."

"Good thinking," I said. "And you remember to count to ten in Russian every time your mum says something annoying."

"Why Russian?"

"It takes more concentration. And if that doesn't work, think of Matt and all the fun you're going to have when you get home."

The taxi driver blasted his horn outside, and Inga disentangled herself.

"I'm not sure that's a good idea," she said, trundling her suitcase to the front door. "If I start thinking about what I'd like to be doing with Matt, I'll be heading straight for the airport to come home."

"See you in a week," I said, blowing her a final kiss.

"See you, gorgeous," she said, flashing me a smile, and then she was gone, the front door closing behind her, her boots clomping down the garden path.

I stood there, waiting for the taxi to disappear. Then I locked the front door, put a ready meal in the oven and went upstairs to unpack my suitcase. I wasn't going to see my great-aunt Alice at all. Great-Aunt Alice didn't exist. I wasn't going anywhere.

When I'd first met Inga in the halls of residence at art college before our course started, she was in the process of dumping a long, very unsexy nightdress into the kitchen bin.

"Early Christmas present from my mother," she explained. "I think she wants me to live like a nun. Fat chance of that." She turned to grin at me. "I'm Inga, by the way."

I smiled back. "Lily."

She stuffed the nightdress and its packaging further down into the bin and let the lid thwack closed on it. "And have you got a controlling mother like me, Lily?" she asked, turning to look in my direction.

I walked over to the kettle—I'd come into the kitchen to make myself a cup of tea—and filled it at the sink. "No," I said, "I lost my mum four years ago."

"God, I'm sorry," Inga said. "What did she die of?"

At that point, of course, I had no idea Inga and I would quickly become such good friends. I'd seen her around before, and she was stunningly pretty and confident, while I was more of a background kind of a person, not wanting to draw attention to myself. So I trotted out the usual lie I told when I was asked about my mother.

"Breast cancer."

"Gosh," she said, "that's awful. Poor you."

When our course started, just by fluke, Inga and I were given neighbouring workspaces, and we got into the habit of going to the college canteen for coffee breaks together. I discovered that her father—whom she'd adored—had died in a car crash two years previously, which was when her mother, who was Danish by birth, had decided to return to Denmark.

"Mum tried to insist I go with her. I mean, no way. I've always lived in England. Sure, we've always visited Denmark a lot, Mum's family are there, and it's a cool place and all that, but this is my home. Besides, Mum and I have never really got on. Not the way me and Dad did."

She had an intent way of looking at me over her coffee cup, her eyes a brighter blue than the sky on a faultless summer's day. "What about you after your mum died? How did your dad cope with it?"

I didn't have to lie about that. I'd never known my father, and for various reasons, I'd never been curious about him.

"Mum was a single parent," I said. "I've never met my father."

"Wow," Inga said. "So, what happened to you after your mum died, then?"

But there was no way I was telling her the details about that. Art college was my chance for a new start; I didn't want the awful recent years intruding on it. So I just shrugged. "I took care of myself."

I was still cautious back then, I suppose. Reluctant to become too attached to anyone in case they vanished from my life. But Inga—with her enthusiastic invitations to join her for a drink, go to the cinema or the theatre, or to see an art exhibition, quickly wore me down. We could chat for hours on end about art, about boys, about everything. It was like a miracle to have a friend like her, to have met someone who so obviously cared what I thought and felt.

One night when we'd had a lot to drink at a music gig, Inga started talking about how she'd always wished for a sibling growing up, and I found myself telling her I had a sister, Violet, whom I hadn't seen since I was seventeen years old. That she'd been taken into care after Mum died, and we'd lost touch. When Inga's eyes widened and she began pumping me with questions, I soon regretted saying anything. So I told her it was painful to think about, and then some other friends joined us, Inga just gave me a sympathetic shoulder squeeze, and the moment passed.

Sometimes I wondered whether, if I could rewind time and be back in that kitchen, watching Inga dumping that nightdress from her mother in the bin, I'd tell her the whole truth about what happened to Violet and me. Inga was such a generous friend; she certainly deserved my honesty.

But I couldn't rewind time. The lie was a tangled mess I couldn't bring myself to dwell on, and I couldn't risk Inga thinking I was some kind of weird freak she'd better avoid. So, I left the lie where it was and said nothing. Because, after all, being honest would require me to confront past events myself. And why would I want to do that? No, far better to just get on with my life. To make new memories.

Except for times like Christmas, when I was incapable of forgetting.

So, with my suitcase back under my bed and dressed in my cosiest pyjamas, I went downstairs to eat—a TV dinner without the TV, since I didn't bother to turn it on, loath to watch the usual seasonal diet of Christmas specials and repeats. A cup of tea, a spot of washing up so my plate wouldn't be encrusted with dried-on lasagne, and then I took the first of the sleeping tablets from the stash I'd hoarded earlier in the year when I'd told my GP I was suffering from exam stress.

Ten ought to be enough to take me right through Christmas if I rationed them, enough to block out the memories and the nightmares.

I could only hope.

3

A year and a half on from that first meeting with Alex and Matt, I was still dating Alex, and Inga was still dating Matt. Alex had proved to be good, undemanding company, and somehow, when he'd suggested we get a place together, I'd found myself saying yes. Now we were living together in a rented flat near the train station, and Inga and Matt had a bungalow to the north of the city. We still saw each other as a foursome as much as we could—going out for drinks, cooking each other meals, walking in the woods or on the coast. And this summer we were taking our first holiday together.

North Wales was Alex's suggestion. I didn't find out until later that it was mainly because there was a giant zip line over a disused quarry near the cottage we were renting—a zip line Alex had always wanted to try out. He'd kept quiet about it until after we'd booked. Probably because he knew about my fear of heights.

I'm not sure whether Alex thought he'd be able to persuade me to give the zip line a go when we were actually in Wales, but if he did, he was soon disappointed. No way was I doing that. Just thinking about it made me feel nauseous.

The others were keen, though, so I went along with them anyway and bagged myself an outside table at the café with a fantastic view of the mountains.

"Are you sure you'll be okay here on your own?" Alex asked.

"Come on, Lil. Come with us! You'll forget all about your fear of heights when you're whizzing over the quarry. Don't be so boring," Inga said.

"That's a bit harsh, Inga," came from Matt.

All three of them were togged up in harnesses, jumpsuits and crash helmets about to travel at a hundred miles per hour over the disused quarry. I was where any sensible person would be—seated at a reassuringly immobile table with plentiful supplies of coffee and chocolate.

"You do remember how I was when you bought us those gallery seats at the Theatre Royal, don't you?" I asked Inga.

I certainly did. I swear my face was green. I'd probably worn holes in the arms of my seat I'd clung on so hard. I can remember absolutely nothing about the play we went to see.

"Maybe you should have stayed at the holiday cottage?" Alex said with concern, bumping me with his helmet as he tried to give me a hug.

"I'll be fine. I've got coffee, chocolate, and my sketch pad. What else could I want?"

"Sounds boring as hell," said Inga.

Matt looked at his watch. "Why don't we leave Lily in peace?" he suggested. "It's almost time for the briefing talk, anyway."

Another hug and helmet bump from Alex. "See you afterwards. I'll text you just before we go so you can spot us."

"Okay. Have fun, all of you."

"See you on the other side," said Matt.

"Later, loser," said Inga.

Finally, they were gone, and it was just me and the crazy people zooming intermittently overhead on the zip line.

I sipped my coffee, enjoying the sudden peace and quiet, opening my sketchbook but not picking up my pencil. Thinking about Inga in an effort to get my thoughts back to the present. There was something different about Inga on this holiday. She seemed . . . restless. Wired.

As if being in Wales was the most exciting thing ever to have happened to her.

And being in Wales was nice. The views from the cottage we were staying at were stunning, the light on the mountains constantly changing—one minute picked out in sharp detail by the sun, the next obscured by mist. There was a good supply of board games to work through, and Matt was an amazing cook, preparing restaurant-quality food for us every evening. I loved the way he put so much into his meal prep, breaking into song every now and then, laying the loaded plates down on the table with a flourish. Matt was an impulsive hugger, scooping you into his arms for a squeeze when you passed by. He did it to us all, even Alex. Especially Alex. And I know Alex liked it, even if he complained and said, "Get off, Matt, you big dolt."

We were having fun, the four of us. I definitely laughed more since Alex and Matt had come into my life. The other week, Alex had brought me breakfast in bed wearing the rooster tea cosy Inga had bought me for Christmas on his head and nothing else.

"Breakfast is served, mademoiselle," he said, setting the tray down on the bedside table with one hand behind his back like a high-class butler. A butt-naked butler.

Needless to say, my eggs had gone cold, abandoned as we giggled and romped about in bed.

There was no doubt that Alex was good for me, but the only thing was, with Alex in my life, I didn't get much time to be alone. I shouldn't mind, but somehow I did. Every time Alex had to work late, my heart leapt with excitement, making me feel like a high-class bitch. It had nothing to do with not liking Alex's company; it was just that the lack of mental space was affecting my creativity. I wasn't painting nearly as much as I used to. Even when I went into the box room I used as a studio, I was aware of Alex somewhere in the house, waiting for me to be finished. Which totally stifled any creative instinct.

God, maybe I was destined to be alone.

Smiling at myself for being so dramatic, I picked up my pencil. I had these couple of hours to draw at least. And Alex and I would work things out. After all, what was wrong with someone trying to make your life better? Someone asking if you were happy. Arranging little treats. Making plans. Someone who made you their priority. It was certainly a novelty for me, given my past. I needed to get used to it, that was all.

Maybe I should find a studio outside our home. The box room was tiny. And dark. Though God knew how I was going to afford to pay for a studio when I sometimes struggled to find the rent.

But I'd worry about that later. Right now, I was going to draw the mountains from the safety of the café.

But the second I picked up my pencil, at least three families joined me in the café, sitting at the other tables and instantly surrounding me with excited children's voices.

"Where's Daddy, Mummy? Is that Daddy?"

"I can see him!"

"No, that's not him. He won't be down for a while yet, I don't think. Sit down, Milly. No, Jacob, you can't have another ice cream. Not until this afternoon."

Soon, the café was full, and there weren't enough seats for everyone. When a mother with four children eyed the empty seats at my table I smiled and offered them to her. She accepted gratefully. The two children she assigned to my table were less grateful, though, sliding into the seats and looking balefully at me as if I might be an axe murderer. I considered making conversation but decided against it, turning my seat further round to face the mountains more directly, my pencil moving over the page.

Three people swooped overhead on the zip line.

"Is that Daddy?" I heard the younger girl say.

"Not yet. It's too soon."

A pause, then, "Does anybody die doing the zip line? Will Daddy die?"

"No, course not, silly. He promised to take us paddle boarding this afternoon, remember?"

My pencil carried on moving, but I wasn't thinking about what I was doing any longer. The older sister's tone had been so caring; so reassuring. She could just as easily have said much the same words in a mimicking, *you're so stupid* kind of a way, but she hadn't. She'd been loving; looking out for her baby sister. The way I'd tried to look out for Violet.

The memories had been pushing to crowd into my mind all day, stirred by us being up somewhere high, no doubt, but now there was no stopping them. All of a sudden, I was ten years old, back in my childhood home, and Mum was telling me I had to take Violet out.

Mum was wearing her new dress—the short one with the low neckline. I knew what that meant. Ronnie, her boyfriend, was coming round.

"But I'm meeting my friends!"

One day, that was all I'd wanted. One day of being like everyone else my age. Of not being different.

"You can still meet them. Vi won't be any trouble. She'll go to sleep in the buggy. Come on, quick, sharp."

"It's not fair."

"Lily, I'm not asking you, I'm telling you. Take your bloody sister out. And don't come home until five o'clock, okay?"

She turned her back on me, conversation closed. Violet was already strapped into the buggy, face bright, saying, "Park, Lil. Park." It wasn't her fault our mother was a selfish cow. It wasn't my fault, either, but so what? One way or another I always got lumbered, and I loved Vi too much to just storm off and leave her and Mum to it.

I checked the contents of the bottom of the buggy and wasn't surprised to find Mum hadn't put all the stuff Violet might need in there—drink, snack, hat, changing bag. So, I got the things together myself and headed out just as Ronnie pulled up in his expensive car.

"Off out somewhere, girls?" he said, as if he didn't know. As if he hadn't spoken to Mum on the phone. Said something like, *"Get shot of those girls of yours, won't you? Then we can have some real fun."*

I didn't bother to reply. I loathed Ronnie with a passion. He was even worse than Dan, his predecessor, and that was saying something. At least Dan's gaze hadn't roamed over my body anytime Mum was in another room.

It was a scorching-hot day. The type of day when the pavement radiates heat, and the birds are eerily absent from the skies because it's too hot to fly. Violet was kicking her legs, happy to be outdoors. That would probably all change when she realised we weren't going to the park, but she'd get over it when she saw where we were going.

What with getting Violet's stuff ready, I was five minutes late arriving at the meeting place. To my relief, my friend Jasmine and her two brothers, Harvey and Leo, were still there when I puffed up to them.

"Thanks for waiting."

"We wouldn't have if we'd known you were bringing her," said Harvey, stabbing his finger in Vi's direction.

"Yeah," agreed Leo. "She stinks."

Violet had stunk last time I'd brought her along because her nappy had leaked, and Mum hadn't put any clean nappies in the changing bag. There were some today, though—I'd put them there myself.

"Not sure if you'll be able to get the buggy through the hole in the fence," Jasmine said, sounding irritable. "Why'd you bring her?"

"Mum made me."

"Mum made me," mimicked Harvey unpleasantly in a baby voice.

"Come on," said Jasmine impatiently. "Let's go."

Jasmine led the way, her long legs striding out. Harvey slouched along after her, hands in pockets, giving me and Vi a wide berth. Leo picked up a stick from the side of the road and bashed just about everything he passed with it as he walked along—wall, postbox, dropped tin can, which he sent clattering into the gutter. He even poked it in a pile of dog poop and gleefully threatened me with it until Jasmine told him, "Leave it out, Leo."

Shrublands Manor, where we were bound, was a mile or so away. Turns out Mum was spot on about Vi falling asleep in the buggy—she was fast asleep when we got there. People paid a fortune to get into Shrublands to walk around the gardens, but Harvey had recently discovered a hole in the fence leading into the woodland, and this was where we were going to get in. Only, Jasmine had been right about the buggy not fitting—not upright, anyway. The hole was just about big enough to squeeze through on your belly. Watching the others emerge on the other side, I cursed Mum and Ronnie all over again.

"Maybe if you left the buggy there?" Jasmine suggested. "Nobody'll nick it."

But I couldn't be sure about that, and leaving aside the grief I'd get if it disappeared, I'd never be able to get Vi home without it.

So, I lifted Vi out, waking her up and causing her to start up a whimpering protest. Then I held her, awkwardly folding up the buggy one handed so I could slide it through to Jasmine along with the changing bag. Harvey and Leo had already scarpered—we could hear them smashing a way through the undergrowth with sticks.

"Hurry up, Lily. We'll lose them. And make her shut up, can't you? Somebody'll hear us."

"Shh, Vi. It's okay," I said, handing my little sister to Jasmine through the gap in the fence. "It's really exciting in here. You'll love it, I promise you will."

Violet was squealing inconsolably in Jasmine's arms.

"She's like a flipping fish," Jasmine said, holding on to Vi's wriggling form with difficulty as I pushed myself through the hole in the wire fence, snagging my T-shirt as I did so.

Then I was through, taking Vi from Jasmine. The buggy was folded up and hidden in some rhododendron bushes, Jasmine had the changing bag over her shoulder, and we were off, following the trail the boys had cut through the trees.

I carried Vi until we reached open parkland, and then I put her down and she toddled gamely next to me, her tears forgotten as I pointed out a herd of deer.

"Look, Vi, it's Bambi."

Her little face lit up. She adored Bambi. "Bambi!" she squawked. "Bambi!"

A wave of love for my little sister swept over me as she trundled along, arms outstretched in a huge Bambi embrace. She was so cute. Even Mum noticed it sometimes—when she wasn't too wasted. I looked around for Jasmine to share the moment with her, but she was gone, racing ahead after her brothers, who were making their way towards a lookout tower.

"Come on, Vi," I encouraged. "We're going up the hill. We'll be able to see all the Bambis from there. I'll count them for you. I bet there are more than a hundred."

Gamely, Vi tried to keep up. But soon she was saying, "Lil carry. Lil carry."

So, I had to pick her up and struggle up the hill with her. When I arrived, panting, Vi's changing bag was dumped by the entrance to the tower, and Jasmine, Harvey, and Leo were nowhere in sight. I guessed they'd gone up the tower, but there was no way my legs would have taken me up there, even if I'd wanted to go, which I didn't. So, I got Vi's drink from the changing bag and sat panting while she guzzled it, wondering whether I'd be able to steal a sip or two myself, looking back the way we'd come. No deer were in view. Not one. They were hidden by the brow of the hill.

"Bambis," Vi said, also looking back. "Bambis gone."

"They haven't gone; we just can't see them from here."

We'd be able to see them from the top of the tower, but I hoped she wouldn't think of that. I'd never been keen on being up anywhere high. I had to steel myself just to go up the steps to the top of the slide. Besides, Vi's little legs would never make it up all those steps.

As I rummaged in the changing bag for a distraction snack, Jasmine, Leo, and Harvey appeared at the top of the tower, waving down at us.

"Woo-hoo!" Leo called.

Vi pointed at him. "Boy!" she said. "Boy up!"

"Yes," I agreed. "Boy up. Wave to him."

We waved. Only Jasmine waved back. Then, shortly afterwards, we heard the three of them shrieking as they tore back down the steps, their feet clattering as they sped as fast as they could go, finally tumbling breathless and laughing out of the door at the bottom.

"Go on, Lily," said Jasmine. "Your turn."

"I can't. I have to look after Violet."

"I'll look after her. Go on, the view's amazing."

"No, it's all right."

"She's chicken. Lily's chicken," said Leo.

"I am not."

"Prove it, then."

"Go on, Lil, Violet'll be okay with me," Jasmine said.

So, because I was suddenly sick of always being different, always being the one who said, *"No,"* or *"I can't,"* I went, followed by my sister's cries of distress, convincing myself she'd soon settle. That my friends would be proud of me when I got back down. That the view from the top would be worth it. That there was nothing to be afraid of. The walls weren't closing in on me. I wasn't going to faint. That I just had to carry on breathing. Take one step at a time.

Fifty-eight. Fifty-nine. Sixty. God, how many more were there? Was I halfway yet?

I stopped, sitting on a step, the stone cold against my bare thighs, Vi's cries spiralling up to me. Should I continue up, or go back down? I couldn't decide. My brain felt squashed. Like it was pressed in the vice Dan had used for his woodwork projects. The vice he'd left in the shed with his tools when he'd left Mum.

"Hurry up, Lily," Jasmine shouted to me through the tower door. "We're waiting for you."

Clinging to the step in front of me, I got to my feet and clambered on, one endless step after another, uncounted now, trying not to think about how I was going to get down again. Thinking only about getting to the top. Of looking down at the others, waving triumphantly. Seeing Vi's smile when she saw me.

Finally, finally, I emerged into the open air. Clinging to the wall, eyes tightly shut, I inched myself round to the side where the others were standing. Opened my eyes. Allowed the seasick feeling of the sky and the trees and the hill and the birds flying over to swim past me for a moment. Clenched my stomach with my arms.

I could look over the top. I could. Except that I couldn't. Not until the sound of Violet's distressed cries punctured my underwater world.

"Vi?" I said, inching closer to the edge, centimetre by painful centimetre. And there she was, far below me, a tiny figure in her pink playsuit. All alone. Where were the others? Where the fuck were the others?

I moved my swimming head to look and saw them running down the hill. The three of them, even Jasmine, not even looking back to check on Violet.

"Lil!" she was crying. "Lil-Lil!"

"Stay there, Vi," I called. "I'll be down in a minute. Don't move."

And it was enough, the terror of something happening to Violet—some accident, or her running off and me not being able to find her—to get me to the stone steps again. To get me bumping down on my bottom. Thud, thud, thud; Violet's cries winding round the tower to me all the way.

"I'm nearly there, Vi. Hold on."

When I reached the doorway, I could barely stand. My head and the whole world were spinning. I had to bend down and puke my guts up by the side of the tower. But all the time Vi was screaming, screaming, so I made myself open my eyes.

"It's okay, Vi. I'm here," I said groggily. Only it wasn't okay, because a strange woman had Vi in her arms, and she and her husband were staring at me accusingly.

"Does this little girl belong to you?"

"She's my sister." Shakily I walked towards the woman, my arms out, ready to take Vi from her. Only she didn't let go.

"Did you really leave her down here on her own while you went up the tower?"

"No, my friends were with her."

"What friends? There was no one here when we got here."

"They left." And they weren't friends. Not any longer.

Violet was screaming her head off by now, her arms stretched out towards me.

"Can you please let go of my sister?"

Reluctantly, the woman did so, asking. "How old are you? We ought to report this."

I turned my back on them, carrying Violet over to collect her changing bag. Some of my vomit had splashed onto it. But I couldn't worry about that. I just had to get Violet away from these people before something even worse than her being left alone at the bottom of the tower happened.

"Shh, Vi," I said, hurrying away, the changing bag bumping against my side. "It'll be all right. I'm sorry you were scared."

"Lil gone," Vi said, still sobbing as if her heart would never mend. She was warm against my chest. Warm and wet. "Lil gone."

"But I'm here now, aren't I? And I'll never leave you alone again." But I did.

~

"The lady's crying."

"Shh, she'll hear you."

"I'm not crying," I told the two girls at the table. "It's just allergies." Allergies. Yes, that was it. I was allergic to memories.

I took a tissue from my pocket and blew my nose. I wasn't surprised when the girls left a few moments later to crowd at the table with their mother and brothers.

My fear of heights had improved slightly over the years. At one time I wouldn't even have been able to sit in this first-floor café and look out at the mountains. In fact, I probably wouldn't even have agreed to come to Wales with all its mountains at all.

My phone bleeped. **Setting off in five minutes**, Alex had typed.

Have fun, I typed back.

I saw them fly over. At least, I think it was them. It was hard to tell since everyone was kitted out the same, and they were travelling so fast. But I could say I'd seen them. They'd never know the truth.

4

Back at the holiday cottage, Alex sat outside on the veranda strumming his guitar, Matt went to the kitchen to make a start on dinner, and Inga and I settled on the sofa with our cups of tea.

"I love Wales," I said, gazing out the window at the view of the mountains.

"Me too," Inga said. "Though I'm not sure I could live here. It rains too much. And besides, I'd always be thinking about Morgan Caddick."

I smiled. Morgan Caddick had been one of our tutors at art college. He'd had a habit of creeping into our studios without us noticing, making us jump out of our skins when he suddenly appeared next to us. *How's it going, Lily?*

"Remember how he was always pushing us to work from the life model?" Inga said. She adopted a stern expression, furrowing her eyebrows, attempting a Welsh accent. "Georgia O'Keeffe may have painted flowers because they were cheaper than engaging someone to pose for her, but we provide life classes free of charge for students here."

"I've never believed that's why O'Keeffe painted flowers," I said, picturing her huge close-up pictures of irises and petunias. "At least, not the only reason anyway."

"Hell no," agreed Inga. "I mean, the woman painted flowers as if they were female anatomy—you know, female genitalia. She'd never have asked a model if she could do a close-up of her you-know-what, would she?"

I laughed. Inga could be such a little Puritan at times, which was hilarious, since, before the advent of Matt, her relationships had rarely lasted more than a few weeks.

I put on an all-purpose American accent, having no idea where Georgia O'Keeffe was from. "Excuse me, life model, would you mind if I painted a close-up of your vulva?"

"See?" said Inga, laughing. "She couldn't do it, could she? I mean, what excuse would she give? The life model would think she was hitting on her."

"It's not that I'm in any way attracted to you, you understand," I continued in the same accent, "or even that I think you have a particularly impressive vulva, but rather because I want to stand out in the overwhelmingly masculine world of art, and painting vulvas would be the perfect way to do that."

Inga was laughing so hard she was writhing about on the sofa clutching her belly. "Oh, stop, stop. My tummy hurts."

But I carried on. "Why, Ms. O'Keeffe, the very idea! I'm not putting my most intimate parts on display for all and sundry! The very idea of it. I suggest you paint flowers like any lady would."

"She was exploring her sexuality, wasn't she?" Inga said when she could speak properly again.

"Definitely. If she'd been born now, she'd just have experimented."

"Which would be a loss to art. Her flower paintings are divine."

"All her paintings are divine. I've always wanted to go and paint in New Mexico the way she did."

"Well, sometime when we can afford to have more than baked beans on toast for our dinner, we'll have to go."

"You never have baked beans for dinner with Matt around. Besides, shouldn't we be searching for our own messages instead of copying other artists?"

"I already know what my message is, though, don't I?" said Inga, her exuberance suddenly gone. "Loss. Every bloody time I start something new, I think I've moved away from it, and there it is again. Pathetic, really."

I knew she was thinking about her beloved father, and I squeezed her shoulder. "It's not pathetic," I said. "It's brave."

I wasn't sure how brave with my art I was myself.

"You're such a talent, Lily," my tutor had told me once at art college. "You have the potential to be really great if you choose to be. But there's something closed off about your work. It's as if you're hiding something. To really get somewhere, I think you have to find the courage to reveal yourself completely."

She'd been dead right. My work did lack something. But nobody wanted to see my everything. Certainly not me.

"It's boring to still be churning out work on the same old theme, not brave. I've got you lot. Honestly, I'd really like to move on. Sometimes I think . . ."

"What?"

"That the only way to break free is to do something drastic."

"Like what?"

She shrugged. "I don't know. Oh, don't listen to me. I'm spouting rubbish, as per usual." She yawned hugely, stretching her arms upward. "God, I'm bushed. Who thought a holiday in Wales could be so exhausting. I swear it was the strain of trying not to see that guy's hairy wart on the train."

I laughed. "It can't have been that bad."

"It bloody was! You weren't there."

I'd decided not to go on the mountain railway up Yr Wyddfa as we'd planned in case my fear of heights spoiled the experience for everyone else. When Alex heard I wasn't going, he decided not to, either, and we'd gone boating instead. Inga, apparently, had been seated in a train compartment opposite a man with a huge growth on his chin, and she'd spent the whole time staring fixedly out the window to avoid looking at it.

"Didn't you want to look out the window, anyway? For the views?"

"Not for a solid hour, no. Besides, there wasn't much to see. It was really misty up there."

"Poor guy."

"Poor guy? He ought to get something done about it. I can't believe anybody wants to look like that." She gave a dramatic shudder. "You certainly had the right idea, lazing about in a bloody boat."

"We weren't lazing about; we were rowing."

"I bet you didn't do too much rowing. I bet you were lying back waiting for Alex to feed you grapes."

"We got some cheese-and-onion pasties from the shop. Does that count? They were right out of grapes."

"And that's another thing that drives me crazy. You and Alex have been gorging yourself on cheese-and-onion pasties all afternoon, and you'll still eat all your dinner. Neither of you ever puts any weight on. It's sickening. I only need to look at a pastie to gain five pounds."

"But you love us really, right?"

"To the bloody moon and back. Anyway, I'm going to have a lie down before we eat. I'm exhausted."

She left, her bare feet slapping up the stairs. Outside on the veranda, Alex was still playing his guitar. I knew he'd stop if I went out there, so I went into the kitchen to join Matt.

"Was the guy's wart as bad as Inga's making out?"

Matt looked up from slicing onions. "I doubt if I'd even have noticed it without Inga pointing it out. I was too busy being wowed by the view."

"She said it was misty."

"It was cloud, not mist. And it was actually quite magical being above the clouds. It felt as if you could walk on them. When they parted for those few minutes, it was amazing to look through them to see the valley."

"It sounds wonderful."

"It was."

"What can I do to help?"

"You could fry these onions while I dice the beef, if you like. We're having stroganoff."

"Sounds delicious. We can have fish and chips one night, though. Or eat out. You mustn't think you've always got to cook."

"I like cooking. It relaxes me."

"You always seem relaxed to me, anyway."

"Do I?"

I nodded. "You do." He did. Matt was a constant. Reliable. Dependable. Slow to be riled. Not that he was boring; anything but. You just knew where you were with Matt, and that was important to me. If I were ever to have a problem, I could go to him with it, I knew that. I could go to Alex, too, of course, but Alex was different. Restless, always on the lookout for the next activity, never quite able to sit still. Which was one of the reasons I hadn't wanted to interrupt his guitar playing. Working tunes out on his guitar was one of the things that did absorb him.

"I've been thinking about possibly making some changes, actually," Matt said suddenly, taking me by surprise.

I looked round at him. "Oh? Like what?"

"I've applied for a new job. In London."

My stomach jolted. I'd only just been thinking about how important our friendship was to me, and now here it was, all about to change. Of course it was. Had I forgotten the lessons from my childhood? You couldn't depend on anything.

"I'm not sure if I'll take it if I'm offered it," he continued, "but I thought I'd keep my options open, you know?"

I didn't believe he meant that. Maybe he thought he did, but I was pretty sure he'd accept the job if he was offered it.

"Wow. What does Inga think about it?"

"She thinks I should take it. In her mind, it's already as good as mine. She's definitely up for coming with me." He saw my face. "She didn't mention it to you, then. Sorry. Maybe she was waiting until she had something definite to say. It's all pie in the sky at the moment."

"Sure," I said. "That'll be it." I tried not to mind, knowing Inga probably hadn't wanted to hurt me unnecessarily. She could hardly base her life decisions on whether I'd miss her or not, could she? We weren't joined at the hip. But suddenly, what she'd just said about needing to do something drastic to break free made perfect sense. She'd been talking about moving to London with Matt. Inga and Matt, both gone. I couldn't imagine it. Stupid, so stupid to have taken their presence in my life for granted.

"Well, good luck," I said, as lightly as I could. "I hope you get the job. When will you know?"

"Probably when we get home. The interview was a few days before we came away. They said they'd let me know in a week or so."

"It's very exciting," I said, stirring the onions in the pan, making sure to get all the pieces that were sticking to the sides.

"Daunting, too, I must confess. But it was always going to be the only real way to develop my career, to work in London. We'll miss you and Alex, though, if we do go."

"We'll miss you too." I turned again, making myself smile, refusing to think about how lonely I'd be without them. "But there are trains, right? We can visit. You can show us round London."

"You probably know London better than I do. You and Inga are always there taking in exhibitions."

The door opened, and Alex came in. I glanced at him but saw no signs that he'd overheard my conversation with Matt.

"I think I'll have a snooze before dinner," he said to me. "Fancy joining me?"

I looked over at Matt. "Feel free," he said. "I can manage here."

Alex and I went upstairs and lay down on the bed. As we kissed, I was thinking about Matt's news, trying to imagine what it would be like with them gone.

When we started to make love, my mind wasn't really on it.

"Sorry," I told Alex. "I guess I'm tired after all that rowing."

"You hardly did any rowing," he protested, but he pulled back good humouredly, cradling me against him. "Have you ever thought what it would have been like if you'd ended up with Matt instead of me?" he said next, taking me by complete surprise.

I turned to look at him. "Whyever would you ask that?"

He shrugged. "The two of you have a sort of ease with each other."

It was true, we did. We always had. "We all love each other, don't we?"

"Sure. But I love you and Matt the most. Inga's sort of like an irritating little sister."

I laughed. "You're crazy about her. So is Matt."

"He seems to be. And what about you? Are you crazy about me?"

I wasn't fooled by his casual, jokey tone of voice. For all his outgoing personality, I'd seen quite early on how fundamentally insecure Alex was. And even if I hadn't, his mother made sure I knew.

"You won't break Alex's heart, will you, Lily?" she'd said one afternoon shortly after our first meeting, when Alex and his dad were in the living room watching football. "I can see how much he cares about you, and, if you don't mind me saying, I sense a sadness about you. Some secret sorrow you've yet to deal with."

I didn't know what to say to that. For one thing, I hadn't realised I was so transparent, and for another, it wasn't what you'd expect the mother of the boy you've only been dating for three months to say. So, I ignored what she'd said about me—because I didn't know her, and there were limits—and just said casually, "We're still just getting to know each other, Janice."

She smiled, squeezing my shoulder. "Sorry, I know this is awkward. Alex would be furious if he knew I'd said anything. Some—his dad in particular—would say I overprotect him. Perhaps he's right. But old habits die hard. Alex may be a man now, but he's still my baby."

I racked my brains for what Alex with his middle-class, happy-family background had needed protecting from and couldn't think of a thing. "If it helps," I said, "I don't have any plans to hurt Alex."

"You know I adore you," I said to Alex now, and I suspected that, with Inga and Matt gone, we were about to become even more important to each other. But I still didn't mention anything about Matt's news, and it occurred to me that I was doing exactly what his mother had always done—protecting him.

The way I'd always protected my sister. Until the day I hadn't.

5

"The owner of the cottage popped by while you were all asleep," Matt told us when we ventured down to eat.

"Checking up on us?" asked Inga.

"Just seeing if we had everything we needed."

"Checking up on us."

Matt dished up the beef stroganoff. "Actually, I think she's a bit lonely. She told me she's a widow in about her third sentence. I almost felt I should invite her to dinner."

"God," said Inga, "I'm glad you didn't. We'd have had to tidy up."

It was true. The place was a complete mess. None of us, apparently, had the tidy gene, at least, not when we were on holiday.

"How old is she?" I asked, curious. Matt had dealt with the booking, and the key had been under the doormat.

"Only about forty, I think. Her husband died in a farming accident. He was crushed by a hay bale."

"That's awful," said Alex.

"Depressing is what it is," said Inga.

Matt shook his head. "I know. It made me think how we have no idea what's going to happen second to second. One minute he's at the kitchen table eating lunch with his family, the next he goes out into the barn and bam, the hay bales topple, and he's gone."

"Jesus, Matt. We're on holiday, for Christ's sake," Inga said.

"Sorry. Just sharing my thoughts."

There was a pause while we all started to eat. I couldn't stop wondering whether there was a moment when the guy had known he was going to die, or whether it had just happened to him, and he'd been oblivious. A farmer, a family man, just finished his lunch. Had he looked up at the critical moment? Seen the bales falling? Had there been time for him to think about his wife? His kids? A man like that wouldn't have been blind drunk like my mother was when disaster happened. He'd have been lucid. Aware.

"Did I ever tell you about the time I heard my uncle speaking to me?" Alex said into the silence. "I told you, Matt, I know."

"You did, mate, yeah."

"What d'you mean, you heard him speaking to you?" I asked, glad to be pulled from my miserable reflections.

"It was a few weeks after I finished school. I had this crap factory job, processing chickens. Completely vile. Anyway, I went in one day with a serious hangover, and there's all this machinery going, all these women chatting and laughing, me in the middle of them, we've all got those blue protective hats on, and the women are taking the piss because I look as if I'm going to die right there on the conveyor belt. Get processed and packaged like the chickens."

Inga burst out laughing so hard she almost choked on her food. I had to slap her on the back. "It sounds like hell," she said when she could speak again.

"It was, it really was." Alex shook his head. "I couldn't eat chicken for years afterwards."

"How does your uncle come into this?" I asked.

"Well, I heard him, honest to God. I'm standing there, trying not to die, trying to work, and I hear his voice, loud and clear as if he's right next to me, speaking into my ear. So, I turn to look for him, but he isn't there. Nobody is."

"What did he say?"

"*It won't always be like this, Alex. Things will get better.*"

We stared at him. Goose bumps spread down my back.

"It was really weird, you know? But what with feeling so shit, I didn't think too much about it. I mean, I was so hungover, I could have hallucinated anything. But when I got home, Dad told me Uncle Jim had died in a car crash that day."

"Ooh, spooky," said Inga.

"Were the two of you close?" I asked.

Alex shook his head. "Not really. The guy barely spoke to anyone. He has to be the most silent person I've ever met. I tried telling my dad what had happened, but he didn't want to know. Actually, I think Dad was part of the reason I wasn't close to Uncle Jim. I think Dad made his mind up about Jim when they were both young, and that was that. No second chances."

I could believe that. Alex's father was a man of strong opinions. The first few times we'd met, I'd definitely felt under scrutiny. Fortunately, he seemed to have decided to like me.

"We can never really know what's going on with people, even if they do speak to us, can we?" I said, thinking not just about Matt and Inga's secret, but my own secrets too. The dirty truth about my past I'd chosen not to reveal to these, my closest friends, in case they were so appalled they stopped loving me. "We can guess, and we can base those guesses on our experience of them, but maybe everything's just a half truth, seen through a veil."

They were all staring at me. I'd probably been a bit intense.

"We share everything, though, don't we?" Inga said, making it worse, and my stomach squelched with guilt.

But then I saw her glance meaningfully at Matt and realised she was speaking about her own situation. "Unless it's a secret that's not ours to tell, anyway."

"Sorry, Lily," Matt said. "I asked Inga to keep my news to herself until I was surer something was going to happen. I was surprised she managed to keep quiet, though, I have to admit, you two being as close as you are."

Alex was frowning by now, and I reached over to squeeze his hand.

"What news?" he asked.

"Matt had an interview for a job in London before we came away," Inga told him. "If he gets it, we're both moving there."

Alex's fingers gripped mine. Hurting me.

Matt sighed. "Sorry, mate. It all happened so quickly. To be honest, I didn't think anything would come of my application."

Alex rallied. Smiled at his friend. Withdrew his hand from mine and forked up some stroganoff. "That's fine, no problem," he said, but I could tell he was hurt. Because I was, too, even though I had absolutely no right to be when I was keeping secrets of my own.

"I hope you get the job. That's . . . well, it's exciting. When will you know?"

"When we get home, I think."

But it turned out to be sooner than that. Much sooner. Matt got a phone call officially offering him the job the next morning. By which time Alex had had time to recover.

"Mate!" he said, bear-hugging his friend. "That's fantastic! I'm so pleased for you. For you both. You'll love living in London, Inga. Won't she, Lily?"

~

The day we waved Matt and Inga off, Alex and I took a train to the coast and walked along the beach with the sprawl of a fairground behind us, on the promenade. We could hear people screaming as they got soaked on the water chute. The rumble of the cars on the rollercoaster's elderly, wooden tracks. This part of the beach—the ugly part, away from the sand dunes—was deserted. It couldn't have been less like the beach at Catterline where Joan Eardley had painted the fishing nets hung out to dry, but the sea was beautiful anyway. And just ours.

"We won't see any seals here," Alex said, his hand in mine.

"No. But I bet they're here, anyway, keeping an eye on us."

Far out to sea the waves were breaking on a sandbank, frothy white in the middle of a solid expanse of grey blue. A black-backed gull flew over, squawking, on the lookout for fish.

"Why d'you think they kept it a secret from us?" Alex asked, sounding wistful.

If Inga and Matt had been here with us, the four of us would be laughing, pretending to push each other into the water. Dodging the breaking waves like children.

"I don't know. Maybe we're just all growing up. We can visit them, though. We'll always keep close."

"You think so?"

"Of course. You know we will."

The tide was going out. We took off our shoes and walked on the wet sand, leaving our footprints. Then Alex said suddenly, "Say, why don't we move to London too? I'm sure we could get work. You'd be near all the important galleries."

I didn't want to move to London. I didn't want to move anywhere. London was super expensive, and it was difficult enough to get by as it was. Norwich was a small, friendly city—the type where you could entrust your neighbour with your new address and be sure she'd pass it on if anyone enquired after you.

"I'm sorry, Alex. I don't want to move to London. I like it here. This feels like home to me. But maybe . . ."

"Maybe what?"

"Maybe we could try and buy somewhere together? I know you're not keen on our flat. What d'you think?"

He kissed me, his face clearing. "I think old Uncle Jim was right about my life," he said. "It did get better. A lot better. In fact, I'd say it's about flipping perfect."

A group of children suddenly rushed down onto the beach from the fairground, their excited cries interrupting our romantic moment. Two of the boys began hurling pebbles at a couple of seagulls resting on the beach, causing them to squawk and fly away.

"Hey, don't throw rocks at the birds," Alex shouted at them.

"Excuse me," their mother said crossly to him as she joined them. "They're my kids. If there's any telling off to do, I'll do it."

And she herded them off, after shooting another scowl in Alex's direction.

When they were out of earshot, Alex and I looked at each other and laughed.

"God," he said, "they're doing it again, and she's just letting them. Why do people have kids if they're going to let them turn into little shits?"

"I have no idea."

"Let's not have any little shits ourselves," he said.

"It never has been on my wish list," I said.

Alex squeezed my hand. "Okay, it's a deal. No little shits. Now, come on, let's go and get some ice cream."

6

At first Inga seemed really happy living in London—keen to take me and Alex on a tour of Camden Market when we visited for the weekend. Full of all the exciting job opportunities she'd applied for. Talking proudly of how well Matt was getting on in his new job.

Matt looked tired—apparently he worked long hours—but when he showed us the plans for the office building his company was designing, I was seriously impressed. If you had to work in a high-rise in the city, you'd want to work in that one. It was beautiful, with its angles and curves. A rival to the Shard.

The four of us went for a walk on nearby Hampstead Heath before it was time for me and Alex to catch the train home, and as the boys went on ahead, I took Inga's arm and hugged her close. "It's all going well for you, then, living here?"

She shrugged. "Yeah. It'll be a lot better when I get a job, you know? Something to get me out of the flat for a bit. But, yeah. It's great to see all the exhibitions as soon as they come out instead of having to wait. How about you and Alex? Is that going okay?"

"He missed Matt like crazy at first. But I've been encouraging him to play more sport."

The way Inga smiled and squeezed my arm told me she'd heard the words I hadn't spoken out loud. That I'd encouraged Alex to join another football team so I'd have some time to myself.

"I miss you," I said, but I said it with a smile, because I was glad things were working out for her.

"Me too. Maybe we could meet somewhere halfway sometime? Cambridge, maybe? For a bit of shopping? Or does your teaching course take up too much of your time for that?"

I'd started an evening course to become qualified to teach art to adults after Inga left, and now I spent a large part of my weekends completing assignments. I hadn't picked up a paintbrush in months.

"It's only part time, but it is pretty full on. I'm not sure I can afford Cambridge just now either. Things are pretty tight."

Inga sighed. "Don't you sometimes wish you hadn't been born creative? That you were the type who was happy filing or working in a supermarket?"

I'd done both jobs in my time and was currently temping for an insurance company doing soul-destroying data-inputting work. The completion of my teaching qualification couldn't come soon enough. At least then work would be related to something I loved. Yet did I wish I wasn't creative? Not when I was in the zone and nothing else in the world existed, no. Art—and Violet—had been the only things that had got me through my bleak childhood.

"Sometimes," I said, pushing aside memories of myself filling sketchbook after sketchbook with drawings and paintings in an effort to express my frustration and despair. "Come on, enough of this depressing chat. Let's race the boys to the top of the hill."

"Christ," Inga said. "Do you want to kill me?"

But she joined in, anyway, and we took Matt and Alex by surprise, tearing gleefully past them and ending up in giggling—and no doubt sickening to any observers—couple clinches at the top when Alex and Matt caught us up and tackled us to the ground.

Then Alex sprang to his feet saying, "Let's roll all the way back down!"

And we did, like four overgrown kids, Inga moaning, "If I roll over some dog shit, I'm going to fucking kill you, Alex Hammond."

As I rolled, my nose picked up the scent of the grass and crushed clover, transporting me back in time and reducing the squeals of the other three into the distance. I was with Violet, all those years ago at Shrublands Manor, risking feeling nauseous all over again by rolling down the hill with her to distract her from the trauma of being abandoned at the tower.

"Again, Lil! Again!" Violet yelled when we reached the bottom, loving it.

"Come here, terror," I'd said, grabbing her when she tried to run back up, pulling her wriggling body down on top of mine, her arms around my neck, her blond curls tickling my face.

"You have some harebrained ideas, Alex," Inga said loudly, snapping me back to the present, making a great show of checking every item of her clothing to make sure it was dog poo–free.

Matt hung back with me, putting a friendly arm around my shoulders. "You look miles away. You all right?"

I blinked away the memories and pushed myself affectionately into his side. "Sure. All good."

It was extremely tough, saying goodbye to them all over again at Liverpool Street Station. They were Matt and Inga, the other halves of us.

"Thanks for a really fun weekend." Alex's voice was determinedly chipper. "Great to have the crew back together."

"We'll always be together, mate," Matt told him, giving him a bear hug. "Even when we're apart."

It was my turn next. "Take good care of her, won't you?" I whispered to him as we hugged, and when he kissed my cheek and squeezed my arm, I knew it was his way of saying he would.

There were tears in my eyes when I hugged Inga, her body almost as familiar against mine as a lover's. "Call me."

"Tonight too soon?"

"Tonight's perfect," I said, and Alex and Matt lifted their eyebrows at each other and laughed.

Alex and I walked home from the station instead of getting a bus. The moon was out, sending glittering reflections on the river, and I think we needed a non-transport-based transition before we got home.

Where the river curves around the ancient tower that was once a part of the city wall, we cut up a steep, grassy hill to a viewpoint overlooking the flood-lit cathedral and the distinctive cube of the castle.

I was panting before we were even halfway up, my East Anglian leg muscles unaccustomed to hills and still tired from running up the hill on Hampstead Heath. "Tell me again why we're taking this route home?" I asked, stopping to catch my breath, hands on my hips.

Alex smiled at me through the darkness. "For the view. Oh, and so I can get you alone."

I opened my mouth to say we were usually alone these days, now that Matt and Inga had gone, but I didn't get the chance to speak the words because Alex grabbed me.

"So I can do this."

He kissed me, blocking the view of the cathedral and the stars, pulling me down onto the grass, and I kissed him back, holding him, pressed into the ground by his weight.

"I love you, Lily," he said, moving back slightly to gaze down at me.

"I love you too," I said. "Even if you are squashing my as-yet-undigested chicken rogan josh."

"How to kill a romantic gesture, directed by Lily Best," he joked. "Coming to a cinema near you."

I laughed. "Sorry." I reached out to stroke his hair back from his face. "And I'm sorry, too, for not wanting to move to London. I'm happy living here."

He kissed the end of my nose. "Me too. Maybe it was time for the four of us to be apart more, anyway. Do our own thing."

"Maybe. I was thinking actually, you should do an open-mic night or something. Play your guitar to an audience."

"I'm not good enough."

"You're much better than you think."

"And what are you going to be doing while I'm stepping up and being brave?"

"I'll be supporting you, of course. Sitting at the front, being your groupie."

"Well, naturally. But what are you going to do to expand your comfort zone while I'm making a tit of myself onstage?"

"Alex," I reminded him, "I've got my teaching practise test next week. That's enough comfort-zone expansion for anyone, believe me. Now, shut up and kiss me again."

I rolled on top of him, my hands slipping inside his clothing, our passion soon taking us away from the thought of anything but the here and now. And later at home, while Alex slept, I painted a picture of us rolling together on the crushed grass—a fused unit, with the cathedral and the landmarks we'd visited in London that weekend flying through the air away from us.

The following week I did my teaching practise test in front of my fellow students, and although my voice was shaking and my mind froze at one point, so the presentation was a bit clunky, I did it. And people seemed reasonably engaged. Best of all, I knew that now I'd done it once, I'd be able to do it again. For real, this time. And although teaching wasn't creating art, it was a thousand times better than data inputting or waitressing.

If Inga hadn't been in London, I'd probably have gone out with her to celebrate my achievement, but she was, so I went out with my fellow survivors from the course instead. All of us were high on relief and drank far too much. And I got talking to Amy, an aspiring writer, who I'd sat next to in training sessions a few times.

"We ought to try teaching together sometime," she suggested. "Find a way to combine words and images."

"That's a great idea," I said, something sparking inside me at the suggestion. "My boyfriend's a part-time musician, if you want to include music as well."

Amy grinned, displaying a cute gap between her two front teeth. "My boyfriend works for the council—he's in charge of recycling. Not sure how he'd be any help to the project. Except maybe for clearing up after us if we make a mess?"

We both burst out laughing at that, our amusement fuelled by the amount of wine we'd consumed, and from then on we became firm friends, and my parting from Inga became a bit easier to bear.

7

Christmas was soon juggernauting towards me, as out of control and unstoppable as ever. Inga and Matt had decided to spend the holiday season in London, so there was nobody to distract me from the relentless festive cheer except Alex, and Alex had no idea whatsoever that I needed to be distracted. Though he probably wondered every now and then why I was alternately over quiet or snappy, even though I tried very hard not to be either. All I wanted to do was sleep or run away, and although I knew life would be much easier if I just told him the truth, I didn't have it in me to do it.

One thing was certain, I wasn't going to be able to use my Great-Aunt Alice card very easily this year—not now Alex and I were living together, a fully-fledged couple. It had been different last year, because we'd only been living together for a matter of months, so I'd got away with it. But this year Alex would expect either to visit Alice with me or to drive down to Hampshire before Christmas to bring her back to spend Christmas with us and his family. So, short of inventing a brand-new lie, I was stuck with actually celebrating Christmas.

The idea filled me with dread. But it was one day, that was all. Well, two probably because Alex had agreed we would stay over at his parents' house on both Christmas Eve and Christmas Day. But it would be fine, surely? Alex and his parents were all so outgoing they wouldn't notice if I was quiet. And Alex was good for me in so many ways. He loved me. He deserved for me to do something good for him, he really did. Even if he wouldn't be aware what a huge deal celebrating Christmas with him and his family would be for me.

So I told Alex that Great-Aunt Alice had a friend coming to stay this year and we didn't need to visit her. Alex accepted it without question, which made me feel like an utter shit, because of course it would never occur to him that I'd be anything less than absolutely honest with him.

Alex's parents gave us a warm welcome when we arrived on Christmas Eve.

"Come in, come in, lovely to see you, Lily. Let me take your coat. Goodness, your hands are freezing. Go and stand in front of the fire to get warm. Hello, Alex, darling."

Alex kissed his mother. "Hi, Mum. I see you've gone for the minimalist effect with the Christmas decorations again."

"Your mother doesn't do minimalist, son, you know that. The fridge is so full I'm sure it's going to crash through the floor into the cellar," said Alex's dad. He turned to me. "Should you hear a loud thud in the night, Lily, that's what it'll be."

"Don't listen to him, Lily. I'm sure your sleep won't be disturbed by anything. In fact, speaking of sleep, I've got a surprise for you two. Come upstairs, I'll show you."

"It can wait until they've had a sherry and a mince pie, can't it, Janice?"

"It's all right, Dad," said Alex. "Mum's got me intrigued. Lead on, Mum."

So we followed Janice upstairs, where she threw open a bedroom door with a flourish. "Ta-da!"

As Janice spread her hands to indicate the bed, I looked, not realising the significance at first, just seeing a bed. A comfortable-looking bed, but just a bed, nevertheless.

Then Alex exclaimed, "Mum! You bought a new bed!"

Ah. So that was what the fanfare had been about.

Alex turned to me. "I was expecting us to be sleeping in my old single bed together. Either that or my old single and a mattress on the floor." He went over to kiss his mum on the cheek. "This is fantastic, Mum. Thank you."

"Yes," I said. "Thank you, Janice."

She smiled. "You're both very welcome. Right, let's go down and see about that sherry. Or we have heaps of other drinks if you're not a sherry drinker, Lily. Alex tells me it's your birthday tomorrow too?"

I forced a smile. "Yes, it is."

"I always feel sorry for people with a Christmas birthday. Did you feel left out as a child, or did your parents give you double the amount of presents?"

"Sometimes I felt left out, yes." Which was the understatement of the year.

Both Janice and Stanley were lovely to me. It wasn't their fault that the Christmas-hits album playing in the background as we settled down to play board games was the exact same album Mum had been playing that fateful Christmas day I'd gone out to meet my friends, ignoring Violet's pleas for me to stay at home. And it wasn't their fault, either, that all evening I felt like an actor playing the part of Lily at her partner's parents' house, playing games and laughing along with family banter.

By the time Alex and I went up to bed, my head hurt from the strain of pretence, and my jaw ached from smiling a fake smile. Alex hadn't seemed to notice anything was wrong, and I was glad about that, mentally awarding myself an Oscar for my acting skills, wondering how on earth I was going to keep it up all the next day as well. I wasn't sure I'd be able to sleep for worrying about it, but finally I did drift off.

But two hours later, Alex was shaking me awake because I was screaming my head off.

"Lily! Lily! You're having a nightmare. It's all right, I'm here. You're safe."

I was panting, choking, my senses overwhelmed as I tried to struggle from a horrific re-enactment of the events of that distant night. Alex was bending over me—I could see him, feel his touch on my arm, but it was as if he was behind some kind of a veil, and the terror was a living thing, clawing at me, trying to push me under again into the nightmare.

Somebody knocked on the bedroom door. "Whatever is it? Is everything all right?"

"Lily had a nightmare, that's all. Sorry we woke you, Mum."

Alex was stroking my hair as he spoke, gentling me out of the horror. Or trying to.

"Are you all right now, sweetheart?"

Somehow I managed to push myself upright, leaning back against the headboard, my pyjamas drenched in sweat, my heart still slamming against my chest.

"D'you want to talk about it?"

Sleep was impossible. Without the sleeping tablets, the nightmares had come straight back. Would come again if I went back to sleep. No amount of rationalisation or distracting games of Trivial Pursuit could change that.

"It . . . it's . . . Auntie Alice," I lied. "I dreamt something dreadful had happened to Auntie Alice. That she needs me. It was all so real, it was like . . . a premonition."

I picked up my phone from the bedside table.

"Lily," said Alex, "it's two o'clock in the morning. You aren't seriously going to call her, are you? It was a nightmare, that's all. I'm sure she's fine. We'll call her in the morning to check, but I'm sure there's absolutely—"

He broke off as I got out of bed and began to pull my clothes on. "Lily, what are you doing?"

"I have to go to her. I have to check she's okay."

"It's the middle of the night."

"I have to, Alex. I'm sorry."

Alex was starting to look really freaked out now. I could hear the rumble of his parents' voices in the next room. I was making a scene, being ridiculous. But the thing was, I wasn't capable of doing anything else. I had to get out of there as soon as humanly possible. I had to escape.

"This is ridiculous, Lily." There was an edge of frustration in Alex's voice now. "How are you even going to get to Hampshire? It's Christmas, for goodness's sake. Even if it wasn't the middle of the night, there are no trains running."

I left the bedroom and began to make my way downstairs. Alex followed me, dressed only in his boxer shorts.

"Look, give your aunt a ring if you need to set your mind at rest. If something has happened, I'll drive you there myself."

He took hold of my shoulders, the frustration gone, leaving only love. "We're a partnership, you and me, Lil. You don't have to do everything on your own anymore. I'm here for you. I'm here."

He was too good for me. Too good to be lied to. Tears suddenly sprouted from my eyes. He pulled me to him and held me while I sobbed. Behind him, I caught a glimpse of his mother in her dressing gown, a worried expression on her face.

"Are you sure everything's all right, Alex?"

"It's fine, Mum. Go back to bed."

"Are you sure? Shall I make a pot of tea?"

"Honestly, we're fine. Thanks."

"Well, all right, then," she said uncertainly, making her way back upstairs.

"Tea might not be such a bad idea, eh?" Alex said to me after she'd gone. "Let's go into the kitchen."

I sat at the kitchen table, dumb with misery, while Alex scurried about making tea, dressed in his father's gardening coat from the peg by the back door, and I decided with a sense of dread that it was time to tell him something approaching the truth.

Alex placed two mugs of tea on the table and sat down opposite me, reaching for my hand. "D'you want to phone your aunt?" he asked.

I couldn't meet his eyes. "There's no point."

He stroked my fingers. Brought them to his lips. "It might put your mind at rest. It was just a nightmare, though, I think. A horrible one, to have kept you in its grip like that. You looked as if you were still there, Lil. Still in it. It scared me."

"I'm sorry."

"Don't be silly, it's not your fault. None of us can help what we dream, can we?"

I gave a shaky sigh. "There's something I haven't told you, Alex. Something you don't know about me."

He frowned, looking worried. "What?"

"I . . . hate Christmas."

He flapped a dismissive hand, his expression clearing. "Well, you're not alone, are you? Lots of people say that."

"No," I said, "you don't understand. Christmas is . . . traumatic for me. Those nightmares. They're not a one-off." I took a deep breath. "Alex, something really bad happened to my family one Christmas. Something that comes back to haunt me every year." I steeled myself to look up at him, encountering bafflement and concern in his eyes. He opened his mouth to ask a question, but I covered his lips with my fingers to silence him.

"Don't ask me to talk about it, Alex. Please. I just can't. But, you see, because of what happened, I don't do Christmas. I never have since then."

"What do you mean?"

"I mean, I shut myself away until it's over."

He frowned. "What about Great-Aunt Alice?"

I shrugged. "There is no Great-Aunt Alice. I made her up."

"But Inga said . . ."

My gaze dropped to the table. "I lied to Inga too. To everyone. I'm not proud of it, it's just . . . what I have to do. I stay at home over Christmas. Or I book myself into a hotel. Then I wait it out. Sleep. Drink. Do whatever I need to do to get through it."

I looked up again, taking in his bewilderment. "I realise that makes me sound like a crazy person. Sometimes I think I am exactly that. Or at least someone who needs therapy, anyway. But that's just the way it is. Only this year, with you wanting me to come here so much, I thought I'd give it a try. I hoped being with you would make a difference. Make it bearable. But it hasn't, Alex, and I'm really sorry, but I have to leave."

Alex was still staring at me across the table. "I can't take this all in, I really can't."

More tears trickled down my cheeks. "I don't blame you."

"What shall I tell Mum and Dad?"

"Whatever you need to. Whatever you think best. Look, don't ruin their Christmas. Stay here."

But I didn't need to see his expression to know that Christmas for this household was already ruined. Janice had gone to so much trouble to make everything perfect. She'd bought us a brand-new bed, for goodness's sake! Me leaving would cause a strained atmosphere it would be impossible to ignore. But I couldn't help that. If it were possible for me to stay and pretend everything was okay, I would. But it just wasn't.

"I can't leave you on your own in this state. And it's your birthday tomorrow. I'll tell Mum I—"

"No, Alex. I'll be all right. I told you; I'm used to it."

He sighed. "I'll get dressed and take you home."

"Thank you."

When we reached our house, Alex turned the engine off and made to open the car door, but I put out a hand to stop him.

"Go back, Alex. Go back to bed. Tell your parents I'm sorry. That I hope they understand."

He looked at me, his eyes sad under the streetlight. "This isn't just a fling for me, Lily," he said.

My heart squeezed inside my chest. "I know that."

"Then you should know you can trust me."

Tears spilled down my cheeks. "I do. I do know that."

"But not enough to confide in me, eh?" He sighed. Raked a hand through his hair. "We ought to be dealing with this together, whatever it is. It shouldn't still be affecting you all these years later."

"I know." I did know. Sort of. But what guarantee did I have that opening up the excruciatingly painful can of worms would make any difference? Ignoring the whole thing, stuffing the memories down inside me, had served me reasonably well so far. I supported myself. I painted pictures. I'd just got a new qualification. I had my friends. Alex. I was doing okay, really. Except for the Christmas thing.

He sighed. "Will you at least promise you'll speak to someone? Get some help?"

But I couldn't promise that. Just the thought of bringing that night into appalling Technicolor made me want to run. To vomit.

"Don't pressure me, Alex. Please."

"I'm sorry, I just . . ."

"Look, I'll try, okay?" I lied. "That's all I can say."

He nodded. "Okay." His voice was so sad, it made my heart turn over. Especially when he said, "Happy birthday for tomorrow."

I opened the car door. "Night, Alex. Happy Christmas."

I went upstairs and got into bed. Not that I expected to sleep. Which was just as well because I didn't. Instead I lay there imagining Alex having to deal with the aftermath of my flight the next morning. Defending me in the face of his parents' disappointment and annoyance. Poor Alex. I groaned, burying my face in the pillow. I didn't deserve him, I really didn't. Would he even have got involved with me if he'd known what he was taking on? If he had any sense, he'd be lying sleepless in bed himself, trying to decide how to dump me.

Not that he would. Deserve it or not, Alex adored me.

I wanted suddenly to talk to somebody. No, not to somebody, to someone. To Violet. My sister.

It was hardly surprising my thoughts turned to her, tonight of all nights. I thought about her almost every day anyway—more so since Inga had moved away. And now it was Christmas.

Where was she? Still abroad? Back in the UK without having told me she was home? I wondered whether she was thinking about me too. Whether she was happy. Alive. But of course she was alive. I'd have heard if something had happened to her. Wouldn't I?

Violet had finally got in touch with me again three years ago, before she went travelling. She called me out of the blue after years of silence, asking me to meet her in a café near the station. I hadn't known what to expect when I showed up. What to feel, even. I was a bundle of excited nerves, my gaze sweeping round the tables, searching for her. And there she was, sitting at a battered metal table, drinking a bottle of Coke as if it were beer. Alive. Real. Within reach.

My little sister.

I couldn't, mustn't start blubbing. My hands needed to stop shaking too. She wouldn't want any of that. I was meant to be the one in control in our relationship. So, I waved to her, pointing to the serving counter, indicating that I would get a drink before I joined her. Giving myself time.

She looked so different. Of course she did. She was a young woman now. And yet I could still see in her the little girl who'd followed me around everywhere, demanding attention. I'd given it to her mostly, putting aside my sketchbook or my homework to listen to her, to paint her nails, fix her something to eat.

Joining my sister with my coffee, I wondered if she still thought about those times—Violet and Lily against the world—or whether the events of what happened afterwards had obliterated all those memories.

"It's been a long time, Vi. It's so good to see you."

Where have you been living? Why haven't you been in touch? God, Vi, I've missed you so much. D'you think about that night as often as I do? Are you okay? Tell me you're okay, Vi. I've been so worried.

Somehow, I don't know how, I managed to keep the questions in. Violet didn't say it was good to see me too. Just knocked back more of her Coke and shrugged, giving me no indication why she'd contacted me again. I supposed I shouldn't feel hurt, but I was, deeply. It was as if roles had somehow reversed—that it was me with the puppy-dog eyes now. But she'd got in touch, hadn't she? Suggested we meet. That had to mean something.

"So, travelling, eh?" I said in an overbright voice. "Where are you headed first?"

"France, to work on a campsite for the summer. Then maybe Italy. I don't know yet. Depends what happens. Who I meet."

I nodded as if it was fine not to have a plan. To tumbleweed your way through life. Well, it was, when you were Violet's age.

"You will be careful, won't you?"

Violet's eyes were a dark, dark brown, not green like mine and Mum's.

"I can take care of myself."

She sounded hardened. Toughened up by the foster care system in ways I didn't want to think about.

"I'm sure you can."

We'd seen each other now and then at first, after she'd been fostered out, but it wasn't so easy. Something seemed to go wrong at every foster home Violet was placed in. Almost as if she was deliberately sabotaging them.

For the first year, she'd begged me to let her come and live with me, but there was no way the local authority was going to sanction that, even if I'd felt capable of it. I was only sixteen, after all. Not much more than a child myself. In the end, she stopped asking. Our meetings became less and less regular, until eventually, they dried up altogether.

"I'm really sorry, Lily," one of her foster carers told me over the phone. "But Violet doesn't want to see you just now." The poor woman babbled on with excuses about new schools and homework pressure, but I didn't really listen, knowing they were all fake. I knew why Violet didn't want to see me. Because she blamed me for everything that had happened. I knew it because I blamed myself too.

Lying in bed with Alex's ruined Christmas on my conscience, I remembered how Violet and I had struggled to find anything to say to each other in that station café. How every topic of conversation was a minefield. How she asked me nothing about my own life, as if she had no interest in what I'd been doing since she'd seen me last. How it was almost a relief when it was time for her to go and catch her train. And how, at the same time, I'd wanted to run to the station after she'd left to beg her not to go, consumed by a mixture of overwhelming love and terrifying helplessness. Exactly the same way I'd felt as a nine-year-old, trying to rock her to sleep in my arms.

After she'd left to catch her train, I'd made my way home, a complete emotional wreck.

Violet. How I wished she were here now, asleep in the spare bedroom. That we could wake up in the morning and reinvent Christmas together, just me and her. And, yet again, as I'd done so many times, I wondered where she was. Whether she was happy. Whether she was safe.

8

With my secret about Christmas out, I knew I had to tell Inga as soon as possible. She mustn't, couldn't find out from anyone but me. So, as soon as the festive season was over, I phoned her to confess.

"So Aunt Alice was all a lie?" she said, staggered. "The cold and the smell of cat wee? Everything?"

It was like the Violet admission all over again. Only much worse. I was bitterly ashamed of myself. "Yes. I'm so sorry."

"I worried about you all the time, Lil. I lay awake imagining you freezing fucking cold all over Christmas. I made you those gloves to take with you, and I can't even knit!"

"I know. I'm sorry."

There was a pause, then she said, "They were awful, though, those gloves, weren't they?"

I laughed, a tear dripping down my cheek. "They were both for right hands."

"And the thumbs were far too long."

"Only three inches or so."

We laughed together, then I said, "I shall never, ever throw them away, Ing."

I heard her sigh on the other end of the line. "What the fuck happened to you that was so bad you had to go to those lengths, Lil?"

"I can't talk about it," I said. "I really can't, I'm sorry. I only want to forget it. Most of the time I do. It's just that at Christmas, I can't."

"Shit, Lil. That really sucks."

"Don't think badly of me. Your friendship means everything. You know that."

"I could never think badly of you, sweetie. I only wish you'd felt you could talk to me, that's all. Have you spoken to Alex about it?"

"No."

She sighed. "Poor Alex. Poor you. Though I'm glad you haven't had to go and sit in an icebox and play patience with an old biddy every year."

"It was canasta, not patience."

"What?"

"We played canasta, not patience."

She laughed, filling me with relief. "Well, that's all right then. But seriously, Lily, if anything terrible like whatever it was ever happens to you again, promise me you'll tell me about it."

"I promise." It was an easy promise to make. Because I was pretty sure nothing as bad as that could ever happen to me again.

Anyway, it turned out I wasn't the only one to keep secrets in our friendship. Three months later, just as the spring flowers were starting to put in an appearance, Matt phoned in the middle of the day, and I could tell from his very first words that something was badly wrong.

"Lily?"

"Matt? How are you? Alex is at work, I'm afraid."

"It was you I wanted to speak to, actually. How are you?"

"I'm okay. Good. We both are. Matt? Is something wrong?"

He sighed. "It's Inga. I think she's feeling really low."

"She didn't get that job, then?"

He sighed. "No, she didn't. Or the others she applied for. They have thousands of applicants for the kind of thing she's after. And then there's her mum, of course."

Inga had called me the previous month to tell me her mother had lung cancer. They had never been close, the two of them, or not since Inga's father had died, anyway, and she hadn't really wanted to speak about it, apart from the bald facts that her mum was receiving treatment, and the prognosis was uncertain. "It's too depressing, Lily. She's outraged about it, as if for some reason there's an injustice that she couldn't smoke forty cigarettes a day for most of her life and get away with it."

"You knew she went to Denmark to see her mum?" Matt said.

"I knew she was planning to, but I haven't heard from her since she got back. It didn't go well, then?"

Matt sighed. "She won't talk about it. But no, I don't think so. She's alone too much. I think that's part of the trouble. I've been trying my best to get home earlier, but it's really difficult. Everyone stays late here, and then there's the tube journey home. She really misses you, Lily."

I felt a lump in my throat. "I miss her too," I said, because it was true, I did. My new friendship with Amy was lovely, but there was nothing like a long-term friendship—a friendship within which you've grown and tested the waters together.

"I was wondering whether you'd be able to visit for a few days? I think she could do with seeing you."

"Of course," I said, my mind already running through train times and cancelling any arrangements I'd made. Amy's birthday party. Bugger. But she'd understand, I knew she would.

Matt sounded relieved. "You'll be able to get the time off work?"

"Sod work. It's only a crappy temp job, anyway. I'll get another one if they don't like it."

"What about your college course?"

"I'm up to date with my assignments. It's fine, Matt, honestly."

"Thank you. I really appreciate it. I'm really worried, you know? I just can't seem to reach her. I'm out of my depth."

I'd always thought of Matt as strong—he was a big man with a deep voice—one of life's doers and organisers. A coper. An achiever. I hadn't seen this vulnerable side of him before. And that made me wonder what else I didn't know about him. Whether some of that strength and capability was a front. But I didn't think about it for long because I was too worried about Inga.

I was even more worried when I got to London and saw her. Grey faced and ill looking, she was still in her robe at midday, the curtains in the living room closed.

When we hugged, Inga's arms seemed weak, as if it was an effort to hold them up. And when I went to make us tea, she waited on the sofa for me to bring it to her, instead of leading the way to the kitchen to make it herself, keeping up a constant stream of chatter the way she would normally do.

"Sorry Matt's dragged you here."

"Don't be daft. I'm surprised you didn't call me yourself."

She shrugged. "Didn't like to bother you."

"Since when has moaning to each other been a bother for either of us?" I set our tea down on the coffee table and nestled against her on the sofa. "I'm so sorry about your mum."

"Yeah," she said. "It's shit. She's always been a bit anal about her hair, spending a fortune on shampoo and conditioners, and now it's coming out in clumps."

"She's not coping well, then?"

"Er, no." She sighed. "And I am sympathetic, obviously. Not that she wants my sympathy. Honestly, Lil, if I was deluded enough to think this might bring us closer, she soon put me right about that. I might just as well have stayed here and sent her a text saying, *'bad luck about the cancer.'*"

She looked at me, her pain undisguised. "She didn't want my sympathy at all. Wasn't interested in my carefully chosen gifts. Certainly didn't want to talk about the past or be reconciled with me or any of the dumb things I imagined on the plane over. I'd booked the hotel room for three nights, but I almost didn't go to see her after the first time. The first thing she said to me was, 'You shouldn't have come.'"

"People say that, though, don't they? To be polite?"

"Yeah, but she meant it."

Inga looked down at her robe, her fingers plucking at the silky material. I noticed some sort of food stain on it that hadn't been there when I'd last seen her wear it.

"I'm so sorry," I said again, feeling utterly helpless. I knew all about getting zero emotional connection from your mother, but what good did that knowledge do, really, except to provide empathy?

"Don't be. It's my own fucking fault, being deluded enough to think a little thing like cancer might be character transforming." She took a deep breath, swiping tears from the corners of her eyes. "And, anyway, the cancer wasn't the only reason I went."

"No?"

She shook her head, the strands of her unwashed hair moving in greasy clumps, tears suddenly streaming down her cheeks.

"What is it?" I said, suddenly afraid. "Has something happened?"

She nodded. "You could say that. I . . . I was pregnant. I had an abortion while I was in Denmark."

My jaw dropped. My stomach churned. "An abortion? Christ, Inga."

Her eyes were suddenly urgent. Appealing. "Matt doesn't know, Lil. You mustn't tell him."

I was shocked at that, remembering his voice on the phone. Strong, loving Matt, asking me to come here because he was so worried about Inga. Oblivious to the fact that she'd just aborted his child.

Inga's eyes switched from appealing to challenging. "Don't tell me you wouldn't do the same thing if you were in my position, because I know you would. I couldn't risk Matt wanting to keep it. You'd be exactly the same with Alex."

I wasn't sure if that was true or not. Like Inga, I didn't want to have children, but the idea of deceiving Alex like that appalled me so much, I thought I probably would tell him. But perhaps you could never be sure what action you'd take unless you were in that situation. Which was why I was so consistently careful about protection. I'd thought Inga was too.

"Did you forget to take your pill or something?"

"No, I came off the pill. I didn't think it was helping with my depression. We've been using condoms."

"I see. And did it help with your depression?" I wasn't really sure why I was asking the question. It was sort of irrelevant now, wasn't it?

She shrugged. "I'm just a bit poleaxed. Worn out. Tired of being stuck in this flat with nothing to distract me. I've got too much time to brood. Lil, I think . . ."

"What?"

Inga's eyes filled with tears again. "I think I want to come home. Living in London isn't what I thought it would be. I haven't managed to get a decent job, and I can't face going back to waitressing. I've got all this time to be creative, and I never lift a fucking finger. Even before this happened, when Matt gets home, I've got nothing to talk to him about. And now, well, it's even worse."

I thought of all the women I'd met through my various jobs who'd used reasons exactly like this to start a family—plugging the emptiness of their draughty lives with new life. Inga had done the very opposite of that. In a way I admired her for standing by her principles, but I couldn't help feeling unspeakably sad about it, thinking how lonely it must have been to do it all on her own. How awful to have had to arrange it behind Matt's back.

What would he have said if Inga had felt able to tell him she was pregnant? Would he have supported her decision? Or, deep down, did he want to be a father?

"I can't imagine you and Matt not having anything to talk about together. He's so worried about you, Ing."

She made an impatient gesture. "Matt tiptoes around me like I'm made of glass," she said, covering her face with her hands. "It's unbearable. I'm a total bitch to him, and he just takes it. All of it." She burst into sudden tears.

"Oh, sweetie, come here," I said, and I drew her as close to me as possible, as if to try and absorb her pain.

When Matt came home from work, he enfolded me in one of his bear hugs. "Thanks so much for coming, Lily."

I hugged him back, feeling the tears close. "You two need to talk. I'll go for a walk."

He frowned, his eyes searching mine. "There's nowhere much to walk around here. And it's not that safe to wander the streets alone after dark. Stay in here. Watch some TV. Inga and I can go into the bedroom to talk."

So, they went into the bedroom while I sat in front of the TV with the volume up loud, hoping against hope Inga would find the courage to tell Matt the truth. If she didn't, I was going to have to keep it secret from Matt for the rest of my life, and I was already keeping so many secrets from him. From everyone.

Finally, when I couldn't stand hearing the rumble of their voices any longer, I put the front door on the latch and phoned Alex from the communal landing of the apartment block.

"How's Inga?" he asked straightaway.

I could hear a football match on TV in the background and imagined him with his feet up on the coffee table, beer in hand.

"Not good. She and Matt are talking, so I came outside. I think Inga wants to move back."

"Give up on London? Really? That would be fantastic!"

"What about Matt's job?"

"He'll sort something out. Don't worry about Matt. He loves Inga. He'll do whatever it takes to make her happy. The crew back together again. It'll be great."

And suddenly it occurred to me that it wasn't just Matt I was going to have to keep the abortion a secret from if Inga didn't come clean. I was going to have to keep it a secret from Alex too.

"Lily? Are you still there?"

"Yes, I'm here."

"Look, you worry about everybody too much. They'll be okay. When d'you think you'll be home?"

"I'm not sure."

"I miss you."

"You're all right. You can watch football in peace without me there."

"I can do that when you are here. You just leave me to it and go and do some painting. The difference is, I know you're here, in the house when you do that. That you're going to emerge at some point with a smear of paint on your cheek and your hair sticking up, and we'll go to bed and spoon together so I can go to sleep."

I had to smile at that. "Alex, you always go to sleep the second your head hits the pillow. My not being there won't make any difference."

"I go to sleep, but not with the same joy. I love you, Lily."

"I love you too."

"And Matt and Inga love each other. It will all be okay. I promise."

9

Inga never told Matt about the abortion. She did tell him she wanted to move back to Norwich, though, and they gave up their flat in London. Matt applied for a job at his old company, but, although they took him back, he had to take a demotion. Outwardly, he was stoical about it.

"I'll give it a few years, and then I'll set up my own business. It'll be fine."

I often wondered how it must really feel to have his work directed by someone in the role he used to fill, but Matt seemed as cheerful as ever—at least when he was with us—so I gradually stopped worrying about him and did my best to stuff my knowledge about the abortion to the back of my mind.

I was busy with my own life, too, of course—getting used to a schedule of teaching and lesson preparation. In reality, because I only felt really confident about teaching if I spent ages preparing my sessions, I didn't get much more time to be creative than I had before when I was data inputting or serving people their meals.

The courses I taught were all art based, but they varied immensely according to who I was asked to deliver them to. Many were aimed at retired people taking up a new hobby, but some were out in the community, working with groups with some kind of need or disadvantage. I liked those the most, although they could be challenging.

Even with some teaching experience under my belt, I still got things wrong sometimes. And I always worried about whether what I was doing really helped people the way it was intended to, especially when I started my art sessions at a women's refuge. These art sessions were directed at families, so I had to think of art activities suitable for a variety of ages. It was important, valuable work; work it meant a lot to me to get right. And I didn't always manage to do that.

There were four children in the art group next time I went there—Tabby, Rose, Leesa, and Jack. There were supposed to have been seven kids and seven mothers, but I wasn't surprised when some of the group didn't turn up. The previous week had gone so badly, I'd had nightmares about it afterwards.

"How lovely to see you all," I said, beaming at the mums. "I wasn't sure anyone would be back after I turned your kids into mini Shreks last week." I shuddered at the memory, drenched all over again by horror and disbelief. It had been awful. Truly awful.

"It was cool," said Teri, Leesa's mum.

"I haven't laughed that much in ages," said Catherine, Rose's mum.

"Yeah, don't worry about it, Lily," said Izzy, Tabby's mum.

Jack's mum, Trish, was busy dealing with Emily, Jack's baby sister, and said nothing except, "Sorry, Lily, I'll have to give her a feed."

"Of course," I said, "that's fine." I expected her to feed the baby right there, but she stood up and went to a corner of the room, calling out to her son as she went.

"Stop making so much noise, Jack."

But Jack, who was running around the room with his toy car making *brm brm* noises, paid no attention.

"You did look stressed, though," said Izzy.

"You really did," agreed Catherine.

"I was," I said with feeling. "Has the dye come off yet?"

"Tabs, show Lily your hands," said Izzy, and Tabby turned her hands palms up. There was still a distinct green tinge to them.

"Mine are greener than yours," said Rose, putting her own palms alongside Tabby's.

"Mine are the greenest!" sang out Leesa.

Oh, God. All their hands were still really green.

"I am so sorry," I said. "I should have guessed the rubber gloves would slip off their hands because they didn't fit properly. D'you think that's why the others haven't come today?"

"What, in case you've got something else messy for us to do?" said Catherine.

"They've just got appointments and that, Lily," soothed Izzy. "Nobody minded."

I had, though. A lot. I would never forget my horror when I saw the floating rubber gloves and realised the kids' hands were plunged right into the tub of green dye mixture. I never wanted to look at a tie-dye scarf again. Whatever had possessed me to think tie-dye was a suitable art project for families?

"You're all very kind," I said now, smiling round at them all and thinking how different it could have been if they'd decided to complain. Though I guessed there was still time for one of them—perhaps one of the mums who hadn't come along today—to do just that.

I pulled myself together. "Anyway, so today we're going to make some wax scratching pictures."

"Not with hot wax, though?" asked Catherine.

"No, no, don't worry!" I reassured her quickly. "Just wax crayons. No mess, I promise. Look, I'll show you how it's done, if you all want to watch?"

I pulled my piece of paper closer. "The first thing we do is draw a lovely, brightly coloured picture on our piece of paper."

Jack was still running round the room making *brm brm* noises for his car. When his circuit brought him close to the table, I smiled at him. "I know, I'll draw Jack's lovely red car," I said, and proceeded to sketch it out, pleased when Jack stopped running to watch.

"There," I said, when it was finished. "Now, we cover our picture all over with the black wax crayon like this."

But I hadn't thought things through, because the second I began to scribble over the red car with black, Jack burst into noisy tears and tugged at the sheet of paper, screaming, "No! *Brm brm.*"

"Jack!" called his mother from the corner of the room. "Don't be naughty."

"No, it's all right," I said. "Here, Jack, you can have it. I'll do another picture." I gave him the picture of a car, and he ran off with it to show his mum.

"I know," I said, pressing on, still determinedly cheerful, "I'll draw a lovely rainbow, shall I?"

I quickly drew a rainbow across a fresh sheet of paper in fat, bright strokes, aware that Rose was starting to fidget. Maybe I should have got them to get started instead of demonstrating? But that hadn't worked so well last week, had it? And after that fiasco, I'd wanted everything to be perfect. And clean, definitely clean. But clean didn't necessarily mean interesting.

I sped up, filling in the colours of the rainbow quickly until the whole page was covered.

"Now, I'm going to cover my picture with black crayon. Don't worry, it will end up looking beautiful by the time I've finished!"

I hated my overbright tone of voice. The hint of desperation in the way I said it would look beautiful. It had better.

"You kicked me!" Rose complained to Leesa.

"I didn't!" said Leesa. "Mummy, I didn't!"

"She did."

Oh, God, they were clearly bored.

"Girls, please," said Izzy, and she sounded so tired. These sessions were supposed to help, not to create more stress.

"Come on, girls," I said quickly. "Help me to cover the rainbow right up. Here's a black wax crayon for you all."

Tabby and Rose were soon attacking my rainbow with gusto, tongues poking out with concentration. Only Leesa was sitting back, her black wax crayon on the table in front of her, not taking part.

"The rainbow was so pretty," she said, sounding tearful. Oh, God, she'd probably had so many things destroyed in her short life already. In its own way, this wax crayon scratch picture activity was as potentially harmful as the tie-dye one had been.

"Don't worry," I said. "We'll see the rainbow again very soon. The next bit is the really fun part. After we've covered everything in black, we're going to take one of these lolly sticks, and we're going to scratch through the black like this. See? Isn't it beautiful?"

I demonstrated, moving the edge of the lolly stick so it removed the black wax crayon to reveal the jewel-like colour beneath. Sneaking a glance at all of their faces, I saw them smile, one by one. Phew.

"Do you want to have a try?" I asked Leesa, offering paper. "You don't have to draw a picture; you can just draw patterns or coloured blocks to cover with the black."

Which was what I should have done myself.

The girls were delighted with the magic revealed by scraping with the lolly sticks. They wanted to do it all over again as soon as they'd finished, bent over their work, fiercely concentrating. Looking up with gap-toothed smiles to share the magic with their mothers.

And their mothers relaxed, taking the opportunity to let their shoulders soften. Leesa's mum did her own picture, covering her sheet of paper with yellow, orange, and red, then scraping back the black to make a pattern of stars and planets. A galaxy of optimism.

"That's beautiful," I told her, and she smiled faintly.

"It's make-believe. But thank you, it was fun."

Jack came over to the table, toy car clutched to his chest, and picked up a black wax crayon. He started to scribble.

I was pleased he was taking part. "That's it, Jack," I said. "Go for it!"

But then he picked up a lolly stick and wanted to scrape away a pattern the way the others were doing. Only it wouldn't work because he hadn't put any colour beneath the black. Soon he was screaming with frustration, and before I could show him what he needed to do, an unpleasant smell—clearly from his nappy—filled the air.

"Sorry, Trish," called Catherine, "Jack needs changing. Want me to do it?"

Baby Emily was asleep now. Trish carefully got to her feet and began to come over. "No, it's all right, he'll only kick off if I don't do it. Will someone hold the baby for me?"

She was looking straight at me, so I automatically put my arms out. Seconds later the precious bundle that was her daughter was in my arms—snuffling and surprisingly heavy—stirring for a few seconds before she settled again. Two months old.

I gazed down into Emily's face, wondering whether it was her birth that had given her mother the impetus to leave an abusive relationship. I had no way of knowing because I didn't know the background stories of any of my workshop participants at the refuge. There was no need for me to know. My role was to run art workshops to help them to connect with their kids. To help them find creativity and hope through making something together. That was all.

"You look like a total natural, Lily," Catherine told me, nodding towards me and the baby.

"She does, doesn't she?"

"Next thing we know she'll be on maternity leave and these workshops will get cancelled."

I did know my way around babies, it was true. But even so, their words had taken me somewhere I didn't want to go. Right back to my thin-walled childhood bedroom with my baby sister crying next door. Suddenly the baby seemed to have doubled in weight. I wanted to give her to one of the mums; to say, *"Here, could you hold her, please? I have to get the paperwork out of my bag."*

I did have to get the paperwork out of my bag. Even at sessions like this, at the women's refuge, we tutors were supposed to get students to complete paperwork. We didn't get any funding for the courses unless the participants set themselves some "measurable goals" and reflected on their progress. And now the girls had finished their pictures and were beginning to look bored again. Very soon everyone would drift off, leaving me literally holding the baby.

"Ladies," I said, "please don't go without filling out your forms. Just a sentence or two about what we've done today and what you got out of it."

I bent to pick up my bag from the floor next to my chair, encountering Emily's soft, downy head with my cheek as I did so. Inhaling her milky, unique-to-a-baby scent. With only one hand, it was a struggle to undo the flap of the bag to reach the paperwork.

"Here, let me help," said Catherine. But she didn't take the baby from me. Instead, she rummaged in my bag. "You got any pens in there? Oh, yeah, I see them. Here you go, girls."

The trio of women settled down to write, their daughters drifting away from the table. For a very brief moment there was perfect peace. Just the sound of pens moving across paper and the gentle breathing of the contented baby in my arms.

Then the door opened to signal the return of Jack and his mum, and very soon the little boy was running around the room with his car again making his *brm brm* noises, and Trish reached to take her daughter back from me.

"Thanks, Lily," she said, and she looked so very tired I wanted to ignore the fact that she hadn't completed her perishing form and to tell my boss all over again that all this red tape and form filling had no place at a women's refuge.

Not that it would do any good. I already knew what she'd say, because I'd heard her say it plenty of times before. *"Presumably, you want to get paid for the work you do, Lily? No forms, no funding. It's as simple as that."*

It wasn't her fault, I supposed. She hadn't put the rules into place. She'd probably felt just like me when she first started out. Probably still did, beneath that tough exterior. Take it or leave it was her attitude. She knew as well as I did that there were plenty more struggling artists hungry for a bit of part-time teaching to help them get by. With a prestigious art college in the town, I was dispensable. If I left because of my principles, someone else would soon take over from me while I was struggling to afford to eat. And besides, leaving the paperwork aside, I did enjoy the work. When I wasn't dyeing children's hands green, anyway.

I always cycled when I worked at the refuge. Cycling got me to places quicker than the bus—I knew all the time-saving cycle tracks and cut-throughs in the city. But after a session at the refuge, I usually pushed my bike back home, taking a little detour so I could walk along the path near the river. I needed some space to leave behind all those faces. The emotions. The undisclosed histories. And doubt, too; there was always plenty of self-doubt about whether I'd done the best job I could have done or not.

Gradually, as I walked along through the scrubby piece of woodland that led to the river, my bike wheels tick-ticking beside me, I became aware of the birdsong or the rustle of a squirrel in the treetops, and I was able to let most of those faces and emotions go.

By the time I reached the bridge across the river, I usually only had the children left in my head. The children were always the hardest to forget.

I stopped on the bridge to stare down at the moving water, my bike propped against the wrought-iron structure. Alex had introduced me to the game of Pooh sticks from the Winnie-the-Pooh books when I first brought him here. You both found a stick and dropped it into the river. Then you rushed to the other side of the bridge to see whose stick emerged first. I was crazy with joy when I won the first time we played.

"You threw your stick out a bit when you let it go!" Alex protested. "You're supposed to just drop it."

So, next time, I just let it fall. And I won again. Pooh sticks champion of the world, me.

That day, straight from the refuge, I imagined the children I'd been working with that afternoon playing Pooh sticks. Leesa, Rose, and Tabby, concentrating, their tongues protruding the way they had when they'd made their wax scratch pictures. Jack, demanding to be picked up.

Had anyone ever played Pooh sticks with any of them? If not, I hoped somebody would very soon.

I picked up a stick and dropped it in, crossing to search for it from the other side of the bridge. But I never saw it emerge because something else caught my attention. One of the reeds just where the river began to bend, moving in an unnatural way that had nothing to do with the gentle breeze. A kingfisher, staring down into the river, on the hunt for fish.

I gasped, watching it. It almost made my heart stop it was so beautiful.

Sapphire, cerulean, turquoise—my artist's mind searched fruitlessly to describe that exact blue. I switched it off and just accepted the gift of the sight—the utter treat of the bird's perfection. And then the kingfisher launched itself from the reed and flew straight towards me, ducking beneath the bridge. I dashed to the other side to watch it fly right up the river. Then it was gone, lost in the shadows of the overhanging branches.

I got onto my bike—because walking was too slow now—and made for home, my legs pumping, the trees and the river rushing past me, a huge smile on my face, the problems of the women and children in the refuge tucked away until next time. I slowed down only for dog walkers and their charges, smiling automatically when they thanked me, my whole focus on what colours I would use to recreate the experience of that kingfisher. How I would incorporate it into the painting I was working on.

So it was a surprise when I got home to find Alex already there, home from work early, the house filled with the smells of cooking, the kitchen with the sounds of sizzling and chopping. Just in time, before Alex could look up and see my expression of disappointment, I remembered that Inga and Matt were coming to dinner. The kingfisher would have to wait.

"Hi, sweetheart," he said, looking up with a smile. "Did you have a good day?"

"Perfect," I replied, dumping my bag down and going over to kiss him.

10

Matt and Inga arrived ten minutes late—they were always ten minutes late—and greeted me with kisses, hugs, and, in Inga's case, perfume. She'd rarely worn perfume when she'd been an artist, but now she was an estate agent—*"It's not selling out, Lily, it's growing up. And besides, viewing properties is a perfect job for someone as nosy as I am"*—she wore perfume and full make-up all the time. It made her seem different, but you didn't have to scratch far beneath the surface to find the old Inga, albeit a happier version of her. She'd got the estate-agent opportunity via a temporary typing job at their offices—clearly they'd recognised her suitability and had taken her on as a trainee. The rest, as they say, is history. Though it still surprised me, shocked me even, that somebody could give up making art and still be happy, because I knew I'd feel completely lost—as if I'd abandoned a fundamental part of who I was—if I were to do it.

Over dinner, Inga talked about some of the properties she'd recently viewed, and then Matt told us about some new clients he'd started working with.

"So, I go to meet these new clients, and they've done a rough sketch of the layout of the inside of their new house to give me an idea of what they want. And there's this strange square room marked out downstairs—too small to be a study, not a utility or a cloakroom because those are already marked on the sketch. The room's labelled PC, so I rack my brains to think what that could stand for, because I don't want to look ignorant, but I just can't think what it is, so I have to ask."

"And what was it?" asked Alex.

Matt grinned at us. "A padded cell."

"A padded cell?" repeated Alex.

Matt nodded. "I kid you not."

"Why would they want a padded cell?"

"They didn't say, and I didn't like to ask."

"Did they want a dungeon too?" asked Alex. "A torture chamber?"

"No, just a padded cell."

"Are you going to give them one?" I asked.

"Of course. So long as there's planning permission and it fits building regs, the client gets what the client wants."

I wondered, as I'd done many times before, if he minded that. Whether he missed the status of working for his old London firm. Whenever I brought the subject up with Alex, he told me I worried too much, and Matt was fine. But I'd noticed that Matt seemed to drink more than he used to. And I'd read in the newspaper about his old firm winning a prestigious architecture award for a new building in Docklands, so I couldn't help worrying.

"Sometimes I think you worry about Matt more than you worry about me," Alex had said once, only half joking.

"Should I worry about you, then?" I asked. "Is there anything wrong in the world of insurance advice?"

He grabbed me and pinned me against a wall to kiss me. "No, my life is utterly perfect. Or it would be, if you'd stop fretting about Max's career and come upstairs for a quickie."

"How are you settling in to your new home?" I asked now.

"It'd be better with less nature," Inga said. "Those bloody wood pigeons I told you about are back again, *woo hoo hooing* on the roof at all hours. I swear, until we moved to the countryside, I had no idea how fucking noisy it was. Owls hooting, foxes barking, tree branches clattering." She shuddered. "You can keep your sounds of nature. Give me a padded cell any day."

I'd questioned Inga's suitability for country living when Matt had first bought the house to the north of the city. The changes he'd made to it were incredible—so light and spacious, with amazing views of the surrounding countryside. But ever since they'd moved in, Inga had practically worn the road out driving to and from the city. But then she did need to travel a lot with her work.

Alex cleared his throat. "If it's okay, I . . . well, I've got something I want to say. Something I've wanted to say for ages. Well, ask rather than say, I suppose. And I can't think of a better time to do it, when we're together with the people we both love most in the world."

He looked suddenly nervous. Terrified, even.

"Alex," I said, my heart suddenly pounding, desperate for something, anything, to stop him from speaking. For Inga to rant about owls again, or to break into another one of her anecdotes about property viewings. For the ceiling to fall in. Anything to hold back what I sensed Alex was about to say. Yet at the same time there was a strong feeling of recognition unfurling within me. My subconscious had known this was a possibility for a while.

So, why the fuck hadn't it warned me?

"Lily," said Alex, staring into my eyes. "I adore you. I want to spend the rest of my life with you. Will you marry me?"

I was aware of Matt's steady gaze on us both. Of Inga's swift intake of breath. But mostly, I was aware of the love and hope streaming to me from Alex's face.

Time slowed right down. A series of images flitted through my mind. Me, standing on the landing in our house, gazing regretfully into my studio as Alex called to me from downstairs. The two of us walking hand in hand along the beach together the day Matt and Inga moved away, with the screams of the people in the fairground drifting towards us on the breeze. Me, hurrying home in the early hours of Christmas morning, a sick, ominous feeling growing in my belly with every step I took.

My hands began to shake.

"Lily?" he said, and I emerged from my memories to see his kind face focused on mine. His arms waiting to embrace me; to hold me safe forever.

"Yes, Alex," I said. "Yes, I'll marry you."

11

Inga screamed with excitement. Alex jumped onto the table, narrowly missing the salad bowl, and swung himself down in the space beside me like someone dismounting from the pommel horse in the Olympic games.

"Really?" he said, his face inches from mine. "That's really a yes?"

I nodded. He kissed me—a suction cup smacker of a kiss. Then he fumbled in his shirt pocket, brought out a ring and slid it onto my finger where it twinkled brightly against some black oil pastel I'd missed under one of my nails when I'd washed my hands.

"Congratulations, you two," said Matt, getting up to kiss first me, then Alex, a kiss that turned into back slapping, hand shaking, and much brotherly laughter.

"Wow," said Inga, embracing me in turn. "Just wow. I'm so happy for you both."

"Thank you," I said, ignoring what looked like questions on her face. *"Did you have any idea about this? Are you sure you want to say yes?"*

"This calls for champagne," she said. "Do they sell champagne in your corner shop?"

"No need," said Alex smugly. "There's a bottle in the fridge."

"To Alex and Lily!" Matt toasted us after the cork had been popped and the glasses filled.

"To Alex and Lily."

"Are you happy?" Alex asked me in bed, after Matt and Inga had gone home.

My face ached from smiling. My head from the champagne. I wanted to say, *I think so, yes. I just need some time to process it all. It was lovely of you to ask me, but I wish we'd talked about it together first. That you'd asked me when we were alone.*

But I didn't say any of that.

"Yes, I'm happy."

Alex beamed at me. "Good. Come here."

We made love, the easy passion of two people who have learnt how to play each other's bodies. In the morning, there was a text from Inga. Call me. Let's meet. Soon. I knew she didn't want to discuss bridesmaid dresses or hen parties. She wanted to grill me about my feelings. But I wasn't entirely sure what they were myself, so she would have to wait.

I had to go to a staff meeting that morning. I never had enjoyed them; all the other tutors seemed to have known each other forever, bandying jargon and acronyms about all over the place, speaking about learning outcomes and self-evaluation. They were always polite to me; friendly, even. But, feeling out of my depth as I did, I tended to keep myself to myself. Or at least, I usually did. But that morning, my manager spotted my engagement ring the second I stepped foot in the meeting room, and the first five minutes of the meeting was given over to congratulations. Well, it felt like five minutes. Ten, even, with everyone looking at me and oohing and aahing at the ring. I had never been so popular.

"I didn't put you down as the marrying type," my manager said.

It was difficult to know what to say to that. "Didn't you?"

"No. You seem too independent."

"What a gorgeous ring," somebody else said. "Have you set a date yet?"

"Not yet, no. Alex only asked me last night."

"Oh, how romantic! Did he get down on one knee? My husband almost fell over when he asked me. It was so funny."

Etc.

I was quite glad when the meeting got underway. Not that I absorbed much of it. I was too busy trying to make sense of what had just happened. It was as if, by agreeing to marry Alex, I'd joined some sort of a club. As if I was suddenly like other people. Which only drew my attention to the fact that I never had felt like that. As a child and a teenager, it had been what I wanted more than anything—just to be an ordinary kid, demanding the latest toys before moving on to plaster my bedroom wall with posters of pop stars. To have parents who nagged when I wore my skirts too short or developed a liking for black lipstick.

I never had managed that because Mum hadn't cared what I did. Well, she hadn't cared much about anything, really. And until that last disastrous night, I'd been too busy looking out for Violet to do much in the way of rebellion. I was used to being on the sidelines; being different.

Twisting the ring round and round on my finger, I attempted to pinpoint exactly what was wrong. I loved Alex. We'd been together for a while now. Marriage was the logical next step, especially as we'd just bought a house together. Everything was fine. I just needed to get used to the idea, that was all.

I was meeting Alex for lunch in the city after my meeting finished. I arrived at the café first and managed to get a table by the window. I soon saw Alex walking across the square from the covered market, blond hair flopping about in the wind. It needed cutting; he always left it a bit too long between appointments, so it was as if he had two identities—the floppy-haired dandy of a man he was now and the short-haired serious man he was when he had it all cut off. The longer hairstyle made him look boyish. Which he was. Alex loved fooling around and making jokes. He hadn't changed much at all in the time since we'd met.

I saw him notice me. Watched his face light up. His pace quicken. Then he was inside the café, bending to kiss me, grabbing hold of my left hand to take a look at the ring nestled there on my finger.

"You haven't lost it yet, then?"

"No, Alex, I haven't lost it."

He grinned. "Good. How was your meeting?"

"Very dull. I'm not sure I even know what it was about, to be honest."

"Sounds like all the meetings I've ever been to. What d'you want to eat? I'll go and order."

The café was a large space inside a building that housed the library, with tables spread inside and outside. It was a popular place, especially at lunchtime, and I'd only got a table by the window because somebody had just been leaving when I arrived. There hadn't been time for anybody to clear our table, so, while Alex went to get our food, I stacked up the used crockery and moved it to another table a few metres away. As I did so, a voice hailed me, and I looked over to see Trish with her two children.

It was good to see her, and I smiled and went over. "Hi, Trish. How are you?"

"We're okay, thanks. Just been in a long queue at the council offices. I promised Jack a hot chocolate because he was a good boy, but I'm busting to go to the loo. You couldn't watch him and hold Emily while I go quickly, could you? Sorry to ask. I didn't plan this very well."

"Of course, it's fine."

"Thanks. Be a good boy for Lily, Jack. Mummy won't be long."

I sat down at the table, holding the baby, who seemed to stiffen slightly in distress as she saw her mother walk away. I bounced her up and down on my lap a bit.

Jack held his hands in front of his face, then pulled them away again, saying, "Peep-bo!"

I pretended to be scared. Jack laughed. More encouragingly, baby Emily seemed entertained too. So, I placed her carefully in the crook of my arm and picked up a menu from the table, using it to hide my own face. Then I moved it aside. "Peep-bo!"

She gave a gurgle of laughter, so I did it again. She laughed again, the sound making me smile. "You like that, don't you?"

"Me do it too!" said Jack.

"Okay," I said, "let's both do it."

So, we both peepboed the baby, who seemed to find it even funnier than ever. When Alex came over, all three of us were laughing.

"Hello," he said, "who do we have here, then?"

"Oh, Alex, this is Jack and his baby sister, Emily. They're both in one of my art classes. Mummy's just gone to the loo. Jack, this is my boyfriend, Alex."

I ought to have said *fiancé*, not *boyfriend*, but Alex didn't seem to notice.

"Very pleased to meet you, Jack," he said.

"My hands went green," Jack told him, and Alex laughed.

"Did they? And was that Lily's fault?"

Jack nodded seriously. "I like blue best," he said.

"You'll have to tell Lily to use blue dye next time," Alex said.

"Stop it," I told Alex, and he laughed.

Emily began to whimper again, so I continued with our game of peep-bo, while Alex told Jack that blue was his favourite colour, too, and they started to list all the things they could think of that were blue. When Trish returned to the table I introduced Alex to her. It was several minutes before we returned to our own table.

"You're really good with kids," Alex told me as I bit into my sandwich.

"You have to be with my job," I said.

"Come on," he said. "That wasn't just work. You really liked them."

I shrugged. "They were both being cute. What's not to like?"

"It's just nice to see another side to you, that's all," he said. Then he went on to talk about something amusing one of his friends at work had said that morning, and the subject was dropped.

But later on, at home, Alex said, "I was thinking, maybe we should move into the back bedroom. Turn the front bedroom into your studio."

I frowned. "Why would we do that? We only recently finished decorating in there."

We were watching TV, sitting side by side on the sofa, drinking our post-dinner cups of coffee. Alex didn't look away from the screen. "I know, but there's quite a lot of traffic noise, isn't there? Besides, the back bedroom has the little room off it."

The Victorian terraced houses in our street all had the same small box room off the second bedroom. It could only be accessed through the bedroom and was too small to be used for anything much more than storage. At the moment, I had my finished paintings stacked in there.

"What would be the benefit of that?" I asked Alex, still missing the point. "D'you fancy having a walk-in dressing room or something?"

He smiled, giving me a nudge, still not looking away from the TV. "No, silly," he said. "I just thought we could use the small room for a cot when the time comes."

I stared at him, aghast. He was still watching TV, but I sensed he wasn't trying to avoid my gaze. He looked quite relaxed. Quite unaware he'd just dropped an enormous bombshell.

Jesus. I'd told him I didn't want kids. Inga had even said it the night we met. We'd both agreed not to have any "little shits" that day on the beach. Where the hell had this come from?

"Don't you think?" Alex prompted me when I still didn't answer, and he was turning towards me when his phone started ringing.

He picked it up from the coffee table. "It's Dad," he said.

I wanted to tell him to reject the call. Tell him we needed to talk. Right now. But it was too late.

"Hi, Dad. Everything all right?"

But it soon became clear that everything was not all right at all. That whatever Alex's father was telling Alex was about to totally eclipse what I'd been about to say to Alex about his plans for the small bedroom.

By the time Alex ended the call, his face was completely drained of colour. He turned hollow eyes in my direction. "It's Mum," he said. "She's got breast cancer."

12

It turned out Janice had put off going to see her doctor when she'd first noticed a lump, and now the cancer had spread. Appallingly, it was too late to do anything except find a balance that would prolong her life for a few more months while leaving her as comfortable as possible. Her decline was rapid.

Alex was devastated. In shock. He spent most of his free time at the hospital with his mother and supporting his father as much as Stanley would allow him to. And when Alex got home, he poured his sadness and frustration out to me.

"Dad's so angry all the time. He's convinced Mum's not trying to get better. That all she needs to do is think positively and she'll be cured. It's ridiculous. What was the point of us paying for a second opinion if he's just going to ignore it? He even shouted at her today. It was awful, Lil. I was this far from hitting him." He held up his thumb and forefinger to indicate how close it had been.

It was all too easy to imagine retired high-achiever Stanley not taking the loss of his wife well. She was the backbone of their relationship. "He's probably in denial, don't you think? He just can't stand the thought of losing her."

"Well, neither can I," Alex said passionately, his eyes filling with tears. "If there was anything I could do, I'd do it. I just want her last months to be as peaceful and as happy as possible. Why can't Dad see that?"

I held him in my arms. "He's hurting, that's all. You mustn't fall out with him; he'll still be here after your mum's gone. I know you've always been closest to her, but you don't have a bad relationship with your dad, do you? Not normally. He won't be able to go on denying it all forever, and then he's going to really need you."

Alex sighed, rubbing his face. "I guess so. God, I'm glad I've got you, Lil. I don't know how I'd cope if I was dealing with this on my own. Will you come with me when I go to see Mum next time? She was asking to see your engagement ring."

"Of course."

Janice seemed to have lost a third of her body weight since I'd last seen her. Dreadfully frail, her eyes dark in her shadowed eye sockets, she was a husk of the woman who'd once challenged me not to break her son's heart.

"Hello, Lily," she said after Alex had kissed her. "This is a turn up for the books, isn't it?"

"It's come as such a shock to us," I said, knowing I sounded pathetic, but having no clue what to say to her.

She laughed—a short, bitter-sounding laugh. I noticed there were dark roots in her hair. I hadn't even guessed she wasn't a natural blonde. "A shock," she said. "Yes, that's one way of describing it." She began to cough, her whole body racked by it. Alex quickly held a beaker of water to her lips.

"Take a sip, Mum," he said, supporting her head, and she did.

"You've been through all this before, haven't you, Lily?" Janice said when she could speak again. "With your own mother."

I felt the blood drain from my face as I nodded. How awful to be confronted by your long-ago lie in circumstances like this.

When I didn't speak, she patted my hand, assuming the memories were too painful to talk about. Then she said, "Anyway, I'm so sick of thinking about it. Of talking about me. Thinking about treatments and time scales and blood counts. Let me see that ring of yours, Lily. Alex said he chose it himself. I hope he did you proud."

I held out my hand, the diamond on the ring sparkling in the light from the window.

Janice looked at it, her breathing laboured. "It's beautiful," she said. "Good choice, Alex."

Alex's voice cracked. "Thanks, Mum."

"All you need to do now," she said, looking from him to me and back to him again, "is get married quickly, so I can be at the wedding."

Alex and I exchanged glances. Janice had two months to live at the very most.

"Don't look like that, both of you," she said with a measure of her old strength. "I know it means you won't have time to plan the wedding of your dreams, but you can always have a second bigger affair after I'm gone. It would mean so much to me, to be there. To see my darling boy set up for life with the woman he loves." She paused, a single tear trickling down the side of her face into her hair. "After all, I won't be around to meet my grandchildren, will I? And that breaks my heart, it really does."

I felt sick.

Alex began to sob. "Oh, Mum."

Janice held out her arms to him, and he went into them.

"There, there. I'm sorry to upset you. It's just that, with so little time left, I have to say what needs to be said, don't I?"

She looked at me then, over Alex's heaving shoulders, her eyes searching for reassurance. Confirmation. It was my cue to say something. Anything. But I wasn't sure I could. I don't think I'd ever been more grateful to see anyone than I was to see the nurse entering the ward with a trolley of medical equipment.

"Time to take some more bloods, I'm afraid, Janice. Perhaps your visitors could wait outside?"

Alex pulled himself together, and we trooped outside to the waiting area to sit hand in hand on orange-plastic chairs. He was hurting so badly, and there was so much more pain ahead of him. So far, as far as

I could tell, Alex had barely experienced pain in his life. It was going to change him forever. Force him to grow up.

After a moment, he cleared his throat. "Would that be all right for you? What Mum suggested? Bringing the wedding forwards? I know it will be a big rush, but we'd still be married, wouldn't we? And I think . . . well, I would like Mum to be there. In fact, I can't imagine getting married without her being there."

I longed for another interruption. For someone else to come along.

Miraculously, my phone bleeped. I reached for it from my bag, like a lifeline. It was a message from Amy, suggesting we catch up for a drink soon. I didn't tell Alex that. Instead I put my phone back in my bag and stood up.

"Sorry," I said. "Can we talk about this tomorrow? That was my manager, reminding me she wants a report about my work at the women's refuge for a meeting tomorrow. I'd forgotten all about it with everything that's happened. I'll have to go and finish it. Sorry. Will you be all right here on your own?"

Alex looked at me. "I won't be on my own, will I? I'll be with Mum." A tear rolled down his cheek. He wiped it quickly away. Attempted a brave smile. "I'll be fine. You go and get your work done. I'll see you later."

"Okay, thanks. See you later. Give your mum my love, won't you?"

"Wait," he said. "How will you get home?"

The hospital was a few miles out of town, and we'd come in Alex's car.

"I'll catch a bus. There are loads from here. I can think out my report so I'm ready to start work as soon as I get home."

"Okay."

I kissed him. "Bye, love. See you later."

Then I left my sad, bewildered-looking fiancé on his own in his hour of need and took my cowardly, lying butt out to the bus stop at the front of the hospital. And when the next bus to arrive was headed in the direction of Matt and Inga's house, I took that one instead of waiting for the one that would take me home. I couldn't just go home and sit there waiting for Alex to get back. Couldn't paint with all this churning around in my mind. I needed to talk to someone. If I didn't, I might just explode.

A heavily pregnant woman with a young child got on the bus. She looked happy, not careworn, and I wondered what had taken her to the hospital. She certainly hadn't just visited her fiancé's dying mother by the look of her.

They took the two empty seats in front of my seat.

"Can we have burgers tonight, Mummy?" asked the little girl, who looked about five.

"No, we're having chicken casserole, remember? Mummy put the slow cooker on before we came out."

"I like burgers more."

The woman stroked her daughter's hair. "Don't worry, I'm sure there'll be plenty of burgers when the baby comes. Pizza too. Mummy and Daddy will be too busy to do much cooking, I expect."

"Can the baby come soon, Mummy?" asked the girl.

The woman laughed. "Oh, so you're in a hurry now, are you? Now you know you'll get burgers when the baby's here?"

The little girl nodded, giggling. "Burger Baby."

"You are not going to call your little sister Burger Baby, young lady."

The girl giggled some more. The woman in the seat adjacent to theirs caught my eye and smiled, shaking her head. I smiled back.

"Come here, trouble," the mother said, pulling her daughter into her side and planting a kiss on the top of her head.

The little girl snuggled, contentedly sucking her thumb, entirely confident she was loved, so openly loving of her mother, even one who wanted to feed her healthy chicken casserole instead of burgers.

I wondered what the woman's work was. Whether she had work. Whether she'd given it up or gone part time after she'd had her daughter, or if the little girl had gone into full-time childcare before she'd started school. Whether it sometimes seemed to the mother as if her life was one long scramble to fit everything in, and there was no time for herself.

If she was sometimes overwhelmed, or whether she was usually perfectly content with her lot the way she clearly was today. Then I rummaged in my bag for my phone and plugged myself into my music, closing my eyes to blot everything else out.

At Matt and Inga's house, my knock was answered by Matt.

"Lily, hi. What a lovely surprise. Inga's not back from work yet, but come in, come in."

It was a relief somehow, to have Matt to myself. A treat. If Inga was here, she'd probably ply me with questions I didn't feel up to answering.

"You look as if you were just going out," I said, taking in his walking shoes and the jumper thrown around his shoulders.

"I was just going out for a walk before I cook dinner. Touring the estate, you know?" He smiled. "Want to come?"

I nodded, realising I couldn't think of anything I'd like better. "Yes, please."

"Great. Want to borrow Inga's walking boots? She's barely worn them."

"No, that's okay. My trainers will be fine."

"All right, then." He stepped out of the house and pulled the door closed. "How did you get here?"

I fell into step beside him. "I caught a bus. From the hospital. Alex is still there."

"Ah, yes, poor Janice. How's Alex taking it? Sorry, daft question. I imagine he's in bits?"

I nodded. "He is, yes."

"They've always been really close, Alex and his mum. We used to tease him about it at school, but really, I think we were probably jealous."

We were heading across the lawn towards the trees at the edge of the property. A slight breeze was blowing, and I could hear it soughing in the fir trees. I let out a deep breath I hadn't been aware I was holding in.

"How about you?" Matt asked me gently. "How are you doing?"

"Oh, I . . ." As I began to speak, a ghost glided along the edge of the trees, head turned down towards the ground, searching for prey. "Was that an owl?"

"That was our barn owl. It's the tawny owls that really drive Inga crazy. They're not out just yet. Inga would say they deliberately wait until she's gone to bed."

But I was too entranced by the barn owl to want to discuss Inga's dissatisfactions. It was still gliding along, turning its round face this way and that as it listened for its prey. Stunningly beautiful.

"He's hunting for the voles that live along the stream bank," Matt told me, and as he spoke, the stream came into view, a glittering strip of silver flitting in and out of the shadows of the line of trees.

"Poor voles," I said.

The owl flew off, and we stopped at the edge of the stream to watch it flowing, the water bubbling as it caught on some large stones, the peaceful sound a balm for my troubled mind. Out of nowhere, a memory sprang into my mind. A long-ago day with my mum before Violet was born.

"My mother and I made a dam on a stream like this one day. I was about seven, I think." I spoke without thinking, probably as a result of the raw emotion of the last few hours, taking myself by surprise before I could stuff the memory back down inside me the way I always stuffed childhood memories down.

Matt was looking at me, his smile a prompt for me to talk about it. "Sounds like a special day."

"It was," I said, Matt's expression somehow making the impulse to drift along like the stream into my memories less reckless than it would normally feel.

It had been a rare day when everything coalesced to be perfect. Sunny weather, no school, Mum awake, and well. Food in the fridge, no boyfriend imminently arriving.

"Come on, kiddo," she'd said. "We're going for a picnic."

I was excited as I dressed in my favourite summer dress, running downstairs to help Mum pack some supplies before we left to catch a bus to take us to the outskirts of the city. Once there, we spread our blanket, laid out our edible treasures, and ate while looking out at the view of the cathedral spire and the distant city. Birds were singing. Wildflowers bobbed about in the breeze. A stream babbled somewhere nearby. And best of all, Mum was smiling.

"Let's have a paddle," Mum said when we got too hot, so we went down to the stream and took off our shoes.

"Tuck your dress up into your knickers so it doesn't get wet," Mum said, helping me to do it, and then we paddled, the icy water delicious between our toes.

"Come on, let's make a dam," said Mum. "My dad showed me how to do it when I was your age."

We collected sticks and fallen branches and piled them up across the stream, Mum directing where they should go, until finally the water was deep enough to make a pool.

"That's worn me out," Mum said, and she took herself off to have a nap, leaving me to get lost in a world of make-believe, pretending the dam was hot coals I had to run across, making sticks breach the dam and topple down imaginary rapids. I was so absorbed I didn't notice my dress had come free from my knickers and was now soaking wet and filthy with mud from the stream bank. Oh, no. Mum was going to be cross.

With apprehension settling on me, I turned my back on the happy hours spent playing in the stream to find Mum asleep on her back on the picnic blanket, her mouth open, an empty wine bottle lying beside her.

My heart sank still further. She wouldn't want me to disturb her, I knew that. But the sun had gone behind a cloud, and I was shivering in my wet dress.

"Mummy?" I said quietly.

There was no response. I couldn't even hear her breathing.

"Mummy?"

I shook her, suddenly panicked, and when she still didn't move, I shook her again. "Mummy!"

Suddenly she snapped into abrupt wakefulness. "Jesus Christ, Lily, I was asleep."

By now I was really shivering. "I'm cold, Mummy."

She struggled upright, mimicking me. "*I'm cold, Mummy.* Well, you shouldn't have got your lovely dress wet, should you? Look at it. It's ruined. You always have to fucking well go and spoil everything, Lily, don't you?"

"Lily?" Matt said. "Is everything okay?"

I wiped away tears I hadn't known were falling, thinking about what I'd learnt from that day by the stream and countless other days like it. To keep my feelings and my needs to myself. To avoid conflict at all costs.

Matt put an arm around my shoulders. "What is it? Tell me."

"Let's just say that day started out well and ended badly."

"I'm so sorry."

He waited; a listening pause I knew I could fill with stories of my sad, neglected childhood if I wanted to. And to be honest, the idea of letting go, of unburdening myself to Matt was very tempting. I could imagine the way he'd listen to me; carefully hearing out my story. Offering comfort after I'd finished.

But then what? I'd be vulnerable, the past out in the open. And Matt would think of me that way: poor, broken Lily with a drunken mother.

So, I took in a shuddering breath, saying, "Oh well, it was a long time ago."

"You're shivering. D'you want to go back to the house?"

I shook my head. "No, it's fine. I need to go soon. Alex will be back from the hospital."

"I'll drive you home. Unless you want to wait to see Inga?"

I supposed seeing Inga must have been the reason I'd caught the bus here from the hospital, but somehow that wasn't what I wanted any longer. "No," I said. "I'd better go. A lift home would be great. Thank you."

But Matt made no move to go back to the house. "Look," he said, "tell me to butt out if you like, but is there something else bothering you? You seem . . ."

"All over the place? Fraught?"

He smiled. "No, just a bit troubled, that's all."

I sighed. "Janice has asked me and Alex to bring our wedding forwards so she can be there."

"God, poor woman."

"I know. It's so sad. But I . . ."

"Don't want to be rushed?"

I shook my head. "No, I don't. But Alex wants to do it. He says we're getting married anyway, so why not earlier? But there are things we need to talk about, the two of us. Things I don't want to bring up while he's so upset about his mum."

"Is this about having children?"

I whirled round to look at him. "He told you about that?"

"Not in any big announcement way, no. Just in passing. We were out together, and there was this new dad with a baby strapped to his chest, and Alex said, 'D'you think I'd look good in one of those?' You know, like the harness or the carrier or whatever it's called was an item of clothing or something. And I said, 'I don't think those things come with a baby, mate.'"

It was funny. Except that it really wasn't.

"I don't want to have children. I thought I'd always been really clear about that. But I guess I can't have been, can I?"

Matt sighed. "Look, I adore Alex. But sometimes he's got selective vision. When we were in India, the poverty and suffering seemed to just pass him by. He was too fixated by the sights and sounds to notice it, whereas it was all I could see."

I pictured the two of them in India; imagined myself there with them. "I'd be the same as you, I think," I said, and he nodded.

"Yes, I think you would."

It was an oddly intimate moment, this acknowledgement that we were similar to each other, and suddenly I remembered Alex, in Wales, pointing out how at ease Matt and I were with each other. The slight snag of insecurity in his voice as he'd said it.

Darkness was beginning to gather. The silver highlights on the stream were gone, and the birds had settled down for the night. Alex would certainly be home now, wondering where I was. I was surprised he hadn't texted or called yet. Then I remembered my phone was off from being at the hospital. I ought to hurry home. Yet I didn't want to. I wanted to stay here, in Matt's reassuring, comforting presence, enjoying that feeling of kinship. Of being understood.

And suddenly, out of nowhere, I found the courage to speak. "My mother drank," I said into the silence, my voice shaking slightly. "She'd drink, and then she'd pass out and leave my little sister crying to be fed."

"Jesus, Lily."

Matt's arm went around my shoulders, anchoring me.

"I'd hear Violet through my bedroom wall. On and on. I'd go and try to wake Mum up, but I couldn't. So, in the end, I learnt how to feed my sister myself."

"God, how old were you?"

"About eight."

"Bloody hell."

He held me close. I felt tears start to slide down my face. It was a relief to have spoken the words out loud. To be understood. Comforted. But there was guilt, too, plenty of it. Because there'd been so many chances to tell Inga and Alex about it, and I never had.

"I just can't imagine how that must have been for you." He shook his head, pushing me away slightly to look at me. "How can we have been friends for as long as we have and not known this about you?"

I sighed, wiping my wet cheeks with my hands. "It's not something I find easy to talk about. And I suppose I don't want to dwell on it. It's all such a long time ago."

"That kind of thing never leaves you, though, does it?"

"It doesn't seem to do, no. I feel . . . I feel as if I've already been a mother, you know? Taking care of Violet like that. And it was hard, Matt. So hard."

"Of course, it was. You were a child, for Christ's sake! God. Does Alex know about this? Have you talked to him?"

I shook my head, feeling ashamed. "No. Please, don't tell him, Matt. Or Inga. I know I have to. And I will. Just when I'm ready, okay?"

He nodded. "All right. But do it soon, okay? I really think, if you tell him about it, he'll understand better."

I was doubtful. Alex's childhood had been the stuff of dreams. Loved, provided for, his every need and whim anticipated. "Maybe."

"Have I ever told you about my dad?" Matt said suddenly.

"Not really, no."

"He was a workaholic. Either away or too whacked from running his business to interact much with us kids. Mum was always shushing us, making us play quietly with the TV volume down low. If I ever become a dad I'll make sure I'm there for my children. Not that it's likely I ever will, because Inga doesn't want kids, either, as you know."

Shit. Immediately I thought about the baby he had no clue about. The baby that was still very much on my conscience because I'd had to keep quiet about the abortion. Here I was, taking comfort from Matt, confident enough of his regard to spew out secrets I'd never told anybody before about my past, when all the time I was keeping a huge secret from him. And I'd just asked him to do the very same thing for me. Jesus, what a mess. A dirty, stinking mess.

"What . . . ," I started, trying to speak normally, stopping to lick my lips. "What d'you think about that?"

"You mean about not becoming a father? I don't really think about it, to be honest. It's just the way things are. Like I say, until very recently I'd no idea it was in Alex's plans either."

He turned to face me in the darkness. "You have to speak to him, Lily. Not just about not wanting children, but about the wedding too.

Janice has always been really good to me, but it's wrong, what she's asking of you."

The feeling of intimacy was back again. That feeling of being fundamentally understood. But this time it was tempered by my shame. Matt deserved better.

I looked down at the ground. "Some would say I'm selfish not to give her what she wants, when she's dying."

"You can't just get married and have a child to please other people."

I nodded. He was right; I couldn't. But it was one thing to know it, and another thing to try to convince Alex.

13

"I'm here if you ever need to talk. You know that, don't you?" Matt said when we stopped outside my house.

"Thank you," I said, emotional all over again, kissing his cheek.

He kissed mine. "Good night, Lily."

"Night, Matt."

When I got home, the lights were on in the house. As I'd expected, Alex was home before me. The front door opened as Matt's car drove away.

"Was that Matt?" Alex asked, staring up the road.

"Yes." I thought quickly. Conjured up a lie. "I went to the library to write my report in the end. Matt passed me when I was walking home."

"You should have asked him in."

"I did. He had to get back."

We went inside. Alex closed the door. "What made you go to the library?"

I shrugged. Took my jacket off. Hated myself. "Change of scene, you know? I remembered on the bus that I had the memory stick with me. Thought it would help me focus."

"And did it?"

I nodded. "Yes. All done. Want a cup of tea?"

"No thanks. I had one while I was waiting for you. Want me to make you one?"

"No, that's okay. I can do it." I walked past him. "Are you hungry?"

"Not in the least."

"Me neither." Lying to the man you share your life with can take the edge off your appetite, I suppose.

I felt like shit. Especially when Alex followed me into the kitchen and carried on with the conversation he'd started at the hospital.

"You should have seen Mum after you left. The wedding's really given her something to focus on. She reminded me there's that community centre near their house we could use for the reception. You know, the one where we went to see that play that time? I know it's a bit rough and ready, but you and Inga could make it nice, couldn't you, with your artistic flair? Oh, and Mum said you can wear her wedding dress, if you like? You've seen it, haven't you? Classic, stylish. Not an eighties meringue or anything like that. We thought it'd save a bit of money. Speed things up, too, if you haven't got to shop for one. You're the same size, aren't you, and you'd look gorgeous in anything, anyway."

The kettle had boiled, but apart from taking a mug from the cupboard, I'd done nothing to make my tea. My face was turned away from Alex, but he must have caught something of my gathering tension because he broke off to say, "Sorry, it was just so good to see her fired up about something. You don't mind, do you?"

I turned then, feeling about a hundred years old, my body suddenly aching and heavy, as if Matt and I had gone for a long hike instead of a gentle saunter around his garden. "Alex," I said, "we need to talk."

I reached for his hand. Led him back to the sitting room.

"I'm sorry. It feels as if Mum and I are taking over, doesn't it?" he said, eyes searching my face as we sat down on the sofa, so wide off the mark it was as if we were complete strangers instead of long-term lovers.

"It isn't that. It's the whole thing. Bringing the wedding forwards." I took a deep breath. Made myself look at him. "I can't do it, Alex."

He was frowning. "Why not? It's only a few months earlier than we planned."

"I know, but . . ."

"You should have seen her face, Lil. She was so happy."

I couldn't speak. Alex filled the silence.

"Look, I want her at my wedding, okay? Christ, I want her at all the major events of my life." His voice cracked. "But I can't have that, can I? Because she's fucking dying."

"I'm so sorry, Alex."

He swiped an angry hand across his eyes. "If you were really sorry, you'd agree. Why won't you? Is it because you don't want a dying woman spoiling the wedding photos, or what?"

I recoiled from him. "Of course not. What do you take me for? You know I'm not like that."

"I'm not sure about anything at the moment," he said spitefully.

I took another deep breath to pull myself together. "It's got nothing to do with the type of wedding or the wedding photos or any of that crap. None of that stuff is important to me."

"What is it, then?"

I sighed. "Like I said, there are things we need to talk about. Things I'd hoped we could deal with sometime in the future."

"You mean after Mum's dead?" Alex said bitterly, and once again, I flinched.

It was what I'd meant, but put like that, it sounded brutal. This was no good. Alex was overwrought, not in any kind of frame of mind for this discussion.

"I think we ought to talk about this tomorrow," I said. "When we've both calmed down."

Alex shook his head. "Oh, no. Neither of us will be able to sleep with this—whatever it is—hanging over us. Come on, tell me. Tell me what's wrong."

I studied my fingers for a moment. Found the courage to dive in. "It's about children. Alex, I don't want to have them. I never have done. And you . . . suddenly you're all, *we can put a cot in the small bedroom*, and I . . ."

He stared at me with disbelief. "That's it? Really? Lily, that was nothing. Just a stupid daydream. Forget about it."

"Alex, I saw your face. It wasn't nothing."

He sighed. "Well, all right, I guess I just assumed that one day, somewhere along the line . . . I mean, people say they don't want kids all the time, don't they? And then they get older, and they change their minds."

"I'm not going to. And I can't marry you if you're waiting for something that's never going to happen."

He took my hands in his. "Look, I just want to marry you, Lil, babies or no babies."

I looked into his eyes, trying to read them, searching for something to convince me he meant it. "You say that now, but . . ."

"I say it because it's true." He pulled my hands up to his mouth. Kissed them. "I honestly can't imagine my life without you."

It would have been so easy just to accept that. To allow myself to be convinced and to let him lead me upstairs for some reassuring make-up sex. But the subject was just too important to gloss over.

"But can you really imagine living your life without being a father, Alex? Because I'm honestly not going to change my mind. And if deep down, you're going to regret committing to someone who can't see children in her life, then . . ."

He stared at me. Dropped my hands as if they'd suddenly become something deeply unpleasant. "What are you saying? This is crazy. I make one little slip-up, and suddenly you want to break up with me? It was one throwaway comment, that's all."

Wait a minute, I wanted to say. *Who said anything about breaking up?* But then I supposed that was just what I was saying. If Alex wanted someday to be a father, and I didn't want to have kids, then the brutal truth was that there was no future for us.

My throat was suddenly bone dry, my hands shaking in my lap.

Alex was looking at me as if I was a stranger, suddenly angry again. "The thing about you is you never do show your true feelings, do you? You're closed off. Daren't let yourself feel anything. Won't talk about things that upset you. That's the real reason you don't want kids."

It felt as if he'd kicked me in the stomach. "If I do keep things to myself, it's only because they're painful," I managed.

"You think my mother dying isn't painful?" he said bitterly. "The fact that you apparently don't give enough of a shit about her to do something that would make her happy in the last few weeks of her life?"

"Your mother has always adored you," I told him quietly. "She may not be around much longer, but you'll have a million memories of how much she cared."

"Well, bully for me, eh?" he spat out, then sighed, running his fingers through his hair, trying to pull himself together. "Look, I know you were very young when your mum died, but . . ."

"My mum was an alcoholic," I burst out. "A wasted alcoholic who went on binges for days on end. I was a kid, but I had to take care of Violet because there was no one else to do it. Only I can't have done a very good job, can I? Because I have no bloody idea where she is. She could be dead, for all I know." My voice ended on a sob, and I knuckled the tears away, reaching for a tissue in my pocket.

Alex was staring at me. "Jesus," he said. "Why don't I already know about this?"

I shook my head, suddenly exhausted. "I don't know. Maybe because it was easier to forget about it? To live in the present? Pretend it never happened?"

"But we're a partnership, Lil. Lovers. We're supposed to tell each other everything."

He reached out to pull me against him, holding me. "Look, I'm so sorry you had to deal with that. You were a child. It was awful. Wrong." He pulled back to look at me. "But, Lil, it wouldn't be like that if we had a child together, would it? He'd be part of me and you. Or she. Part of our lives. You wouldn't be on your own. Hell, I could even be the main caregiver, so you had all the time you needed to paint."

Nobody who's never been neglected or abused can ever really understand, that's the trouble. Just as nobody who isn't an artist can ever really grasp what a creative person needs to be able to create.

"It isn't only about having the time I need to be creative; it's about having the mental space. It's not wrong to want children, Alex, but it isn't wrong to not want them either. It's a choice. And I choose not to have them. That's it, that's all."

Alex sat and looked at me. My heart was suddenly beating very fast. He'd wanted me to open up, but now I'd expressed my thoughts and feelings in no uncertain terms, and by the look on his face, he couldn't cope with it.

He shook his head. "You know what," he said at last, "I think all this is just an excuse. I think you wanted to break up with me anyway, and this is just a convenient out for you."

I couldn't believe he thought that. It wasn't in the least bit true, and suddenly the contrast between the way he was acting, and the way Matt had received my confession about my mother's neglect slapped me in the face. As he'd said, we were a partnership. Alex was supposed to be the one who understood me and gave me comfort.

"That's not fair, Alex. And it's not true."

"Not fair?" He got to his feet, heading for the door. "Breaking up with me when my Mum's about to die, that's unfair. But d'you know what? I can't deal with this right now. I'll tell Mum we won't be getting married anytime soon."

Jesus. How was this happening? It didn't feel real. And yet there was Alex, at the door, so it must be.

Then he stopped, putting his head in his hands. "Oh, God, how am I going to do that? She's already going through so much. This will destroy her."

"I'll tell her," I said. I'd be the bad guy so Janice could hate me. It was the least I could do.

~

It played out pretty much exactly how I'd imagined it would when I went to the hospital the next day. Janice was lying back in bed with her eyes closed when I arrived, looking so frail it was difficult to believe she'd have been able to attend a wedding even if we had gone along with her plan.

I hesitated in the ward entrance, feeling like a total shit, uncertain whether to stay or not. Then her eyes opened.

"Lily," she said. "Where's Alex?"

I sat down in the chair next to her bed. "He's at work. I wanted to come and see you on my own. How are you feeling?"

"That sounds ominous," she said, ignoring my last question.

I didn't say anything straightaway. I'd rehearsed my words on the way over, but now, face to face with her, none of them seemed right. It might have been easier just to have got married to Alex rather than put myself through this.

"You'd better say it, whatever it is."

So, I did, my voice shaking but resolute. I told Janice that Alex and I wouldn't be getting married in the next few months. I didn't tell her we were breaking up, perhaps because, despite what Alex had said the previous night, I couldn't quite believe that was going to happen. By the end of it, there was no mistaking the dislike on Janice's face. And I wondered whether, deep down, she'd always felt that way about me.

"You always have been selfish, Lily," she said. "I sensed that about you right from the start. I don't know what happened to you in the past—if you've ever told Alex about it, he's never confided in me. He wouldn't do—he's too loyal. But whatever it was, it left you lacking somehow. Withdrawn. Self-obsessed. I've never forgiven you for the way you wrecked Alex's Christmas like that, after we'd all gone to so much trouble to make you welcome. But to deny a dying woman's wish, well, that's taking things to a whole other level, it really is."

Her voice may have been weak, but it was still whip sharp, and it found its target.

"I'm sorry. It's just that Alex and I have some issues to work through, and I can't just—"

If Janice had been able to move towards me, she would have. Instead, her eyes did it for her. "Look, if you're going to break my boy's heart, then do it now, while I'm still here to pick up the pieces. Please. He deserves better."

Maybe he did. Maybe Janice was right. I was scarred by the past. Defective. Focused on my art to the detriment of anything else because when I was painting or drawing I lost some of the pain I carried with me always.

Tears were suddenly streaming down Janice's cheeks. "The pity of it is, I won't be around to see who he replaces you with." Her eyes narrowed spitefully. "Because he will replace you, Lily, as quick as you like. My son is a catch, even if you can't see it." She closed her eyes. "Now, I'd like you to leave, please."

So, I left. And when Alex returned home from visiting his mum after work, he went straight upstairs to pack a bag.

"I'm going to stay with Dad for a bit. I think that's best," he said, avoiding my gaze.

I didn't want to ask if he was planning on coming back or not. Whether this was it. I couldn't believe me and Alex were really over, I suppose. Everything had happened so bewilderingly quickly. So, I stayed silent, following him back down the stairs.

"Call me, won't you?" I said. "If I can do anything at all."

He looked back at me from the door, lips twisting resentfully. "Anything you want to do; that's what you mean, isn't it, Lily?"

"Alex," I started to say, "that's not fair."

But he didn't answer. Didn't even look at me. Just went out the door and slammed it shut behind him. Leaving me on my own to deal with the wreckage of my life as best I could.

I didn't deal with it at all well. Once I'd craved some time to myself to be creative. Now I had all the time in the world, but I couldn't so much as pick up a pencil or a paintbrush. Not even to express my sorrow and despair.

Inga visited me the day after Alex had left, demanding to know why I hadn't called her straightaway. Anyway, she soon forgot about being indignant and just held me, allowing me to do whatever my misery directed me to do. Talk, sit in silence, sob in her arms. Her support was deeply comforting. But then she left, and she wasn't there in the long, lonely nights when I tried fruitlessly to sleep, wondering how Alex was.

Janice died three weeks later. As soon as Inga told me, I phoned Alex. When he didn't pick up my call, I texted and sent a sympathy card, attempting to put into words everything I was feeling. Alex didn't respond to any of it.

I wasn't invited to the funeral. I heard from Inga that Alex's father didn't want me there, and I guess Alex can't have wanted me there, either, otherwise he'd have fought for me to come.

Wanted or not, I hated that I wasn't there to support Alex. I wanted to comfort him. To talk to him about Janice and all the ways she loved him. Remind him that she would always be with him because of the way she brought him up, her love and care shaping the man he'd become.

I still couldn't paint, even with the flood of feelings clamouring for expression. I tried, a few times, but it seemed pointless. All I wanted was for Alex to poke his smiling face around the studio door and ask, "Want a cup of coffee? *Happy Valley* is about to start. Shall I record it, or are you coming down?"

Then, on the afternoon Alex was burying his mother, my creativity suddenly returned. It came from a dismal, joyless place, but it did come. I painted me and Alex naked, sitting back to back, our knees up to our chests, curled away from each other. I used burnt sienna, carmine, magenta, and crimson—the colours of blood and flesh. Then I mixed some greens and painted a plant growing up from the ground—bindweed, wrapping around us, tying our legs and arms to our bodies, separating us into two tethered bundles. My hair was loose in the painting, not scraped back into a ponytail as it was in real life, flying around my shoulders as if caught in a wind machine. It would only take one strong gust to send me toppling over, rolling away from Alex forever.

By the end of the afternoon, I was as wrung out as if I'd been to the funeral, tempted to slash the canvas to ribbons with a knife. But the painting told a truth I sensed I should preserve, so I closed the studio door and went downstairs to cook pizza with painty fingers, still dressed in the painting overalls Inga always said made me look like Bozo the Clown.

Inga herself came round when I'd finished eating, still wearing her black funeral clothes.

"Where's Matt?" I asked when I saw she was alone. "Does he think it would be too disloyal to come round and see me?"

"Don't be daft," Inga said, giving me a hug. "You know he isn't like that. I wanted to see you on my own, that's all. That's okay, isn't it?"

I nodded, pitifully glad to see her. "I'll put the kettle on."

Inga produced a bottle of wine from her bag. "I think we can do better than that, don't you? I'll get some glasses. Then you can show me what you've been painting."

I didn't really want her to see the painting, but, Inga being Inga, she wouldn't take no for an answer, and we trooped upstairs to the studio with our wine.

Inga gasped when she saw it. "Bloody hell, Lily. I mean, it's fucking brilliant. But bloody hell."

I wasn't surprised she was shocked. I was, too, seeing it again.

In the painting, Alex's skin was toned and suntanned beneath his plant tethers. Mine, on the other hand, was flayed, stripped to the bone, blood pooling on the ground beneath me.

I didn't realise I was crying until Inga held me. "Come here, you," she said, and I began to sob, great shudders of emotion ripping through my body.

"This will pass," Inga soothed me. "I know it may not feel like it now, but this will pass. You won't always feel like your skin's been ripped off. Lil, this is the most powerful thing you've ever painted. Hideous and shocking, but utterly amazing. It must have been so therapeutic to paint." She held me at arm's length. "Promise me you'll never destroy it. It will be in an exhibition of your work one day. Reproduced in art books. I mean it."

I couldn't bear to look at the painting any longer. "All right," I said, mostly to end the conversation. "I promise. Come on, let's go downstairs. Tell me about the funeral."

"From what I can gather," Inga said later, "Janice would have been too ill to attend your wedding even if you had brought it forwards. She ought never to have asked you to. It was selfish of her."

"I suppose dying is an excuse to be selfish. How is Alex? Was he . . . did he hold up okay?"

"He's . . . how you'd expect. Bowed down by grief. Like someone knocked him over and propped him upright again. Half the person he was because you weren't with him."

"I wanted to be."

"I know you did, sweetie." She sipped her wine, holding my hand in her free one, reminding me of how I'd comforted her in London that time. Now, here we were, our roles reversed.

She put her glass down. "Look, you should probably know, Alex wasn't at the funeral on his own. He was with an old school friend. A female school friend. Felicity. Fliss. She was . . . comforting him, shall we say? They left together."

I'd never heard either Alex or Matt mention anyone called Felicity. I wanted to know everything about her. Nothing about her. I imagined them fucking. Her offering him the comfort I'd wanted to offer.

"Me and Alex are really over, aren't we?" I said, starting to cry all over again, realising that, despite everything, a part of me must have been in denial these past few weeks.

Inga sighed. "It does seem that way, yes. I'm so sorry. Look, let's go out somewhere. Get drunk. Forget about all this."

"I can't."

"You can. You should." She gave me a little push. "Go on, scrub that paint off, dry your tears, and put on something sexy."

I allowed myself to be bullied. Probably because of the mention of getting drunk. Suddenly I craved oblivion more than anything else.

At the second place we went to—after a lot more wine and several shots—we ran into Harry, one of Inga's work colleagues, with his friend Patrick. With Inga and Harry launching straight into work gossip, Patrick and I were left together. He was blond, like Alex, but there the similarity ended. There was no little-boy-lost expression on that chiselled face. It was the face of a man who knew what he wanted and was confident he would get it. And judging by the way his gaze roamed over my body, he wanted me.

"So," I said. "Are you an estate agent too?"

"No way," he said. "I'm an IT consultant." He saw my expression and laughed. "I know it sounds boring, but it's not. At least, not to me. But let's not talk about work. Let's dance."

So we did. And when we weren't dancing, we had shouted conversations with each other. Made suggestive eye contact. Kissed, right there amongst the dancers, me reckless from the drink and a determination to push the past miserable weeks out of my mind. I was very glad Inga had persuaded me to come out.

Whenever I glanced over at her, she and Harry were leaning in towards each other, smiling and laughing. I couldn't help thinking about Matt.

"Inga has a boyfriend, you know," I told Patrick. "A live-in partner."

"Sure she hasn't forgotten that?" His smile was lopsided, his mouth pulled up more on one side than the other.

I shook my head. "Matt's lovely," I said. "Harry's out of luck."

"What about you?" he asked, pulling me into him, his cock rock hard against my body. "Have you got a boyfriend/live-in partner waiting for you at home?"

I let my hands stroke up the nape of his neck to the soft buzz of his hair. "Nope. I'm completely single. Unfettered. Free."

"Well," he said, "how about we go back to yours, then?"

It was very tempting. But Inga and I had a rule about not leaving each other alone in situations like this. Because of Matt and Alex, it had been a very long while, indeed, since we'd needed to act on that rule, but it was a rule, nevertheless.

"Inga and I came together. I can't go off and leave her here."

"She looks like she knows what she's doing," he said. "But let's go and see what she says."

We went over. Patrick spoke before I could. "We're ready to make tracks. You guys coming?"

Harry's arm was around Inga now in a way I knew Matt wouldn't appreciate. I wasn't sure why Inga hadn't shrugged him off yet. Poor Matt.

Inga saw me looking and got to her feet, hitching her bag onto her shoulder.

"Sure, time to go."

The four of us stumbled out of the club to the taxi rank laughing. A taxi pulled up straightaway. Patrick opened the door for me. Inga smiled approvingly in my direction—her message clear. *Go and fuck away your heartbreak, kiddo!* It was precisely what I intended to do. But it still didn't feel right to leave her.

"You can sleep on my couch," I told her. "Drive home in the morning."

Inga flapped a hand. "Don't worry about me. I'll probably call Matt and ask him to come and get me."

So I kissed her goodbye, gave her a hug, and got into the taxi. Patrick kissed me all the way home—hot, passionate kisses.

By the time we got back, I was on fire. The front door had barely closed before Patrick pressed me against the wall, still kissing me deeply, his hands pulling up my skirt. Then I caught sight of Alex's jacket hanging up in the hallway and suddenly needed to come up for air.

"D'you want a coffee?" I said, pushing back a little.

"No," Patrick said, holding my hips. "I want a tour of your house. Specifically, your bedroom."

I smiled. "Sure. It's this way."

"Up the stairs?" Patrick teased, holding my hand as he followed me up. "I would never have guessed."

In the bedroom he picked me up and threw me onto the bed. The smell of oil paint and turpentine was filtering in from the studio—if I could smell it, I was sure Patrick could, but he didn't mention it, too absorbed in divesting me of my clothes and kissing me so hard I didn't know where my breath ended and the kiss started.

The room was suddenly spinning. Too much wine. I would have a hangover to end all hangovers in the morning. In fact, it felt as if it were starting now. As if I'd be sick, if I wasn't careful. Either that or start sobbing my heart out.

A tear ran down my cheek. I quickly wiped it away before Patrick could see it, but more followed—too many to hide, spurting from my eyes like a sprinkler system.

He pulled back. Looked at me. Raised an enquiring eyebrow. "No?"

"Sorry. I just broke up with my boyfriend. I thought this was what I wanted, but . . ."

"I get it." There was a strong note of frustration in his voice. He slumped onto his back away from me. "Shame you didn't realise while the taxi was still here."

"I really am sorry."

He hauled himself off the bed. I hadn't removed any of his clothes, so he only had to slip his feet into the shoes he'd kicked off.

"No problem," he said, looking down at me. "See you around, Lily."

He left, his feet clattering down the stairs, leaving me spread-eagled on the bed, the tears wetting the pillow, my mouth burning from his kisses.

God. *God.*

I tore the rest of my clothes off, shrugging into my cosy, unwashed pyjamas, and called Inga, needing to speak to her. There was no answer—her phone was either off or on silent. But what could she do, really, anyway, except lend a sympathetic ear?

This was how it was going to be from now on—me dealing with things alone. I might as well get used to it.

14

I got through the next few weeks by painting every free minute I got—anything and everything. There was nothing else quite as raw as that first painting of me and Alex, which I'd hidden from myself behind a stack of old paintings, but everything I did was still expressive and cathartic—painting after painting made with barely any conscious thought, just responding to my feelings. A psychoanalyst's dream, no doubt.

Alex phoned around two months later. It was a shock to hear his voice.

"We need to talk about sorting the house out," he said. "Shall I come round?"

Instinct told me a neutral location for our meeting would be best.

"No," I said quickly. "Let's meet in the park."

Alex sounded doubtful. "Sure. Though I could do with collecting some of my things."

"You can come and get them afterwards."

"All right. The bench overlooking the fountain at eleven?"

I looked around at the clichéd unwashed dishes and discarded pizza boxes—a testament to how well I was coping without him. "Can you make it twelve?"

"Okay, see you there."

As well as clearing up, I took a little trouble with my appearance before I went to meet Alex. I didn't want him to know I hadn't been sleeping. That I was grey faced from painting through the night. Stressed because I couldn't apply my brain to my teaching planning and subsequently turned up to sessions having forgotten half the art materials or some critical piece of paperwork. That I'd lost weight because I kept forgetting to eat and I was just so fucking sad and lonely, despite my friends coming round to keep me company as often as they could.

So I made an effort, choosing something flattering to wear, putting on make-up, conditioning my hair so it shone. As I set out for the park, I had no idea whether any of it had worked or not. Whether I looked fine and in control. A person dealing well with a sad situation. I'd hardly been able to face looking at my poor broken reflection these past few months—but I'd done my best today, which was all I could do, and that knowledge gave me enough courage to walk past the park's herbaceous borders and up the steps to the fountain.

Alex was already there—seated on a bench, looking at his phone, wearing new clothes, I noticed—a dark-green jacket and a pair of cream cargo pants. He didn't see me straightaway, so there was time to notice his hair was freshly washed and even longer than he usually wore it. It suited him. He looked good; not like a grieving man who had recently broken up from a long-term relationship. More like someone who had embarked on a new chapter of his life. He didn't look like someone who'd been pining for me at all, and that hurt. A lot.

He looked up. Saw me. Stuffed his phone into his jacket pocket. Stood.

"Hello, Lily."

"Hi, Alex."

There was a moment where we just stood there, unsure how to greet each other. Then, at the exact same moment he moved to kiss my cheek, I drew away to sit down on the bench.

Alex sat, too, leaving three feet of space between us. "How are you?"

But I wasn't going to tell him the truth about that. I had my pride, after all. So I nodded. "Fine, thanks. You?"

"I'm . . ." He spread his hands. "You know, getting there. Working my way through the stages of grief. Trying not to be annoyed because Dad seems hell-bent on sticking in the anger stage."

I nodded, easily able to imagine his father like that. Anything to avoid the inevitable despair. "You are what you are with grief, though, aren't you?" I said. "There's not much deliberate choice involved."

He looked at me. I wondered if, like me, he was uncertain whether or not we were only talking about his mum.

Alex sighed. "That's true. But even so . . . It's time to move on. I can't stay living with Dad. That's why I wanted to see you. To discuss selling the house."

He looked at me. My cue to deliver my carefully prepared and partly fabricated speech.

"Yes. Well, about that. I've got a friend moving into the house on the weekend." Amy. I hadn't actually asked her yet, but I was pretty sure she'd say yes. "And I'm starting some weekend work in a few weeks' time, so—"

Alex frowned. "Teaching? On weekends?"

Care-assistant work at the hospital, mopping up sick and emptying bedpans mostly, no doubt. But maybe there could be an element of teaching involved? Showing the patients how to keep positive in dire circumstances, perhaps? Who was I kidding? There wasn't going to be any teaching involved. It was just going to be a hard slog. But I didn't have any choice, did I? If I didn't want to sell the house, I'd need to give Alex his share of what we'd already paid off on the mortgage. And no mortgage company was going to give me a mortgage if I only had my teaching salary. I was lucky to have got the extra work.

"It's allied to teaching, yes," I lied. "Anyway, the important thing is, once I've started that work, I'll be able to take on the mortgage by myself. I'd like to stay living there if I can."

I focused my attention on a boy cycling round and round the fountain, trying to outrun the spray, laughing gleefully every time it hit him. But I could still sense Alex's searching gaze.

"If you're working that much work, when will you have time to paint?"

When, indeed.

I forced myself to look away from the boy. Shrugged. "I'm sure it will sort itself out somehow." I wasn't.

When he still looked doubtful, I said, "Look, it's fine. It will be fine. Don't worry about it. How about you? Will you buy a flat?"

Now it was Alex's turn to look away. "I'm not sure. Possibly. The thing is . . ."

Surely he wasn't planning to move in with his new girlfriend? Not already?

"I know about Felicity," I said, wanting to get it out of the way. To get it over with. "Inga told me."

He nodded. "Of course she did." He sighed. "Look, I didn't plan for it to happen. When I left, I wasn't even sure it was permanent. I just needed some space. Then Mum died, and Felicity was . . . well, she was just there, I suppose, at first. But she was really so good to me. So kind. Things just . . . well . . ."

I spoke quickly. "That's great, Alex. You don't need to explain. I'm happy for you."

There was a moment's silence.

"She's not you, Lily," Alex said quietly. "Felicity's not you."

I made an attempt at a smile. "That's not necessarily a bad thing, though, is it?"

It was true—at least for Alex. He always had wanted more from me than I was prepared to give. The baby issue had just brought that into sharp focus.

I got to my feet. "Listen, I hope it works out for you with Felicity. I wish you both all the very best, I really do. Now, I'm off to meet a friend, so feel free to go and collect some things. I'll be in touch about any paperwork you need to sign once I've sorted the mortgage out. Bye, Alex."

"No, wait," he said. "Don't go. There's . . . well, there's something you should know."

I turned. "What?"

"Fliss. She . . . well, she's pregnant."

Fucking hell. I blinked, with no clue what to say. Or to think. Or feel.

"Well, that was quick."

Alex looked embarrassed. "I know. Actually, I think it must have happened the first time we . . ."

I had a sudden memory of Alex leaping onto the kitchen table the evening he'd proposed. So much for grand gestures.

"Well, congratulations. I'm very happy for you."

Alex looked as if he wanted to laser beam my eyeballs, he was so determined to read my expression. "Do you really mean that?"

Of course I didn't fucking mean that. What was wrong with the man? It was just something you said, because you wanted the whole miserable meeting to be done with. When you needed to get away from someone as fast as was humanly possible.

"Of course," I said, summoning superhuman skills from somewhere to back the lie up with a kiss. "You'll be a wonderful father."

"Thanks. I hope so."

He opened his mouth to say more, but I was at my absolute limit of pretence, so I just lifted my hand and turned to walk quickly away. "Sorry, Alex, I'm going to be really late to meet my friend. Good to see you. I'll be in touch soon. Bye."

Jesus. Nobody wanted to know they were so easily replaced, but had that actually been pity in Alex's face? Had he really thought my maternal instincts would somehow be magically kickstarted by the news that he'd impregnated somebody else? Well, they hadn't, and they wouldn't. I only wished I'd got out of our relationship sooner and saved all that unpleasantness with his mother.

He was right. It was time to move on.

15

Soon everything was sorted. The mortgage was in my name only, Alex had moved his things out, and Amy had moved in as my lodger. Unfortunately, I was also working six or seven days a week, and I was so tired my teaching was suffering.

Life was just work, largely sleepless nights, then more work. Mine and Amy's paths didn't cross very often, but when they did, I tried not to moan about my situation. The last thing I wanted was to make her wish she'd never moved in. Matt was away with work quite a lot, and Inga seemed distracted whenever I saw her. I didn't know if she was missing him and didn't like to say so to me because I was dealing with my break-up from Alex.

Anyway, I struggled on as best I could. Until my boss called me in to see her.

"I understand you're going through a difficult time at the moment, Lily. I was so sorry to hear about your engagement ending. But the thing is, when we're involved in such important work, we simply cannot allow our personal lives to get in the way. I popped into the women's refuge on Monday and was told that on several occasions your sessions have been . . . well, *chaotic* was the word used, I think."

I opened my mouth to speak, but she leant towards me across her desk, cutting me off before I could say anything.

"These poor women have had enough chaos in their lives, Lily. Our art sessions should be an oasis of calm for them. An opportunity for them to just be. To express themselves and have some fun. To forget everything."

"I know, I—"

"Do you, Lily? Do you really understand what's at stake here? It wasn't easy to get us into that refuge, you know. I had to overcome a great deal of doubt and resistance. And it's a huge thing for a woman to sign up for one of our courses. When she signs up, she's making an investment in herself. Telling herself she's worth it. And at a time when her self-esteem is likely to be at rock bottom, the importance of that cannot be underestimated. I won't allow all that hard work and potential for good to be put at risk because your life happens to be at a low ebb at the moment."

She sat back, lecture delivered. "Which is why I've decided to take you out of delivering community-based courses for the time being."

I stared at her, horrified. "You're cancelling my teaching?"

"Not at all. I've some more leisure-based courses coming up soon. I'd normally give them to Ruby Wallace—you know Ruby, I think? But she's going to take on your community courses, including the one at the refuge."

I nodded, still stunned. I ought to be thanking her for not firing me altogether, I supposed, although I couldn't view the prospect of taking on more leisure courses with much enthusiasm. They were aimed largely at retired people and were more like a social club than anything else. Entertainment. But there was nothing wrong with that, and I couldn't afford to be snobby about it. I'd enjoyed feeling as if I was making a real difference to people's lives, though. Except that I hadn't been doing that lately, had I? I'd just been making a mess. And my boss was right. Those women deserved so much more than that.

She stood up, the interview over. "I'll be in touch with further details once they come available, Lily, okay? And do try to get some sleep, won't you?"

I'd been scheduled to teach that afternoon, but suddenly I had several hours with nothing to do ahead of me and no desire to go home yet. With no fixed purpose, I wandered into town, cutting through the park near the shopping centre. I'd always liked this particular park; it had some spectacular trees, and I walked along the meandering pathways, taking them in, appreciating their shapes and colours. The music their leaves made in the breeze. Diverting myself from my problems. Then, suddenly, I saw Matt, seated on a bench beneath a magnificent copper beech tree eating his lunch.

We caught sight of each other at the same time.

"Lily!"

"Matt!"

He put his sandwich down on the bench and got up to hug me. I hugged him back, hugely pleased to see him.

"How are you? It's been ages since I've seen you. I haven't been avoiding you. Work's been mental."

"It must be difficult for you, though," I said. "I'm sure you still see Alex."

"I do. But that doesn't mean I can't see you. We must sort something out very soon."

Close as we'd always been, Matt and I had rarely met up on our own. Either Inga or Alex or both of them had always been there too.

He moved his sandwich for me to sit down.

"I'd like that," I said, smiling, taking him in, reassured to see he was exactly the same, aware the same could not be said about me.

"Want some of this?" he asked, holding up his sandwich. It was a doorstep, stuffed full of ham, cheese, and tomatoes.

I really shouldn't steal somebody else's lunch, but I hadn't eaten. And besides, this was Matt.

"Yes, please."

He smiled and broke the sandwich in half, handing me my share. "Here. I'll even throw in a napkin too."

"You're too generous."

"I know. I can't help myself. Anyway, how've you been? Inga says you're working all hours these days."

I swallowed a mouthful of sandwich. "Well," I said, "I was until today." I told him about my recent interview with my boss. "Maybe I ought to have let the house go," I said. "It's a struggle to pay the mortgage on my own, and I'm so tired with all the extra work. That's why my teaching's suffered. She's right. It's not fair to those women."

"None of this is fair to anyone, is it? Certainly not to you."

I felt tears in my throat.

"I only wish there was something I could do to help."

"It's just good to see you," I said.

"It's good to see you too. Really good. And maybe this will turn out for the best, you know. If these new courses are less stressful for you to teach, that can only be good, can't it?"

"Maybe," I agreed. "I'll have to let you know. How's your work going?"

He shrugged. "I'm working on a difficult project at the moment. The couple can't agree on what they want. Keep drawing me into discussions. *'It would be better if we blah, blah, blah, don't you think, Matthew? No, I'm sure Matthew thinks we should blah, blah, blah.'*"

"How are you dealing with it?"

"I say something technical about steel girders or spiral staircases, mostly."

I smiled. "And country life? How's that going? I haven't seen Inga for a few weeks, what with my extra shifts."

Matt frowned. "Inga's not been well, actually. Some bug, I think. She's had to have a few days off work."

"Oh, no. I'll have to give her a ring."

Matt caught my eye. "I don't think she's depressed again. Nothing like that. She's happy, I think. Or she was, until she got poorly."

"She never has coped well with having anything wrong with her."

"World's worst patient," he agreed.

We munched on our sandwiches for a while, watching a squirrel run through the daisies and shin effortlessly up a tree.

"What's it like working at the hospital?" Matt asked, crumpling up the sandwich wrapper. "Apart from being exhausting."

"It's not that bad. The work isn't glamorous, but the people are nice. Well, mostly nice. Patients are either pathetically grateful or peevish and complaining. I can understand both attitudes, really. I mean, they both describe me, don't they? Pathetically grateful for the extra money, peevishly complaining that I can't stay in bed at the weekend. Just as well Amy's out for the count when I leave for work, or she'd be on the receiving end of all my moaning."

"Amy, that's your new flatmate, right? It's so odd to think you're living with someone I haven't even met yet."

"I know. You'll have to come over for dinner when Inga's feeling better."

"We'll bring dinner to you," Matt said.

I smiled. "All right, deal."

~

In the end Inga dropped round a few days later, before we could arrange an evening for her and Matt to bring dinner over. I was pleased to see her but also selfishly wary, because she looked pale and peaky, and I couldn't afford to catch anything to keep me off work.

"This is a nice surprise. Amy's just put the kettle on. D'you want a coffee?"

Inga dumped her bag beside the armchair she usually sat in. The armchair Amy had taken to sitting in. "Have you got one of your herbal concoctions? Peppermint? Gooseberry? Something like that?"

"Is gooseberry tea even a thing?" I asked. "I thought you despised herbal teas."

She threw herself down on the armchair. "People change."

"I think I've got some peppermint tea," I said, registering how tired she looked.

"Perfect."

When Amy and I came back with the teas, Inga had her eyes closed.

"Should we tiptoe back out?" asked Amy.

Inga opened her eyes and sat up straighter, taking her tea. "No, it's all right, I'm not asleep. Just bushed. How are you, Amy? Settled in all right?"

"Yes, thanks."

"There's something different about the place," Inga said with a frown, looking around her.

"I brought a few cushions with me," said Amy. "I'm a bit of a cushion fan."

"No, it's not that, it's the smell. Normally it stinks of oil paint and turpentine."

"I've been using acrylic paints," I said. "Not surprisingly, Amy wasn't keen on the oil-paint stink. Not that I've had time to do much painting lately. Well, none, actually."

Inga was frowning. "But you love oil paints." She turned her gaze towards Amy. "You do realise my friend is an actual genius, don't you? She needs to create with whatever medium she needs to create with."

"Inga," I said, because her tone had been quite severe.

"I didn't tell Lily to stop using oil paints," Amy said. "She offered."

"Well, she would, wouldn't she?" Inga retorted. "Lily's the type to let people walk all over her given half the chance."

There was an awkward silence. Part of me was worried about what Amy was thinking, and the other reeling from what Inga had just said about me.

Amy stood up. "I think I'll take my tea upstairs," she said. "I've got teaching prep to finish."

"Something I said?" Inga asked sarcastically as she left, her voice a little too loud.

"Of course it bloody was," I hissed, angry with her. "She's right, I did offer to use acrylics. And I don't let people walk over me."

"You hate acrylics."

"Well, it's time I stopped hating them, then, isn't it? I need to have Amy living here more than I need to paint with oil paints."

"Don't be cross with me."

"Don't be a bitch, then," I snapped right back, but was horrified to see Inga's eyes fill with tears.

"Oh, God, I'm sorry," I started to say. "I didn't mean to snap. I'm just so tired, Ing, what with working at the hospital and . . ."

But she interrupted me. "I'm pregnant again."

"What?" I stared at her, unable to believe what I'd just heard.

"I'm pregnant."

My heart squeezed with dread. "Shit, Inga."

"I know."

Jesus, Matt. It had been so awful the last time, keeping Inga's abortion from him. I shook my head. "I can't keep it from Matt. Not again. Please don't ask me to, Inga. I just don't think I can do it."

She looked at her hands. "It . . . the baby isn't his."

I just stared at her, unable to comprehend what she was telling me.

So, she said it again. "The baby. It's not Matt's."

I shook my head. "Are you sure?"

She nodded. "Positive."

I shook my head again. Or maybe I'd never stopped shaking it because my mind was like a whirling fairground ride as it tried to make sense of what Inga had just told me. She'd slept with someone else. She'd been unfaithful to Matt. Was pregnant by someone else. I literally had no idea how this was possible. Kind, beautiful Matt, who'd never been anything but good to her. To all of us. A sudden wave of anger ripped through me. I clenched my hands together to stop them shaking.

"I can't believe this," I said. "Whose is it? When did you . . . ?"

But suddenly I had a flashback to Inga cosying up to Harry on that ill-fated trip to the nightclub when I'd ended up back here with Patrick, and with sick certainty I knew.

"Shit," I said. "It's not Harry's?"

She nodded, tears in her eyes. "Yes."

"God, Inga."

She held her head in her hands. "I know. I fucking know, all right? You don't have to make me feel a million times worse than I already do."

I waited for a moment to calm down, processing it all. I wasn't very good at maths, but I didn't have to be to work out that Inga must have slept with Harry more than once. That she must have been having an affair. Then I asked, "Have you told him? Harry?"

"No."

"Are you going to?" But even as I asked the question, I already knew the answer. Inga hadn't even told the man she loved when she was pregnant with his child, so why would she tell someone who was just a fling? She would get a quick abortion, and Harry would never know anything about it.

"No, I won't tell Harry," she confirmed. "He's not exactly father material. Besides, he's transferring to the Cambridge office soon."

I gaped at her. Father material? Did that mean . . . ? "Wait a minute. Are you planning to keep it this time?"

Her face fell. She brushed tears from her cheeks. "I don't know. Yes. I think so. It feels . . . I don't know, as if the universe is trying to tell me something."

The universe was probably telling her she ought to get better contraception. That she shouldn't be unfaithful to someone who loved her the way Matt did. I felt sick.

"I've not said anything to Matt yet."

"You'll have to, though, won't you?"

The anger simmering inside me had probably been reflected in my voice because Inga was suddenly defensive.

"I'm not stupid, Lily. I do know that. I haven't exactly got much choice, have I? I already don't fit into lots of my clothes. And with Harry being Black . . . What? Don't look at me like that."

"I'm not looking at you like anything." But I knew I probably had been, because I was just so fucking appalled by the possibility that, had Harry been white, Inga might have passed the baby off as Matt's.

No, I was jumping to conclusions. That can't have been what she meant.

"You always said you didn't want children."

"I didn't. I don't." She began to cry again. "I just can't go through another abortion, Lil. It was hideous. I felt like a murderer." She looked up at me, her expression resentful. "I was hoping you'd support me. I'll need you to."

"Oh, Ing," I said with something close to despair. "Of course I will, but . . ." My voice trailed off, a cold fist clenching around my heart at what that support might mean. Babysitting. Listening to Inga moaning about night feeds and teething problems. The possibility of my close bond with Matt gradually ebbing away as I did so. I couldn't bear it.

But this was Inga—my best friend, my family. I was angry with her now; furiously angry, wondering whether I'd ever really known her if she could behave like this. Yet at the same time I knew my anger would blow over. I loved Inga, so I'd end up supporting her in any way I could. And besides, she would make new friends to do all that stuff with. Mum friends.

I wanted to cry, though, because I was just so damned sad. "Whatever made you do it?"

Inga was already crying, and when she wiped a tear away, another instantly took its place. "I don't know. I'd had too much to drink, that first time anyway. Too much. Work is . . . well, it's fun. There's all this supercharged banter flying around the office when there's no customers about. But it can be stressful too. Harry and I . . . well, it's always been a bit flirty between us, if I'm honest. Harmless stuff, but exciting, you know? It made me feel good. Better than I've felt for years. And he taught me a lot about the job when I started—I appreciated that."

Another flash of anger. "You slept with Harry because you appreciated him training you to do your job?"

Her eyes flashed at me through her tears. "Of course not. Nothing would ever have happened between me and Harry if we hadn't run into him at that nightclub. At least, I don't think it would. I don't know,

Matt and me, it's all got so . . . well, grown up, I suppose." She started crying again. "I'm not old, Lil. We're not old. I don't want to be all paint colours and dinner parties, not yet."

She blew her nose. "But the irony is, Harry's all set to be paint colours and dinner parties anyway—he's off to Cambridge to move in with his girlfriend. So I'm sorry if I offended your lodger by sticking up for your right to use stinky oil paint in your own home, but I'm a bit on edge at the moment, and I want at least one of us to have the kind of life we want."

I closed my eyes at that, doing my best not to think how utterly different my current life was from the life I wanted.

"Harry or no Harry, there won't be any bloody banter at work after I've had the baby, will there?" Inga continued, wiping her eyes. "It'll all just be rush, rush, rush; got to nip into the shops in my lunch break to get formula and fucking breast pads and rush back at five o'clock to relieve the child minder."

"You're quite sure about keeping it, though?"

Inga drew in a big shuddering breath, pulling a sodden tissue apart with her fingers. "I've picked up my phone so many times to call the abortion clinic I've lost count. But I never dial, Lil. Not one fucking digit. I just sit there and stare and stare at the card. So, yes, I guess I'm sure about keeping it, even if it's by default. I'm either brave or crazy— I'm not sure which. Jesus, I'm going to get fat, aren't I? I'm going to have melon tits. I'll be up every night feeding it. Changing its nappies."

She began to properly cry then—great gushing tears and shuddering shoulders.

The last bit of my anger drained away. I held her. "Shh . . . it'll be all right," I soothed, even though I couldn't really see how it would be, at least, not for quite some time, and I remembered the four of us on our holiday in the Welsh mountains—me, Inga, Alex and Matt. The innocence of us, eating the meal Matt had prepared and talking about Alex's experience of hearing his uncle's guiding voice. Out of all of us,

Matt was the least changed, perhaps because he'd always been so strong. And now, through no fault of his own, the rug of his life was about to be pulled from beneath him. I couldn't bear to think about how hurt he was going to be. It broke my heart; it really did.

"Shit, Lily, how am I going to tell Matt?"

"I don't know." I didn't. I only knew she had to do it as soon as humanly possible. "But please, do it as soon as you can. I don't want to know about this and still see him. He's planning for you two to bring dinner over here soon."

"I'll make some excuse. Put him off. Tell him you're too busy with work or something. Don't look like that. I will tell him, but in my own time, okay?"

I looked at her, wanting to object. To insist.

"I don't know why you're so worked up about me keeping Matt in the dark for a few weeks while I get my head together, anyway."

"Because he's my friend. I care for him."

Inga frowned at me. "*I'm* your friend."

"You both are. You're Matt and Inga."

"You were Lily and Alex, and look how well that turned out. But if you two hadn't split up, and you'd shagged someone else and got pregnant, I wouldn't tell Alex about it before you were ready for me to."

We were getting angry again. "I haven't said I'd tell Matt. I've asked you to tell him as soon as possible so I don't have to lie to him, that's all. You're the one who just told Amy I let people push me around. This is me not being pushed around."

She looked at me. "I think I preferred the old you," she said.

And when she stood up to leave, I wasn't sure whether to call after her or scream at the top of my lungs with frustration and despair. In the end, I did neither thing. I went to bed and lay there in the dark thinking about Matt. Imagining his face as Inga told him the truth. Wondering what would happen next. Oh, Matt. Poor, poor Matt.

～

When Matt texted a few days later to set a date to come round with food, I knew full well Inga still hadn't told him, because I'd texted her only that morning to ask her and had received an abrupt reply by return.

Soon, ok?

So, the day before they were due to come—my first night off in a week—I phoned the agency to volunteer for an extra shift. Then I sent Matt a message to cancel, saying work was short staffed and I wouldn't finish until around midnight. It wasn't a total lie—work was always short staffed, and they'd accepted my offer to do extra hours with enthusiasm. But I still felt bleak about it.

"I didn't think I was going to see you tonight? I thought you had the night off?" my favourite patient Beryl said when I went onto the ward.

Beryl was eighty-five, an ex–botany professor with weeks to live. I'd been rostered onto the Coronary Care Unit several times and had got to know her well enough for her to talk to me in quick snatches about her adventures—the field trips to far-flung countries in search of rare specimens. Her close encounters with civil wars, earthquakes, and terrorists, none of which had managed to snuff her out. And now a failing heart was about to succeed where they'd failed.

Beryl's voice was croaky. She had a constant, insatiable thirst because of her medication.

"I wasn't rostered to work, no," I said. "My plans changed."

Beryl's eyes were the observant eyes of a woman who had spent her life noticing minute details and infinitesimal changes. "Happens to us all," she said. "I was supposed to be the keynote speaker at an international wildflower conference next year. Now they'll be delivering my eulogy."

I busied myself with checking her blood pressure and made a note on her chart. Beryl was very matter of fact about her illness and her imminent death. I hadn't quite got used to it yet, but I knew she wouldn't appreciate mawkish sympathy.

"I bet it would have been a good talk."

"Oh, indubitably," Beryl said, then frowned at me. "You look tired, my dear, if you don't mind my saying so. You ought to have said no when they asked you to work."

Beryl's tone was so kind. I'd never had a grandmother, or at least, not one I knew, but if I had, I'd have wanted her to be like Beryl, and I had a sudden desire to sit on the edge of her bed to spew the whole thing out—Inga's infidelity and pregnancy. The fact that she hadn't told Matt about it yet, and that I was getting increasingly anxious about Matt realising at some future date that I'd known about it all along. But it wouldn't help to unburden myself to poor Beryl. She had enough to deal with as it was. Besides, nothing except Inga doing the decent thing would help.

"I'm all right," I told Beryl brightly. "Don't worry about me."

"Ah," Beryl said. "The classic response of someone used to dealing with things on her own. Believe me, I know."

"What about your son?" I asked. "He seems very helpful." I'd met him once when he'd been visiting his mother.

"Of course he is. But he's also married with three children and a stressful job. I've never liked to bother him with my problems unless I absolutely can't help it. I think you're the same."

I smiled a little at that. "Maybe."

Beryl smiled back. "Definitely." She looked at me. "So, come along. It does no good at all to keep one's demons bottled up."

With that, she sat there looking at me, waiting patiently for me to unburden myself. And I might have done just that because Beryl was so kind and so special, and I did badly need to talk to someone. But then Sister Brown looked into the ward with a frown, reminding me I had lots of other patients to see to.

"I'd better get off," I said to Beryl. "But thank you. Sleep well."

"Come back to talk any time you like," Beryl said. "I'm not going anywhere, well, at least until I die, anyway, and I've been told I'm a good listener when I'm not waxing lyrical about ghost orchids or crested cow-wheat."

When she squeezed my hand, I squeezed hers back, feeling emotional. It was all I could do to stop myself from throwing myself down onto her bed to sob my heart out, but I managed it somehow, moving on to the next ward to help an elderly patient use a bedpan.

My shift dragged on, finally finishing at midnight, after the buses had stopped running. I'd come by bike because of the lack of buses, and I was just unlocking it when someone called to me.

"Lily?"

I whirled round. "Matt!"

He was holding a takeaway bag, smiling at me. "I brought your meal to you here as we couldn't bring it round earlier. I thought you'd be hungry when you finished your shift."

It was such a kind thing for him to have done, I was beyond moved. I wasn't convinced it would even have occurred to Alex to do such a thing when we were together, and Matt's thoughtfulness made me want to cry. Especially when I searched his face, trying to gauge whether he knew yet or not, and all I could see was concern for me.

I swallowed. "That is . . . so . . . Thank you."

"Come on," he said, looping the takeaway bag over one of my handlebars and taking hold of the bike. "Let's shove this in the back of my car. I'll run you home."

Matt's face was all shifting planes and angles in the passing streetlights, his hands strong and capable on the steering wheel.

"Inga okay?" I asked. It was a question I'd normally ask, but somehow, with everything I knew, it felt loaded.

Matt, being completely innocent of everything, just sighed. "I still don't think she's a hundred percent, to be honest. You've seen her recently, haven't you? What did you think?"

Fortunately for me, he carried on speaking, not waiting for me to reply. "I told her to make an appointment at the doctor's, but you know how she is."

There was affection in his voice as well as worry. He trusted Inga. Loved her. The truth was never going to occur to him on its own. The pressure of my unwanted knowledge was like a clamp pressing down on my head. I loved Matt. It was just so wrong for him to be hoodwinked like this.

"Are you sure you're all right, Lily? D'you want me to pull over?"

"No, it's okay. Bit of a headache, that's all. Long shift."

"Sure you don't want me to stop for a bit?"

"Sure."

He carried on driving, and we didn't speak again until we reached my street. What could I say that didn't feel like lying by omission, after all? And Matt, I assumed, was keeping quiet because of my headache, which was becoming more of a reality by the second.

By some miracle, there was a free parking space outside my house. As Matt pulled into it I saw the lights were still on in the sitting room. Amy must still be up.

He got out to take my bike out of the boot.

"There you go."

"Thanks." I took a deep breath. Looked up at him. "You need to talk to Inga, Matt. She . . . she's not too happy right now. I . . . I can't . . . Look, please don't mention I said anything. But . . . just talk to her. Please."

Matt stared at me, his gaze as penetrating in its own way as Beryl's, taking in my worry and concern. He took my hand. Squeezed it.

"I will. I promise."

I could feel tears in my eyes. Blinked quickly. Started pushing my bike towards the house. "Thanks so much for driving me home."

"Anytime, you know that." He reached into the car, pulling out the takeaway bag. "Don't forget your dinner."

"Thanks." I hooked it over the bike handlebars knowing I wouldn't be eating it. Hungry as I was, my churned-up stomach would reject anything I tried to feed it right now.

"See you soon, Lily."

I reached over to kiss his cheek, somehow managing to do it without meeting his gaze. "Bye, Matt."

"Bye, Lily. Take care."

I propped my bike against the house wall and fumbled for my door key, listening to him drive away. Even if Matt didn't say anything about my prompting him, Inga was bound to guess anyway. I hoped she wouldn't be too angry with me. I hoped Matt wouldn't be too heartbroken. I hoped they both knew that, no matter what happened, I would always be there for them. Prayed that I could still be friends with them both. That Matt wouldn't react so badly he moved away, out of our lives forever.

Bone weary and emotional, I turned my key in the lock and pushed my bike into the house. To find my sister sitting on the sofa, waiting for me.

16

The bike clattered against the wall. The takeaway bag fell to the carpet. "Vi!" My little sister was sitting on my actual sofa next to Amy, her legs curled up under her as if she sat there every day.

Quickly, I hurried over to take her in my arms before she could vanish in a puff of smoke, having to bend awkwardly to do it, inhaling her scent—something spicy, something lemony—her shoulder blades fragile beneath my fingers.

Violet suffered my embrace for a full ten seconds before she pushed me off.

"No offence, Lil, but you stink of hospitals."

There it was, the familiar cocktail of hurt and guilt inside my chest, but at least now there was a fair helping of relief too.

The words poured from me. "Where have you been? What have you been doing? Why haven't you been in touch?"

"Jesus, can I at least have another cup of coffee before I answer all that? And some of that curry I can smell if you aren't planning on eating it?"

"I'm sorry, Violet," said Amy, "I didn't think to offer you anything to eat, what with it being so late."

Poor Amy. I didn't suppose she felt she could just go to bed and leave Violet waiting for me and she was normally fast asleep in bed by eleven o'clock. She must be exhausted. And sick to death of my friends and family.

"Can I get myself a plate? I'm guessing the kitchen's through there?"

When Violet got to her feet I saw a large, fading bruise on her cheek. A hint of a black eye.

My mouth engaged before my brain. "What happened to your face?"

She stared at me with angry eyes, letting her hair swing forwards. "I fell," she said, her tone saying, *"Mind your own fucking business."*

"Are you all right, Lily?" Amy asked when we were alone. "You're shaking."

I struggled out of my jacket. Tossed it onto the back of a chair. Thanked the gods, social services, my old neighbour, whoever it was that had passed my address on to Violet.

"Yes. It's just been quite a night, one way or another. And it's been so long since I saw Violet."

"Four or five years, she said."

"Something like that. You've been chatting, then?" Of course they had. Had I expected them to have just been sitting in silence for hours, waiting for me to get back?

"Yes, she's been entertaining me with stories of her adventures abroad."

I nodded, less concerned at the moment with my sister's adventures than I was with the bruising on her face. "Did she tell you how she got the black eye?"

"*She* got drunk and walked into the edge of a door," said Violet, returning with a plate and fork and holding out her hand for the takeaway bag.

I picked it up and gave it to her, watching as she opened the foil trays and helped herself, leaving deposits of curry and rice on the coffee table.

She began to eat, then looked up at us. "What is this?" she asked. "A spectator sport?" The words were tossed off—irritable rather than jokey.

Amy made for the door, taking her cue. "I'll leave you guys to it. I've got an early start tomorrow."

I nodded, smiling, doing my best to act like a normal person. "That's right, you're teaching in Fakenham, aren't you?"

She nodded. "And you're in Cromer starting that new course?"

"Yes."

She smiled. "We're proper jet-setters, your sister and I, Violet."

"Aren't you, just?" said Violet, mopping up curry sauce with a torn off piece of chapatti.

"Well," Amy said, "I hope it goes well tomorrow, Lily. Good to meet you, Violet."

"Night, Amy."

"She seems nice," said Violet, after she'd gone.

I frowned. Violet had made it sound like a criticism.

"What? I said she seemed nice," said Violet, rifling through the takeaway bag. "Didn't you get any naan bread?"

"Take a look in the bag. It was bought for me; I don't know what's in there." I sat down in the armchair opposite her, suddenly feeling totally wiped out by the events of the day. "Where have you been all this time, Vi?"

Violet was wearing a loose-necked top that left one shoulder bare. She shrugged the naked shoulder. "India, China, Vietnam, Brighton, Lewisham . . ."

"Lewisham? When were you in Lewisham?"

"Ever since I got back to the UK six months ago. Some friends have a squat there."

I stared at her, hurt. "Why didn't you get in touch?"

"You've been busy with your life, anyway, by the sound of it. Teaching. Dumping your boyfriend, from what Amy tells me."

"I didn't dump Alex."

"No?"

"No. We split up because we wanted different things. It's complicated. I don't really want to talk about it. Not now, anyway. Tell me about some of the countries you've visited, what you've been doing."

She looked at me. "It's complicated. I don't really want to talk about it."

"Vi, don't be like that."

"Like what? You want to know about the world, you go out and discover it yourself."

I sighed. Vi had been a bit snarky when we'd met at the café before she'd gone travelling, but this was on a whole different level. Where had my sweet, loving sister gone? What had happened to make her so defensive? "If you must know, Alex and I broke up because he decided he wanted kids, and I . . ."

"Don't tell me. Your experience of taking care of me was so good, you don't want to repeat it in case looking after your own kid doesn't match up?"

That hurt. I took a breath. "Vi, I willingly took care of you."

"Oh, yeah."

I had a sudden, vivid flashback to meeting up with Violet with one of her foster mothers six months after she'd been taken into care. Of Violet launching herself into my arms, clinging and sobbing. *"Please don't send me back, Lily. Please don't send me back. I want to live with you. Please."*

I'd held her, heartbroken, desperately trying to think of a way I could take care of her but unable to come up with any ideas at all. I was sixteen—too old to go into the foster-care system. All I had was one tiny room in the seedy hostel I'd been placed in, which I shared with ten other young people, most of whom I wouldn't want my eight-year-old sister to come within a hundred yards of.

The foster mother came to my rescue. Sort of.

"Lily can't take care of you, Violet. She hasn't got anywhere for you to stay. Besides, she's only a child herself really."

Never mind that it was technically true. I'd looked after Violet all her life, so what was different now? That was what would be going through Violet's mind, I knew it. She hugged me even tighter. "Please, Lily. Please."

In the end the foster mother practically had to drag Violet away, kicking and screaming. She certainly wasn't in any hurry to arrange for Violet and me to meet up again, and I had no idea whether Violet had begged to see me or not. All I knew was that by the time I did get to see my little sister again months later, a force field had gone up—a coldness and a distance that had never been there before and which Violet seemed determined I would never break down.

"I've just never wanted children, that's all. I'd be an awful mother. Half the time my mind's on my art. I'm always in a daydream, creating art in my head."

"Is that why you're working in a hospital? Because you want to do your art so much?"

I frowned at her sarcasm. "No, Vi, that's so I can live. It's not easy to make money from selling paintings. Besides, having children wasn't the only reason Alex and I split up. We just weren't a good fit for each other any longer. But I can't say it hasn't been hard, because it has. I still really miss him." I sighed, rubbing my tired face with my hands. "It's good to see you, Vi. I wish you'd got in touch sooner."

Another shrug. I doubted whether I'd ever find out what she'd been doing in Lewisham. And probably very little about her travels around the world—how she'd survived, who she'd met, what she'd seen. But perhaps that was just as well. And it didn't really matter, anyway, did it? She was here. She was safe.

"Are you crying?"

I was. "I do seem to be, yes."

"Most people smile when they're happy about something," Vi said, pushing her plate away. "Anyway, where am I going to sleep? I'm guessing there's only two bedrooms. Unless Amy's in your room, and you and her are an item? Is that one of the reasons you and Alex aren't a 'good fit' anymore?"

She yawned a huge yawn, stretching her arms up to the ceiling, the bruise on her face picked out by the overhead light.

I didn't bother responding to the dig, even though it hurt. Vi's bitterness towards me didn't seem to have calmed down any, so there would probably be plenty more where that came from. "You can sleep on the sofa. I'll get you some bedding."

She was out like a light almost as soon as I'd thrown a duvet over her. My little sister. All grown up now. Though, asleep as she was, I could still see traces of the little girl who'd sat on my lap while I read her a bedtime story.

"Are you going to stand there watching me all night?" she asked drowsily.

I smiled. "Good night, Vi."

"Night, sis."

I got ready for bed myself, then lay there in the darkness, not trying to sleep. Vi back, after all this time. I wanted to call Inga to tell her about it. But I couldn't, because besides the fact that it was two in the morning, Inga was probably right in the middle of breaking Matt's heart thanks to what I'd said to him earlier. Shit, what a night. What had I done? Inga was going to kill me. I just hadn't been able to bear Matt not knowing the truth. I'd only just about managed to keep quiet the last time.

I longed suddenly for someone to speak to about it all. Not just about Matt and Inga, but Violet too. Alex, I supposed. But then, Alex had only ever known a few bare facts about Violet, hadn't he? I'd never told him what happened that night, so he'd never really understood. Maybe, if he could meet Violet now, he might. Only he wouldn't be meeting my sister anytime soon because I wouldn't be speaking to him anytime soon.

I wrapped my arms around my body, accepting the bald truth that there was nobody to share the news of Vi's return with right now. That it would have to be enough to hold it in my heart.

Had Vi really fallen against the edge of a door when she was drunk? It was certainly possible. So why was it so much easier to believe somebody had hit her? I could even picture it; see Vi's head snapping back from the force of a fist making contact. But that was a memory, wasn't it? Mum, not Vi. Alec? Grant?—I couldn't remember which of them—had hit her fairly frequently, often when Vi or I were in the room. Mum would hide away for a week or so, then carry on as if nothing had happened.

I thought of the women I'd met when I was working at the women's refuge, wondering if they were all still living there, or whether they'd found homes now. If only Mum had taken me and Vi to a refuge to get help to make a new start. What would our lives have been like if she had? If she'd been given help and counselling to try to change her patterns of behaviour? A safe, secure base to make a fresh start? But then, Mum would probably have abused the system and ruined it all for us—smuggled alcohol in. Had a party. Fallen out with the other women. Victim as she was, she was also capable of being the aggressor.

No, Mum would never have fit in at a refuge. She hadn't wanted to escape. Would have sworn blind she had nothing to escape from.

Inevitably, because I'd slept badly, it was hard to wake up the next morning. Amy, bless her, knocked on my door.

"Lily? Shouldn't you be getting up to catch your train? Cup of tea outside your door."

I sat up to look at the clock as I heard Amy go downstairs. Shit. There was no time to drink tea. Or to have breakfast. Dressing quickly, I charged downstairs with my teaching things, leaving them at the bottom of the stairs while I dashed into the bathroom. By the time I emerged, Amy was ready to leave, standing outside the closed sitting-room door.

"No sign of my sister yet?"

Amy shook her head. "No, I think she's still asleep." She looked at the canvas I'd propped against the wall. "You aren't thinking of taking that on the train, are you? It looks a bit windy out today. Sorry I can't give you a lift to the station."

"Don't worry, I didn't expect you to," I said, eyeing the canvas doubtfully. It was one of my old seal paintings—I was taking it to illustrate what I wanted my students to do in the session. If I'd been more organised I'd have taken photographs to show them instead, but it was too late now. If I messed around getting a good image, I'd miss the train for sure.

"Anyway, see you later. Hope it goes well."

"You too."

Amy let herself into the darkened sitting room to reach the front door. I picked up the canvas and the rest of my teaching things and followed her. The blind was still down, but I could see Violet in the half light, still fast asleep.

"Vi?"

When she didn't stir, I shook her gently. "Violet?"

"What?" A grumpy croak.

"I have to go to work now. There's a spare key on the kitchen counter. Help yourself to any food you can find to the right of the fridge. The stuff on the left is Amy's. Don't touch that, okay?"

No answer.

"Okay, Vi?"

"Got it. No food on the left."

I nodded. Not that Violet could see that with her eyes closed. "That's it. See you later. I'll be back around four."

Half an eye opened. "I might be gone by then."

"Gone where?"

Violet yawned hugely. "To Nottingham, to look for my dad."

"*What?*"

"I told you that last night, didn't I?"

"No, you didn't."

I would most definitely have remembered that.

"Well, I got a lead he might be living there, so I thought I'd look him up." Violet opened her eyes—finally—and saw my expression. "What? What's wrong with that?"

There was so much wrong with it, it was difficult to know where to start. Like why on earth she would want to look up somebody who'd never bothered to play a part in her life—somebody who'd left when Violet was only months old, a person our mother had always described as a useless drug addict. But there was no time to get into it now. If I missed my train and failed to turn up for my teaching, that would probably be the end of my career with adult education—Community Department, Leisure Department, or whatever other department they came up with.

"I've got to go, Vi," I said. "Please stay a bit longer so we can catch up properly. Please. Or if you really can't, then at least give me a way to keep in touch."

"All right."

"Promise me, Vi."

"All right!" she snapped, turning her back on me, eyes closed, face pressed into the sofa cushions.

I sighed. "See you later then."

I headed for the door. She didn't answer.

Amy was right. It was breezy. It was a nightmare negotiating the canvas to the station. Gusts of wind kept turning it into a sail, practically lifting me off my feet, making me bash into other pedestrians, parked cars, and brick walls. When I finally turned into the station, there was only a minute to go until my train left, and I still had to negotiate the automatic ticket barriers with the canvas. Thank God I'd bought my ticket in advance.

I ran up the platform, calling to the guard to wait, pulling open the nearest door and hauling my belongings in after me. Then I stood for a moment to catch my breath, my bags and the canvas dumped in the space next to the luggage racks.

Finally, after I'd recovered a bit, I took my phone from my bag to see if there were any messages from Inga. Only to see I had ten missed calls from her. Shit. With Vi turning up, I'd forgotten to take it off silent after my shift.

"Inga?"

"Where've you been? I've been calling and calling."

"I'm sorry. My sister turned up after work, and I forgot to unmute my phone."

"Violet turned up?"

"Yes. It turns out she's been back in the country for months, but only just bothered to get in touch. Are you all right?"

Inga sounded angry. "No, I'm not bloody all right. Matt was packing when I called you last night. He's gone to a hotel. Why did you have to tell him, Lil? I said I'd do it in my own time. I wasn't ready for it."

"I didn't tell him," I said, but there was no conviction in my voice.

"You as good as told him. He confronted me as soon as he got in. Kept on at me until I broke and told him. It was awful. He was so hurt."

Of course he'd been hurt. What the hell had she expected? He'd have been hurt whenever he found out. Poor Matt. I hoped he was all right.

"I'm sorry," I said, but, as hard as it had been, I knew I'd probably do the same again. Matt had deserved to know.

"Yeah, well, look, I've got to go now. I was just leaving for work. I'll call you later, okay?"

When she hung up, tears filled my eyes. I knew she was upset, that she was cross with me for forcing the issue. And we were never cross with each other, Inga and me. I sniffed, worn out by emotion and lack of sleep.

The wind was even stronger in Cromer, coming straight off the sea. By the time I reached the community centre where I was teaching, I was sweating and exhausted, and there was a small tear in my canvas from where it had been blown against the corner of a broken flint wall. The painting meant so much to me—it captured the joyful movement of the seals in their natural habitat. It also reminded me of the night Inga and I had first met Alex and Matt. And now it was damaged, just like our relationships.

Matt would be able to repair it—he was good at things like that. If he didn't decide to up sticks and move to a different city to get over all this. If seeing me didn't remind him too much of Inga. If, if, if.

Oh, God. Alex was gone from my life, Inga was mad with me, and Violet was like a prickly, defensive sea urchin. If I didn't see Matt much anymore, I'd not only miss him like crazy, I might well fall apart altogether. And why the hell had I thought it was a good idea to bring the canvas today, anyway? I could have sat down and cried, right there on the high street, but I had to be an adult and press on to the community centre to teach my course.

When I finally arrived at the centre, I paused on the threshold, giving myself a talking to. I was an inspirational tutor on a mission to share my enthusiasm and my skills with a receptive audience. *Not* a recently ditched woman whose long-lost sister had just turned up out of the blue and whose friends were currently going through hell. The tear in my canvas could definitely be repaired, as could my life.

I pushed open the door and went in. The centre manager was waiting for me.

"Hi, I'm guessing you're Lily, the art tutor?"

"Yes, that's right. I hope I'm not late?"

It had taken me longer than I'd expected to walk from the station, especially with the painting flapping about.

"Not at all. Your students are all here—they do like to arrive early to chat—but you've got time to make yourself a quick coffee to take in with you. I expect you could do with one as you've come from Norwich. Let me show you the kitchen."

Coffee made, I paused on the threshold of the classroom, to arrange a smile on my face. Then I pushed the door confidently open. Unfortunately, it was heavier than I'd expected it to be. Coffee sloshed down my leg.

"Ow!"

The buzz of conversation in the room abruptly stopped.

"Are you all right, dear?" A grey-haired lady rushed over to take the dripping mug from my hand. "I think you'd better mop yourself down before that stains. I'm Percy, by the way—it's short for Persephone—and this is, well, everybody."

I looked out at a sea of faces—well, nine or ten probably, but with coffee dripping down my trouser leg, feeling humiliated by my disastrous entrance, it seemed like a sea. "Hello, Percy, everyone. I'll just go and . . ."

When I returned with my soggy, sponged-down trousers, my coffee had been replenished, and the seal painting was hanging in a place of pride on the wall. Everyone was so absorbed in looking at it, they barely glanced in my direction.

"It makes you want to be a seal, doesn't it?" Percy was saying dreamily, her chin cupped in her hands, and I smiled, suddenly relaxing, sensing that this class was going to be okay.

As the hours passed, the grey heads emerged as people—Iris, a recently retired shop manager, Clive, who had wanted to train to be an artist but who had been persuaded by his parents that banking was a more secure career. Jean, who wanted to paint with her grandchildren.

I told them all how I'd got into painting seals and that trying to capture movement and observing the rhythms of nature could be a good way to free yourself up and to get away from a restrictive obsession to make everything photographically accurate. With my guidance, those who were able to do so stood to make sketches from my seal painting, moving their whole arm instead of just their hand, putting their whole body into the marks they made on paper.

"Wait 'til I tell my wife I've been doing modern art," Clive said, pleased as punch when I told him he'd captured the dancing movement of the seals perfectly.

I was tired as I made my way back to the station later, but relieved the session had gone well, already thinking about what to do with the class the following week.

It was only when I was on the train that everything else returned to sour my mood again. I sighed, gazing out of the window at the passing Norfolk landscape, then pulled my phone out to check for messages. Nothing from anybody. Not from Violet, Inga, or Matt. God.

I sent Inga a text.

Hope you're ok. Will call later. XXX

Then I put my phone away and went back to staring out of the window. Only at some point I must have closed my eyes because suddenly we were arriving at Norwich station, and the guard was telling us the train terminated there and not to forget to take all our belongings with us. So, I hauled myself up, retrieved my bags and the canvas and trooped along the platform to negotiate the automatic-ticket barrier again. Only to find, when I emerged from the station building, that it was raining—and not just a light drizzle my painting might recover from, but torrential rainforest-like rain, bouncing off pavements, sending people scurrying across the station car park with unlikely items held over their heads in a futile attempt to stay dry.

Shit. There was nothing for it but to join the very long taxi queue, which was going to eat right into my earnings for the day.

When I finally got home, dripping wet despite the taxi, it was to find the house in darkness. Amy had probably dropped in to see her parents on her way home. But where was Violet? Had she broken her promise and left already? I checked the kitchen worktop—the spare key had gone—then I changed my clothes, towel-dried my hair and made myself a cup of tea, sitting in the same spot on the sofa Violet had taken last night. The duvet was screwed up on the armchair—the only sign, apart from the missing key and the faintest trace of that spicy, lemony scent she'd been wearing, that Violet had ever been here at all.

Tears filled my eyes. I blinked them away, lying back against the cushions, the stresses and triumphs of my day eclipsed as I wondered when I'd see Violet again. Whether she'd just slipped out somewhere locally, which might give us the chance to reinstate our relationship, or whether she was already in Nottingham on the trail of her father.

I'd never been interested in knowing my own father, but Violet had always wanted to know about hers. She'd come home from school one day—no doubt after being exposed to other kids with two parents—and asked me whether I knew who and where he was. The only time I'd asked Mum where he'd gone, she'd said he was *"That fucking useless, drug-taking wastrel? Who bloody cares?"* so I didn't tell Violet to speak to Mum about it. I don't remember exactly what I said. I probably fobbed her off with some rot without actually lying to her—but whatever it was, it had clearly done nothing to dissolve my sister's happy-ever-after fantasies of a loving dad, because here she was, nearly twenty years on, still hankering after him.

If Violet had gone to Nottingham, she'd done so without leaving me her phone number, so the ball was in her court. I might harbour dreams of us working on our relationship and becoming closer again, but as usual, Vi held all the power. She would get in touch, or she wouldn't, and there wasn't a thing I could do about it. After my initial surge of joy when I'd let myself into the house and seen her here on the sofa, it was an utter letdown.

But if I couldn't do anything about Violet at the moment, I could do something about Matt. Even if it was just to phone him to check up on him. It wasn't being disloyal to Inga to make sure he was all right.

He answered on the second ring. "Lily."

"Matt. I've been thinking about you all day. How are you?"

"Inga told you, then? Of course, she did. How am I? Angry. Sad. Bulldozed. About what you'd expect, I suppose when you discover your partner's pregnant with another man's child."

It hurt so much to hear the pain in his voice. That note of extreme weariness I'd become so familiar with myself lately.

"I'm so sorry." It was all I seemed to say lately and completely inadequate. But it was true. I was sorry. Sorrier than I could say. He didn't deserve this.

"I feel like such an idiot, Lily. If you hadn't said what you said last night, I'd have coasted on without a clue. God, even when she was telling me, actually saying the words, it didn't click at first. I thought she was telling me *we* were pregnant. That we were having a baby together. I was so busy trying to get my head round the fact that I was going to be a father, I didn't register what she was actually saying. That she'd fucked somebody else. Was pregnant by somebody else."

"Oh, Matt . . ." I couldn't say I was sorry again.

"Did you know about it, Lily?" He sighed. "I know I shouldn't ask. I get that you're in a tricky position, I do. But . . . did you?"

A wave of shame washed over me. Along with another sense of panic that he might blame me. That I might lose my closeness to both Matt and Inga over this. "Not for a long while, no. I swear, Matt. Then, when she did tell me, when I knew she was pregnant, I begged her to speak to you. She said she would. She promised. But she kept on putting it off. I suppose she knew . . . what would happen when she did tell you."

"What really gets to me is knowing she could have got rid of the baby—gone off somewhere to have an abortion without me knowing anything about it. That we'd have continued on together, Matt and Inga, me worrying that she didn't seem herself, perhaps—but never having a clue what she'd done."

Oh, God. Even if he forgave me for not telling him this time, the sword of Damocles would still be hanging over me. Were Matt ever to find out about the abortion—if he and Inga had a row sometime in the future and it came out, my friendship with Matt would still potentially be on the line. And there wasn't a damn thing I could do about it.

The front door opened. Amy. She gave me a little wave and walked through to the kitchen, closing the sitting-room door behind her. As tactful and considerate as ever. I really was lucky to have found her as a flatmate.

"She's just not who I thought she was for all those years, you know?" Matt was saying. "Not if she can do this to me. And I can't stop thinking about all that wasted time."

He was almost making Inga sound evil now, and she wasn't. Just misguided. Impulsive to the point of reckless at times. She'd never set out to deliberately hurt Matt, I knew that.

"She really loved you, Matt. I'm sure she still does."

"Yeah. Just not enough, eh?" He sighed. "Look, I've got to go. I appreciate you ringing, though, Lily."

"You will keep in touch, won't you?"

"Of course. Take care."

Did he really mean that? Or was it just the kind of thing people say? I wanted to push further; to arrange something definite, but it was too late. Matt had gone, and my stomach suddenly felt as if something had died in it. My phone was warm in my hand. As if it had been heated up by what I'd concealed from Matt. I put it down on the coffee table and put my face in my hands for a minute. Then I went to find Amy.

"Hi. How did your session go?" she asked.

"Really well, thanks. It's just everything else that's a mess. Matt and Inga have broken up."

Amy looked shocked. "Oh, no. That's terrible."

"And my sister seems to have left without saying goodbye." I noticed Amy still had her jacket on and was now holding her purse and a shopping bag. "Don't tell me she ate your food? I told her, nothing from the left of the fridge."

"Well . . ."

"God, I'm sorry."

"It's fine, don't worry about it. I needed to get some things, anyway. Is there anything you want?"

To turn back the clock twelve months?

"No, thanks."

There was a knock at the door. Had Vi lost her key? I went to open it, but it wasn't Vi at all, it was Inga, her face flushed. Still angry with me, by the looks of it.

"Inga," I said. "Hi. How are you?" What a ridiculous question. How could she be anything but wrecked, desperate and sad after splitting up with Matt?

She pushed past me into the living room. "How the hell d'you think I am?"

I closed the front door. "I'm so . . ."

"You're so sorry. I know. You said."

She'd been drinking, I could tell.

"You didn't drive here, did you?"

Her eyes flashed at me angrily. "So what if I did? And don't try and tell me I ought not to be drinking because I'm pregnant."

"Well . . ."

"No, don't you dare. I mean it. Why the fuck didn't you let me speak to him in my own time, Lily? Why?"

I sank down onto the sofa. "Because Matt's always so good to me. To everyone. I just . . . I couldn't bear to live a lie. I told you that, over and over."

"We were friends first, Lily. It feels like you chose him over me."

I shook my head at her, feeling suddenly exasperated, angry, and desperately sad. "We're thirty, not three, Inga. I care about you both. I don't want to have to choose between you. Why didn't you tell him straightaway, as soon as you knew?"

Inga slumped down next to me, her face in her hands. "Because I was waiting to see if I'd miscarry, idiot."

"Oh, Inga."

"What? Plenty of people do in the first few months. I thought . . . if I lose it, I wouldn't have to tell him. It would be like it never happened."

I remembered what Matt had just said about how he and Inga would have carried on together with him in complete ignorance. I couldn't believe Inga had been waiting, perhaps hoping, to miscarry. It was the kind of thing a schoolgirl would do. But what did I know? I'd never been in her position.

Inga swiped at her eyes. "Jesus, Lily, you should have seen his face when I told him. So cold. He's never looked at me like that before. He hates me."

"He'll have been hurting, that's all. He doesn't hate you. He loves you."

"You wouldn't think so if you'd seen his face. It was the same way Mum looks at me sometimes. Like I'm a crushing disappointment to her. But let's face it, I'm a crushing disappointment to everyone. Aren't I? Especially myself."

Since I was so disappointed with Inga myself for the way she'd treated Matt, I didn't, at that precise moment in time, have an answer to that.

But what was done was done, wasn't it? Inga would be mad at me for a while, I'd be disappointed in her for a while, but I didn't really think the two of us were going to end our friendship because she'd made a mistake, and I'd forced her hand to come clean about it.

"You wait," Inga went on. "My child's going to take one look at me and my life and ask to go back again."

I tried to smile. "She won't."

"He," she said, her fingers plucking at one of Amy's cushions.

A rush of emotion. "You know the sex?"

She nodded. "Mm-hmm. I had a scan the other day."

"Oh, Inga, that's . . ." I wasn't sure what the right word was.

"Definite," she supplied. "That's what it is. This little fucker is coming into my life, disaster zone or not. And you're going to be Auntie Bloody Lily, all right?"

I nodded, tears dripping from my eyes. "All right."

17

Several months on from that conversation in my sitting room, I was in the delivery suite with Inga about to become just that—Auntie Lily. Despite an inauspicious start, Inga had sailed through pregnancy, looking glowing and fantastic, carrying on at work almost until the last minute. Sometimes it had occurred to me that she might be in denial about it all; that she did her level best not to think about the fact that she was about to become a mother. If you can be in denial about that when you turn up to house viewings looking as if the prospective house buyers might need to phone the emergency services at any minute.

But one thing was for certain, if she had been in denial, that all ended now. Because this baby was coming.

"Everything's fine," I said inadequately, feeling out of my depth. "You can do this, Inga."

"Easy . . . for . . . you to say," Inga said bad-temperedly, panting. "Aargh!"

Inga had asked me to be her birth partner quite early on in her pregnancy. I'd felt obliged to accept—she'd only just forgiven me for hinting to Matt about the baby. Besides, with her mother in Denmark, there really wasn't anybody else. Plus this was Inga. *Inga.* Of course I had to do it. Even though I did feel supremely underqualified and unequipped for the job.

With zilch experience of childbirth, all I could offer was encouragement, a deaf ear to the cursing, and gritted teeth to cope with the pain of having my hand clutched so hard my fingers were in danger of breaking. Inga was clearly in absolute agony, and if I'd had the slightest craving to have children myself, the experience of being in that delivery room would have cured me of it, no problem at all.

But maternal or not, wanting a baby myself or not, I'd have had to be some kind of a machine not to be moved when Inga's baby boy finally entered the world. When I first saw his dark, bewildered eyes and full head of black hair, and clapped eyes on Inga's expression as she gazed down with the deepest joy at him in her arms.

"Oh, my God, he's perfect, Inga," I breathed, and she beamed at me.

"He really is, isn't he?" she said as the baby stared at her, frowning, seeming to drink her in.

"D'you think he's trying to work out whether I'm a good bet or not?" she asked.

"Of course you're a good bet; you're his mother," I said, although I, of all people, knew it didn't necessarily follow.

"D'you want to hold him?"

I couldn't say I didn't want to, not with my best friend holding her firstborn out to me like a precious gift. Inga didn't know that a baby, for me, was like a portkey in a Harry Potter movie, transporting me someplace else as soon as I held it. To dark times. To a baby too heavy in every possible way for my eight-year-old arms.

It hadn't always been like that. When Mum first arrived back from hospital after having Violet, I couldn't stop gazing at the bundle in the carry cot. My new little sister, fast asleep, her mouth slightly open, looking exactly like the doll Katy Brown had brought into school one day. Except that this doll's chest was magically rising and falling—I could see it. She was a living, breathing human being in miniature. Perfect.

I reached out one hand to touch her closed eyelids, wanting them to spring open the way the eyes on Katy Brown's doll had done, and Mum whisper-yelled at me. "Don't touch her, Lily!"

Startled, my hand sprang back, accidentally jolting the baby, causing her eyes to open just the way I'd wanted them to. Only I hadn't pictured the cries of distress that came with it, or the way that perfect face would screw itself right up into a look of reproach.

"Now look what you've done!" Mum said, not bothering to whisper any longer. "She's gone and woken the baby up, Kevin."

"I can see that," Kevin said, not budging from the sofa.

"Well," Mum said, "can't you do something about it? I've just given birth. I'm fucking whacked."

"I would do, babe, but I'm not exactly kitted out with the right equipment, am I?" And he pulled at the front of his T-shirt to emphasise his point.

I wasn't equipped to give Inga's little boy what he wanted, either— for surely, even if he didn't start rooting around against my useless breasts for milk, he would sense my reluctance to hold him.

"He won't bite," Inga told me, noticing my resistance. "At least, I bloody hope not, since I've got to breastfeed the little bugger."

The baby made a snuffling sound as I took him from her, opening his mouth in a huge yawn before lying perfectly still. My arms accommodated him easily—a reflex action or muscle memory that came with the knowledge that his black hair would be as soft as duckling fluff and that, should I bend my head, he would very likely smell of sweet milk even though he hadn't yet suckled. He was perfect, his whole life ahead of him. I thought of all the things he had to learn, including the things he might have to accept that he might never know, like who his father was. Just as I had done.

"Bloody hell, Lily," Inga said, holding her arms out to take him back, "it's meant to be me who gets emotional, not you."

She did get emotional, though, not long afterwards. One moment she was fine, gazing gooily down at the perfection of her son's face, and the next she was sobbing, her body shudders jolting the baby.

"Oh, Lil, I wish Matt were here," she said, looking up at me with tragic eyes. "I wish I hadn't stuffed up."

I squeezed her hand, my own eyes leaking tears as I gazed down at the little boy who was so unmistakably Harry's son. "I know."

Had he been Matt's, it was effortlessly easy to imagine Matt here in the room with us instead of away on a possibly deliberately timed holiday to Spain. Grinning all over his face, picking the baby tenderly up, his movements confident, his face blazing with love. It wouldn't matter that he hadn't been sure whether he wanted to be a father or not. He'd have loved his child when he was here, I knew he would. With all his heart. It was the only way Matt knew how to love—with everything he had, holding nothing back.

"Do you think he'll ever even get to meet him?"

I wasn't sure. Somewhere along the line, Matt would inevitably encounter Inga and her son. But deliberately? Maybe after he'd got over his break-up with Inga to the point where he wasn't at risk of getting sucked back into their relationship.

"I'm sure he will," I said, more confidently than I felt. We'd met up a few times since their break-up, me and Matt, so I knew how sore he still was about it all. "Matt's not malicious, is he? He'll want to make sure you're okay. Anyway, have you decided what you're going to call this little guy?"

"I was thinking about Noah?"

I wasn't used to Inga's sentences having a question at the end of them—to her being cautious or doubtful about anything. I was sure the outspoken person who rarely hesitated to voice her opinions would return at some point, but I supposed the little guy in her arms was always going to demand some compromise from her, just by nature of his existence.

"Noah sounds perfect," I said, and Inga gave me a watery smile.

"Shit, Lily," she said. "I've really gone and done this fucking thing, haven't I?"

I laughed, tears dripping down my cheeks. "Yes, you have," I said. "You really have."

Noah began to stir, his whimpers quickly turning to cries of distress.

I searched Inga's face, half expecting to see panic or resentment, relieved only to see focused love and tenderness.

"Here, little one. Come to Mummy."

And I cried and smiled all over again when little Noah latched straight onto Inga's breast like a champ and began to suckle, ignoring the childish voice inside my head that wanted to point out that, now that Noah was quite rightly Inga's priority, our friendship would never be quite the same again.

18

I thought about Violet's father on the bus journey home from the hospital. Apart from that time when he and Mum brought Violet back from hospital, I didn't have many memories of Kevin. Which probably meant he hadn't played much of an active role with Violet. Certainly, I couldn't remember him changing nappies or feeding her, or anything like that. I could only really remember him suddenly not being around, and Mum finding it harder and harder to cope.

Had Violet managed to track him down? I'd heard nothing at all from her since she'd left. If she had found him, had she got what she wanted from the experience? Staring out of the bus window at the passing traffic, I wished all over again that she'd left me her phone number so I could keep in touch. That my sister was as keen as I was for us to be a proper family again.

Oh, God. If only I didn't have to teach in Cromer the next day. If only I could sleep for a week.

If I didn't sleep for a week, I did sleep reasonably well that night, worn out by the emotion of the day. And as I slept, I dreamt all over again about Mum bringing Violet back from the hospital. About eight-year-old me looking down at her in her carry cot. Only when I looked, the baby wasn't Violet at all, it was Noah. Noah with his dark-brown eyes; a mini-Harry. Then, in my dream, there was a knock at the front door, and it was Matt, just returned from a holiday, wheeling his suitcase behind him, sunglasses on top of his head, his expression reproachful.

"Why didn't you tell me the baby had come, Lily?" he asked. "You should have told me."

Dream Matt was right, I thought as soon as I woke the next morning. I did need to tell him. He was away somewhere, I knew, but even so, I had to try to reach him.

I called him from the train with the lush Norfolk countryside passing by outside, imagining him seated on a hotel balcony somewhere with a very different view.

"Lily, hi."

"Hello, Matt. How are you? Where are you?"

"In Barcelona, walking along the beach on my way to breakfast. How about you? You sound as if you're travelling."

"I'm in a train, on my way to Cromer."

"You're teaching there today?"

"Yes. Matt . . ."

"I can guess why you're ringing. The baby's arrived, right?"

"Yes, a little boy. Noah. Eight pounds, two ounces. Mother and baby doing well."

"Noah." There was so much sadness in his voice. I wished he were there with me. I wanted to hug him. To be enveloped in one of his bear hugs. Words were entirely inadequate for this situation. I wanted to physically show him how much I cared. That I was there for him.

"How was it? The birth? Is Inga all right?"

"The midwives said it was very quick, although it didn't feel like it to me. She's okay. I think she's already forgotten about the trauma of it all, to be honest. When are you home?"

"On Thursday. But I'm still off work on Friday. Want to meet up for a drink?"

My heart lifted. "Yes. I'd really like that."

"Great." A pause, then he said, "I can't see her, Lily. Not yet."

"I know."

"But I could look at a photo or two, if you have any?"

"Of course I have."

"I'll call you when I'm home. Thanks for ringing, Lily. I appreciate it."

"Bye, Matt. See you soon."

But when Matt and I did meet up, it wasn't to go for a drink. Because on Friday evening, two days after I'd accompanied Inga and Noah home from hospital in a taxi, I received a text from Violet.

Found my dad. Come with me to meet him?

I phoned her right away. To my relief, she answered.

"Hi."

I put a rein on all the *why the hell haven't you called*s and the *I've been so bloody worried*s with difficulty, saying only, "It's great news that you've found him, Vi."

"I know, right?" There was a smile in her voice. My heart swelled at the sound of it.

"Where are you?"

"Nottingham. At the Premier Inn, near the station. We're meeting up tomorrow morning at nine. Can you come?"

I had no idea how I was going to get to Nottingham by nine in the morning, but I did know I was going to manage it somehow.

"Of course. Where are you meeting him?"

"In the Starbucks just down the road."

"I'll meet you in the hotel foyer at eight forty-five. We can walk down together."

"Okay, see you."

"Oh, and Violet . . ."

But it was too late; she was gone. I didn't even know what I'd wanted to say, not really. *Don't get your hopes raised too much? I hope it's everything you want it to be? You know I love you, no matter what, don't you?* Any of it would have done. I just hadn't wanted to let her go so soon. Not when she sounded so happy. But I would see her tomorrow, because she wanted me to go with her when she met the father she could never remember knowing. That was big. Huge. Wonderful.

I pulled my tablet towards me to start to research trains to Nottingham. Then, as the website was loading, I called Inga. I'd promised her I'd go round on Saturday morning, just as I'd gone round every day since she'd got home.

I called her. When she answered, I could hear Noah crying in the background.

"How's it going today?"

"Well, he's not exactly a happy bunny at the moment, as you can hear. No idea why. I've tried everything. But that's new motherhood, right? Solving the puzzles? The midwife's coming round again later, so hopefully she'll be able to shed some light."

I'd been searching for trains to Nottingham, but now I stopped clicking to really listen to my friend's voice. Inga sounded tired, but philosophical as well. And help—in the form of the midwife—was on its way. She'd be all right without me for a little while, surely.

"I'm glad the midwife's coming. Look, something's happened, Ing. Violet's been in touch again."

"Has she now. Where is she? Marrakesh? The Yukon?"

"No, Nottingham."

I wasn't surprised when Inga laughed—Nottingham did sound rather tame compared to some of the places Violet had got to on her travels. But, with a meeting with her unknown father in the offing, I was willing to bet Nottingham was currently the most exciting place on the planet for my sister.

"The thing is, she wants me to meet up with her there tomorrow. She's managed to track down her dad, and she wants me to go with her for moral support."

"So, you're calling me to see whether *I* can manage without your moral support while you give it to her?" Inga said dryly.

I sighed. "I suppose so, yes. I don't imagine I'll be away long. You know Violet. And I'm teaching on Tuesday, anyway, so I'll have to get back for that."

The search results popped up. There was a train from Norwich to Nottingham in half an hour. It would be touch and go whether I'd be able to catch it, but I'd like to. Go tonight, stay at the hotel, make sure I was there in time for Violet instead of a last-minute rushed journey first thing in the morning.

Noah's cries were louder now. "It's fine," Inga said. "I'll be fine. You go."

Afterwards, I wondered whether I'd allowed myself to be reassured because I wanted to be. Whether, if I'd been in the frame of mind to listen more carefully, I'd have picked up on a worrying note of fragility in Inga's voice. But at the time, I just accepted her reassurances and told her I'd see her and little Noah very soon. Then I ended the call and dashed about stuffing things I'd need into a bag, wondering whether I was crazy to even think I stood a chance of catching the train.

Then, when I was ready to leave, I pulled the door open to find Matt on the doorstep, just about to knock. For a millisecond I stared at him in bewilderment, a rush of pleasure sweeping through me at the sight of his smiling face. Then I remembered our arrangement to go for a drink. Shit. How the fuck had it slipped my mind, even for a second? I'd been looking forward to it so much.

"Why do I think you've forgotten we were meeting up?" he said, his gaze on my backpack. "Unless you've decided we should go for a hike instead of for a drink?"

It was so good to see him. Disappointment flooded through me, replacing the pleasure. If I was going to catch my train, we'd have to rearrange our meetup.

"Sorry, my sister got in touch. I've been waiting to hear from her for ages, and she's asked me to meet her in Nottingham tomorrow morning. I'm just on my way to the station." Quickly I filled him in on Violet's quest to track down her father.

"Well, why don't I drive you?"

"To the station?"

"No, to Nottingham. We can chat on the way."

I paused, taken aback, not wanting to be a bother or a burden.

"It's no trouble, Lily," he said. "Honestly."

I looked at him and realised that he meant it. That he really didn't mind. He wouldn't end up wishing he'd never offered to help out. That it was safe to say yes, and I didn't have to deal with this situation all on my own.

"Thank you," I said. "That would be amazing."

"Well, come on, then," he said. "Let's go."

"How will it go tomorrow for Violet with her dad, d'you think?" he asked when we were on the road, heading out of the city.

"Oh, God, I so hope it goes well for her. But I don't know, I really don't. I was eight or nine when Kevin left. I'm not even sure why he went; whether it was something between him and Mum, or whether it was just the reality of having a screaming baby in the house."

I saw him flinch a little as I said that, and could have kicked myself, knowing I'd made him think about Inga.

I reached out to put a comforting hand on his leg. "Sorry. That was tactless of me."

"I keep trying to imagine Inga dealing with a newborn, but I just can't somehow do it. I mean, this is a woman who complained incessantly about screech owls disturbing her sleep."

"I know."

"I used to have to gentle her awake with a cup of coffee. And not just any old cup of coffee, but a coffee made with exactly the right freshly ground beans in her special mug. I'm not kidding, no other mug would do. The sodding shower had to be free when she wanted to use it, and woe betide the world if the shower mat was already wet."

I laughed a little at that—I couldn't help it. But it wasn't funny, really, and I wanted to give him another comforting squeeze. I didn't, though, because we were on the dual carriageway now, and a lorry had just pulled out to overtake another lorry just at the start of an incline, forcing everyone to slow right down, and Matt needed to concentrate on his driving.

"Bloody idiot," said Matt, and I chose to believe he was talking about the lorry driver, not Inga.

"Maybe you can put your own needs and desires to one side more easily if it's your own flesh and blood," I suggested.

"Maybe," Matt said doubtfully, sighing. "Does the baby look like Inga at all?"

I pictured little Noah. "He has her mouth. And her jawline, I think. I've got photos on my phone if you want to take a look when we stop."

"Sure. There's no point hating him because of what he represents, is there? He didn't ask to be born, poor little bugger."

"No," I said, my thoughts returning to my baby sister. To all that perfect, fresh potential carried back from the hospital. "He didn't."

The lorry finally managed to pull clear of the other lorry and switched back to the slow lane. I looked up into the driver's cab as we passed by. Saw a man with short, grey hair and a double chin. Somebody's grandfather. Somebody's husband. Not far off from retirement. He didn't look like an idiot, and yet he drove like one, perhaps to relieve the boredom.

Had that been why Inga had so recklessly slept with Harry? Because she was bored? Matt wasn't in the least bit boring, though; not unless you counted being nice and considerate and supportive as boring, which I didn't.

Would he ever forgive her? Knowing Matt as I did, I thought there was a fair chance he would. Probably not enough for them to get back together—that ship seemed definitely to have sailed—but enough perhaps for him to become Uncle Matt, a fun, loving role model for Noah. I couldn't imagine the same for me and Alex's child, but that was different, because I doubted whether Fliss would welcome me, Alex's ex, into their lives.

I sighed, thinking of the four of us, and all the happy times we'd spent together. The close bond we'd shared. I'd been mourning the loss of that closeness far more than the ending of my relationship with Alex. Alex and I hadn't been right for each other, I could see that now.

"Have you seen that much of Alex?" I asked Matt.

"Not lately, no, not really. It's awkward, to be honest, with Fliss there. Fliss and I . . . well, let's just say I remember her too clearly from school. She was one of the cool kids, and I most definitely wasn't." He smiled wryly in my direction. "No chance of blending in, either, when you're a good foot taller than everyone else."

Instantly I was back in my own school days, never having the right uniform, the right equipment, a proper packed lunch. Always having to pretend so hard not to care about the bullies and the petty school rules that put a spotlight firmly on my family situation.

"School stank for you, too, then?" I said.

"Let's just say it was something I wanted to forget all about as soon as I left. Still want to forget about, thank you very much. Unfortunately, it seems to be Fliss's favourite subject. It's as if her school years were some kind of a golden era for her."

"The baby will change all that when it comes, though, won't it?"

"Hopefully. Alex is certainly excited about becoming a dad, anyway."

"I'm happy for him," I said, bringing Matt's glance in my direction.

"He always asks about you when we do manage to meet up."

Coming close on the heels of my memories of the four of us sharing happy times together, I felt a pang somewhere between my heart and my stomach. "What do you tell him?"

"That you're working hard. That your teaching's going well. That you're painting when you can."

I sighed. "Which hasn't been often lately. I miss it."

It wasn't just my painting I missed. It was the routine of my old life. Having a group of friends that were like family. How stupid I'd been to take it all for granted. To wish for a moment to have time to myself to be creative.

"I really miss the four of us doing stuff together."

Matt sighed. "Me too."

But as we drove on in silence, I wondered bitterly whether we'd really been as close as I'd thought we were, the four of us. After all, Alex must have always been hiding his desire to have kids. Inga must have had a creeping dissatisfaction about her relationship with Matt. So maybe that tight-knit, friends-forever unit had all been an illusion? I didn't want to think that, though, to have all those happy memories tarnished.

"It's great that Violet's asked you to be there for her," Matt said, and I turned my face to look out the window, hiding my expression from him.

God. If he wasn't careful, I was going to cry. "It really is. I hope . . . I really hope this marks a new start between us."

"I don't know why it shouldn't. However this turns out for her, I should think it will be emotional. Violet's going to need her big sister."

I glanced at him. "How do you always know the absolute right thing to say?"

He shook his head. "I don't, believe me. Jesus, half the time I don't even know something needs to be said. I just sail on with life without a clue that everything's falling apart."

"Oh, Matt," I said, and he laughed; a weary laugh, totally lacking in humour.

"Don't worry, I'm not really a cynical git. Well, at least, I'm trying not to be. Most of the time I succeed."

"I hope . . . ," I started. Broke off, started again. "I hope seeing me doesn't remind you of everything."

He shook his head. "No. It's not something you need to be reminded of, is it? It's with me all the time, anyway. Really, Lily, I'm fine. Time's a great healer and all that."

When at last we reached the outskirts of Nottingham, I put the address of the hotel into my phone so I could direct Matt. By the time we arrived it was ten thirty in the evening, and the hotel only had one room left. One room with one double bed.

"You take the room," Matt told me. "I'll find somewhere else."

"No, I'll give Violet a call. I can share with her."

But there was no reply from Violet's phone—it was switched off. "Probably out clubbing somewhere," I said, feeling unjustifiably annoyed.

"Honestly, Lily," Matt said. "I don't mind trying to find somewhere else."

I looked at his tired face. "No, we can share. We've done it before."

We had, but not without Alex and Inga. And it had been on a camping trip, in a big tent, not a hotel room for two.

Matt nodded. "All right, if you're sure."

"I'll sleep on the floor," he said as we rode up to the sixth floor in the lift.

"Don't be daft," I said. "This isn't the nineteen thirties. You know, *It Happened One Night*, when Clark Gable strings a blanket across the room between him and Claudette Colbert for decency's sake?"

He laughed. "I can't say I've seen that film," he said. "But I can find some string and a blanket from somewhere if you want me to."

"No," I said, as the lift pinged for our floor and the doors opened. "That's all right."

"I didn't realise you were such a fan of old black-and-white movies," he said as we walked along the corridor.

"I was in a film club when I was at art college," I told him, looking at the door numbers as we passed. "We saw all the classics."

Inga had gone along with me; we'd bonded over such films as *The African Queen*, *Casablanca* and *All About Eve*. But I didn't mention that to Matt.

Oh, Inga. Stringed blanket or no stringed blanket, I was glad she didn't know that me and Matt were about to share a bed.

"Here it is," said Matt and used the key card.

The door opened. We went in together, and I dumped my backpack on the bed while Matt shrugged out of his jacket and headed for the bathroom.

What would it be like, going to sleep together? Fine, surely. This wasn't a rom-com, was it? Matt and I weren't an item. We were friends, and he was only here because he was a kind man supporting me while I did my best to help my sister.

The TV remote was by the bed. I switched the TV on. It was a news report about a major fire in a factory in Spain.

Shit.

I sank down on the edge of the bed and stared at the huge flames licking the sky; the distressed family members wailing as they looked on, their loved ones clearly trapped inside the inferno; and I felt sick.

I should turn the TV off. Get rid of the image. I tried never to watch news reports of fires because they inevitably took me back to that long-ago Christmas night—the night of my sixteenth birthday. But somehow, this time, I couldn't tear myself away, and before I knew it, I was back there, and the smell of burning seemed to come into the room. I remembered the smoke. The tide of panic rising inside me. The screaming.

"Mum! Violet!"

I'd wanted to launch myself into the flames to try to get to them, but strong hands held me back, making me utterly powerless. Just like the people on TV now, wailing and crying for those trapped inside.

So many years had passed, but everything about that night was still so totally vivid to me. I hadn't talked about it to anyone—not to therapists, not to my best friend, not even to Alex, who I'd expected to spend the rest of my life with. Certainly not to my little sister, the one person who really knew about the hell of that night. It was all still too painful. Too raw.

Until recently I'd locked away the memories of the fire deep inside myself and thrown away the key. It was the only way to function.

But if I was ever going to do more than function, if I was ever going to be truly myself with the people I loved, then maybe I would have to talk. To speak the awful, dreadful words and to finally set the traumatic memories free.

Could I start now, with Matt? Matt, who'd listened so carefully when I told him about Mum and me on that summer picnic that had gone wrong. But a failed picnic was a very different thing to a terrifying, life-transforming fire.

Dry mouthed, I watched the efforts of the firefighters to get the blaze under control, remembering how Beryl had tried to persuade me to talk about my demons. Imagining her here now, egging me on. *"Talk about it, pet. Tell him the truth. It's time."*

Yes. I'd do it. But how to start? *"A dreadful thing happened to my family when I was sixteen."* Or, *"I've seen a fire as bad as that."*

I still hadn't decided on my opening line when Matt left the bathroom and came to stand beside me.

"Bloody hell," he said, reading the information line below the images, "that's right near where I've just been for my interview."

What the fuck?

"You went to Spain for an interview?"

The footage of the fire came to an end. Back in the newsroom, the newsreader began to talk about a downturn in the economy.

Matt looked at me, slightly shamefaced. "Not entirely, but yes. Well, all right, I built my holiday around the interview."

Well, then.

I nodded, the moment for my big confessional heart-to-heart vanishing in a puff of smoke.

Matt, living in another country. Jesus.

Suddenly desperate to escape the room, I picked up the kettle to take it to the bathroom to fill it.

Matt put a hand out to stop me as I passed by. "I wasn't going to keep it as a big secret, Lily. I just saw the ad and thought, why not? That if I switched countries, I might get some perspective. Be able to make a new start." He sighed. "I'm just kind of making my life up as I go along at the moment, you know?"

Like I did pretty much every day of my life. Not that that made his decision any easier to accept.

"When will you hear whether you've got the job or not?" I managed to ask. Then I remembered our holiday to Wales, and his big announcement. "Or do you already know?"

"No, I haven't heard anything yet. I should get a call in the next few days if I've been successful, I should think."

I continued on past him towards the bathroom with the kettle. "Well, I wish you all the luck in the world." I did my level best to make my voice bright. Had no idea whatsoever whether I'd managed it or not. "If anyone deserves it, it's you. What's the project? Oh, wait a minute, let me fill the kettle, then you can tell me all about it over a cuppa."

Acting, acting, acting. Pretending I hadn't just cranked myself up to a position where I was finally going to tell someone I trusted about that long-ago night from hell only to have the chance of unburdening myself ripped away by yet more devastating news.

In the bathroom I turned on the tap, managing to splash myself when I put the kettle under it. Oh, God. Everything in my life was broken. Everyone but me was getting on with their lives. Matt, Alex, Inga. All of them moving on. While, scratch beneath the surface, and I was pretty much the same person I'd been at sixteen.

The kettle was filled. Overfilled really, for two cups of tea. But I needed more time before I could face Matt again if I was going to put on any kind of successful front. So I put the kettle down on the side of the sink and locked the door, pretending to go to the loo. Leaving it as long as possible.

"If I do get the job, you can come and visit me as often as you want to," Matt said when I eventually left the bathroom. "I'll be back in the UK regularly too."

I set a smile on my face and plugged the kettle in.

"Sure. I love Spain. You won't be able to keep me away. Now, what d'you want? Tea or coffee?"

Matt told me all about the housing project the job was focused on, and I think I managed to show enough enthusiasm and interest. I asked some questions, anyway, and he answered them. Then he found a comedy show on TV—I have no idea what it was—and we watched a couple of episodes before we got ready for bed.

And, if I hadn't quite got over the shock of the fire on TV and hearing Matt's news by the time Matt switched the light out, I was feeling slightly less churned up as I settled back against the pillows.

"D'you remember that camping trip we went on to Scotland?" Matt asked me in the darkness.

"Of course I do," I said, smiling at the memory.

We'd all slept in one big tent together, and I could vividly remember the jokes and the laughter. The rustling as Inga unearthed a midnight snack.

"Alex tried to convince us the animal we could hear outside was a lion escaped from that zoo up the road."

I laughed; a quick bubble of laughter that soon dried up at the thought that those innocent times were well and truly behind us.

Matt sighed beside me, obviously thinking exactly the same thing. "Night, Lily."

"Night, Matt."

I turned on my side, away from him, tucking my hand under the pillow the way I liked to do when I went to sleep, listening to him breathing beside me, the sound of someone moving around in the room next door reaching me faintly through the wall, making me remember other times when I'd shared a bedroom. When Mum and her current boyfriend had been rowing downstairs—whoever it was, there always seemed to be rows—and I'd take my duvet into Violet's room to sleep on the floor next to her bed.

Vi. Her voice had been so lit up when she'd told me over the phone about meeting up with Kevin. God, let it go all right. Let Kevin show up tomorrow. Show up and be kind. Give my little sister what she needed from the meeting.

I fantasised then about Violet being transformed by something going well in her life, her eyes bright with the happiness of discovering a new family member. Me and her sharing something special. Starting again. And sometime along the way I fell asleep next to Matt.

Only to be plunged straight into a dream about a fire.

Matt shook me awake. "Lily? You were having a nightmare."

You can pretend to be okay all you like when you're awake, but when you go to sleep and your subconscious takes over, it's quite a different matter.

I woke to find my face soaking wet, my throat as raw as sandpaper, and I guessed I must have been screaming and crying in my sleep.

"It's all right," Matt soothed, his arm around me, and I breathed deeply, trying to stem the flow of tears.

I could still see flames inside the building of my dream, licking at the windowpanes. "It . . . it was the fire on telly."

Now I was awake, memories were quickly taking over from the nightmare, and I couldn't stop sobbing and shaking.

Matt moved closer, holding me. "Shh . . . it's all right. I'm here," he said, and somehow that made me want to cry even harder because the way he was talking and holding me was so exactly what I needed.

"I . . . I'm sorry," I said eventually. "Sorry I woke you."

"Don't be daft," he said. "Here, let me get you a tissue."

He got up from the bed to make his way to the bathroom through the darkness. On his way back, he collided with something and cursed.

"Are you all right?" I asked. "D'you need the light on?"

"No, it's fine," he said. "Here."

"Thanks." I took the tissue from him and used it to wipe my face. He sat close to me, his shoulder against mine. "All right now?"

I nodded. "Better."

"Want a cup of tea?"

I could say yes. We could sit up in bed and drink it, and I could do what I'd planned to do earlier on—tell Matt all about my sixteenth birthday. How I'd plotted and planned for weeks to get Teddy Newsome's attention, and nothing and nobody was going to stop me going out with my friends to celebrate. Not even my little sister's pleading. *"Please, Lily. Don't go. Please, don't go."*

I'd woken up that Christmas morning with the feeling that everything was going to be different from now on. Not with my family—I wasn't misguided enough to think Mum would suddenly stop drinking. That she'd have found the energy, money, and desire to have bought me a birthday present. To be awake to wish me happy birthday.

No, I didn't have any unrealistic expectations like that. But I did think Teddy Newsome, the older boy I'd had a crush on for months, might finally look in my direction. And as I got dressed, I was full of plans for how I was going to get his attention and what I would say after I'd been successful.

And then I went downstairs, and Violet had made me a Happy Birthday banner and strung it up for me above the kitchen door. She was waiting there for me, a smile splitting her face right in two, and I tried not to think about her standing on one of our ultra-wobbly kitchen chairs to pin it up, or to notice that she'd left the *n* out of *sixteenth* so that it read *Happy Sixteeth Birthday, Lily.*

"Did you make that all by yourself?" I said, scooping her into a hug. "Thank you, Vi. It's beautiful."

"D'you really like it?"

"Of course I do. It's fantastic. My best birthday present ever in the world."

And she'd grinned and hugged me back.

"Happy Christmas, Vi. Come and open your present."

She ripped the paper off the tiny teddy bear I'd wrapped up for her, kissing it and proclaiming it was called Mr. Cuddles, and I laughed, pleased she was so happy with my gift, blissfully unaware that this was the last proper day we would spend together.

I went out to meet my friends that evening, ignoring all my little sister's pleas. I left my sister all alone with Mum, knowing Mum would inevitably get drunk.

I had let Violet down so very badly; no wonder she barely got in touch with me.

Except she had, though, this time, hadn't she? She'd asked me to be here to meet her dad with her. That meant a lot. More than me relieving my guilt by spewing it all out to Matt.

"No," I said to Matt, "it's okay. Let's go back to sleep."

"Sure?"

"Sure."

So Matt got into bed, and I lay on my side, and he lay in the same direction and held me.

The way Alex used to.

"Is this okay?" Matt asked.

A part of my mind knew I should say no. But after the nightmare, it was just so comforting to be held. So I said, "Yes, it's fine."

But within seconds I was thinking about another film where a platonic couple shares a bed. *The Proposal* with Sandra Bullock and Ryan Reynolds when they're pretending to be a couple prior to a sham wedding so the Sandra Bullock character won't be deported. The Sandra Bullock character massaging his shoulder, pretending to be loving, when his mother brings them breakfast in bed.

Lying in the darkness now, I could see the expression on the Ryan Reynolds character's face as he realises he's enjoying it, and his mind is saying, *wait a minute . . .*

But that was just a movie. Matt was not going to start massaging my shoulder, and we weren't pretending to be anything but what we were. Friends. Friends on borrowed time too. Because I was sure Matt would get the job in Spain. Why wouldn't he? He was good at his job, and he was bound to have been impressive at the interview. Yes, he'd get the job. Then he'd be gone.

And, anyway, Matt was already asleep.

So I closed my eyes, focusing on my own breathing to help me to relax. And within seconds, I was asleep too.

19

Matt was up and dressed by the time I woke.

I sat up quickly. "I haven't overslept, have I?"

"No," he said with a smile. "There's plenty of time. I just thought I'd get out of your hair while you dressed. I'll see you downstairs in the lobby, shall I?"

I pulled the duvet up to my chin, suddenly aware of the skimpy T-shirt I was wearing. "Sure. I won't be long."

When Violet turned up five minutes late, at eight fifty, her gaze went straight to Matt.

"Is this Alex?" she asked, staring.

"No, this is my friend Matt. Matt, meet my sister, Violet."

"Hello, Violet."

"Just friends, eh?" she said. "I'll believe you. Thousands wouldn't."

That was the thing with my little sister. I adored her, longed to see her, and then when we did meet, she drove me crazy within minutes. It was frustrating in the extreme. As if, because we'd never been teenagers together, we were having to make up for lost time now.

I opened my mouth to make another rebuff, but Matt placed a reassuring hand in the small of my back. "I'll leave you both to it. Call me when you've finished, Lily. See you later." Then he smiled and walked away.

I watched him go for a moment—a decent man intent on finding a decent cup of coffee. A man who would draw glances whatever country he lived in. But I wouldn't think about the future and his probable move to Spain. Not now. I needed to focus on Vi's meeting with her dad. Even if Violet and her smug expression were the most annoying things on the planet.

"What are you pretending to be just friends for?" Violet asked.

"Because we are just friends."

She shrugged. "Could have fooled me. It's obvious you feel something for each other. And who cares? You're not with your boyfriend any longer."

"I told you; Matt and I aren't together. I'm not with anyone at the moment."

Violet shook her head, giving me an *I know better* smile, and I sighed, leaving it.

"Anyway, how are you feeling?"

She shrugged. "A bit shagged out. I was up late dancing. Found a great club. Nottingham's cool."

"I meant, how are you feeling about meeting your dad?"

"Can't wait. In fact, we'd better make tracks, hadn't we? If we don't want to be late?"

She said it as if I was the one holding us up, but I just lifted my eyebrows and let that one go too.

We didn't speak much as we headed for the café. Violet was walking quickly, head down, the heels of her shoes staccato on the pavement, her body tense. I wanted to tell her not to get her hopes up too much. To take things as they came. To basically be a killjoy big sister so she wouldn't get too hurt if things didn't turn out the way she wanted them to. But I knew Violet wouldn't want to hear all those warnings, so I kept quiet and hoped and prayed for the best.

There was no one who looked as if he was Kevin in Starbucks when we arrived. Just a couple of businessmen and an elderly couple.

"Why don't you grab a table while I get us some coffees?" I said to Violet.

"Yeah, cos a coach-load could suddenly turn up and fill the place out," she said sarcastically, not budging from the counter.

The café door opened. A man came in. I heard Violet's swift intake of breath. My gut told me this wasn't Kevin, and my instincts were proved right when the man went over to join the elderly couple. Their son, by the looks of things.

"It would be good to get a table by the window, wouldn't it? So we can see Kevin when he arrives?"

"All right." She went, looking as if it hurt her to do what I'd suggested, but by the time I got to the table, Kevin still hadn't shown up.

"He's late," Violet said.

"Only by a few minutes. It's a busy time of day."

"Nine a.m. was his idea, not mine."

I didn't bother to try to find another excuse for Kevin. The guy hadn't seen his daughter since she was a baby. Traffic or no traffic, he ought to be here on time. There were no excuses.

Then suddenly the door opened again, and there was a man with long, mousy-brown hair and a wary expression wearing a T-shirt that showed off muscular arms. And despite all the years that had passed, I knew it was Kevin.

He came over, the wary expression stretching into a smile. "Blimey, look at you," he said, not to Violet, but to me. "You must have been nine or ten when I last saw you, but I'd still have recognised you anywhere. How are you, Lily?"

Why was he speaking to me instead of Violet? Hugging me, not Violet?

"Hello, Kevin," I said, moving deliberately to one side so he had to look at her.

"Whereas you look pretty different to when I last saw you!" he said to her. If it was meant to be a joke, it wasn't in the least bit funny. I expected Vi to make some sarcastic crack, like, *I couldn't find a Babygro in my size,"* or, *"What d'you fucking mean? I was a baby when you took off!"* But she didn't say anything like that. Instead, she just smiled a polite, very un-Violet-like smile, and somehow that upset me much more than her rudeness would have done.

"Can I get you a coffee, Kevin?" I asked, deciding to give them some time alone.

"Oh, thanks. A double espresso, please. Here, I'll give you the money."

I moved quickly away as he started to scrabble about in his pockets for change. "No, that's okay. I'll get it."

There was a small queue at the counter. I deliberately turned my back on Violet and Kevin, focusing my gaze on the display of cookies, willing the two of them to connect.

It was impossible to tell whether they'd made any progress or not when I returned to the table with Kevin's coffee, and when Kevin immediately began asking me what work I did, I wished I hadn't come with Vi, after all. I'd come because she'd asked me to, but my presence was turning out to be a hindrance, not a help. Violet was getting fidgety, turning her cup round and round on the table and swinging her crossed leg, her gaze lowered to the froth on her drink as if it was the most important thing on earth. I ached for her, easily able to imagine how much she was hurting. How desperate she was to hide that fact.

Suddenly she scraped her chair back and got to her feet. "I need the loo," she mumbled, and off she went, leaving me and Kevin alone together. I watched him watch her go, searching his face to try to detect some kind of emotion. Any kind of emotion. But still, what he said when he finally turned in my direction came as a surprise.

"You know she's a user, don't you?"

"I beg your pardon?"

He jerked his head in the direction of the toilets. "Violet. She's a user. Probably taking something right now. Takes one to know one, as they say. I've done a lot of drugs in my time. Not any longer; I'm clean now."

"Violet doesn't take drugs."

He couldn't be right, could he? No. He was just a useless piece of shit who didn't care who he hurt.

"Didn't you notice how she couldn't keep still? The look in her eyes? Desperate for a high."

"She was nervous about meeting you, that's all. She hasn't seen you since she was a baby. This means a lot to her. Everything."

Kevin looked suddenly shifty. "Ah. About that. I can't do it, I'm afraid."

"What d'you mean?"

He sighed. Sipped some coffee. "I've got three other girls. Grandkids too. My wife knows nothing about Violet. I probably should have told her, but, well, I didn't. And now . . . I just can't do it. I'm sorry."

I was shaking with anger. Was so furious I wanted to shove him right off his chair. "Why did you agree to meet up with her then?"

He shrugged. Oh, that shrug. "Curiosity, I suppose. And she seemed like a kid who wouldn't take no for an answer."

"Well, I wish you'd tried harder. She's going to be devastated."

Another shrug. "She'll get over it. Let's face it, I'm hardly much of a prize, am I? Look at me. I scrape a living together, live in a shitty falling-down house. She's not exactly missing much."

My coffee was getting cold. I had no desire whatsoever to drink it. My mind was too busy scrabbling about, trying to think of a way to get Kevin to change his mind. He was right; he wasn't much of a prize. The exact opposite, in fact. But Violet deserved to have the right to decide that for herself, and I'd do anything to make this useless excuse for a human being let her do that.

"Look . . . ," I started to say, but he interrupted me.

"Have you heard anything from your mum?"

And bam, the question sent me straight back to the aftermath of the fire. To the wrecked house, still smoking. Me yelling to the firefighters, "Where's my mum? She was in there, I tell you! She was in there!"

One of them, an older fatherly guy, came over and placed a big, dirty hand on my shoulder. "There was no one in there except your sister, love." I could see Violet, over by the ambulance with a blanket around her shoulders. She was crying, looking over in my direction. I couldn't go over, not until I knew what had happened to Mum.

"We've done a thorough search," the firefighter went on. "I promise you, your mother's safe."

Safe, but absent. Gone out God only knew where and left her eight-year-old daughter alone in a burning house. Never to be heard from again.

"Why should I have heard from her?" I asked Kevin bitterly now. "Why would I even want to?"

"I just thought, you know, over the years, things might have mellowed." He sighed again, moving closer to me across the table. "Look, I can see your sister needs someone in her life. That she's searching for someone. But it can't be me, I'm really sorry."

With that, he drained his espresso cup and pushed his chair back.

I stared at him, shocked. Panicked. "Wait, aren't you going to speak to her yourself?"

"It's best if you do it. If I tell her, she'll only make a scene."

"She won't."

"Come on, Lily, we both know she will."

"Oh, and that's based on five minutes' acquaintance, is it? Or are you counting how she cried as a bloody baby in that assessment too?"

"Goodbye, Lily," he said, turning away. "Give your sister my very best for the future."

"Kevin!" I called after him, desperate, but it was too late. He was gone, out through the café door, past the shop front and out of sight. Just as Violet returned from the toilet.

"Where's Kevin?"

My expression no doubt said everything. "He . . . had to go."

She snatched up her shoulder bag from the back of her chair. "What did you say to him?" she yelled. "What the fuck did you say to him, Lily?"

"Vi . . ."

But she was running out of the café, pausing to stand on the pavement, looking desperately about, not knowing which way to go.

I joined her. Tried to touch her arm.

She flinched away from me. "Don't you touch me!" she screamed. "Don't you fucking touch me!"

"Vi, listen to me, I tried to get him to stay."

"I should never have asked you to come with me. Just because you haven't got a father yourself, you didn't want me to have one. You were fucking jealous!"

"That's not true, Vi. Please, come back inside. Let me tell you what he said."

"No! Fuck off, Lily. Just fuck off!"

She walked quickly away—as it happened in the same direction Kevin had gone in. Not that it would do her any good, because even if she managed to track him down, which I doubted she would, his mind was made up. Bastard.

I walked aimlessly along for a few minutes, not knowing what to do or where to go, my brain blasted by it all. Vi's outburst. Kevin's utter selfishness and cruelty. The fire on TV. Remembering the way Violet and I had been parted that night—Vi taken off to hospital to be checked out, me taken by a social worker to the hostel that would become my so-called home for the next few years. *Where's my sister? I want to be with my sister!* No amount of reassurances that she was okay, that the trip to hospital had just been a precaution and she was on her way to a caring foster family had made any difference. *"Violet'll be calling for me. She needs me!"* And I had needed her too. Badly. Just as, last night, I had needed Matt.

All around me, people were hurrying to work. There were cars, buses, trams. Noise. The busy hubbub of a big city starting the day.

I stood on a quiet corner to get myself together, my shaking hands reaching up to rake back my hair, trying to think. This was now, not back then. Violet was still a vulnerable woman, it was true. But she wasn't the completely helpless child she'd been back then. And she'd end up going back to the hotel at some point, surely? We had to check out by twelve. I could wait for her in reception. She had my phone number, didn't she?

If I wasn't careful, I was going to crack up. The memories and old hurts I'd stuffed down inside myself for so long were building up and up inside me, like a pressure cooker about to blow. It was all too much. Vi hadn't even given me the chance to tell her what had happened—she'd just assumed Kevin's departure had been my fault. I guess it was easier to blame me than to accept a second rejection from him. I got that; I did. But understanding it didn't make it any easier to take, and, if I wasn't going to go under myself, I had to stop putting Vi first every single time. I had to think about myself.

I'd said I'd call Matt when I was finished, but I hadn't expected it to be so soon, and I was reluctant to inflict this latest crisis on him, even though I knew he'd offer words of comfort. Hold me, maybe, the way he'd held me last night, after the nightmare. Poor bloody Matt. It would be better for him if he did get the job in Spain. I couldn't dump all of this on him.

"Lily?"

I turned, and there was Matt himself, seated at a table outside a café, a newspaper open in front of him.

"Meeting finished already? Where's Violet?"

I took the chair opposite his, tears already filling my eyes despite my resolve not to burden him. "Oh, Matt, it was awful. Kevin didn't want to know. He showed up, barely spoke to Violet, and left. And she's somehow convinced it's all my fault."

Just as I'd know he would, Matt listened. Sympathised. Expressed opinions about Kevin that matched my own. It was comforting, of course it was. Sometimes, many times lately, I thought Matt was the only reliable, dependable thing in my life.

"Why don't you text Violet? Tell her we'll be in the hotel foyer at eleven thirty?" he suggested, and I did. Then we whiled away a few hours exploring the city, me doing my best not to worry about my sister or to wonder, when Matt's phone rang, whether it was the company in Spain to say he'd got the job.

"My mum," he said, ending the call. "Reminding me it's Dad's birthday next week."

"I don't imagine you'd forgotten," I said.

He shook his head. "No. I bought him something in Barcelona."

Barcelona. Jesus. Matt may be reliable and dependable, but he wasn't going to be around much longer. It was almost a relief when it was time to go to the hotel to meet Violet.

Inevitably, she didn't turn up at the appointed time, though. And so, going against all my instincts, I told Matt we should set off for home.

"She's got my phone number, and she's a big girl now, isn't she?" I said, justifying my decision.

"She travelled round Europe on her own, as well, didn't she?" Matt reminded me. "I'm sure she'll be okay. But whatever you want, Lily. If you'd prefer to stay another night, that's fine. I don't need to rush back for anything."

"No," I said. "Let's go." After all, Violet had made the decision to ignore me when I'd tried to explain. She was her own worst enemy. But knowing that didn't make it any easier to drive away.

Matt and I talked now and then on the way home, but not much. I guessed he could probably tell I was wallowing in the misery of things not turning out well in Nottingham.

"I bet you wish you hadn't offered to drive me now," I said bitterly as we passed King's Lynn, an hour away from home.

"Of course not," he said. "I was happy to be there for you; you know that. Anyway, I'm not sure how much help I was."

"It would have been bleak without you," I could have said, which was the truth. But I didn't, because I didn't want him to know how utterly devastated by everything I felt, and because I didn't want him to start feeling guilty about going to Spain if he were to be offered the job. To be a burden to him. Difficult or not, I needed to find the strength to

deal with things on my own. It was pretty much what I'd always done, anyway.

When we finally pulled up outside my house, I turned to him.

"D'you want to come in for a coffee?"

"No, I'll get home, I think. Back to my owls."

I smiled weakly. "Say hello to them for me, won't you? And let me know when you hear anything from Spain."

He nodded, pulling me in for a quick hug. "Will do."

Inside, there was a note waiting for me from Amy. *Gone to visit my parents for the weekend. Hope all's well?*

I folded the note up and put it on the coffee table, hoping she wasn't mad I hadn't left a note for her before I dashed off to Nottingham, feeling both sorry and glad she wasn't home. Sorry because I didn't feel like being on my own; glad because I didn't want to have to talk about the disaster of the last few days.

I kicked off my shoes, made myself a cup of tea, and sat on the sofa to drink it. I ought to check on Inga. Check my emails. But I did neither of those things. Instead, I sat, sipping my tea, worrying about Violet. Was Kevin right? Was she using drugs? I couldn't bear to believe it. But if he was right, should I have stayed in Nottingham and made sure she came back here with me? Helped her get clean if she needed me to? But I wasn't sure how I would have even found her if she wasn't answering my texts and calls, let alone persuade her to come with me. She had my number if she wanted me. Or did she? For the first time it occurred to me that Violet might have lost her phone. Had it stolen, even. Sold it to buy drugs.

Oh, God. I closed my eyes tight shut, resisting the urge to scream. Even if I did give Inga a ring, I wouldn't be much help to her in this state. And anyway, I wasn't entirely sure what she'd think of me and Matt going off to Nottingham together, especially if she found out we'd shared a room. So, I sent her a text, saying I was back and that I'd pop round in the morning. Then I took my empty cup into the kitchen, poured myself a glass of wine, and went upstairs to the studio, suddenly needing to paint so badly, the impulse couldn't be denied. Not to produce anything good. Not to follow on sensibly from the work I'd made last time I'd been in the studio, whenever the hell that had been. Just to whack some paint about. To express my worries and frustrations through splatters and swipes of colour.

It was perhaps no big surprise that many of those colours were flame red, ember orange, and charcoal black. Sheet after sheet of paper covered with flickering flames with brightly coloured Nottingham trams riding through them as I imagined Violet hopping onto one to escape everything—me, Kevin, rejection. I painted the café we'd met in like a footprint, squashing Violet beneath it. A man—Kevin—jumping up and down on it, a speech bubble coming from his mouth. *Has your mother been in touch?*

I painted and I painted into the early hours of the morning, half-crazed, seeking relief, escape, I don't know what. Not looking at any of my paintings because I was afraid I'd see a kind of madness in them.

And finally, I closed the studio door, went into my bedroom, and fell into bed. Only to dream about fire again, my paintings somehow coming to life, complete with smells and smoke tearing at my throat. I woke on a scream, no Matt to comfort me this time, just me and the memory of Kevin's question going round and round my brain. "Have you heard anything from your mum?"

When I reached for my phone, I saw my hands were still covered in dried-on paint. At least I'd used acrylics, not oils, so the bedsheets weren't covered in it.

Without much hope, I googled my mother's name. It wasn't the first time I'd done it, though it had been years since I'd last tried. Because every time I did, it brought me face to face with Mum's abandonment of me and Vi, and I wasn't sure whether I wanted to find an obituary, which would explain her silence, or evidence that she was alive and well.

Nothing ever showed up, anyway, and it didn't now. A few women on Facebook with the same name whose profile pictures couldn't be turned into images of my mother no matter how long and how hard I stared at them. Nothing anywhere else on social media.

What had I expected, really? What had I even wanted? Even if I did find her, I was never going to be able to forgive her, was I? It really was time to move on. There was never going to be a happy ever after to our story.

I left my search and checked my emails instead, still waiting for the nightmare to recede enough for me to go back to sleep, scrolling through emails from mailing lists I needed to unsubscribe from, the adverts that had slipped through into my inbox instead of going to my spam folder. There was one email with the title *Christmas Exhibition Opportunity*—surely another spam email. Then I saw the sender's name. It was from Diane, one of my students in Cromer—the one who had a husband with an art gallery in Norwich—and I clicked on it to open it.

Dear Lily,

We've had an unexpected cancellation for an exhibition due to take place at the Bond Gallery, Norwich, for two months from the end of November and wondered if you'd be interested in taking the slot? I showed Ken, my husband, some photos of your work, and he was very impressed. We'd like to give you first refusal if you could reply asap.

An exhibition! I knew the Bond Gallery—it was an amazing space. But it was large. Would I be able to get enough paintings together for an exhibition that size? It was a tall ask. But it was such an opportunity; and it would definitely be an excellent distraction from my troubles. How good of Diane to think of me; to have that much faith in me. Though if she were to take a look in my studio and glimpse the work I'd just produced, I was pretty sure she'd withdraw her offer pretty damn quickly. Was I just setting myself up to be embarrassed and humiliated if I accepted Diane's offer?

20

I hadn't replied to the email by lunchtime as I made my way round to Inga's house, doubts about whether I'd be able to produce enough suitable paintings within the time frame still crowding out my excitement about the opportunity.

And in any case, I forgot all about the exhibition when Inga opened the door because I was shocked by the state of her, though I did my very best not to show it. Her T-shirt was stained with milk, her hair was lank and unwashed, and the deep circles around her eyes spoke of a severe lack of sleep.

"Come in, come in," she said in a whisper. "But for fuck's sake be quiet. I've finally got him to sleep."

"D'you want me to come back later?"

"No, it's fine. Just close the door quietly after you if I fall asleep drooling in the middle of a conversation."

I smiled. "Will do. So, how's it going?"

Inga flapped a hand to indicate her dishevelled appearance, a pile of baby clothes on the sofa, a stack of unwashed plates and cups on the coffee table. "As you see. All pretty normal, as I understand it. I managed to get to the corner shop yesterday. Only took an hour to get out the door. Never imagined I'd think of a trip to One Stop as a big day out, but there you go."

"Well, if I can help out in any way at all, let me know, won't you? Want me to do some washing up?"

"No way, far too noisy. If you really want to be helpful, you can talk to me about something other than babies. Absolutely any fucking thing else. How did it go with Violet in Nottingham? Did you go there on the train?"

"No," I said uncomfortably. "Matt drove me."

Inga lifted her eyebrows, hastily stifling a hurt twist of her mouth. "That was nice."

"Yes, it was good of him, wasn't it?" I heard myself talking politely, as if to a stranger. Wasn't sure how else to speak about it. Became aware of being in uncharted territory. Wondered whether Inga felt it too.

"How is he?" Inga sounded polite too.

"He's all right."

"Is that it? All you're going to tell me?"

Ah, that was more natural. More like Inga. But I didn't want to tell her about Spain, not until it was confirmed. *If* it was confirmed. It wasn't my news to share, after all. And I could hardly tell her what Matt had said about his doubts about Inga as a parent. Or the fact that we'd shared a hotel room.

I shrugged, feeling uneasy and off-kilter about keeping things from her. "He was Matt. It was good to have him there. Especially as things didn't go so well with Violet."

The sound of crying started up from the back room. Noah was awake.

Inga closed her eyes, looking utterly exhausted. "Jesus, why doesn't that kid ever sleep?"

"D'you want me to go and get him?"

Her eyes flicked open. "No, I'll leave him just for a little while. He might go back off. So, it didn't work out well with Violet?"

"No." I didn't really feel like going into it, not with Inga like a coiled spring, listening to the note of her son's crying to try and judge whether he meant business or not.

"Kevin wasn't interested in connecting with Violet. I don't know why he even bothered to turn up. He made a run for it while she was in the loo. Left me to break the news to her myself. She stormed off God knows where. Matt and I looked for her for a while, but then we had to come home."

The crying went on and on. It didn't sound as if Noah was going to go back to sleep anytime soon, and in the face of that distressed wailing, my problems with Violet seemed insignificant.

"Sorry," Inga said. "I can't really concentrate on anything properly when he's like this."

"It's fine."

Inga got up with a heavy sigh, looking as if her limbs were a lead weight. She soon returned with a squirming, wailing Noah in her arms. "Could you just hold him for me for a minute while I go to the loo?"

"Sure."

I took the baby from her, looking down into his face while Inga went to the bathroom. He was such a beautiful little boy—or would be, if he wasn't screwing his face up so badly. Maybe he just needed burping. There was a muslin cloth amongst the pile of washed bodysuits. I pulled it out, draped it over my shoulder, and lifted Noah up there, swaying gently as I patted his back. Seconds later, he gave an almighty baby belch. Ah, that had been it, then. Wind.

Still swaying and rubbing his back, I began to sing softly, transporting myself back in time to the days when I'd held Violet like this, remembering for once not the panic and anxiety of having to take care of her, but the joy when something I tried worked. The times when Violet was bathed and fed and ready for bed. When she smiled, or closed her eyes, her cheek on my shoulder the way little Noah's was now. It hadn't all been bad, taking care of my sister. I had loved my little ally. My constant companion.

Nothing like the hostile, accusing woman who'd stormed out of the café after Kevin, convinced I'd deliberately tried to sabotage their reunion. And I thought again about what Kevin had said about Violet using drugs. Wondered for the umpteenth time where she was, whether she was all right.

Inga came back from the toilet. "Oh," she said. "You got him back to sleep."

"He had some wind. He was okay after he brought that up. He'll probably settle back down now."

"Yes. Thank you."

Something about the way she took the baby from me and carried him carefully into the next room made me wonder whether I ought to have left Noah for her to sort out. I hadn't meant to take over, my instincts had just kicked in.

"Everything all right?" I asked when she finally returned.

"Sure. He's fast asleep. Well done."

Now there was no mistaking her tone of voice. She was definitely narked.

"I'm sorry if I overstepped a line."

Inga sighed, running a tired hand through her hair. "You didn't. It's just . . . you have a way of making me feel inadequate sometimes, you know? You break up with Alex, and you're fine. You'd never get accidentally pregnant, and I've done it twice. You're talented, and you keep at it, producing the work, even when you're holding down two jobs. You're fucking impressive, Lily, and sometimes it's a lot to keep up with. And it would just be good if I had a better idea about how to keep my baby happy than you did, that's all."

I stared at her, wondering how anyone could have such an inaccurate view of me, not really knowing where to start with putting her right. But then I saw that her eyes were almost closed and remembered that her body was pumped full of post-childbirth hormones.

"Why don't you take a nap while Noah's asleep? Here, lie down on the sofa. I'll get you a throw."

Inga lay down silently, placing a cushion beneath her head and tossing the rest to the floor. "That's another thing," she said drowsily when I returned with the throw and covered her with it. "You've got the patience of a fucking saint."

I picked my bag up from the floor and headed for the front door, holding back tears with difficulty. "Sleep well, see you soon," I whispered, but Inga didn't hear me. She was already asleep.

It was a lonely walk home. All the way I asked myself how my best friend could have got things so wrong about me. Okay, so I was careful about contraception because I was so sure I didn't want children, but as for sailing through my break-up with Alex, surely Inga knew how lonely I'd been these past months? How badly it hurt to have been so quickly and easily replaced by Fliss? She'd seen me, after all. But maybe I'd been good at putting on some act, because Inga didn't seem to know it. Maybe keeping things locked away inside myself was my coping mechanism. Like a Jenga tower, where the whole thing topples if you remove the wrong piece.

As for me coping with balancing out work and painting, that was a complete joke. Okay, so I'd managed to keep painting over the years; I hadn't given up art altogether the way Inga had. But I had a shift at the hospital starting in two hours and three days solid teaching I hadn't prepared properly for after that. The only art I'd produced lately were the crazy, wine-induced ravings currently scattered over my studio floor. I produced art because without creativity filling up my mind and my time and my heart, I was in danger of staring into an abyss. But right now, when Inga was tired and vulnerable, caring for a newborn baby, wasn't the time to tell her any of that. I could take care of myself. After all, I'd been doing it all my life.

It had been lightly raining ever since I'd left Inga's flat, but suddenly the heavens opened, and I ducked into a convenient bus shelter. As luck would have it, a bus was just approaching, splashing through the puddles on the road. I hailed it, climbing the stairs to take the seat right at the front—Violet's favourite seat when we were kids.

Gazing out of the bus window at the rain-drenched streets, I focused on the people hurrying along under their brightly coloured umbrellas, trying to resist re-entering the rabbit hole of worrying about my sister. Violet didn't want my help. She'd thought she had, meeting

Kevin, but she'd soon discovered she was wrong. And now Inga didn't seem to want my help either. It was stupid for that to make me feel so profoundly lonely. I wanted Inga to be okay, didn't I? It was a really good thing if she felt she didn't need quite so much help.

Jesus, I really needed to stop feeling sorry for myself.

On impulse, I took out my phone and dashed off an email in reply to Diane.

> What a wonderful offer. Thanks so much. I'd love to accept the exhibition.

I panicked the second after I'd hit send. Shit, shit, shit. How the hell was I going to find the time to finish the amount of paintings I'd need for an exhibition?

My phone beeped. I thought it might be Diane. But it was from Inga. One word. **Sorry.**

I quickly typed a reply. **That's okay. Take care. Love to you both. See you soon. L X**

21

The following weekend—a very rare work-free weekend for me, which I planned to use to get some painting done, after I'd given myself the luxury of a lie-in—Inga phoned at nine o'clock in the morning.

As soon as I answered, she jumped right in with what she wanted to say without bothering with any chit-chat. "Lil, I am so, so sorry for being such a bitch to you the other day."

"That's okay," I began, but she interrupted me, her words splurging out in a frantic rush.

"No, it's not. It's not okay at all. Especially as I'm about to beg you to come over to take the baby out for a little bit. I don't care if you're better at looking after him than me. I don't sodding well care if you're a former nanny to the royal fucking family. In fact, it would be good if you had been, because I bloody well need you, Lily. I'm so goddamned tired. My eyelids feel sandpapered. I practically need nails to keep them open. If I don't get some sleep soon, I'm going to go crazy. He just won't sleep, Lily. He won't sleep."

"Of course I'll come," I said, mentally closing my studio door until another day. "If you're really sure you want me to."

"Lily, I'm surer than the surest thing on the planet. That's how sure I am."

"Okay, I'll be with you in an hour."

When I arrived at her flat, Inga was cradling Noah in her arms. She looked as if she hadn't slept since the last time I'd seen her.

"Thank you so much for this, Lily."

I reached out to take the baby from her. "Are you sure everything's all right? Has the midwife checked him over?"

"Yes, yes, clean bill of health."

"And what about you? No chance you've got the baby blues?"

Inga shrugged wearily. "Can we talk about it later, after I've had some sleep?"

It was a crisp, sunny day. I decided to head to the park because there was a café there.

Noah fell asleep on the way and was still sleeping when we got there, which meant I could stroll peacefully along the paths beneath the trees and past the herbaceous borders with their last blooms of the season. As I walked, I did my best to stay in the moment, to absorb the autumn colours and enjoy the sunshine on my face, not to think about the last time I'd been there—to meet with Alex after our split—or to worry about not getting paintings done for the exhibition, or whether Inga needed professional help or not. Trying just to drink in the colours and the sunshine and the feeling of satisfaction that Noah was, for the moment, content.

I hadn't seen or heard from Matt since our trip to Nottingham, and I wondered whether he'd heard about the job in Spain or not. Maybe I should call him, find out. If he didn't have anything much on this weekend, perhaps we could meet up.

I took my phone out of my bag and found his number, then hesitated before hitting the call button. He'd have called me if he had any news, wouldn't he? And he was hardly going to want to spend time with me when I had Noah in tow. Inga might need me to care for him for a bit longer than just this morning. And Matt and I had only seen each other a few days ago, after all. If he did get the job in Spain, there'd be weeks, or maybe months between our meetings.

I stood beside the steps to the ornamental pond, still undecided, wondering how things had suddenly become so complicated, impatient with myself for overthinking it. Matt could either say yes or no to us meeting up. What was the problem? And if he couldn't meet up, I could get on with some painting the way I'd planned to this weekend after I'd returned Noah.

The weather decided the issue for me, the heavens suddenly opening, forcing me to make a run for it to the café, hoping against hope all the way that Noah wouldn't stir in the changed surroundings. But of course he did, almost immediately, so I quickly ordered my coffee and retreated to a table in a far corner in the vain hope we wouldn't disturb people too much there. Then I took a now wailing Noah from his buggy and held him to me, rocking him slightly and crooning into the soft down of his hair.

When someone approached the table, I assumed it would be one of the serving staff with my coffee. But it wasn't. It was Alex, of all people, with a baby strapped to his front.

"Alex!" I said, stunned, my eyes riveted by the baby.

"Hi, Lily," he said, smiling down at me, his gaze moving curiously to Noah. "Is this . . . ?"

"This is Noah, Inga's son." I moved the baby slightly so Alex could see his face. Saw Alex's surprise that the baby was mixed race. "Wow," he said finally. "He's gorgeous. Well done, Inga."

"I'll pass that on to her," I said, looking once again at the pink-dressed bundle against his chest.

"This is Lola."

Well, how bloody awesome. Alex now had everything he'd always wanted. And I wasn't bitter about being so easily wiped from his life. No, not at all.

I stretched my mouth into a smile. "Congratulations, Alex."

"Thanks." He indicated the spare chair at my table. "Mind if we join you?"

It was the very last thing on earth I wanted. But I heard myself speaking lightly, saying, "If you're sure you want to. Hopefully, he'll settle soon, but if not, I'll have to take him home, I guess. Inga's been breastfeeding so far."

Alex shook his head. "Gosh, it's all so grown up, isn't it? I would never have put Inga and *breastfeeding* in the same sentence this time last year."

Me neither.

"I'll just go and order."

By the time Alex got back, I'd managed to rock Noah to sleep again. If only my mind was as peaceful. I wasn't looking forward to chatting with Alex at all.

"I'm impressed," Alex said. "I'd have been in a state of panic if it had been Lola crying like that."

"He isn't my baby, though, is he? That must make it easier."

He nodded, acknowledging the truth of that. "How is Inga?"

I didn't feel like sharing Inga's current state of desperation with him, so I said simply, "Tired. How about Fliss?"

A shadow crossed Alex's face; a shadow that gave me a sense that all was not paradise with Alex's new relationship. It was mean for that to give me a flicker of pleasure, but it did.

"Same. Tired, emotional, inclined to snap at me over the slightest thing. I'm actually amazed she let me bring Lola out on my own, to be honest. She finds fault with most of what I do for the baby." He sighed. "But you probably don't want to hear about all that."

I didn't. And yet, at the same time, I did. The way you might want to pick at a wound to see whether it has really healed.

Noah stirred in his sleep, and, after a moment, began to cry. I put him over my shoulder to massage his back, aware of Alex across the table, watching my every move.

"What?" I asked as Noah's eyes closed again.

He shrugged, smiling that lopsided smile of his. "Nothing. You're just a natural, that's all." He looked down at his own beautiful daughter, dropping a kiss on top of her head. "I just wish . . ."

"Don't," I interrupted him before he could say more, unable to bear the prospect of him raking over the coals of us having children together again. "You have what you wanted now, Alex. Look at her; she's absolutely gorgeous."

He nodded. "She is. Fatherhood is amazing. It's just such a tragedy that Mum couldn't be here to meet her." Tears filled his eyes. Began to slide down his face.

Oh, God.

Alex wiped the tears away with the back of his hand.

"She would have been besotted, your mum," I said.

More tears. "She would, wouldn't she? It's so sad that this little one will never know her." He sniffed, looking at me with reddened eyes. "Fliss can't really understand that, I don't think. The way I can be so sad and so happy at the same time. It makes her . . . impatient."

I didn't fucking want to talk about Fliss, but somehow heard myself saying something comforting as if I were some superhuman patron saint of cheering up ex-boyfriends. Habit, maybe. Alex and I had been together for a long time, and for years I'd been the one to cheer him up when he needed cheering up. It had been hard not to be able to do that when his mother died.

"Maybe Fliss has never lost anybody."

"She hasn't, that's it. Or a part of it, anyway." He shook his head. "I don't know, this all happened so quickly, there was no time to really get to know each other."

My coffee had gone cold. And suddenly my superhuman powers abandoned me. There was no more free space in my heart or my mind to listen to Alex's sob story about his relationship. Noah would soon wake up and need Inga. It was time to go.

"I'm sorry, Alex," I said, doing my very best not to jolt Noah as I stood up. "I've got to go."

"Lily, wait."

I got to the café door with the buggy, still holding Noah against my chest. A woman opened the door for me, and I smiled, thanking her. Got outside, thanking the weather gods that it had cleared, and walked quickly away. Or, as quickly as I could do, holding a baby to my chest and pushing a buggy with one hand.

Unsurprisingly, Noah woke up again and began to cry. No doubt I was clutching him too tightly.

"Shh, it's all right, little one," I said, stopping to lower him into his buggy, covering him with his fleecy blanket.

Alex caught up with me. "Look, I'm sorry," he said. "Can we just walk together for a bit?"

I glanced up at him. Saw that he had a lot more he wanted to say. Decided I didn't want to hear any of it. "No, sorry," I said, "I have to get this little one home. Inga will be wondering where we are. See you around, Alex, and congratulations again."

22

"Are you okay?" Inga asked when we got back, carefully taking her sleeping son from the buggy and going to sit down on the sofa.

"It should be me asking you that. Did you sleep?"

"Like the proverbial dead. Thank you so much, Lil. You literally saved my life. Or Noah's life, I'm not sure which. But don't deflect. You look as if you were mugged while you were out. Something happened, didn't it? Wait a minute, don't tell me, you had an epiphany moment. Noah worked his magic on you, and now your hormones are on the rampage. You've abandoned all thoughts of being an artist, and you're on the hunt for a man to churn out babies with."

I had to laugh at that. "No, nothing like that. I ran into Alex in the park. He had his new baby with him. Lola."

"Shit."

I nodded. "Exactly. It was just that. Shit. Not because of the baby, but because—" I broke off, my feelings too confused to continue. I missed Alex, and yet, at the same time, I didn't miss him at all; at least not him on his own. I missed the four of us, together, a unit. Family.

"Oh, babe, I'm so sorry. Come over here."

She held out her free arm, and I went, squeezing into the space next to her on the sofa to be hugged.

"Look at me," she said after a moment. "I've got twins. Though for the life of me I can't think how the fuck I gave birth to a big one like you."

I laughed, relieved and glad to hear her sounding like the old Inga. "Twit."

She smiled at me kindly. "Takes one to know one. So, what did you feel, then? When you saw the boy wonder?"

I sighed, still uncertain what I was feeling. "I'm not sure, really. Panic, mostly, I think."

"Not a sense of regret, then? That you didn't have his babies? That it wasn't your baby he was being all gooey about?"

"No." I sighed. "If I regretted that, I'd have to regret being the person I am, wouldn't I?"

"Never regret being you, babe. You're an absolute star."

"Hardly."

"You are. Look at you, dashing over here to take my son off my hands so I could sleep my way back into sanity. You're perfect, absolutely perfect."

"That's not what you said the other day," I reminded her.

"I've already apologised for that. And I think it's very unfair of you to bring up the tortured ramblings of a postnatal single parent on the edge."

I pulled back to look at her. "Are you on the edge? Because, if you are, please get some help. I'll come over whenever I can, but . . ."

She put up a hand. "Listen, I'm sure every new parent feels like they're on the edge at some point, don't they? Why should I be any different? I'm hardly the only single parent in the world. But excuse me, I think we were discussing your emotional needs, not mine. What d'you want to do about Alex?"

I shrugged. "What can I do? I'll just have to avoid him, I suppose, at least for a while. Things will settle down in time."

"Is he happy, d'you think?"

"As a dad? Blissfully. With Fliss? I'm not so sure. But it doesn't make any difference, does it? We can't go back. It was just awkward, seeing him, that's all. But hey ho. Onwards and upwards and all that."

Noah began to stir, and Inga took her arm from around my shoulders to pull up her T-shirt. "You forgot to mention your stiff upper lip," she said. "Oh, and the fact that every cloud has a silver lining."

I smiled. "Or that good things come to those who wait?"

"Exactly," she said, fitting Noah to her breast and smiling down at him with a tenderness that reassured me more than any of her words could do that the two of them would be all right.

"The ball's in your court as far as your future's concerned, babe," she said, looking up to turn the smile onto me. "There are other fish in the sea, apart from Daddy Alex. Just don't hide your light under a bushel and remember that it takes two to tango."

"Oh, God," I said, laughing aloud at her stream of idioms, thrilled the tension between us had gone and our friendship was back on track again. "I'm off to get on with some painting since you're obviously feeling so much better. That's if I can still remember how to paint."

Inga smiled. "Of course you can remember, babe. It's just like riding a bike."

I was almost home when my phone rang. I smiled, thinking it was Inga with another helpful idiom to cheer me on my way. But it wasn't Inga; it was Matt.

"Matt, hi."

"Hi, Lily, how are you?"

"Fine, fine. Just on my way home from Inga's." I wanted to tell him how worried I'd been about her. But of course, I couldn't. Matt might be the person I'd be able to speak to most easily about my worries, but he was also exactly the person I couldn't speak to about this particular worry.

So, when he asked, "How is she?" I just answered, "Fine, fine," and waited for him to tell me why he'd called, guessing it would be with news about the job.

It was.

"Good," he said, "that's good. Listen, I wanted you to be the first to know. Spain just rang. I got the job."

And just like that, my heart, which was already piled high with regrets about Alex, worry about Inga and Violet, and stress about the forthcoming exhibition, felt utterly crushed, right down to my purple Dr. Martens boots.

"Lily?"

"Yes, I'm here. That's fantastic, Matt. Wonderful. Congratulations! I'm so pleased for you! When d'you start?"

"Not until the New Year. I'll probably go before Christmas, though. Spend a bit of time settling in and sorting things out before I start my job."

"Christmas in Spain!" I gushed, aware that I sounded a bit manic. "How wonderful!"

"Says the world's worst Christmas-phobe," Matt teased, and suddenly tears sprang to my eyes, and I knew I'd have to end the call if I didn't want to sob my heart out.

"Listen, Matt," I said, "I've got to go, but well done again. I'm so pleased for you. Speak soon, yes?"

23

I made my way home and straight upstairs to the studio. Painting was the very last thing I felt like doing. My head was aching. A hundred and one things were thrashing around my brain, a hundred and one things I couldn't bear to think about, especially why I was so upset about Matt going to live in Spain. But I had an exhibition to prepare for and a free weekend to paint in. So, I painted.

It was pretty much like the last time I'd been in the studio—a sort of protracted art-therapy session that left me feeling exhausted—but at least it was something, and on Monday morning I went back to work feeling as if I hadn't totally wasted my time off. Even if I couldn't use anything I'd produced this weekend, at least it had stopped my mind blowing up.

I was working at the hospital that day and was pleased to see Beryl the botanist sitting up in bed when I did my rounds. Every day I was rostered onto that ward, I half expected her bed to be empty, the sheets turned down. Either that or occupied by someone new.

"Hello, dear," Beryl greeted me. "You look tired again, if you don't mind my saying so."

I smiled. "Shh. I've only just got to work. I'm supposed to be full of energy."

She smiled back. "I won't tell anyone if you don't. Were you painting?"

"Yes, getting ready for my exhibition, or trying to. How are you feeling?"

She flapped a hand. "Oh, like someone on her way out. All very dull. How's that friend of yours? The one who had the baby?"

I pulled a face. "Feeling the strain of doing it all by herself a bit, I think."

Beryl nodded. "I know just how she feels. I brought my son up on my own too. It's tough being responsible for making all the decisions, always being the one to have to sort things out because there's no one else to do it."

"Well, you did a good job, from what I've seen of your son."

"I did my best. Even though I did drag him with me around the world. Still, he didn't know anything else, so I don't suppose it did him any harm. Do check up on your friend, though, won't you? Postnatal depression can be as dark as the Veryovkina Cave. That's the deepest cave in the world, by the way, in case you were wondering."

"Thanks, Beryl, I will," I said, starting to move on to the next bed, thinking, as I always did after any interaction with Beryl, how sad it was that such a bright life force was about to be extinguished. Someone else precious to me soon to be gone from my life.

"And take care of yourself, too, dear," Beryl called after me. "All work and no play makes Jill a dull girl."

I looked back. She smiled at me, her eyes twinkling. "Or something like that, anyway. I can't quite remember exactly how it goes. But the message is the same, isn't it. Go out dancing, or for a walk by the sea. Let your metaphorical hair down a little."

I laughed out loud at that. "Okay, Beryl. I promise to try."

"You do that, dear. You do that."

It was a long shift, so I didn't get the chance to call Inga until the next morning. I knew Inga would laugh when I told her about Beryl's metaphorical-hair advice, and I was smiling myself when I dialled. But Inga didn't reply. So I tried again half an hour later, and half an hour after that. Still no reply. Was something wrong? Blast. I would have to go round there to give myself some peace of mind.

I could hear Noah crying right up the street. Or at least, I assumed it was Noah, and Inga's neighbour—who was outside putting a bag of rubbish in her wheelie bin—confirmed it for me when I reached Inga's flat.

"He's been crying for hours on end, he has, poor little mite. I did try knocking, to make sure everything was all right, but she didn't answer. I wouldn't mind, but my Ted will be home soon from his shift, and he'll be needing his sleep."

I wasn't sure what to say. *"Thank you for your concern? Babies do cry, you know?"* So, I just smiled, glad when the woman went back into her house.

There was no reply to my knock, so I phoned. But once again, it went to voicemail.

Jesus, Inga hadn't just gone off somewhere and left him, had she? No, she would never do that. Inga was a good person. She wasn't wilfully neglectful and cruel. She wasn't like my mother.

Inside the house, Noah's cries were getting increasingly frantic. Just when I was considering breaking a windowpane, I remembered the time Inga had once left a key for me under a plant pot in the garden. Maybe it was still there? It was. Seconds later, I was letting myself into the house.

"Inga?"

I found Noah in his Moses basket in the sitting room, red faced, wet through, his eyes red slits of distress.

"Here, little fella," I said, picking him up. "It's all right. You're all right." Although clearly it wasn't, and he wasn't.

Clutching his wet little body to me the way I'd held Violet's all those years ago, I went in search of Inga with a sinking sense of dread and, thank God, found her in bed. Her head, or what I could see of it beneath a pillow, was turned towards the wall, but she was here. She hadn't left little Noah on his own.

"Inga? Are you ill?"

"Make him stop, Lily," she said, her voice muffled. "Please, make him stop."

Noah was rooting around against my chest. There was no mistaking what he wanted. "He needs you to feed him, Ing," I said, as Noah, no doubt sensing his mother's proximity, began to cry even louder.

"I can't, Lily," Inga said, sobbing. "I just can't. Please, can you do it?"

Jesus, she really did need help. Not because she was neglectful the way Mum had been, but because she was clearly ill.

My brain clicked into overdrive. "Have you got any formula?"

"No."

"I'll go to the corner shop and get some," I said.

"Please take him with you," Inga said. "Please."

Noah's cries were so loud now that panic was pummelling at my chest the way it had done when I was a child. But there wasn't time to think about that now, and I pushed the memories away.

"Come on, baby," I said to Noah. "Let's get your nappy changed, and then we'll go and buy you some lovely formula, okay?"

At least there were nappies. And cream to soothe Noah's red, raw skin.

The buggy was in the hallway. I strapped Noah into it and fastened the straps, reversing it out of the door and down the front step.

Inga's neighbour was outside again, washing her front windows. "Everything all right, is it?"

I gave her a tight smile, hoping she wouldn't be straight on to social services as soon as I got down the road. "Yes, all fine, thank you."

I walked quickly away, unable to dismiss her as an interfering busybody because Noah had obviously been lying in hours of accumulated wee, crying to be fed, and it was all absolutely bloody terrifying. Inga needed to get some help and fast. But right now, Noah was my priority. Getting some milk inside the poor little bugger.

Inside the shop, Noah's desperate crying drew the glances of other customers our way. Formula, formula. Where was the bloody formula?

Please, God, let them have some. Bingo. Two brands. God only knew which was the best, but in the circumstances, I didn't suppose it mattered much which one I chose.

I'd paid and was heading back out onto the street when it occurred to me that I had no idea whether or not Inga possessed any feeding bottles or teats. God, I hoped so. I'd have to go to the city to buy those, and Noah was absolutely starving hungry, his cries five hundred times worse than when we'd gone to the park, causing me to panic, sucking me right down into the past, to a place of abandonment and helplessness I wasn't sure I'd ever properly recovered from.

"Lily? Is that you?"

I looked up, startled. The woman smiling at me outside the shop was familiar, but, in my current whipped-up state, I couldn't for the life of me remember who she was.

"Gillian?" she said. "From the art workshops?"

At the women's refuge. Last time I'd seen Gillian, she'd had a huge bruise on her face, badly covered up by concealer.

"Of course. Hi, how are you?"

She nodded, smiling. "I'm good, thanks; really good. You had a baby! We wondered why you disappeared on us."

"Oh, no," I said. "He's not mine. I'm looking after him for a friend. I just came out for some formula."

"He does sound hungry, poor little chap."

"He is." Noah's desperation made me more forthcoming than I'd probably have been in other circumstances. "And I'm not a hundred percent certain my friend has any feeding bottles at home."

"Well, listen, I've got some if you need some. I mind my friend's baby when she has appointments to go to. I'm at number sixty-eight, just round the corner from here. I'll only be a couple of minutes in the shop if you want to come round?"

I didn't have to think twice about it. "That would be amazing. Thank you so much."

"No problem. Back in a minute."

While Gillian went into the shop, I called Inga to let her know what was happening, leaving a voicemail when she didn't answer. Sent a text for good measure, hoping she was managing to get the rest she so clearly needed. Minutes later we were at Gillian's flat, and she was popping the kettle on. "May as well feed him here, Lily. Give me the formula, I'll make it up."

It was good to be taken care of; to feel confident enough to leave Gillian cuddling Noah while I popped to the loo. And finally, finally, the bottle was ready, Noah was in my arms with the teat at his mouth, and I was praying he would take it. God, the relief when the crying finally stopped. I wanted to burst into tears, and I wasn't his mother. Poor bloody Inga.

"Thank you, Gillian," I said with a weak smile. "Thank you so much. You're a lifesaver."

Gillian smiled back. "You're welcome. It's magic when the crying stops, isn't it?"

I nodded. "It really is. How's your little boy?"

"Sam? He's doing all right, yeah. At school, you know. Getting into a routine. Making some mates. We liked your classes. Pity they stopped. That teacher who came instead wasn't the same. Too . . . formal, you know?"

I smiled. "You mean she didn't dye your kids' hands green?"

Gillian laughed. "No chance of that. She never got any of us doing anything as adventurous as tie-dye. To be honest, most of us stopped going."

"I'm sorry to hear that." I really was. The art classes had been a chance for the women to forget about all the heavy stuff going on in their lives, exactly the way painting and drawing in my bedroom had always been a source of escape for me when I was growing up. "Do you still see any of the others?"

"Not really. Most people don't want to be reminded about those times when they move on, I suppose. Me, I don't want to forget. If you start forgetting what happened to you, there's always a danger of drifting back, isn't there? Or at least, that's the way I see it."

I wasn't sure any longer what camp I fell in regarding forgetting the past. Always, before, I'd done my best to stuff bad memories away, unwilling to relive them in case their poison seeped into the new life I was making for myself. But just lately that was getting harder and harder to do, and in a way, perhaps Gillian was right. Maybe you did need to have old scars on view to remind you of how far you'd come. Not that, sometimes, it seemed as if I'd come very far at all.

Noah was still suckling, but less urgently now, his mouth stopping every now and then as he dozed, before starting up again. I gazed down at him, seeing Inga in the definition of his features, wondering what she saw when she looked at him herself; what she must be going through to have ignored him the way she had.

"Your friend's not coping so well, then?" Gillian asked, reading my mind.

"She doesn't seem to be, no. I'm worried about her, to be honest. I'd better get back there as soon as he's finished his bottle."

"She'll get through it, don't worry. She's one of the lucky ones, having a friend like you to look out for her."

My phone rang inside my bag. I was grateful for the interruption because Gillian was being so bloody nice I was really close to blubbing.

"Shall I fetch your phone for you?"

"Could you? It might be my friend."

But it wasn't Inga. It was Amy.

"Amy, hi. You're back."

"Hi, yes, I just got in. Lily, will you be home soon? Only your sister's here."

"Violet?" It was a stupid thing to say—I only had one sister. But I just couldn't believe it.

"Yes."

"Oh, that's . . ." I looked down at Noah. Amazingly bad timing was what it was, even though it was a relief that Violet had turned up, seemingly against all odds. "Is she there? Can you put her on?"

"She's showering at the moment. She seems . . . well, in a bit of a state, if I'm being honest."

What kind of a state? I wanted to ask, but now wasn't the time to quiz her, not with the teat slipping from Noah's mouth and Gillian looking on, not eavesdropping, but unable to stop overhearing the conversation.

"I'll be back as soon as I can," I said. "But I'm dealing with a bit of a crisis at the moment, so I might be a few hours." My mind raced as I tried to picture the contents of the freezer. It had been a while since I'd been shopping. "I think I've got a frozen lasagne she can have if she's hungry. I'm really sorry to dump all of this on you, Amy."

"That's okay," Amy said, but her voice sounded rather flat as she ended the call, and I prayed Violet hadn't said or done anything unpleasant.

"More problems?" Gillian asked as I tried to get Noah to take the teat again.

I sighed. "My sister's turned up. Which is great, because we didn't part on good terms last time we saw each other, but she can be a bit of a pain in the ass, and my flatmate's there on her own with her."

"And you're here, dealing with another crisis."

"That's about it."

Noah was still resisting the teat. I put him over my shoulder to burp him. "I'd better get this one home. Thanks again, Gillian."

She flapped a hand. "No problem, anytime. It was great to see you. Oh, and Lily?"

"Yes?"

"Make sure you've got someone to take care of you while you're sorting everyone else out, won't you?"

I did almost blub at that. It was sound advice, but right now, I just couldn't see who that someone might be.

24

When I got home—having extracted a solemn promise from Inga that she would contact her health visitor/midwife/doctor as soon as was humanly possible, I found Amy just on her way out of the front door. When I saw she had a holdall with her, my heart sank.

"Are you off somewhere again?"

"Yes, back to Mum and Dad's, just for a bit."

"What's Violet done?"

"Nothing, honestly." But she wouldn't quite meet my eyes, and I wasn't sure I believed it. "My parents just invited me, and your sister said she was going to crash in your bed, so I let her have mine. It's no big deal."

It was, though; it really was. So, I gave her a big hug and said, "You're a really good friend, Amy. Sorry my life's such a stuff up at the moment."

She did smile at that. "It's not you, is it? It's all those others." Then she trooped down the garden path to her car, and I had a sick premonition that the next time I saw her here, it would be when she came to collect her stuff prior to moving out. A premonition that got stronger when I went into the house and the pervading smell of oil paint hit my nostrils. Shit. I'd forgotten to use acrylics over the weekend.

There was no sign of Violet downstairs, only evidence that she'd been there—a plate with traces of dried-on lasagne abandoned on the coffee table, a wet towel dropped on the bathroom floor. I cleared them both up, wondering what had brought my sister here. How long she would stay this time. Then I crept upstairs. Amy's bedroom door wasn't quite closed, so I pushed it open further to peer inside. Violet's holdall was lying open on the bedroom floor, its contents spilling out onto the carpet. Violet herself was fast asleep in Amy's bed. Her hair appeared to be a different colour, but I couldn't be sure in the half light, so I just stood there, drinking her in, a lump about the size of a house brick lodged in my throat. It was such a profound relief to have Violet here; to know that, for the moment, at least, she was safe.

She didn't look as if she was going to wake up anytime soon. It was only seven thirty in the evening, but I decided I'd fix myself something to eat and go to bed too. God only knew I was tired enough, and what with everything, I could sleep for at least a week.

But Violet woke up before I could go to bed, staggering downstairs to give me a glimpse of her newly dyed purple hair just as I was turning the TV off. She looked tired—there were dark circles beneath her eyes—but she also looked amazing.

"Hi," I said. "Your hair looks great. It really suits you. Did you sleep well?"

My sister was wearing only a thin pair of shorts and a vest top and looked painfully thin, her collarbone exposed and fragile looking. She shrugged, not acknowledging my compliment about her hair. "Okay. And before you say anything, I didn't chuck your mate out of her bed."

"I wasn't going to say anything," I said. "I saw Amy when I got back. How are you? Where did you get to in Nottingham?"

She flopped down on the sofa, hunching her skinny legs up to her chin.

"I was really worried about you, Vi."

"I didn't ask you to worry about me. I have travelled round the world without you."

"I know. But you were really upset in Nottingham."

Violet picked at the skin around her fingers. I made myself stay quiet, waiting for her to speak first. "I went round to Kevin's house," she said at last, and I registered that she'd called him Kevin, not Dad.

"He said . . . well, he said it wasn't anything to do with you. Why he left Starbucks that day, I mean."

I sighed. "I'm so sorry, Vi."

She shrugged. "Nothing to be sorry for. If he can just walk off like that without even talking to me, the man's a shit. Better off without him, aren't I?"

The look on her face. So much bravado. It broke my heart.

"I think so, yes, hard as it is."

She glanced up very briefly. "I really thought he'd want to get to know me, you know?"

"It's his loss, Vi, it really is."

Another shrug. "He's got three other daughters. That's what he said, isn't it?"

"Did you get to meet them?"

"No; everyone else was out. Lucky for him."

"I bet his other daughters are nothing like you."

"I'll never know, will I? Because I'll never bloody well meet them."

I was going to remind her that she'd got me, but she put a brave smile on before I could form the words. "So, anyway, I thought I'd stick around here for a bit. That okay?"

Having her here, safe with me, not having to worry about her, hopefully building bridges and a better relationship with each other—all that would be fantastic. Oh, but Amy, and Amy's rent, which helped me to meet my mortgage payments.

"Of course. Just so long as you remember Amy lives here too."

"I can kip on the sofa. I told her that, but she was all, *'No, no, you take my room,'* so I didn't like to be rude and tell her to shove it."

There was a sparkle in her eyes—just a little one, but a sparkle, nevertheless. It made me want to smile and scream at one and the same time.

"When Amy gets back from her parents', you can share my room with me."

She frowned. "What if you snore?"

"Excuse me, I do not snore. And if I do, you can wear ear plugs. Seriously, Vi, I need Amy's rent, okay? She shares the house, and sharing the house doesn't include not being able to watch TV because the sitting room is cluttered with sleeping sisters."

Violet yawned hugely. "Got it. No annoying the lodger."

"Exactly right. Now, since we both seem to be shattered, let's go to bed."

"Jeez, it's going to be one long party living with you, isn't it? Going to bed before nine p.m. every night."

But she was grinning as she went upstairs, and, as usual, when my sister smiled, my heart did a happy dance. Maybe, just maybe this could be a new start for the two of us?

Two days later, she came home with a dog.

"There was this homeless guy in the city. He said he couldn't afford to keep him anymore. His name's Fitz. Cute, or what?"

It shouldn't be possible for your heart to both sink and soar at the same time, it really shouldn't. A dog on top of everything else? It was the very last thing I needed. But Fitz *was* cute—a scruffy terrier with huge brown eyes who looked as if he was constantly smiling. He made Violet happy, by the looks of things, and a dog surely indicated she meant to stick around? There had been zero chance of us having pets when we were growing up. They'd have starved to death within a week.

"We can keep him, can't we, Lily?" Violet asked me as if she was seven years old.

I liked that word *we*. Like family.

"If we do, you'll have to walk him regularly." But I was smiling, and so was she.

"Of course. What else would I do with such a cute boy? Look at his little face, Lil. Show her, Fitz; show her what a cutie you are."

She picked the dog up and brought him close to my face, and Fitz obliged by giving my face a thorough wash.

It was getting harder and harder to play the big sensible sister. But I tried. "You do realise owning a dog is going to make it difficult for you to just go places, don't you? You'll always have to think about Fitz. And it's hard to find a rented flat when you've got a pet."

She gave me a cheeky smile. "I don't need a rented flat, though, do I? Not when I'm sharing with you. Please, sis. Say yes. You know you want to."

"All right," I said. "Yes. As long as you promise to—"

"Yay!" Violet swept me into a hug before I could finish my sentence, and when Fitz joined in with the excitement, leaping up at us and barking excitedly, I had to laugh.

I should have known better than to believe Vi's promises, though. By the end of Fitz's first week with us, Violet was rarely home when I got back from work, and the poor little dog was inevitably bursting for a wee, to be fed, to be taken out for a walk. It wasn't that I minded any of it; in fact, I liked it. Walking Fitz helped me to unwind, and he was good company. It was just that the date of my exhibition was rapidly approaching, and I'd barely done any work towards it.

I was disappointed for other reasons too. Violet wanting Fitz had seemed like a sign that she wanted us to be more of a family, so it was a letdown that she was hardly ever home to spend time with us. But what had I expected, really? I was eight years older than Violet, with barely any time in my life for socialising or for fun.

At least Amy was still paying the rent, even though she was staying with her parents, so for now, anyway, I didn't have to worry about how I was going to pay the mortgage. Inga seemed a lot better when I popped round to see her and Noah, too, assuring me that she'd spoken to her health visitor and her GP, who'd put her in touch with various groups and activities, so I could relax about her as well. I just needed to get into my studio and get painting, and I'd be fine.

But by the time half term came around and I had a week off from my teaching, Violet's habits seemed to have changed once again. She was suddenly home more often, which might have been nice, only there was usually a ragbag of people with her, lounging on my sofa, laughing upstairs in the bedroom, staying up late.

Shut away in my studio, trying to paint, the laughter echoing around the house made me feel lonelier than ever. And I couldn't help thinking every now and then about what Kevin had said about Vi taking drugs. Had he been right? I didn't see any evidence of it, though. Not when I was home, anyway. And on the rare occasions Vi and I were alone in the house, we were still getting on reasonably well together, so I was reluctant to bring up any topics that might spoil that.

Then, one evening in early November, I went to work at the hospital with an article I'd found about a rare orchid living at the summit of an extinct volcano in Indonesia to show Beryl, only to discover that she'd died in her sleep. Somehow, it came as a total shock, even though I'd always known she didn't have long to live. I couldn't believe it.

Beryl, gone. I would never be able to speak to her again.

"She didn't know much at the end, bless her," a colleague told me as I stood there staring at the empty, stripped-back bed.

"Sad her son didn't manage to get here in time, though. But I'm sure Beryl had no idea. She just slipped away."

She put a sympathetic hand on my shoulder. "Some of them just get to you, don't they?"

I nodded, wiping my eyes, thinking about Beryl's spark for life. All the intricate, specialised knowledge her brain had held. All of it gone; released to dissipate into the ether. She'd become such a friend to me; a cheery face during the slog of work I didn't want to do. In different circumstances, if she'd had longer to live, I'd have gone round to visit her, wherever she lived, to listen to more tales of her life. She'd have become the grandmother I'd never had, and I'd invite her to the opening of my exhibition as the guest of honour.

But alas, none of that was to be now.

I went about my duties for the rest of the day like an automaton, traipsing wearily home afterwards with some junk TV and a microwave dinner in mind only to find music blaring down the street from Violet's open bedroom window.

There were two pairs of men's boots on the sitting-room carpet, the remains of a Chinese takeaway on the coffee table, and loud laughter coming through the ceiling along with the music. It was like living in a student house, not a home.

I went upstairs without taking off my coat and put my head round Violet's door. Fitz had come up with me, and now he ran straight over to where Violet was sitting on the floor in the gloom. Two guys were sitting nearby, surrounded by half-full pints of beer, flickering tea lights, and an array of what was clearly dope-smoking paraphernalia. The room was filled with smoke and the strong smell of cannabis.

"You know she's a user, don't you?"

Kevin had been right. I had no idea whether Violet's drug use started and stopped with cannabis because Kevin's statement was another thing I had yet to tackle Violet about. Yet another thing I'd put off. If I was honest with myself, I was afraid of my sister; or at least, afraid of angering her, and it occurred to me suddenly that they were one and the same thing.

And suddenly I'd had enough of being a weak, *let sleeping dogs lie* kind of a person, putting up with crap and thoughtlessness, being taken advantage of. Putting off talking to Amy about the rent, treating her—lovely, dependable Amy—like shit because I didn't want to face the consequences.

"Vi, can you turn the music down?" I said, speaking loudly to make myself heard. "It's been a long shift. I need to get some sleep."

"All right, keep your hair on."

As Vi reached for her phone to turn the volume down, I cast another glance over the two guys on the floor. Pale faced and greasy haired, they looked completely out of it—as if they were about to crash to the floor to sleep where they dropped. I didn't fancy going to bed with them in the house at all. Even if I could get to sleep without being disturbed, which I absolutely bloody doubted.

"Actually, can you guys call it a night now?" I said. "It's getting late."

Vi's eyes flashed in my direction. "Oh, here we go. Didn't take long, did it, to start bossing me about? It's ten fucking o'clock, Lily. Ten's not late."

"Maybe not to you, but I've had a shit day at work today, okay? I need to get some rest."

One of the men began to stagger to his feet, shoving cigarette papers into his pocket, almost falling over when they fell out and he stooped to pick them up.

Violet put a hand out towards him. "You don't have to go, Jaeden."

"No, it's all right. Don't want to outstay my welcome."

"Well," said Violet, getting to her feet, "in that case, I'll come with you. Come on, Col, let's leave my sister to her boring life."

"Vi . . . ," I began, my bad temper suddenly falling away, but she turned to scowl at me, nothing but dislike and resentment on her face.

"You know what, Lily?" she yelled. "You can stick your fucking room. Get that pathetic goody-goody Amy back and forget I was ever here. You're good at that, aren't you? Out of sight, out of fucking mind; that's the way it works with you, isn't it?"

All the while she was shouting, Fitz was jumping up and down, barking, and running between me and Violet, clearly distressed. But Violet turned her back on him, and all three of them clattered downstairs.

"Vi," I called after her as Fitz followed on behind, whimpering.

It did him no good. The trio left, slamming the front door after them, leaving him behind.

Wearily I sank down on the edge of Violet's bed. Oh, God. Who knew when I'd see her again now? It had just been too much after the day I'd had, my grief about Beryl. And I'd have had to speak out sometime; I couldn't have gone on treading on eggshells, buttoning my lip every time Vi pushed my limits just a little bit too far.

So much for me and Vi building something together, making a new start, being family. I'd probably just condemned myself to yet more weeks stressing about whether Vi was all right or not too.

I put my face in my hands, utterly spent. Jesus, I couldn't do this any longer; I just couldn't. Taking one measly hopeful step forwards just to get swept back again by a landslide of despair. Like me and Vi were engaged in some kind of hopeless game of snakes and ladders, where the snakes outnumbered the ladders by 99.9 percent, and there was no chance whatsoever of ever winning.

I was so alone with all this. But there was no one to blame for that but myself, was there? Inga didn't even know much about Vi and our tricky relationship. Because I'd never really told her about it. I wanted to suddenly. To call her and spew the whole ugly thing out.

I took my phone from my coat pocket. But I didn't dial. Because Inga might be in the middle of doing something for Noah. Putting him down for the night. Or going to sleep herself. It would be selfish to risk waking them up. And what could Inga—or anybody else, for that matter—do to make me feel better, really? Even Matt, with his uncanny ability to listen and say the right thing, couldn't help this time.

The push and pull of my relationship with Violet was rooted in a sense of abandonment that had always been there—even before the fire and Mum pissing off to who knew where. When Mum had been on one of her drinking binges, I'd been left to my own devices, scratching about for food in empty cupboards, wearing dirty clothes from the bedroom floor. Getting myself to school, pretending everything was all right. Finding temporary solace in drawing pictures and reading stories. Returning home with the vain hope that maybe, just maybe, this time it would be different. I'd smell something cooking. Mum would call to me as I let myself into the house. And sometimes, sometimes, it was like that. But not very often. Not often enough.

After the fire, in that frightening, lonely young-person's hostel, the times I saw my sister were the only bright thing in my life. So when the foster carer told me Violet didn't want to see me anymore, it pretty much blasted me away. No wonder I was so pathetically grateful whenever she sought me out now.

Violet muddied my sight, brought hope springing back. Made me forget what I'd learnt early on in life: that it was a bad idea to let anyone get completely close to you in case they, too, decided to leave.

Fitz pattered back up the stairs, panting and whimpering with stress, jumping up onto the bed to press his shaking body next to mine. I couldn't tell whether he wanted to comfort me, or me to comfort him, but I stroked him, anyway, glad of his presence, wondering about his former owner; how difficult it must have been to give him up. As difficult as it was for me to give up Violet every time she left, no doubt.

"Oh, Fitz," I said, burying my face into his fur. "She's never going to forgive me. Never."

Fitz licked my face as if he understood every word, knew I was talking about what had happened all those years ago, not the recent row. I stroked him for comfort, sensing him calming down along with me, but suddenly there was a knock at the door, and he flew off my lap to run downstairs barking. Quickly wiping away my tears, I rushed downstairs myself, convinced it would be Violet, back again, having forgotten her key. Either that or Matt, responding to some telepathic summons I'd unwittingly sent.

But it wasn't Violet. Or Matt.

"Alex!"

Alex was the very last person I'd expected to see—we hadn't seen each other since that awkward meeting at the café—but I dragged a smile from somewhere anyway. At least he would be company. I might be able to talk to him about my appalling day—the row with Violet,

Beryl dying, how useless I felt. But then I really looked at him and saw he looked dreadful. Worse even than the two guys I'd just ejected from my house. Something must have happened.

"Hi, Lily. Can I come in?"

"Of course." Automatically, I stepped back to let him pass. Fitz surged forwards to jump up at him, barking a welcome or warning me I had an intruder—I wasn't sure which.

Alex recoiled.

"Down, Fitz, there's a good boy."

"You got yourself a dog?" Alex asked, sounding incredulous, trying to shove Fitz off.

"He's my sister's dog. She brought him home last week."

"Your sister's here?"

I nodded. "Well, not right now; she just . . ." Once again I wanted to pour the whole sorry tale out to him. Once again, the expression on his face stopped me. "Is everything all right, Alex?"

Alex shook his head, slumping down onto the sofa; the same sofa on which the two of us had spent evening after evening cuddled up together watching TV. Where we'd occasionally made love. "No, actually, it's not."

Fitz was attempting to climb onto Alex's lap, so I pulled him up onto mine instead, stroking his ears.

"What's happened? Is Lola okay?"

"Yes, she's okay. As far as I know, anyway. I mean, how much can babies absorb about what's going on at that age?"

"What is going on?"

He covered his face with his hands. "Fliss dumped me."

I couldn't believe it. They hadn't been together for very long, and they had a baby. Jesus. "You've broken up?"

He gave a bitter laugh. "That's usually what it means when someone dumps you, isn't it?"

"But why?"

When he shrugged, his shoulders moved like the shoulders of someone much older. Someone stiff and arthritic. "Because she doesn't love me enough, she doesn't think I love her enough, she thinks I'm still in love with you . . . I don't know, take your pick. Oh, and she thinks I'm a crap father."

That couldn't be true, surely? He'd been so besotted with Lola that time we'd met in the café. Knowing Alex, he'd read a ton of books about taking care of babies before Lola was even born. Watched countless videos on the subject.

"I can't believe that."

"Well, you should. Nothing I do for Lola is right as far as Fliss is concerned. She wants to decide how everything's done." He counted off on his fingers. "On-the-clock feeding and nap times, even if that means leaving Lola to cry until my head feels as if it's going to explode. Waking her up at seven a.m. even if she's still fast asleep. Bath time at precisely six fifteen in the evening. If I try to suggest we don't need to be so rigid, she just accuses me of not supporting her. So I just keep quiet, but I guess I didn't make a good job of hiding my feelings because she snapped at me and said she'd be glad when I went back to work. Then I went back to work, and she said I wasn't supporting her. I mean, what does she want?"

He put his face in his hands. "Then, this evening, when I got home, she said she'd been thinking about it, and she thought it would be better if I left. That she'd be better off on her own." He looked up at me, his eyes pleading. "What can I do, Lily? Tell me, what can I do?"

The question ricocheted around my head. *What can I do, Lily? What can I do?*

God. I was so tired; I might dissolve into a pool on the sofa. Lovely, beautiful Beryl had died this afternoon. I wouldn't even be able to go to her funeral because I wouldn't know where it was going to be. I'd rowed with Violet. Again. My exhibition was a few weeks away—a few weeks!—and I still had so many paintings to get done. And now here was Alex, needing me, wanting my advice about how to deal with a situation he'd made all by himself.

"I'm so sorry, Alex," I said. It was inadequate, but it was all I had.

Alex gave a half laugh and shook his head, clearly disappointed with my reaction.

"I'm not sure what else you want me to say," I said.

I might just as well have said what I was really thinking. *I don't know why you came here asking me for help.*

Alex shrugged. "I suppose I just thought you'd listen. That you'd understand. I don't know, that maybe I could crash here for the night or something. I just wanted . . ." He looked me in the eye. "I wanted you, Lily. Because I think that's the one thing Fliss is right about; I'm still in love with you."

Shit.

When he took hold of my hands, I knew with sudden clarity that Alex had come here with complete confidence that I'd kept my life on hold for him, living in limbo, on the off chance that he'd want me back. How fucking insulting. How completely fucking untrue. I wasn't in love with Alex anymore. Hadn't been for a long time.

I snatched my hands from his to cuddle Fitz against me. "If Fliss called you right now to say she was sorry, you'd be back home like a shot. You know you would."

He shook his head, trying to reach for my hands again. "Only because of Lola. I swear, Lily. That little girl . . . I'd literally do anything for her. Even live with her cold bitch of a mother. But it's you I want. You I've always wanted. I was an idiot to let you go."

He was right; he was an idiot. But not for letting me go. For assuming I was some kind of doormat he could walk all over. A bubble of outrage suddenly exploded inside my chest, not all of it directed at Alex. Why the hell hadn't I been clearer about my feelings last time we'd met at the park instead of being all polite excuses and saying I had to get Noah back to Inga?

"You didn't let me go, Alex," I said coldly. "You left. And if you hadn't, you would never have met the love of your life."

He frowned. "Fliss isn't the love of my life, I told you, I—"

I shook my head impatiently. "Not Fliss; Lola. If you and I had stayed together, you wouldn't have Lola in your life."

"She barely will be in my life anyway if Fliss gets her way," he whined bitterly, his eyes big and sorrowful. "Every other weekend and Wednesday evenings, that's what she's got in mind for me. Babies change so quickly. I'll miss so much."

He covered his face with his hands again and began to weep. Suddenly I was very much out of my depth. I couldn't do this anymore. Not on my own. Not anymore.

Now it really was time to phone Matt.

I took my phone to the kitchen to call him. He answered on the second ring. "Lily!" The pleasure in his voice made my heart leap. "Hi. I nearly called you earlier to see if you fancied meeting up, but I thought you were working."

He'd wanted to see me. Maybe I had sent that telepathic message, after all.

"I got back half an hour ago."

"And how was work today?"

I closed my eyes, thinking once again about Beryl. "Awful, actually. But listen, that's not why I rang. Can you come round? Alex is here. He's broken up with Fliss."

Matt sighed heavily on the other end of the line. "I knew it. I never did like Fliss, not even at school. She probably just used Alex to get a baby. Poor sod."

"Can you come?"

"Of course. I can be there in thirty minutes."

"Thank you."

"Are you okay? It can't have been easy for you, having Alex turn up out of the blue."

I sighed, being entirely honest for once. "It wasn't. Life's been pretty crap altogether lately, what with one thing and another. Violet's been staying with me."

"Has she? Well, I hope she was eating humble pie. Though I'm sensing not, from your tone."

I sighed, remembering my initial relief at seeing her. "It was all right at first. We were getting on reasonably well. Until this evening, anyway. Like I said, it's been an awful day at work, and when I get home she's playing music really loudly, and there's these two stoned-looking guys flopped in her bedroom, and I . . ."

"Are they still there?" he interrupted. "D'you want me to turf them out for you?"

"No, it's okay, they've gone. I asked them to leave, actually. But then, of course, Violet shouted at me and stormed out, and who knows when I'll see her again."

"What happened at work today?"

Tears filled my throat. I wanted to tell him, but it was so difficult to get the words out.

"Tell me," he said, his voice intimate in my ear.

"Somebody . . . a patient I'd grown really fond of . . . Beryl. She . . . died this morning. She was ill, she was old. And . . . and I know that's what happens in hospitals, but Beryl was an amazing person, Matt. Really amazing. I didn't know her for very long, but I really cared for her, you know?"

"Oh, I'm so sorry, Lily."

His voice was rich with sympathy. It was almost too much to bear. I swallowed. "Thanks."

If Alex hadn't called to me from the next room, I might have gone on to confide in Matt. To tell him that every time I grew close to somebody it seemed as if I lost them, exactly as it felt I was about to lose him.

But Alex did call to me.

"Lily? Where are you?"

And I did what I always did. Wiped away my tears. Pulled myself together. "Listen, Alex wants me. I'd better go. You'll be here soon?"

"Half an hour, tops. Take care, Lily."

True to his word, thirty minutes later, Matt was at my door. Thirty desperate minutes alone with Alex which I attempted to fill with cups of tea, offers of snacks and any other distractions I could think of.

Outwardly, Matt was the same man he always was when I opened the door to him—smart casual clothes, neat haircut, direct, steady gaze, filling the doorway with his height and broad shoulders the way he'd done countless times before. Nothing different from usual. Nothing new. And yet, maybe because we'd spent that time in Nottingham together, or perhaps because he was imminently moving away, I couldn't help seeing him more clearly. As if we'd been transported back to that Christmas Eve pub and I was meeting him for the first time all over again.

"Thanks so much for coming," I said.

He put his hands on my shoulders, moving in close to kiss me on the cheek, and when he said softly, "I really am sorry about your friend," his voice seemed to vibrate through me.

I shivered. "I'm not entirely sure why it's hit me so badly. As I said, it's not as if I'd known Beryl for very long."

"It doesn't always matter, though, does it? Sometimes you meet someone, and you just click."

I nodded, once again back in that decked-out-for-Christmas city pub, Inga and I wearing our reindeer antlers. What would have happened if I'd been more assertive with Inga that night? If, when she'd said, *"Alex is not going to get down on one knee and ask you to marry him at the end of the evening,"* making sure I knew she fancied Matt, I'd said, *"No, you have Alex. I really fancy Matt,"* instead of being the good, acquiescent friend I usually was?

Inga would have made mincemeat of Alex. They'd have broken up far faster than he and Fliss had. But me and Matt? Would we still be together now?

It didn't matter, though, did it? It was academic. Because I hadn't said anything to Inga that night. I'd given in to what she wanted, putting her first.

"Matt?" Alex called out from the sitting room, beyond the porch. "Is that you?"

At Alex's voice, I pulled myself out of my trance, stepping back to let Matt past.

"Alex, mate," Matt said, going over to his friend.

Alex began to sob all over again. "Oh, Matt," he said, "my life has gone to total shit."

I knew the feeling; I really did.

25

Somehow the next morning, when I took Fitz for a walk after another unsettled night, I found myself heading for a park in the city centre. I was restless, fed up with myself, worrying, despite everything I'd told myself, about Violet and what she was doing. Where was she? In some seedy squat? Sleeping rough on the streets? Shooting up heroin?

All those times I'd sat back to wait for my sister to come home when she'd been on her travels. I ought to have sought her out, flown to meet her, shared some adventures with her instead of passively waiting for her to come home.

Passive just about summed me up. I'd never been curious about who my father was. Hadn't even seriously tried to track down my mother, either, not beyond the odd internet search. She'd never seemed worth searching for, I suppose, after what she'd done. But maybe, if I had done, if I'd managed to save up enough to pay for a private detective, rooted Mum out from whatever hole she was in to demand some answers from her, I'd have been able to finally leave all the shit about my past behind and move on.

I hadn't done any of those things, though. Instead, I'd fallen in with what Inga—my miraculous best friend—wanted. Gone to parties I didn't always want to go to. Bought clothes Inga said I should buy that I suspected I'd never wear. Ignored all my instincts when she begged me not to tell Matt about the abortion. All because her friendship was so precious to me, and I was so afraid of losing it.

My life ever since the night of the fire—long before that—had reeked with fear, and fear had made me weak, living a compromise of a life, hiding in my art or in hotel rooms when things got tough.

And Matt . . . But I couldn't, wouldn't think about Matt and what might have been. If I did, I might just shatter into a thousand pieces onto the pavement.

Another dog walker came towards us, the golden retriever at her side seemingly ecstatic to see Fitz, waving her tail, drawing Fitz in with her enthusiasm.

"Sorry," the dog's owner said. "She does have to say hello to everyone."

I smiled, watching the dogs get to know each other, cheered by the obvious love in the woman's voice.

"Life would be a lot simpler if we were all like that," I said, and the woman laughed.

"You're not wrong there."

We walked on after I'd managed to drag Fitz away, walking over Fye Bridge with its reflections of the weeping willow trees on the bank. I paused for a moment to drink in the movement of the water, the ripples and the shifting colours. Inspiration for painting if I could only switch off my dismal thoughts.

Then Fitz pulled on his lead, and I continued on towards the city.

"It's Lily, isn't it?" asked a voice suddenly, jerking me from my thoughts.

I looked up, startled, and saw a face I'd only encountered once—a face which was now reflected back at me every time I saw little Noah. Harry, here, standing outside Inga's estate agents—his estate agent, too, before he'd moved to Cambridge.

"Harry?"

He nodded, bending to stroke Fitz's head. "The very same."

"I thought you'd moved to Cambridge."

"I did." He straightened, smiling the smile I remembered from that night out. "Let's just say it didn't work out. I'm back here to try and persuade the powers that be to take me back. How's Inga? I hear she's on maternity leave?" He shook his head. "She must have changed. I would never have put the words *Inga* and *maternity leave* in the same sentence."

Was it just his job that hadn't worked out, or his whole life in Cambridge? Had he split up with his girlfriend? It was clear he had absolutely no clue about Noah being his son.

I shouldn't have said what I said next. But what with running into Harry coming hard on the heels of giving myself grief about being too passive, the words just slipped out. "You ought to go and visit Inga while you're here," I said. "She'd love to see you."

Harry looked doubtful. "D'you think? I don't suppose her bloke would be very impressed by some random guy turning up out of the blue."

"There is no bloke."

He frowned. "She's doing the whole parent thing on her own?"

I nodded. "At the moment, yes."

"Wow. What about her ex-boyfriend? What's-his-face?"

"Matt?" I shook my head. "No, Noah isn't Matt's."

Harry smiled. "Noah. Cool name." Then he frowned once again, his gaze sharpening. "Wait a minute, who is the kid's father, then?"

I wasn't going to come right out and say it, but as we stood there exchanging glances, I could see the penny dropping as clearly as if it were a burnished copper thing bouncing and spinning and shining on the pavement right in front of us.

"Jesus," Harry said, and I reached out to squeeze his arm.

"Go and see her," I said. "Forty-seven Arnold Street."

Then I urged Fitz onwards and left Harry and his thunderstruck expression on the pavement outside the estate agents.

I wish I could say I felt cool and confident as I walked away. But I didn't. My heart was hammering like a blacksmith beating the shit out of a piece of metal hot from the forge with every step I took.

Well done, Lily. Bloody well done. This wasn't my life I was practising my assertiveness techniques on; it was Inga's. And I definitely ought not to have said anything to Harry before speaking to her. Why had I done it? Why the bloody hell had I done it?

For fuck's sake. It wasn't because I'd suddenly developed all these churned up feelings about Matt, was it? Because if some subconscious part of me wanted Inga to be happily fixed up so I was free to pursue a relationship with Matt, that was unforgiveable. Stupid, too, because even if Matt did ever start to see me as more than just a friend, Inga would never want the two of us to get together. She'd make me choose between her and Matt as if we were in some soap opera.

Fitz was suddenly pulling on his lead; for a little dog, he was very strong. We were nowhere near the park yet, but something had obviously snagged his attention.

"Fitz! Slow down!" I said, but he paid absolutely no heed to me because someone else was calling to him—a man standing in a shop doorway, bellowing Fitz's name at the top of his lungs.

"Fitzie boy! Fitz!"

Suddenly the little dog gave a lurch more suited to a Great Dane than a terrier cross and slipped his collar, bounding up the road.

Shit. Terrified he'd get run over; I ran after him. By the time I caught up with him, Fitz was in the unknown man's arms, and the man was laughing with delight as Fitz covered him in doggy kisses, his little tail windmilling in ecstatic circles.

I came to a stop in front of them. "He's yours," I guessed. "My sister got him from you."

The man looked in my direction. He could have been anything between thirty and fifty years old with his weather-beaten face and unclean clothes. "Worst thing I ever did, letting her have him. I've missed this boy so much."

Fitz was always so desperate when I got back from work. Panted with stress while Violet and I rowed. "He's missed you too."

The man, suddenly emotional, gazed down at Fitz again, stroking his ears just as I'd done yesterday when I'd wanted to comfort myself.

Then he looked up, wiped his hand on his coat and held it out to me. "I'm Lewis."

I smiled, shaking his proffered hand. "Lily."

He smiled. "She was a flower, too, wasn't she? Your sister?"

"Yes, Violet."

Lewis looked back down into Fitz's adoring eyes again. "D'you think Violet would let me have him back? I'd do better this time. Keep myself clean. Make sure he wasn't out in the cold and the wet. Only, he's family for me, you see."

Family. God, that word. I could have sobbed, right there on the street outside the newsagents. My mind was made up, but what about Violet? Should I wait and ask her first? No, I bloody well shouldn't. My sister had stormed off who knew where without sparing a single thought for Fitz. Lewis might be on the streets, but he loved the dog. Fitz hadn't been in a bad state when Violet had brought him home, had he? And maybe I could do something to make sure he stayed okay.

So, I said, "I'm sure she wouldn't mind at all," and five minutes later, having given Lewis whatever money I had in my purse and extracted a promise that he and Fitz would meet me for a cup of coffee the following week, I left.

Shortly before I arrived home, sans dog, a text came through from Inga. **What the fuck, Lily?** And I guessed that Harry must have arrived at her house.

26

I went round to see Inga a few hours later.

She came to the door in her dressing gown, holding Noah, no make-up on. This wasn't an unusual state of affairs since she'd had Noah, but I knew, whether she'd wanted Harry to turn up on her doorstep or not, there was no way she'd have been pleased for him to see her like that.

She turned her back on me and went inside without a word, leaving the door open.

I followed her, closing the door behind me.

"Inga, I—" I began to say but broke off as Noah began to cry.

Inga jiggled him on her hip, turning to face me. "I can just about get you dropping hints to Matt the way you did, even though it did make the shit well and truly hit the fan. But Harry . . . How bloody dare you, Lil?"

I'd seen Inga angry before, plenty of times. But never like this. Never with me.

I was suddenly chilled right through. "I'm sorry, Ing, I just . . ."

"This is my life, in case you've forgotten."

"I know that."

"Do you, Lil? Do you, really? Because you seem hell-bent on sticking your nose into it."

Noah's cries were really loud now.

"It wasn't like that," I tried to explain. "Look, I know I shouldn't have said anything. I didn't plan to."

She turned her back on me again, heading towards the sofa. "Oh, well, that's all right, then, isn't it?" she said, her voice dripping with sarcasm. "If you didn't plan to." She sat down, opening her robe to feed Noah.

I watched, feeling utterly miserable, terrified I'd gone too far this time. That our friendship wouldn't survive this latest interference. Noting, too, how confidently Inga dealt with Noah now. How easily he latched on. How far the two of them had come these past few months. Feeling proud of her.

"I realise my life must seem pretty fucked up to you at the moment," she said bitterly, still not looking up. "I'm sure you've got all sorts of opinions about what I'm doing wrong with Noah."

It was so absolutely the opposite of what I'd just been thinking that I shook my head, gaping at her. "No, Ing! That's not true at all."

"Of course it bloody is. Why wouldn't it be when I've asked you for help so often?" She wiped a tear from her cheek angrily. "And I'm grateful to you for all you've done. I am. But I really feel as though the two of us are getting there now, you know?"

She looked up, her face vulnerable, despite her strong words. "So I didn't need you to send Harry *fucking hell, why didn't you tell me* Brown round here. You had absolutely no right."

I sank into the armchair opposite her, utterly wretched. "I know. I know I didn't. And I'm so sorry."

"So, what made you do it, Lil? Because I'm struggling to understand here. I thought we were friends."

"We are. Of course we are." I closed my eyes. Opened them again. "It was a stupid impulse. Speaking before thinking." I shook my head. "Life's been really shit lately, Ing. A lot of crap stuff's been happening."

"First fucking time I've heard about it."

I sighed. "I didn't like to bother you," I said. "You've got enough on your mind at the moment."

"Oh, so you decided to shut me out of your life because you think my feeble baby brain wouldn't be able to cope, is that it?"

Had that been it? Possibly. I had wanted to shield Inga from more stress. But it was more than that, though, wasn't it? Misery had made me withdraw inside myself, responding to a deep-seated instinct to deal with shit by myself. And the irony was that, by doing that, by not being open, I'd put my friendship with Inga at risk.

"I have been really worried about you, Ing," I started to say, but she cut through my words, not in the mood to listen.

"So tell me, Lil," she said. "What was so bad in your life you opened me up to potential custody claims and being forced to let somebody else have a say in making decisions about my son?"

I stared at her. "Harry wouldn't do anything like that," I said, horrified. "Would he?"

She shrugged. "Who knows? He might. And before you fucking dare say he's got a right to play a part in Noah's life, I'll say it again. My life. My decision."

I did think it would potentially be better for little Noah to know his father. But she was absolutely right. It was nothing to do with me. And if I'd only stayed quiet, Inga might have got round to telling Harry about Noah herself.

"You know," she said, "sometimes I think you're jealous of me. Oh, I know you talk about not wanting to have a child, but I've seen the look on your face sometimes when you hold Noah. Like you're transported somewhere."

I was. Straight back to my childhood. To Violet.

"Actually, I think you've always been jealous of me," she went on.

I frowned. "Ing, where is all this coming from?" But I knew, deep down in my gut, even before she spelt it out for me.

"Me and Matt. You've always been jealous of me and Matt. Following him everywhere with your eyes. Having special chats. Laughing together. Even when you were with Alex."

My heart was suddenly beating very quickly. "That's not true," I said, even though I couldn't guarantee 100 percent that it wasn't. Not with everything that had happened lately. Things I'd kept from Inga, not because I didn't want to burden her at all, but because I was ashamed. Because I knew, deep down, she'd feel exactly this way. "We were all close."

"We were," she agreed. "But you've always wanted more. Maybe that's why you told Matt I was pregnant, eh? To sabotage the two of us."

Anger suddenly spewed up inside me. "You sabotaged your relationship with Matt all by yourself by sleeping with Harry," I said, the loudness of my voice disturbing Noah from his milk-induced slumber.

Inga got to her feet, holding him against her shoulder, her face red with anger. "Whatever. I can't deal with this right now. Any of it. Because, as it happens, you were right. I have got a lot on my mind. Which you'd know, if you hadn't sent Harry round here, because when he turned up, I was just about to phone you. To tell you my uncle Erik called to tell me Mum's cancer's spread. That she's only got a few weeks left to live. I've got to get me and Noah to Denmark to see her."

My anger vanished as quickly as it had arrived. "Oh, Inga, that's awful. I'm so sorry."

She nodded. "Yeah, it's shit. So, anyway, I need to get showered and dressed. Get a flight booked. So, if you don't mind . . ."

Five minutes ago I'd have offered to take care of Noah while she did those things. But it was obvious that, right now, this was the very last thing she wanted me to do.

So, I stood, wondering whether we'd ever be able to get our friendship back on track after this, feeling sadder than I could remember being in a long time. Which, since I'd been feeling very sad lately, was saying something.

"I guess I'll leave you to it, then."

"Okay."

"I hope it—well, I hope it's not too awful. I . . . I'll be thinking about you."

Inga kept her gaze fixedly on Noah's dark, curly head. "Thanks."

I walked to the door. "Bye, Ing."

"Bye, Lily."

Then I left, closing the door very quietly behind me.

27

I caught a bus home from Inga's house, too spent to walk the way I usually did. Slumped in my seat gazing sightlessly out at the passing houses, my mind churned with every accusation and every angry word Inga and I had hurled at each other.

It had been brewing up for some time, but that didn't make it any easier. And what she'd said about Matt. All this time, even while I'd been swimming around in a soup of sheer denial about it, frantically trying to convince myself Matt and I were still just friends, she'd suspected I had feelings for him. How ridiculous that it had taken her saying it for me to realise it.

Because of course she was right. Of course she was. I was in love with Matt. Had been for a long while. Would it have made a difference if Inga had said something before? Who knew. It might just have meant us falling out earlier than we had. For who knew what was going to happen now? Whether my friendship with Inga would ever be the same again, even after Matt had left for Spain.

"Cheer up, love," said a man walking past to exit the bus. "It might never happen."

A ball of pure fury rose up inside my chest. *It already fucking has!* I wanted to yell after him, but it was too late; the bus doors were swishing open, and he was gone.

"I hate it when people say that, don't you?" the woman seated across the aisle from me said. "Do they expect us to go about grinning like idiots the whole time just for their benefit?"

That, I thought, as I shot her a smile, was precisely my problem. I pretended to be okay when I wasn't. Even with Inga. I really needed to stop doing it. If Inga's reaction was anything to go by, it wasn't helping. It was a defence mechanism, but people didn't love defence mechanisms. They loved real people. People who showed their vulnerabilities and humanity. That was what Inga wanted from me. Or at least, she thought she did, anyway. But what if your vulnerabilities and hang-ups were so overwhelming they were like a sandstorm in a desert, blasting everything away, reshaping the landscape? There was a risk that Inga might not like the real me when she really got to know me. But then, she didn't much like me now, did she? So, if she let me, after she got back, I'd tell her everything.

My phone bleeped inside my bag, and I grabbed it, hoping it was Inga. It wasn't. It was Amy.

> Sorry, Lily. My parents are going away and have asked me to pet-sit. Also, I've decided to save up to buy a flat of my own, so staying with them more permanently makes sense. Is it okay if I come round to get my stuff?

Well, I'd known that had been coming, hadn't I? It was something else I wasn't proud of—stringing Amy along all this time. I ought to have spoken to her ages ago. I'd treated her like shit, and it wasn't good enough. I liked Amy; she was a good friend. If I wasn't careful, she'd end up being somebody else I'd lose from my life.

Just on my way home now. I messaged back. Quite understand. So sorry about everything.

No worries. See you in an hour? she replied.

But an hour later, faced with the reality of Amy with her packed bags, I just couldn't find it in myself to tell her how I was feeling, how crap everything was. It wouldn't have been fair. She'd have felt guilty about leaving. So I did what I'd recently decided not to do anymore—I pretended I was okay when I wasn't.

"It's fine, Amy, honestly," I said when she said again how sorry she was. "Violet's away at the moment, but she'll be back any day."

That was a blatant lie, of course—I had no idea when or even if Vi would be back. Then, just to make sure Amy felt okay about everything, I compounded the lie with another one. "She mentioned a job she'd applied for, actually, so I'm sure she'll be okay to help out with the rent. Sorry it didn't work out as we planned."

Amy smiled, looking relieved. "That's okay. Not that I plan to live back at Mum and Dad's forever, but it'll be fine while I'm saving up, and their kittens are very cute. Though why they imagined it was a good idea to get kittens when they were about to go on holiday is anyone's guess."

"That's parents for you," I joked, despising myself. What did I know about how parents behaved? Normal, nonaddicted ones, anyway.

"Keep in touch, won't you?" Amy said as we hugged goodbye shortly afterwards.

"Certainly will," I said, still with that *I'm okay* grin. "Bye, Amy."

Two goodbyes in a morning. That had to be something of a record.

Though at least the lie about Violet turned out not to be such a lie, after all. Because the very next day, after I got back from my shift at the hospital, I found her in the kitchen, cooking pasta as if she'd never stormed out at all.

I'd already been tired when I let myself into the house. Now I was suddenly completely wiped out. Like I'd aged fifty-plus years.

"Hi," she said. "I'm making carbonara. I reckoned you might be hungry when you got back from work."

Just as if the drugs, the wasted guys, the bitter, cruel words about me and my life, had never happened.

"Hi, Violet, good to see you, Violet, oh, and where the hell have you been, Violet?" I said sarcastically, wondering how the hell I was going to find the energy to deal with this all over again, dumping my bag on the floor.

"Good to see you, too, sis," she said, ignoring the last part of my question.

Giving up temporarily, I left her to her cooking. "I'm going to get changed."

I showered, letting the water run over my face, directing it into the small of my back, which was aching after a day of standing, bending, lifting, my thoughts like birds fluttering inside my brain. God. I'd like to go to sleep and wake up in ten years' time. What next? What fucking next?

When I finally traipsed downstairs in my dressing gown, Violet was just dishing up. The food looked and smelt very good. I wondered wearily where she'd learnt to cook. At one of her foster placements? Maybe she'd been taught by a celebrity chef. Or a lover. Or a lover's mother in Italy. Who fucking knew? I had no intention whatsoever of asking. I was just going to enjoy the benefits and delay the evil moment until me and Vi had another much-needed, and no-doubt-highly-charged stressful conversation.

"This is good," I said as we ate in front of the TV, our plates on our laps.

"Carbonara's my specialty," Vi said. "Where's Fitz, by the way?"

I sighed. Here we go. Vi was bound to be mad at me for rehoming her dog.

"We ran into Lewis in town, and I let him have Fitz back. They'd clearly missed each other, and I just don't have a lifestyle suitable for a dog." I wasn't sure why I was justifying my decision. Probably because I anticipated Vi giving me grief about it. But I plunged on, anyway. "Even before you went away, he was miserable a lot of the time, left on his own when you went out."

Vi was quiet for a while. Then she just said, "Cool," and got on with eating her pasta.

And I was glad that I'd said what I'd said. Relieved, actually, to have got it off my chest.

Miracle of miracles, everything was harmonious for a while—good food, junk TV, companionable silence, me managing not to give vent to everything I'd been thinking and feeling for the past few days. After the week I'd had, still feeling blasted by my row with Inga, it was sorely tempting just to accept it. To keep quiet about what had happened and to enjoy the gift of Violet being here, being nice. Of not feeling so gut-wrenchingly, piercingly alone for once.

But I was trying to be more open now, wasn't I? I wasn't pretending to be okay when I wasn't. And things definitely hadn't been okay between me and Vi last time we'd seen each other. Why shouldn't it all turn to shit again, even if she was being nice now?

So, after I'd finished my meal, I reached reluctantly for the TV remote to switch the soap Vi had put on off.

"Hey!" she said. "I was watching that."

"Sorry," I said. "We need to talk."

I watched the emotions that travelled like quick-fire over her face. Annoyance followed by resentment, then a deliberate attempt to squash both of them down.

"Sure. That's fair. But before you say anything, I'm sorry I was such a bitch. You made me feel small in front of my friends, but I shouldn't have said half the things I said." And she smiled at me—a big, beaming smile that was hard to resist, taking the wind right out of my sails.

"Well," I said, "I'm sorry if I made you feel small in front of your friends. But, Vi, if you're hoping to stay here again, we need to establish some ground rules."

She nodded. "Sure. Write me a list while I wash up." She stood to collect our plates.

"You don't have to wash up," I said. "You cooked."

"Yeah, but you've been at work. Sit. Chill. Work on your ground rules."

Another winning smile, then she shimmied out of the door with our dirty plates like a waitress confident of her tip.

I closed my eyes with a sigh, listening to her clattering about in the kitchen. My sister. No matter what grief she'd caused me, it was still good to have her here. And with everything tied up with Amy, the spare room was now officially free.

It occurred to me suddenly that, if Inga and I hadn't fallen out, I might have sneaked upstairs to the bathroom to call her for advice. *Hey, Violet's back, all sweetness and light, expecting to stay here again. Should I let her?* Inga would say no, I knew she would. But then she was an only child, and she didn't know the history of me and Vi. Hell, she hadn't even met Vi, which was incomprehensible when we'd been friends for so long. Or *had* been friends for so long, anyway, since our friendship was currently uncertain.

It would be nice, actually, to talk to Vi about that rather than about ground rules. To open up and really connect with my sister. Tell her about my stupid decision to drop hints about Noah to Harry. Maybe that way, Vi would feel she could talk to me; I might find out something about her life in those missing years when she'd been abroad. Her hopes and plans for the future.

But we'd never had that kind of a relationship, me and Vi. I was the older sister, the one who gave unwanted advice and did my best to pick up the pieces when things went wrong. Which meant there was no easy way to ask her about her drug taking that didn't feel like an accusation or a pointed finger.

Vi was singing now, a song I didn't recognise; something new, no doubt, aimed at people younger than me.

"Jesus, Lily, you're the same age as I am!" I heard Inga's voice inside my head. *"We're not exactly past it. Or at least, you might be, but I'm certainly not."*

Was she in Copenhagen now? She must be, I supposed. What had the journey been like with little Noah? Had he slept? Or cried the whole time? I wondered whether she'd taken him to meet her mother yet. What that had been like if she had.

I'd know, if we hadn't argued, wouldn't I? Because we'd have spoken, or texted each other, the way we'd done pretty much every day of our friendship.

I picked up my phone, wanting to text her now, and saw that I had a missed call from Matt. Shit, my phone had been on silent during my shift.

There was a voicemail message.

"Hi, it's Matt. My flight's been delayed, so I just thought I'd give you a call. Hope everything's okay and Alex isn't being too much of a pain. He's staying with his dad at the moment, but you know what his dad's like. I don't suppose he's being very sympathetic or offering much of a listening ear. I hope you're managing to get some painting done, that it's going really well. I can't wait for your exhibition. I'll definitely be back for that. Nothing could keep me away. Anyway, take care, Lil. Bye for now."

I played the message again, simultaneously churned up and comforted by it.

Matt. Another topic I'd like to chat to Vi about if we had a different kind of relationship. What I was going to do about my feelings for Matt.

Vi returned from doing the washing up just as the message was finishing playing.

"How's what's-his-name?" she asked, sitting down on the sofa. "Matt, wasn't it? The guy you brought with you to Nottingham."

"He's okay," I said warily, feeling as if she'd read my mind. Surprised that she wanted to bring up the subject of Nottingham after all that had happened. "He's in Spain at the moment."

"That must suck."

It did; she was right.

"I told you before, nothing's happening between me and Matt."

"You're just friends, I know."

She was grinning at me, and I sighed. "It's complicated, Vi."

"Well," she said. "That's life, isn't it? One shit show after another. But I promise, if you say it's okay for me to stay again, things will be different."

"How?"

"I'll be a good girl. I'll do my best to be quiet so you can work. I'll cook for us both." She shrugged. "Whatever you want. You'll see, it'll be fun. You liked my pasta, didn't you?"

"It was delicious."

She beamed at me.

"Well then. Anyway, you look bushed. Go on up to bed. I'll just watch a bit more TV, and then I'll turn in too."

I went, putting aside the feeling that she might be using my tiredness as a way of avoiding any further discussion about ground rules and allowing myself, for once, to be cared for.

Alex came by the next evening. I had the night off and was in the studio painting, doing my best to submerge myself in work towards my exhibition, headphones on, music playing loudly in an attempt to create a creative bubble. Vi had to tap me on the shoulder to get my attention. I pushed my headphones back.

"There's someone to see you, Lil. Big bunch of flowers? Hang-dog expression?" She did an imitation for me. "Says he's Alex."

Oh, God.

"Want me to tell him to get lost?" Violet offered, seeing my expression.

I sighed and put down my paintbrush.

"No, I'd better see him, I suppose."

Vi came with me. Showed no signs of leaving while I said hello to Alex.

"Hi, Lily," he said, holding out the bunch of flowers. "I got you these. To say sorry for the other night. I was a bit drunk."

I took the flowers from him. "Thanks. There was no need."

Violet took the flowers from my hand. "Better get these in water. They look as if they're screaming for a drink."

They did, she was right. In fact, they looked like garage forecourt offerings past their sell-by date. Either that, or Alex had been carrying them around for a while, trying to pluck up the courage to come and see me.

"There was every need," Alex said as Violet took the flowers away to the kitchen. "I was upset, but I shouldn't have dumped everything on you like that." He licked his lips. "But . . ."

My heart sank, sensing what was to come. More stuff about his undying love and him and me getting back together.

Vi returned with the flowers. They didn't look much better in a vase.

"I took the most wilted ones out," she said cheerfully, placing them on the coffee table.

I saw Alex glance in her direction with frustration. Clearly he'd prefer it if she made herself scarce. But she didn't. The very opposite, in fact. She sat down on the sofa instead.

"I'd offer to make you a drink, Alex, but I'm going out soon, and Lily's in the middle of painting. You know, to reach her deadline for her very important exhibition?"

In other circumstances, it might have been funny, but there was nothing funny about Alex's miserable expression.

I opened my mouth to say something along the lines of it being okay, that I'd make him a cup of tea, but closed it again, realising that, yet again, I honestly couldn't think of a thing Alex might have to say that I wanted to hear. Besides that, it was good to have my little sister holding my side, sticking up for me, and I didn't feel inclined to lay that to waste.

Alex left soon afterwards. But a few days later, he was back. And the day after that. Until one day I was upstairs painting—without my headphones on—and I overheard Violet at the door saying, "Look, I don't mean to be unkind, Alex, but you had your chance, and from what I can gather, you blew it. Lily doesn't want to know any more, okay? So we'd both appreciate it if you'd get lost."

Oh, Violet. But, harsh or not, I couldn't have been too disturbed by her blunt manner of speaking because I didn't rush downstairs to waylay Alex and invite him in. I trusted and hoped that, at some future date, we'd be able to meet up and be civil together. We had so much shared history; I didn't want to lose that. But, even without my feelings for Matt, I was completely sure we weren't right for each other, and I didn't want to get back together with him.

Anyway, after Violet's words, Alex appeared to give up, because he didn't come round again.

My sister's considerate behaviour lasted roughly a week; a happy week during which I really started to believe we were getting somewhere, forging a new relationship with each other. Then slowly, bit by bit, Vi started to return to some of her old ways. People were at the house at all hours. Vi's stuff was all over the place. She forgot to wash up.

I was disappointed. Hurt too. Reluctant to say anything in case we argued again. But Vi was nice enough when our paths did cross, and, anyway, I was submerged in my painting any free moment I got, so if Vi did play music a bit too loudly, I put on my noise-cancelling headphones or played music myself.

Painting so intensely helped me deal with Inga not being in touch, or at least it helped a little. I'd sent her a text—*"Just checking in to see how you are."* But she hadn't replied.

I might have been productive, but I was very tired. So it was nice, one evening, to find Violet in on her own and apparently in a mood to share a meal with me. I cobbled together a meal from store cupboard tins and bits and pieces from the fridge, and Vi and I sat side by side on the sofa to eat it. Afterwards, she washed up, which seemed to take her an absolute age, and when she came back, with a cup of coffee for us both, she didn't seem to be able to relax, not even to watch her favourite soap. It was exhausting, watching her pace around the sitting room, picking things up and putting them down again.

I was about to ask her what was wrong, when she suddenly asked, "D'you ever think about Mum?"

My reply came straight back. "Not if I can help it, no. Do you?"

She was holding the boots she'd discarded earlier on her way into the house, one in each hand. "Only every freaking day," she said, and when she turned to look at me, I noticed there was something odd about her eyes. Her pupils, which had seemed fine while we were eating, now looked dilated and strange.

"Vi," I said. "You haven't taken anything, have you?"

Violet dropped the boots onto the floor with a clatter, amicable Vi gone without a trace. "Oh, that's right," she said, face screwed up unpleasantly. "That's you all over, isn't it? Unpleasant subject? Accuse Violet of doing drugs. You'd do anything to avoid talking about Mum. Well, screw you, Lily."

It was a shock, after a period of us mostly getting on, to have her speak like that to me again, and I watched, fighting back tears as she shoved her feet into her boots and headed for the door.

"Vi," I said. "Please don't go."

She didn't bother to answer, ripping the door open and heading out, undone shoelaces trailing.

I went to the door, calling after her. "Vi!"

But she didn't turn back, and seconds later she was off around the corner, out of sight. So I went wearily back inside, wishing I could turn back time, conflicted all over again about having challenged Vi about taking drugs. She'd seemed so weird, though; so strung up. I'd been worried about her. I hadn't known, either, that she thought about Mum so often. Jesus, no wonder she was wired if she did that. She was right; Mum was a topic I tried to avoid.

But there was no avoiding it now. Vi's accusation had taken the lid off my bad-memory jar, and there they all were, tumbling out for my inspection.

The times before I was old enough to walk home from school on my own when Mum forgot to come and pick me up. Letting myself into the house when I was older to find her passed out on the kitchen floor covered in vomit. Her hurrying upstairs with a man I'd never seen before calling out to me to *"Watch some TV."* Burnt meals, empty cupboards, long days when she slept and I had to entertain myself, retreating into daydreams and drawing, drawing, drawing. Pictures of happy families going for walks and holidays, living in perfect houses. Not drunk people shut away from the sunshine in dirty, neglected houses.

All of it peppered with precious days when it was just me and Mum, and she hadn't been drinking, or not enough to make her anything but merry, and she lavished attention on me, brushing my hair, calling me her beautiful girl, making up stories for me. I had lived for those magical days. But they never lasted, and when Violet arrived, they pretty much dried up altogether.

So yes, Vi. I did my best not to think about Mum.

Would it do any good to tell my sister about those times? To be perfectly honest with her instead of trying to protect her? I wasn't even sure she'd believe me, though, the way she was at the moment. I couldn't invent nice memories for her, and if I gave her an edited version, just focusing on the rare good days I'd shared with Mum, I'd be telling her a lie.

Not that I knew what Mum was like now; she might have turned over a completely new leaf for all I knew. If she was alive, that was.

I got ready for bed, not expecting to be able to sleep. Which was just as well, because I didn't, not a wink. Not until I heard Vi come back in the early hours, anyway. As I listened to her stumbling upstairs to bed, I decided I would try to do what she wanted and speak about Mum. Maybe she did need to hear the truth about what it had been like for me. And maybe I needed to tell it too.

But I didn't see Vi the next day. Or the two days after that. She was either asleep or out when I was around. The next contact I had with my sister was a note on a torn-off scrap of paper left for me to find when I got back from work.

Gone to visit a friend. Back for your exhibition.

I stood there holding the note, searching fruitlessly for more meaning in it, frustrated that she hadn't just told me where she was going instead of writing a note. Perhaps, if I hadn't brought up drugs, she might have done. And there I was, right back in the push and pull of what I should and shouldn't have done with regard to my sister.

Worse still, with Vi away, even with my work and my painting, there was way too much time to think. Inga still hadn't been in touch. It was awful to be estranged from her, out of contact, or whatever this was. It was completely wrong. *I* felt completely wrong without her.

Finally, I got angry. Why the hell was I just sitting around passively to see if Inga got in touch, the way I'd always done with Violet? She'd just lost her mother, for goodness's sake—because I assumed that by now Inga's mother must have passed away. If there was even the slimmest chance of Inga coming to my exhibition, I had to talk to her first. I couldn't just let her discover the truth about my lies about the past through my paintings. I had to tell her in person. I wanted to tell her in person. Not just so she wouldn't be hurt, but because I needed to talk about the whole hideous mess with someone I knew I could trust.

So, I phoned her. But the call went straight to voicemail. I popped round to her house on the off chance that she was back and at home—neither of us had ever felt we had to ring ahead for permission to call round, unless we wanted to be sure we wouldn't have a wasted journey. But she wasn't home.

I went for a walk. Came back. Tried again. Still no answer to my knock.

But this time her neighbour was in her garden—the nosy one who'd complained about Noah crying a few months back. "She's away. Family bereavement."

"Oh," I said. "I knew she was going away, but I thought she'd be back by now."

The neighbour shrugged. "Well, she's not. I've taken in two parcels for her too. Huge things, they are. Taking up far too much space in my hallway."

"Sorry," I said. "I'd offer to take them, but don't live around here, and I haven't got a car."

I turned away to make my lonely way home, miserable that Inga had been dealing with her mother's death all this time without me. I walked this time, taking the scenic route. Only it started raining when I was in the middle of the heath with nowhere to shelter. Even the trees didn't help much, because it was late bloody autumn, and they didn't have any leaves. I wasn't wearing a waterproof, so my fleece jacket was soaked through in seconds.

Chilled to the bone, I finally got home. Stripped off my clothes, wrapped myself in my dressing gown. Ran a bath. The plumbing in my house was ancient. It always had been completely inadequate—on our list to upgrade when we could afford it. Baths took an age to run; longer if you stood in the bathroom waiting for the tub to fill.

I left it to do its work and wandered into the studio to look at my paintings. God, was I really going to display these works? Large scale, uncensored paintings that revealed the deepest regions of my heart and my nightmares, the darkest history of my life. As if I'd made them in my sleep. Or somebody had stolen into my house during the night to put those painful brushstrokes down onto canvases.

Sometimes—often, in fact—I seriously doubted I was brave enough to let anyone else see them. But there was no time to do any others, so it was these or nothing. And cancelling the exhibition would be an even bigger statement—to myself and the world—than accepting it had been. God, I needed to speak to someone.

I tried Inga again. Left another message.

I sat there overwhelmed by a compulsion to speak to Matt. I shouldn't, though, should I? Not now I knew about my true feelings for him. And yet . . . I'd have called him before, wouldn't I? When he'd just been a friend to me. I wouldn't have thought about it. If I wanted to speak to him, I'd just have called. Wouldn't I? I couldn't be sure any longer. I'd lost track of what normal was.

To hell with it.

I picked up my phone again. Dialled.

"Lily! Hi."

He sounded genuinely pleased to hear from me. I wanted to weep. "Is this a good time?"

I could hear muffled traffic. Conversation. Birds—parakeets?—screeching. "I'm just on my way to have dinner with my new boss, but it'll take five minutes to get there, and it won't matter if I'm a bit late. It's great to hear from you. How are you?"

I was about to do my usual thing—to pretend I was okay when I wasn't. But somehow, this time, I couldn't do it. "Honestly?"

"Of course honestly."

"Well, I'm not sure I can exhibit any of the paintings I've made for the exhibition, Violet's gone off somewhere again, and Inga and I fell out just before she went off to Denmark, and now she's not answering my calls. You know her mum died? Or at least, I think she's dead. I'm worried about her, Matt. And Violet. I just want to know they're all right, you know?"

Matt was quiet for a moment. Then he said, "I can't do anything about Violet or Inga. I'm sure they'll get in touch when they're ready." He sighed. "I didn't know about Inga's mother. Poor Ing." He sounded sad to have been out of the loop. "But you know how complicated their relationship always was. Maybe Inga just needs some time to process things?"

"Maybe." I hoped with all my heart that was the truth. That after a while, we could carry on as we'd always been.

"And as for your paintings, I wish I was there to see them. In fact, send me a couple of images now."

I thought doubtfully about *Flayed* and *Phoenix*. Did I really want Matt to see that side of me? "No, it's okay. You're on your way to your meeting."

"How long will it take? Anyway, I told you, it won't matter if I'm a bit late."

I was still reluctant. But then he'd see the pictures at the exhibition, anyway, wouldn't he, if I decided to display them? "Okay."

"I'll call you back as soon as I've seen them."

I went into the studio. Took one photo—of *Phoenix*, the painting that was troubling me the most. Remembered—just in time—to turn the bath taps off. Sent the image to Matt. Then sat, biting my nails, for him to call me.

When he did, he didn't even bother to say hello. "Is that your mother at the bottom of the picture?"

Tears filled my throat. I nodded, even though he couldn't see me. "Yes," I answered, my voice faint.

"And that's you, at the top?"

I swallowed. "Yes. Or it's future me, rather than me now. Or at least, I hope it is." I wasn't sure whether he'd understand or not, but he did.

"It will be you, Lily. It will. I'm a hundred percent sure of it. Lily, you must know how good this painting is, surely? It's one of the most powerful paintings I've ever seen. You have to show it in your exhibition. You have to show all of them."

"You really think so?"

"I really do. Promise me you will."

I sighed. "Okay," I said wearily. "I promise."

"Good. Look, my flight's booked for the evening before your exhibition opening. I can't wait to speak to you properly. About the painting. About everything."

I wasn't sure what "everything" meant to him; whether it meant the same as it would to me. Love. Attraction. I didn't even know what I'd do if it turned out that his feelings had deepened the way mine had done. But I did know I wanted to see him.

"I can't wait to speak to you too," I said.

28

By eight p.m. on the evening before my exhibition, all the paintings were finally in position on the gallery walls.

"It looks fantastic, Lily," Diane told me as we stood side by side in the centre of the room, looking around. "You should be very proud." She considered my expression. "But you're looking worried. What's wrong? We can still make changes if you like."

"No," I hastily reassured her. "I think it's as good as it can be. Thank you so much for all your help and suggestions. I'd have never been able to do it without you."

"But . . . ?" she prompted.

I shrugged. "I'm just a bit scared, I suppose."

Diane clapped me on the shoulder with an *is that all?* expression on her face. "There's nothing to be scared of, Lily, trust me. Your work is amazing. You're going to make so many sales. Truly."

Then she walked off to do some final tidying, artist's insecurities dealt with in her mind, and I knew she hadn't understood what I'd meant at all. Of course it would be good to make sales; very good. In fact, my bank account pretty much demanded it. But that wasn't what I was worried about. It was the fact that my whole life was broadcast all over the gallery walls—my mistakes, my vulnerabilities, my deepest traumas, rawly exposed for everyone to see. Things I barely liked to remember myself blatantly on display to invite questions and opinions.

Some of the paintings were safe enough—my seal paintings, and a recent series of seascapes inspired by my love of Joan Eardley's work at Catterline. I'd painted them at night, the waves and the boats on the beach picked out by the lights from Cromer Pier and the promenade. Diane had literally clapped her hands when she'd seen them, declaring them to be *"really saleable."*

No, I wasn't worried about them. It was the paintings like *Flayed* that made me feel vulnerable and exposed. And of course, in a side room, together with a series of framed, preparatory drawings, the giant canvas of *Phoenix*, the painting I'd promised Matt I'd include.

Suddenly, as I walked with Diane to the gallery door, making the decision to display that painting seemed like the most reckless thing I'd ever done.

"See you here tomorrow at six o'clock, then?"

I nodded. "Six o'clock."

"Sleep well, Lily. And well done."

~

Despite being utterly exhausted, I didn't expect to sleep well that night. Violet was still missing; there'd been no word from her at all. Inga hadn't been in touch, either; I didn't know whether either of them would be coming to the exhibition. I did sleep, though; almost as soon as my head hit the pillow. But it wasn't a restful sleep; all night long I had violent, unsettling dreams.

At seven o'clock the next morning, I was having an anxiety dream about the art gallery being savaged by a huge thunderstorm. Heavy rain was lashing down on my guests, forcing them back home to safety. As thunder cracked deafeningly overhead, a huge bolt of lightning suddenly struck the gallery roof and the whole place caught fire, flames licking high into the sky. Inside the gallery, Diane and I clutched each other, terrified, watching as my artworks spontaneously combusted one by one.

The nightmare moved on—now I was out on the street, desperately searching for something, the storm and the blaze of the gallery fire far behind in the distance. But somehow, despite being away from the storm, the clatter of thunder was still reverberating in my ears, louder than ever.

Then a man's voice jolted me awake. "Police! Stand back from the door!"

What the hell?

I sat up in bed, clutching the duvet to me, utterly terrified as boots clumped up the stairs.

Seconds later, two police officers burst into my bedroom. "Stay where you are!"

"What's happening?" I asked, my voice shaking.

The female officer came towards me. "We have reason to believe class A drugs are being sold from this property, and we have a warrant to search the premises."

Drugs? Shit. What the hell?

"If you could get out of bed, please, madam."

Trembling, I did so, reaching for my dressing gown, thinking about Violet and her friends. The unusual hours. The constant knocks at the door. Kevin saying, *"You know she's a user, don't you?"*

Surely Violet wouldn't have sold drugs from my house, even if she'd been taking them herself? She wouldn't do that to me.

But it turned out that she had. Because the police officers were soon pulling little packets of drugs from the toilet cistern, from beneath Vi's mattress, and even from the top of the kitchen cupboards.

All this time, while I'd been painting, doing my best to blot out Violet's noise, she'd been selling drugs. Letting strangers come round to my house to buy them.

Unless one of the undesirable types she'd invited round to the house had hidden them here and Violet wasn't responsible at all? I so wanted to believe it, but try as I might, I couldn't.

"They aren't mine," I said flatly. "I've no idea how they got here."

The police officer ignored me. "Lily Best, I'm arresting you for intent to supply a class A drug. You do not have to say anything, but it may harm your defence if you do not mention, when questioned, something which you later rely on in court. Anything you do say may be given in evidence. Do you understand?"

I nodded, dumbly, because I did understand, only too well. I understood that my sister didn't care about me much at all. She couldn't, if she'd done this. Jesus. I could end up in prison.

"Can you get dressed, please, madam?"

The nearest thing to hand was the dress I'd hung on the back of my wardrobe ready to wear to the private view that evening—swirly skirt, large floral-inspired pattern in reds, oranges, and blues, designed to inspire confidence. So, while all but the female officer searched the rest of the house, I slipped it over my head and stuffed my feet into my paint-splattered Dr. Martens boots. A sweatshirt and sweatpants would have been more suitable, but who cared what I was wearing? Violet had betrayed me, and because of that I was going to be arrested. Shit. I might miss the opening of my show—after all those months of work. All the sacrifices I'd made, all the pain of laying my heart open on those canvases, might now turn out to have been for nothing.

Thank God little Fitz was safe away from this nightmare with Lewis. He'd have been so frightened when the police battered the door down, he'd probably have bolted out into the traffic. As the police officer clipped handcuffs on my wrists and led me down the stairs, it was the only silver lining I could think of.

When we reached the police station, I was booked in, and my possessions were taken away. There wasn't much—my bag containing my purse, my door keys and my phone, and a seal pendant Inga had given me years ago that I rarely took off. I almost cried when I saw the sergeant at the desk slip it into a little plastic bag. I wasn't sure how this could be happening to me, and how, as it was, my best friend had zero knowledge of it. I didn't even know where she was.

But no, I couldn't, wouldn't cry. I must stay strong and get through this. I'd done nothing wrong, after all. They couldn't send me to prison, surely? Where was the evidence? Except for the drugs hidden everywhere in my house.

~

"I've never used any drugs," I said later in the interview room. "Not heroin, not cocaine, not even cannabis. Nothing."

"Then why did we find class A drugs in your home, Miss Best?" asked the interviewing officer.

"I don't know."

"You don't know how several bags of crystal meth ended up on top of your kitchen cabinets?"

"I do not." Even now, I was protecting Vi. Why, when she clearly didn't give a fig about me? But I knew full well why. Because, after all this time, I still felt guilty about the past.

"Well, I suggest you try and think, because I suspect the courts are unlikely to believe somebody broke into your house without your knowledge to plant them there. Have you had any visitors recently?"

Reluctantly, I nodded. "Yes, my sister, Violet."

"Is it possible that Violet hid the drugs in your home?"

I shrugged, dredging up the theory I'd abandoned hours ago. "I don't think so. She had friends come to visit, though. I suppose one of them could have planted the drugs."

"Where is Violet now?"

"I don't know. She went away. I don't know where." It sounded pathetic. Entirely unbelievable.

"Did she say when she'd be back?"

"She said she'd be back in time for my exhibition. I have an exhibition of my paintings at the Bond Gallery. It opens tonight. She said she'd come."

I pictured the scrawled note Violet had left me. No doubt an empty promise.

"Is this your sister?" The officer placed something on the table between us. Violet's passport. They must have unearthed it during their search of the house.

"Yes," I confirmed, even though the name Violet Best was clearly visible, and they didn't need me to confirm it.

The officer stood up. "Wait here, please, Miss Best." He took the passport from the table and left the room.

I sat back in my chair and closed my eyes, thinking about the exhibition. About my guests arriving soon. But most of all, I thought about Violet hiding those bags of drugs around my house. About how little she must care about me. How very much she must still resent me for leaving her that fateful night.

I wanted suddenly to be held. For someone to comfort and reassure me. A tear ran down my cheek. "Can I please make a phone call?" I asked the police officer standing by the door, my voice broken.

But before she could reply, the door opened, and the detective re-entered the room.

"A witness has confirmed that it was your sister he bought drugs from, not yourself," he said.

What? What did that mean?

"You're free to go for now, Miss Best. We'll be in touch if we need to question you further."

I began to really sob then, not just from relief, but because it was proof of Violet's betrayal of me. I'd wanted us to make a new start. She'd just wanted to use me.

"Is there anyone we can call to come and get you?" the detective asked, his tone kinder now.

There was only one person I wanted to speak to.

"It's Lily," I said when he answered. "I'm at the police station. Can you come?"

When Matt arrived, I threw myself into his arms, and he just held me, letting me sob, and for once I didn't rein myself in. I doubt whether I'd have been able to anyway, even if I'd wanted to. And I didn't want to. I needed comfort. Someone on my side.

"Oh, Matt," I stammered, but before I could launch into an explanation, a drunk guy staggered through the entrance doors, and Matt finally pulled back, keeping a firm grip on my hand.

"Come on. Let's go."

"What happened?" he asked me when we were safely in his car.

I found a tissue in my bag. "Violet's been selling drugs from my house. Hard drugs. They found crystal meth hidden all over the place."

"My God."

I looked at him. "How can she have done this to me, Matt?"

He sighed. "D'you think she could be an addict? It would explain a lot. I know it's no excuse for her doing this to you, but if she couldn't help herself, it might explain her actions a bit."

I shook my head. "I honestly don't know whether it's that, or if she hates me." I looked at him. "You saw my painting, Matt. *Phoenix*. The night our house burned down, I was out with a boy. I left Violet alone with Mum when I should have guessed Mum would just forget about her. Mum went out, God only knows where, and the house caught fire with Vi alone in it. She nearly died, Matt, and I don't think she's ever forgiven me for not being there. For putting myself first that night. Maybe she just thinks she's got a right to treat me the way she does."

"But you were a child, weren't you?" he said. "Your mother ought to have been taking care of Violet, not you. You weren't responsible. None of it was your fault. You have to believe that. You have to forgive yourself."

I knew he was right; I'd probably always known that. But knowing it and feeling it were two very different things. But if someone kept on saying it to me, then maybe the guilt I'd been carrying for so long would start to lift.

"I'll try," I said, my voice quavering with emotion. "I promise I'll try."

"Good."

He was gazing down at me, so dear, so familiar. God, how I loved him. I opened my mouth to say something. Closed it again. Because nothing had changed, had it? He may have raced across town to rescue me from one of the shittiest days of my life. Listened to me. Sympathised with me. Held me. But he was still Inga's ex. And right now, I had no idea where Inga was, or even whether she was coming tonight. If she did come, she mustn't think there was something going on between me and Matt. We might never be able to put things right between us if she did.

But resisting the impulse to pour my feelings out was one of the hardest things I'd ever had to do.

"I'd better get to the gallery," I said. "Diane's expecting me at six."

"Want me to drop you off at home first?" he offered. "I can wait for you."

I shook my head. "No, I can fix my hair and makeup at the gallery. If I'm on time, I won't have to make any excuses to Diane." Or tell any lies. I was done with lies.

So, we set off for my big night—the night I'd been working towards for months. I sat back against the seat and closed my eyes, trying to put my pig of a day behind me, to focus on what was to come in the next few hours.

Oh, God. In a way, the prospect of a room full of people studying my paintings, expressing opinions about my paintings, was every bit as terrifying as my day in a police cell.

"All right?" Matt asked.

I opened my eyes. Shook my head. "Honestly? Not really, no. I'm scared. A part of me wishes I'd never agreed to this exhibition."

"That would be a huge shame for everyone else," Matt said.

"You haven't seen all the paintings," I said. "People might think . . . well, I have no idea what they'll think. That I need help, probably. And maybe they'd be right."

"All good art involves self-exposure, though, doesn't it? People will connect with your work. They'll look at it and see their own sorrows, their own challenges. *Phoenix* will give them hope."

"Don't," I said. "You'll make me cry."

The traffic lights just ahead turned to red. Matt stopped the car and looked at me, reaching for my hand. "It doesn't matter if you do cry," he said. "Just as long as you also laugh. So long as you let yourself feel proud of what you've achieved. Celebrate that achievement."

I swallowed, blinking back tears.

"Believe in yourself, Lily. I do, and after tonight, lots of other people will too. You're going to kill it."

The traffic lights turned amber, then green. Matt let go of my hand to set the car in motion again.

"Thank you," I said. "For saying such wonderful things. For coming to get me. For being here."

For being you.

"I told you before," he said. "I'll always be there for you." He shot me a smile. "But I will just abandon you briefly to pop home and get changed after I've dropped you off, if that's okay? I was doing some clearing out when you called me, which is why I'm dressed like this. I don't want to be wearing tracksuit bottoms for your big night."

Clearing out. Of course he was. He was leaving for Spain very soon, and his house would be rented out to strangers. I'd do well to remember that.

"Of course," I said, telling my first lie after deciding I'd never lie again. "No problem at all."

~

At the gallery, Diane was very pleased to see me.

"I'm so sorry I'm late, Diane."

"Only ten minutes late. Don't worry about it, Lily."

She was so kind. Too kind. If she wasn't careful, I was going to spew all my troubles out to her. And while I was starting to realise it might be a good idea for me to share my true feelings with people more, it didn't seem like such a good plan to do it with someone I had more of a professional relationship with. Especially at the start of a very big night for my career. "I'll just go and fix my hair and make-up. Won't be long."

"Sure. I'll have a glass of wine waiting for you."

"Fantastic, thanks."

There wasn't much chance to drink the wine, though. By the time I emerged from the ladies, Diane was talking to a silver-haired man in an expensive-looking business suit.

"Ah, Lily," she said to me, "I'd like to introduce you to Simon Carter. Simon's an avid art collector, aren't you, Simon? He was just asking me about *Flayed*."

It was surreal to be smiling at Simon; preparing to talk to him about my art when I'd just come from being questioned at a police station, but somehow I did it, and by the end of our conversation, Diane was placing a red *sold* sticker next to *Flayed*, and my mind was spinning. Simon had been so enthusiastic and full of plans for the painting. He'd said he was going to show it to some friends of his, and that he thought it very likely could lead to future commissions. How ironic that such a painful period of my life might lead to my being more financially secure in the future. Not having to worry about how to pay the mortgage at the beginning of the month. Or how to pay for groceries when I went shopping.

Turning from the painting, I looked around to decide who to speak to next, when a figure caught my eye in the room where *Phoenix* was hanging. A very familiar, very dear figure.

Inga. On her own, without Noah.

I wondered vaguely where he was, resisting the urge to call out her name. Run to her. Pull her into my arms. But I restrained myself— because who knew if she'd want me to do any of those things after the way we'd parted—and went to stand quietly beside her instead.

She didn't turn to acknowledge me. Didn't speak. So, I didn't either.

I watched her drinking in every tortured brushstroke. The greedy flames, licking the dark sky as they devoured my childhood home. My treacherous mother, at the bottom of the painting, running away from the chaos into a thick, concealing forest. Violet, held back in strong arms as she reached up screaming into the night sky, attempting to catch a bird woman flying from the flames. A phoenix, wings spread, the detailed feathers reflecting the colours of the fire, beating strongly to take me—for the phoenix was definitely me; my head was painted onto the phoenix's body—up and away from pain and disaster.

Little pieces of my soul were embedded into the pigment and texture of every brushstroke. Painting it had demanded—and taken— everything from me. Now, here was that everything on display for the whole world to see. For Inga to see.

And I knew that what she very likely saw most strongly was the hard evidence of those things I'd always kept from her. Everything I ought always to have shared with her, my best friend, had I been able to fully trust our friendship.

Finally, she said, "This is all true, isn't it? I mean, I know you're not secretly a bird or anything, but this really happened to you, didn't it? A house fire. Your mother leaving."

I didn't ask how she knew the figure at the bottom of the painting was my mother, because I'd painted the woman as I imagined Mum would still look if she were here now—as an older version of me.

"Yes."

"You lied about her dying of breast cancer."

It wasn't a question; it was a statement. But I answered it anyway.

"Yes. I'm so sorry."

She shook her head, and I could see the glitter of tears in her eyes. "For fuck's sake, Lily. All these years. Why the bloody hell couldn't you trust me with the truth?"

Shame washed right through me. I'd always taken the easy way out. Lying, refusing to think about that night and its terrible aftermath.

Except that doing that hadn't been the easy way out at all, had it? Not if it made me lose the love and the respect of one of the people I cared about most in the world.

"It wasn't just you, Ing. I didn't tell anybody about it." I gestured towards the painting. "I thought my mum was dead. I stood there watching our house burn down, and I begged and begged the firemen to go back in to search for her. And all the time, she was gone. She went out without me knowing and left my sister all on her own with about a hundred burning candles and she never came back. Violet almost *died*, Ing. Our lives were utterly destroyed. Can you really blame me for not wanting to talk about that?"

Inga swiped a hand across her eyes and looked at me for a moment before turning back to the painting. "I would have told you, if something like that had happened to me," she said, and I knew it was true. *Then maybe you're stronger than me*, I might have said, but she was talking again, so I didn't get the chance.

"It feels as if I've never known you properly all this time if our friendship has never been based on truth."

Panic clawed at my belly. "Don't say that. Please. Our friendship means everything to me. I've missed you so much these past few weeks. You've been gone ages." I paused, waiting for her to say something. When she didn't, I said. "I'm so sorry about your mum. I assume she . . ."

She glanced very briefly at me. "Died? Yes, she's gone. Then, after the funeral, I went trekking with my cousin Olaf and his wife."

I stared at her in disbelief. "Trekking? You and Noah?"

She turned in my direction again, not quite smiling, but almost. "Yes, I do realise how unlikely that sounds."

That almost smile encouraged me. Maybe a little too much. "You couldn't stand hearing owls in your back garden, let alone . . . ," I started to say, but I immediately regretted it, knowing it would remind her of the home she'd shared with Matt.

But Inga just shrugged. "I couldn't, could I?" she said. "Well, somehow, Olaf and Ida managed to convert me. We went to a place called Thy—it's a wilderness park. Olaf carried Noah in the papoose. It was tough, but kind of restful, as well. All that nature; time to think. I wish I'd got to know Olaf and Ida sooner, actually. I could really talk to them about Mum."

I tried to imagine Inga walking in such a place without complaining about it the whole time and couldn't do it. It was far easier to imagine her at the hospital, at her mother's bleak bedside.

"Did you get the chance to speak to your mum before she died?"

Inga seemed to draw back, even though she stayed exactly where she was. As if the privilege I'd always enjoyed of knowing the innermost recesses of her heart had been withdrawn.

"Oh yeah," she said when she finally answered. "We spoke. She said that when I was growing up, we had so little in common she was convinced I'd been swapped at the hospital. That she'd come home with the wrong baby."

I could see her there, seated alongside her dying mother, hearing that, dealing with that, and I wanted to take her hand. But I didn't quite dare to. "I'm so sorry."

Another shrug. "I could have told her how I fantasised every day about being adopted. About my real mother turning up one day to claim me. But you can't say things like that to a dying woman, can you? There are some things you have to keep to yourself. So, I said nothing."

"There are some things you have to keep to yourself." Even if Inga hadn't meant it that way, my guilty conscience made it feel like a dig at me for letting Harry in on her secret.

I'm sorry, I wanted to say. *I shouldn't have interfered.*

But instead I changed the subject. "Where's Noah? Did you find a babysitter?"

Again, that casual, slightly withdrawn tone. "Yes. I can't leave him long, though."

I wanted to ask who she'd left him with, but Diane was approaching us.

"Lily, I'm so sorry to interrupt, but I have someone interested in speaking to you about your seascapes. Can I steal you away for a few minutes, please?"

I didn't want to go, not with everything still unresolved with Inga, with her still so obviously cool towards me.

But Inga smiled for Diane's benefit. "It's okay," she said. "I haven't even looked at your other paintings yet, Lily. I'll catch up with you again later."

So off I went with Diane, a mass of stuffed-down emotions and insecurities, vaguely registering Amy and her boyfriend making their way into the gallery, waving to her, mouthing that I'd see her later. I was pleased to see her here; really pleased. But it was almost as if I was experiencing it all through a thick, choking fog.

Matt arrived hard on Amy's heels—dressed now in smart trousers and a denim shirt. He stood for a moment, looking around. Spotted me. Lifted a hand in greeting. Smiled. Then I saw Inga walk over to him.

"Lily, I'd like you to meet Lorraine and Ian Collins," Diane was saying, forcing me from the fog; from the sight of Matt bending to kiss Inga's cheek.

Somehow I smiled and shook the couple's hands, doing my best not to speculate about what Matt and Inga were saying to each other and to give myself over to their compliments about my seascapes.

By the time I'd finished with the couple, Inga and Matt weren't alone. Alex was with them too. Alex, who I hadn't seen since Violet had told him in no uncertain terms not to come round to my house anymore.

I walked nervously over to them, noticing, to my surprise, that Alex had Lola strapped to his front. Perhaps one thing had turned out all right then.

"Hello, Alex. Hi, Matt," I said, joining them.

Matt bent to kiss my cheek, not giving any sign of how recently we'd seen each other. "Congratulations, Lily. I haven't had the chance to look around yet, but from what I can see, this looks amazing."

I felt like an actor in a play. One I hadn't learnt the words for. "Thank you."

Alex had a bouquet of pink roses in his hand. He held them out to me. "Hi, Lily. Congratulations." As I took them, I remembered the faded garage forecourt flowers and Vi, and the way she'd dealt with them.

"I brought you these," he said. "Stupid idea, really, I suppose. I don't imagine you've got any vases, or any time to arrange them either."

"Not at all. It was a lovely thought."

The two of us were like polite acquaintances, not two people who'd made love on a hillside, overlooking the cathedral. We'd been *engaged*. If it hadn't been for Alex letting slip about his feelings about having children, we might even be married by now.

One of the rose thorns pricked my finger, drawing a speck of blood. I sucked it away, seeing Inga notice, wondering whether she was thinking what I was thinking—that the roses were a lot like my relationship with Alex—beautiful but secretly harmful, destined to slowly wilt and die.

But no, of course, she wasn't thinking any such thing. Not with our argument and everything I had kept from her still lying between us.

"It's good to see you with Lola," I said to Alex. "Are you and Fliss back together?"

"No, not exactly. But she has been letting me see Lola."

"That's great."

"I'm really glad you talked her round, mate," Matt said.

"Well, I had to, didn't I?" Alex said. "I couldn't give up on Lola. Besides, I had some help."

"Who from?" Inga asked.

Alex looked suddenly embarrassed. "Remember my uncle?"

"The one you told us about in Wales?" Inga asked. "The guy who spoke to you in the chicken-processing factory?"

Back in Wales, when the four of us had still been firm friends. Before life had intervened and we'd lost our innocence. When my friendship with Inga had seemed as unbreakable as diamonds.

Alex nodded. "Yes. I had a dream about him. We were at the pub, the two of us. I was the age I am now, and my uncle was the age he was when he died. We were chatting about football, I think, then suddenly, out of the blue, he changes the subject. Tells me Fliss is depressed. That all her micromanagement and doing everything to the clock for the baby are because it's the only way she can see for things not to totally fall apart."

"Blimey, Alex," Inga said, and just for a second, it was almost like the old days; the four of us united again. "What did you do?"

"As soon as I woke up, I went round to talk to Fliss, and she . . . well, she just crumbled and admitted it. Honestly, it was carnage; she's crying, Lola's crying, I'm crying."

"It can be bloody overwhelming, being a new mum," Inga said.

I looked at her, remembering the times she'd been at the end of her rope with Noah, but she avoided my gaze, saying, "Believe me, I know."

I saw Matt look at her. Knew that in other circumstances, he'd have asked whether she was all right.

"I'm getting the help I need now, though," she went on. "So everything's fine. As is Fliss, I hope, Alex?"

He nodded. "Yes, she's getting lots of support now. I think it just helps knowing that she's been feeling the way she has because she's got postnatal depression and not because she's a bad mother. And she's started to trust me enough to have Lola again. Oh, and get this, the thing that settles Lola down quicker than anything else is me playing my guitar to her. Isn't that great?"

I watched Inga reach out to stroke Lola's hair, a gentle, moving gesture that somehow made my heart ache.

"Are you a music fan, then, Lola?" she said, and I remembered Alex strumming his guitar outside the cottage in Wales. Matt and I in the kitchen making dinner, Matt having just told me about the job in London. Me doing my level best to act as if a bomb hadn't just gone off in my life.

A bit like now, really, standing and speaking to my friends when Inga and I still hadn't properly made things up and just a few hours ago I'd been arrested and hauled off to the police station for questioning.

"It is a big thing, you know, to trust someone else with your child," Inga said. "Even when it's their child too."

I wondered whether she was talking about Harry. Whether she'd seen him again. Whether, in fact, it was Harry who was taking care of Noah right now.

"Where is Noah?" Matt asked. "I was hoping to meet him."

Was that really true? Or was it yet another example of Matt's kindness? Whatever, it was a hopeful sign. A sign the two of them might be—if not exactly friends in the future, at least civil towards each other.

But before Inga could answer, someone spoke to me.

"Excuse me. Sorry to interrupt."

I turned to see who it was and saw a familiar-looking middle-aged man I couldn't immediately place.

"I'm Beryl's son," he explained. "Beryl from the hospital? She was one of your patients?"

Tom. Of course it was.

"Of course. Tom," I said, and he nodded.

"That's right."

"I'm so sorry for your loss," I said. "You mum was the sweetest person. I loved our chats."

He nodded sadly. "Thanks. Yes, she loved chatting to you too. Always said it was the highlight of her day when you were on the ward." He paused for a moment, then said, "That's why I'm here, actually."

"Oh?" I couldn't imagine what he meant, but he'd brought a bit of Beryl to my exhibition, so I was really glad he was here.

"Yes. Mum told me about your exhibition before she died. She asked me to come and give you this."

For the first time, I noticed he had something in his hands—a book of some sort—and now he held it out to me.

"It's one of her journals; the one she kept when she went to New Zealand. She wanted you to have it. Made me promise to come and give it to you. She thought it might inspire some paintings."

"Oh," I said, taking it from him, holding it as if it were something uniquely precious. Which, of course, it was. "Thank you. This means so much to me."

He nodded. "She thought it would. Anyway, I won't stop if you don't mind. I have to get back to London tonight. Good luck with your exhibition."

"Thank you. And thank you so much for coming. For bringing this."

"It was my pleasure."

As he walked away, I opened the journal with shaking fingers, and when I saw Beryl's bold, slanted handwriting, tears rushed to my eyes. Instinctively, I looked up, seeking Matt out. Matt, who knew how much Beryl had meant to me, because I'd told him that night he'd come round when Alex was drunk and emotional.

"That's really special, Lily," he said, returning my smile.

I hugged the book to my chest. "It really is."

But then I glanced over at Inga and saw she was frowning.

"You haven't told me anything about Beryl," she said, and it sounded like an accusation. As if it was another thing I'd deliberately kept from her. She was glancing between Matt and me, too, and I knew she'd noticed our closeness.

I opened my mouth to speak, but she stopped me.

"Sorry," she said. "I've got to get back to Noah soon. He'll be needing a feed. I'd better look at the rest of the exhibition. Coming, Alex?"

"Sure," Alex said. "We can talk babies between pictures."

In other circumstances, I might have laughed. These were not other circumstances, though, so I watched the two of them move off together, leaving me alone with Matt, feeling about as bleak as it was possible to feel, noting vaguely that the course Alex was on would soon take him to *Flayed*.

How crazy life was. Not much more than a year ago Alex would have been standing at my side at this exhibition, supporting me, speaking to my guests with me, taking me home afterwards. And now there was a painting about how heartbroken I'd been when he left me displayed on the wall for everyone to see. And even that was out of date, because I'd fully accepted and moved on from our break-up.

"I think," I said to Matt, "Alex is going to flip when he sees the next painting."

"He'll cope," Matt said. "Especially with Lola in his arms. Try not to worry. Enjoy your big night. All your fabulous paintings. Your hard work."

Oh, God.

Had he noticed Inga's expression just then when she'd looked at the two of us? Had he interpreted it the way I had?

Matt nudged me. "Isn't that Violet?" he said.

I looked up, and sure enough, there was my sister, dressed in a dramatic full-length black dress which showed off her purple hair.

She'd come. To support me? To ruin my big night? I had no idea. And it didn't much matter, anyway, did it? Because it would get ruined anyway as soon as I told her I'd been arrested. That she was very likely going to be arrested herself sometime soon. And I had to tell her. I couldn't just make conversation about the exhibition or the number of guests or the bloody weather and not mention the fact that she'd deliberately concealed class A drugs in my home.

I needed, suddenly, to get away. Not from the gallery—I couldn't do that to Diane after all her hard work—but at least to the ladies' cloakroom for a few minutes.

"Excuse me," I said to Matt. "I'll be back in a minute." And I made my way through my guests, doing my best to avoid eye contact with anyone in case I was drawn into a conversation.

When I made it safely to the cloakroom, I found Amy in there, touching up her lipstick.

"Lily!" she said when she saw me, her voice lit with pleasure. "I absolutely love your exhibition. It's fantastic." Then she took a closer look at my face and frowned. "But wait, are you okay?"

I had a sudden desire to laugh. "Yes, I'm okay. Just preparing myself for a confrontation with my sister." I forced a smile. "Don't worry, it's all right. Just a little more drama in the shit show of my life. I bet you're glad you've left me and my messes behind you, aren't you?"

Amy shook her head. "Not at all. You're my friend, Lily. Anytime you need to talk, about anything, you can give me a call. You do know that, don't you?"

Her kindness had me blinking away tears. "Thanks. That means a lot."

She squeezed my hand. "D'you want me to wait and go back out there with you?"

I shook my head. "No, really. I'll be okay in a minute."

"Sure?"

"Sure. Thanks, Amy."

When I emerged from the cloakroom a few minutes later, I could see Matt talking to Alex and Inga again. There was no sign of Violet, so I moved further into the room and spotted her in the room off the main gallery, standing in front of *Phoenix*.

I walked over. Stood by her side, just as I'd done earlier with Inga.

"Well, would you look at that," she said, her voice wickedly sarcastic. "My sister, flying free without me. How absolutely fucking nice for you, Lily."

I sighed. "It's not like that, Violet. You know it's not."

"No? Look at you in that painting. You aren't thinking about me at all. You're headed for the sky with absolutely no thought of turning back for me."

I looked at the phoenix woman in the painting, wings spread, ready to take her up into the beautiful clouds and out over the shimmering sea, and I sighed.

"The painting's just a fantasy, Vi, that's all. It's not real. I've always been there for you. I'll always love you." I looked at her. "Even when you go behind my back and hide drugs in my house. Sell drugs from my house."

She looked away from me, back at the painting.

"How could you do that to me, Vi?" I asked. "The police came to the house this morning. I was arrested."

I was going to go on to tell her there was a real chance she'd be arrested soon, too, but there were tears streaming down her face; tears I hadn't seen since she was a little girl, when she'd begged to go home with me, instead of letting the foster mother take her away again.

"Oh, Vi," I said, reaching out to her, but she flinched away, swiping at her tears as if she despised them.

"You have no idea what it's been like for me all these years, living with what happened that night," she said, and I frowned, moving closer to her because she'd spoken so quietly. "I need the drugs. It's the only way I can forget."

For Violet it had been drugs. For me, it had been art. My friends. Lies. We were both broken.

"Why did you stop wanting to see me?" she asked, swiping away her tears. "Losing Mum, the house, then you, on top of it all. It was too much. It fucking broke me, Lily."

I frowned, shocked by her words. "Wait a minute," I said, "I didn't stop wanting to see you at all. Your foster mother rang to say you didn't want to see me anymore!"

She looked at me pityingly. "And you believed her? That woman was an absolute shit, Lil. She shut me in my room on my own for hours at a time. Made me sit at the table until I'd eaten every bit of her lousy meals. Of course I wanted to see you. I was eight years old, and my fucking world had just ended."

I stood there, reeling as if she'd hit me, remembering the way I'd sobbed my heart out after that phone call. And all the time, the foster mother had lied. She'd known what had just happened to me and Vi, and she'd lied to keep us apart.

"Why would she do such a wicked thing?" I asked.

Vi shrugged. "To make her life easier? Because she was a bitch? I don't know. You should have tried harder, though, Lil. You should have fucking tried harder."

I should have; she was right. I'd only been sixteen, but I'd possessed a bucketful of experience of being let down by adults. I shouldn't have blindly accepted what the woman had told me as the truth. "You do believe me, though, don't you, Vi?" I said now.

She sighed. "I don't know. I guess. It doesn't even matter anymore, does it? That's not why I came here tonight, anyway."

I dragged the back of my hand across my eyes. "Why did you come?"

Her expression changed. There was a glint of something like triumph on her face.

"Vi?" I said. "What is it?"

"I've found her," she said. "I've found Mum."

I reeled back. "What?"

"That's where I've been; visiting a mate in London who's good with computers. He tracked her down in Scotland. She's living in some commune near Stonehaven, in Scotland."

Stonehaven. Literally a few miles from Catterline, Joan Eardley's home. How was that even possible? It was as if I was dreaming all this. I'd wake up soon in my own bed, and the whole of this God-awful day would turn out to have been a nightmare.

I shook my head, wanting to reject the information.

"And get this," Vi carried on. "D'you want to know how my mate found her? There was this old article about Mum's prize-winning vegetables." She nodded at me. "Yeah, you did hear right. All this time we've been picking up the fucking pieces of our shit lives, and Mum's been happily growing carrots and potatoes."

I couldn't speak. What was there to say? It was unbelievable. And yet, at the same time, deep inside me, I knew it was the truth.

When my silence stretched on, Vi shrugged. "It's true. I've seen the newspaper article online. Anyway, I thought I'd go up there. Have things out with her." Her gaze dropped. Then she said, her tone carefully casual, "You could come with me if you like."

But I never got the chance to answer. Because at that moment the police arrived at the gallery to arrest Vi.

"Violet Best," one of them said, while his companion pinned Violet's arms behind her back. "I'm arresting you on suspicion of possessing and supplying a controlled drug. You do not have to say anything, but it may harm your defence if you do not mention, when questioned, something which you later rely on in court. Anything you do say may be given in evidence. Do you understand?"

A sob rose in my throat. I reached out a helpless hand in Vi's direction, watching as she struggled against the officer holding her.

"Please," I said. "Don't hurt her."

"Lily?" Violet said, sounding small and afraid.

Diane appeared at my side. "Lily?" she said. "Is everything all right?"

I had no words to reassure her. Because of course everything wasn't bloody all right. My sister was being arrested in full view of everyone at the exhibition opening. And what's more, her eyes were now blazing at me with utter contempt.

"You told them I'd be here, didn't you?" she spat at me. "I can't believe you did that, Lily. I hate you. I fucking hate you!"

29

I went straight to the police station after Violet had been taken away, leaving the stunned onlookers in the gallery, not even looking back when someone—Matt, I think—called my name. Past the closed shops, up by the side of the market and along the front of city hall to Bethel Street.

When I explained to the officer at reception why I was there, he advised me to go home.

"With a charge like that, there's no telling how long you'll have to wait for news."

I turned away to head for the waiting area, then turned back again, remembering the long hours I—an innocent person—had been detained for, realising he was right.

"Will someone call me, when there's news?"

"Are you her next of kin?"

"Yes."

"Then, yes, someone will call you."

So, I left the police station, passing in front of city hall again, gazing bleakly at the view of the flood-lit castle up on its mound beyond the market and the shops. The castle Mum might have taken Vi and me to as kids had she been a different kind of mum, to ride in the replica of Boudica's chariot pretending to be escaping from Romans. To run off giggling when the ancient stuffed tiger roared at us from its display case in the taxidermy exhibit.

Instead, I'd first gone to the castle with Inga, when we were art students in search of inspiration, swooning at the watercolour collection, enthralled by the mummified cat from ancient Egypt. Inga, my partner in crime, the two of us laughing together, delighting in each other, having fun. All despite my secret sorrow about Violet's whereabouts and the door I'd locked and bolted against the trauma of my past.

Please let me and Inga have fun together again. Take Noah to the castle together when he's older. Or to the coast, seal spotting or making sandcastles, paddling in the freezing-cold North Sea and laughing as we eat ice creams that melt quicker than we can finish them. Let little Noah learn about love just by spending time with the two of us.

It took half an hour to walk home from the city. It was a jolt to see my front door boarded up. How the hell had I forgotten about the police raid? But somehow, with the dramatic events of the evening, I had, and after letting myself in through the back door into the kitchen, I found drawers and cupboards hanging open and piles of my belongings stacked on the floor. Nothing in its right place. A state of chaos.

Just like my life.

I went into the living room. Discovered exactly the same state of disarray there as in the kitchen. Sofa cushions pulled off and uncaringly dumped on the floor. Books all over the place on the shelves. My precious Joan Eardley book tossed face-down on the hearth rug, as if someone had discarded it after flipping through it searching for . . . what? Certainly not inspiration for paintings.

All so utterly sordid. As if my home and my feelings were of absolutely no account. Like I was nothing.

I sank to the floor, picking up the Joan Eardley book and closing it, suddenly remembering the gift Beryl's son had given me before everything had imploded at the gallery. Beryl's New Zealand journal.

Taking it from my bag, I stroked the cover, tracing the sloped writing on the label. *New Zealand, 2015.*

Beryl must have been around seventy-five in 2015. How fabulous that she'd continued doing the work she loved for so long.

Opening the journal at random, I read the first sentence my eyes settled on.

Stewart Island is a veritable birding paradise. Yesterday, at dusk, I glanced up from the Gunnera hamiltonii specimens I was studying to see a kiwi feeding right near me! So adorable. Such a rare treat. I stayed perfectly still and managed to reach in my pocket for my pencil. Hardly the world's best sketch, but it will serve as a reminder of that special, privileged moment. I'm so blessed.

On the opposite page was a sketch of the flightless kiwi bird, intent on feeding, its long bill poking about on the ground. I could picture Beryl drawing it. Could visualise her glee as she transferred her delight onto paper.

Oh, Beryl. If she were here with me now, sitting across from me and saying, *"Come along, dear. It does no good at all to keep one's demons bottled up,"* I'd talk to her this time. Tell her everything. Talk about my lost, frightened sister. The current fragility of my friendship with Inga. My exhibition opening, which had ended in such dramatic disarray. Matt, leaving for Spain. And along the way, I'm sure I'd start to sob, the way I was doing right now. And Beryl would hold me the way I so badly needed to be held, soothing me while I described the lonely, fearful years of my childhood; years filled with responsibility I'd been far too young to shoulder. Keeping my sister safe. Keeping us both afloat.

I closed the journal, stroking the front cover, careful not to let my tears fall on it. Then I put it carefully down to read later, when my mind wasn't as churned up as the sea in one of Joan Eardley's paintings.

I thought again of how incredible it was that my mother was living so close to where the artist had lived and worked; the place I'd always longed to visit. I didn't know what such a coincidence meant, if indeed it meant anything at all. For if it was fate, then it was a very twisted kind of fate.

A text came through on my phone. Inga.

Hope you're OK? Call me in the morning. X

Tears welled up all over again. That kiss at the end of her message made me feel a lot less alone. Gave me hope we'd be able to sort out the issues between us.

I was just typing my reply when my phone rang. It was the police to tell me that Vi had been charged with possession with intent to supply class A drugs and was due to appear at the magistrate's court in the morning.

"Will she get bail?"

"I'd say that's very unlikely. In cases like these, the defendant is usually considered to be a flight risk."

It was all too easy to imagine Vi doing something drastic to escape the consequences of her actions. Stuffing a few clothes in a bag and scarpering. After all, she'd vanished for years at a time already, hadn't she?

"Thank you for letting me know." I could hear my calm voice, asking methodical questions. The shut-off me instead of the new, emotional me. "D'you know what prison she'll be held in?"

"Most likely HMP Peterborough."

Peterborough—two hours away by car. Not that I had a car. But there was a train station, wasn't there? Of course there was. Peterborough was quite a big city.

"Will I be able to visit her?"

"If she fills out a visitor request form for you, yes."

Would she, though? There had been such vitriol on Vi's face when she was arrested.

"But it'll take a while to get that set up. As I say, everything will be decided in court tomorrow. I'll let you know the outcome then."

"Thank you."

After the police officer ended the call, I sat for a while, staring vacantly down at my phone, trying to take it all in. Wondering whether a stint of prison would make things worse for Violet—bring her into contact with the kind of people who'd drag her down further—or whether it might mark a turning point if she had no access to drugs. I had no idea, but one thing was for certain, it was completely out of my control.

Suddenly noticing I had a voicemail message, I played it back. It was from Matt—he must have left it shortly after I'd left the gallery.

"Hi, Lily. I hope you're okay. Well, I know you won't be okay at all, of course not. I'm so sorry. Give me a call when you get this. Any time. Doesn't matter how late it is."

I called him back straightaway, suddenly longing to hear his voice. But despite what he'd said about calling as late as I liked, there was no answer, and the call went to voicemail.

I left a message. "Hi, Matt, it's me, Lily. Thanks for your message. I got back about half an hour ago. Vi's been charged. She's due in court tomorrow. And Matt, they don't think she'll get bail. They think she'll go to prison. Anyway, I'll try you again tomorrow, okay? Thanks for all you did for me today. It meant so much. Bye for now."

Next morning, I was outside the Bond Gallery the minute it opened, on the dot of nine.

Diane didn't give me the chance to say anything; she just took me into her arms for a great big hug.

When we drew back, we both spoke at the same time.

"I'm so sorry."

"I'm so sorry."

Diane smiled. "Lily, it wasn't your fault."

"I know, but even so . . ."

"There is no 'even so.' And look, it didn't make any difference, anyway. See how many of your pictures sold?"

I looked. Saw she was right. There were red dots beside many of my pictures, each one indicating a sale. I choked up looking at them—seal paintings, sea paintings, *Flayed*, all sold. An unkind little inner voice wanted to tell me I didn't deserve it, but I pushed it away determinedly. Why shouldn't I deserve it? I'd worked so hard for this. Even the desperate sketches and watercolours I'd done in my bedroom as a child had contributed something to these paintings. People hadn't bought them out of pity. They'd bought them because they liked them.

"The exhibition's already a big success, and it's only just opened," Diane said with a smile. Then her phone began to ring. "Take a look around and rejoice while I answer this."

As Diane took her call, I was drawn to the side room off the main gallery. To *Phoenix*. I stood in front of it—in the spot where I'd stood so recently with Inga, and then with Vi—taking the picture in all over again. Somehow, now that I knew Mum was alive, it was different. The phoenix's wings beat a little less secure. Vi's desperate lament was more poignant. Mum's backward glance as she hastened away was even more furtive. Had I painted the truth? What had actually happened to mum that night?

Suddenly, I knew I had to find out.

30

I called Matt again from the car-hire centre later that morning while I was waiting to be served. Once again, there was no answer.

"Hi, Matt. It's me again." I paused, not wanting to tell him in public that Vi had been sent to HMP Peterborough to await trial, or that I was about to set off on a trip to meet my long-lost mother. "I've got lots to tell you. Give me a call when you can. If I don't answer straightaway, it'll be because I'm driving. Hope you're okay. Bye for now."

Then, after I'd signed the paperwork for the car and was seated behind the steering wheel, I phoned Inga.

When she answered, I could hear Noah in the background sounding fretful. "Hi," Inga said. "I've been thinking about you. Wait a minute, let me just get the boy latched on, then we can talk."

I waited for a moment until she told me she was ready, then filled her in.

"God, Lily. That's a lot. What you must be feeling! So Violet actually gave you your mum's address?"

"Yes. I'm going up to Scotland to see her. I'm actually sitting in a hire car right now."

I'm not sure what response I'd expected, but it wasn't what I got. I'd imagined her saying, *"Go for it! Tell the bitch exactly what you think of her!"* But what she actually said was, "Are you sure that's a good idea? After all, she's rejected you once, hasn't she?"

An image of Kevin in the Nottingham café returned to me suddenly, him sitting opposite me there, calmly rejecting any further contact with Vi. Hateful, indifferent. A total bastard.

"I'm not going with the expectation of a happy ever after, Ing." I wasn't sure whether I was trying to convince her or myself. "I'm going because I need to hear the truth about what happened. Why she did what she did."

Inga sighed on the other end of the line. "I suppose I can understand that. I just don't want you to get hurt, that's all. Look, keep in touch, okay? And take care of yourself."

"I will," I said, feeling emotional and pathetically grateful that she wanted me to keep in touch. That she was worried about me. "I'm not planning to be away for long. Only a few days. Can I come over when I get back? So we can talk?"

"Lil, of course you can bloody well come over. Noah and I need to give you a big hug. We do need to talk, you're right. But we'll sort things out. I love you, okay? Even if you are an interfering idiot."

The sound I made was part laugh, part sob. "I love you too. I'm so sorry, Ing."

"Save it," she said as Noah made a squawk. "We're good. Really. Though I ought to tell you, Matt gave me a lift home from the gallery, and . . . well, I told him about the abortion."

My body was suddenly chilled right through in the icebox of the stationary car. Shit. I'd wanted Inga to tell Matt the truth for so long, but now she had . . . He'd know I'd kept the abortion secret from him all this time.

Was that why I couldn't reach him? Did he hate me for it?

"It was high time he knew," Inga was saying now.

I swallowed. "How . . . how did he take it?"

She sighed. "He didn't say much, to be honest. But it was obvious he was really upset. It was pretty awful, actually. I guess it might mean we don't see much of each other in the future, which is sad." Another sigh. "I don't know, Lil, in some ways I wish I'd just kept it to myself, you know? But I thought—" She broke off. "But look, we can talk more about it when you get back from Scotland, can't we?"

"Yes, okay," I said, feeling suddenly weary, the nine-hour journey ahead of me a daunting prospect.

Noah's squawks had become cries by now.

"Look, I'd better go," Inga said. "Drive carefully, won't you? Bye, Lil."

"Bye, Ing. See you soon."

I ended the call and put my phone away. Punched the address of the inn I'd booked to stay at in Catterline, Aberdeenshire, into the satnav. Drove out of town and stopped at the first service station to call Matt again.

Once again, he didn't answer. I left another message. "Matt, hi. I've just spoken to Inga. She told me . . . Look, are you all right? Call me, won't you? I'll most likely be driving—I'm actually on my way to Scotland—but I'll call you back as soon as I can. Okay, speak soon. Bye, Matt."

I kept the volume up loud on my phone the whole way to Catterline. But Matt didn't call.

31

The wind was whipping up the sea, sending froth and spray through the air to wet my face. The day after my marathon journey up to Scotland, I was standing where Joan Eardley had stood all those years ago, my ears filled with the sound of shingle scraping against shingle on the beach as the tide drew the water back. Seabirds were squawking in the sky, battling with the wind. And beyond, stretching towards the distant horizon, the heaving, rolling mass of gunmetal grey that was the sea. Cold, wet, loud.

Perfect for taking every other thing from my mind, including the fact that Matt still hadn't called me and that later that day, if everything went to plan, I'd be meeting Mum again after all this time.

Here, on the beach, with its distinctive rows of cottages standing on the cliff behind me, I recalled the images I'd seen of Joan in the 1960s, dressed for the weather in her oilskins; what I'd read about her having to battle her way down from her cottage with her painting equipment, her painting boards catching the wind like a sail. How on more than one occasion one of them had been torn from her grasp and blown away over someone's roof and into their back garden. Even when she'd successfully got a board down to the beach, she'd had to anchor it somehow to keep it on her easel.

And the cold. This morning even though I was dressed in modern-day materials designed for inclement weather, my face was pinched and frozen, and the wind was penetrating every exposed nook and cranny of my clothing.

Come on, then; if you're going to draw, draw.

Suddenly it was as if Joan Eardley was there with me, looking over my shoulder with impatience. So, I took out my sketchbook—a sturdy, hardback one—securing the edges of the pages with the clothes pegs I'd brought for the purpose—and balanced it on my knees to draw the shifting, crashing sea with large, sweeping strokes and scribbles.

You need paint, Joan seemed to say, and she was right. If I'd had paint, I'd have been able to splatter and smudge it onto the paper to better convey the experience of the wild, breaking waves. Later, if it was still light, after I'd been to visit Mum, I'd return here. Something told me I'd need the release of flinging paint about.

The fine spray blowing from the sea grew wetter. It had begun to rain. While I didn't feel precious about my drawings, my pencil and charcoal wouldn't work on wet paper, so reluctantly I packed up my things, casting a regretful glance at the sea before turning to walk back up to the inn, the coming afternoon and all it might hold casting a shadow over me.

~

The farm where Mum lived wasn't easy to find. But, after turning the hire car round numerous times, not a particularly easy procedure on a narrow country road for someone as rusty at driving as I was, I drove up a bumpy track that led to a rambling, redbrick farmhouse with a hotchpotch of outbuildings.

Chickens ran towards me as I got out of the car, and a pair of eager-looking goats in a paddock drew themselves up comically on their hind legs to bleat at me over the fence. I'd never wanted to laugh less, though, comical goats or no comical goats. Was this really where Mum lived? In this place with washing blowing on the line to the side of the house and rows and rows of vegetables growing in neat ranks in the borders?

No, surely Vi's friend must have made a mistake.

As I hesitated, wondering whether or not to go and knock, a battered Land Rover approached the farmhouse from the way I'd come. I watched its progress, one hand shielding my eyes from the sun until it reached me, and the engine died.

The driver's door opened. A man got out, a tall man with long, faded-red hair and a red beard streaked with grey.

"Hi there," he said in an attractive Scots accent. "Can we help you?"

The passenger door opened. Out got a woman. My heart was like a sprinter's on the home stretch.

Mum.

Older, of course, than when I'd last seen her, slumped on her bed with a glass of wine. Grey haired. Plumper. Healthier looking. But most definitely Mum.

By the time I was sixteen, any feelings of love for her had been packed securely away. All I'd ever expected to feel towards Mum was disappointment. Disgust, when she was at her absolute worst. But now, for just a moment, my stupid mind conjured up a fantasy of Mum dropping her shopping bags to the ground, calling out to me.

"Sweetheart?"

Stepping over the mess of broken jars of jam and wine bottles to reach me as fast as she possibly could. Holding me tightly in her arms as if she never wanted to let me go. *"Lily! Oh, God, Lily! It's so good to see you!"*

Then I took in her expression, and stark reality obliterated the fantasy as effectively as napalm. The gaze connecting with mine across the Land Rover's bonnet couldn't have been further from the sentimental fantasy. No love, no transfiguration of joy. Just horror. Fear. Desperate entreaty.

As clearly as if she'd spoken the words out loud, her gaze said, *"Please. He doesn't know about you. Don't tell him."*

And I knew that she hadn't considered either me or Vi worth mentioning.

"Are you lost, lassie?" the man asked.

Behind him, Mum shook her head at me.

"I was a bit lost, yes," I said, stuffing down my hurt, lifting my chin. "But I don't think I am anymore. I think I know exactly where I'm going."

The man frowned, obviously confused. "Oh, is that right?"

"Yes, thanks. I'll be on my way."

Mum stepped forwards. "Would you care to take some eggs with you?" she said. "I was just about to collect them."

I hesitated for a moment. The offer was something, I supposed. Still, I wasn't sure whether or not I should accept. Give her the chance to explain. Make her excuses. Whatever else she wanted to do.

"They're very fresh," she said.

"Take the eggs, lassie," the man said with a smile. "Sharon's right, they are fresh. And they're her pride and joy too. You'll be making her day if you have some."

When he kissed Mum affectionately on the top of her head, it was impossible not to compare the gesture to the way Kevin, Ronnie, or any of her other boyfriends from my childhood had been with her. *"For fuck's sake, Sharon, there's nothing in the house to eat. Talk sense, for Christ's sake, you useless bitch."*

This was a good man. A man who treated Mum decently.

"I'll be inside unpacking the shopping," he said now, taking the shopping bags from Mum before turning back to me. "Would you care for a brew before you go, lassie?"

I shook my head. "That's very kind of you, but no. No thank you."

He nodded. "Bye, then."

And he went into the farmhouse, leaving us alone together.

"The henhouse is this way," Mum said, moving off, as if the whole *selling me some eggs* story was the truth.

"He doesn't know about me and Violet, does he?" I said as I followed her in front of the farmhouse towards a small wooden building.

She sighed, confirming it. "Nobody here does, no."

"Why not?"

She didn't answer. Didn't say anything else at all until we were inside the chicken house, in the relative darkness, surrounded by the smell and sound of the chickens. Then, she asked, "How did you manage to find me?"

"One of Violet's friends . . . ," I started to say, then trailed off. "Does it really matter?"

She shrugged, reaching for a scoop, dipping it into a bag of chicken feed to fill it. Footsteps sounded outside. Mum stiffened, putting up a warning hand.

A woman popped her head round the door. "Oh, you're collecting the eggs, Shaz. I was just about to do it myself."

She looked curiously in my direction.

"Yeah, all in hand, thanks, Belle. Just getting half a dozen for this lady here, then I'll be in. Callum's making tea."

"Great. I'm parched. Starving, too; I'll break open the biscuit tin."

Belle withdrew.

"Look," Mum said. "We can't talk here. Where are you staying? I'll come to you later today. We can talk properly then, okay?"

I hesitated for a moment. Then I nodded. "All right," I said, telling her the name of the inn at Catterline. After all, I'd come all this way. And I still didn't know the truth about that night.

"See you at seven p.m.," I said.

Then I turned and left the chicken shed.

Belle was still out in the yard, about to go into the farmhouse. "Oh," she said, "did you decide against the eggs?"

"Yes," I said, opening the car door. "I decided I didn't need any, after all."

Then I got in the car and drove away.

I went down to the beach with my paints as soon as I got back to Catterline. The rain had stopped now, but I would have painted down there even if it had been torrential. The end result didn't matter. What mattered was letting my feelings out. And, after my encounter with Mum, there were a lot of feelings to release.

Working in a frenzy, I swiped, splattered and dragged the brush across the surface of the canvas. As I painted, I kept seeing Mum leaning back against the pillows on her bed when I'd looked into her room ten minutes or so before I'd gone out the night of the fire; wine glass in hand, in danger of sloshing its contents onto the bedclothes. Inebriated. And yet, somehow, because I'd willed it to be the truth, I'd managed to convince myself she was in a fit state to take care of Violet. That everything would be okay if I went out.

No, I wouldn't think about that. I wouldn't think about anything but putting paint onto the canvas.

When I stood back afterwards to consider my work, the results were wild and messy. Tortured. But, exuberant too. The ocean at its very worst and best, relentless power on display. And I thought once again of Joan, painting here on this beach, a reserved person expressing her emotions through paint exactly as I'd just done. Joan, whose life had been cut tragically short by cancer at forty-two. Who'd only really found reciprocated love in the last year of her life.

I wasn't going to be like that. I wasn't going to let my past dictate my life any longer. I was going to face it—whatever that took—and then I was going to find a way to be passionately creative and productive without being isolated and tormented. To live, with all that living involved. I was going to do whatever it took to repair and nurture my relationships with the people I loved. Inga. Vi. Matt. And I was never, ever, going to merely exist any longer.

But for now, it was time to stop painting. To go back up to the inn to take a shower. Get myself a hot drink and warm up. Prepare myself for the meeting with Mum.

When she approached me at the table I'd chosen by the window, I saw that she'd made an effort with her appearance—a warm floral dress, knee-length boots, and a hand-knitted cardigan that picked out one of the colours of the dress. Hair tied back into a ponytail. Respectable. Unremarkable in the best way. No hint whatsoever that her clothes had once been unwashed, stained with spilt drink or worse still, with vomit if she'd been on a bender.

"Hello, Lily," she said, clutching her bag to her chest, clearly nervous.

"Hi," I said, indicating the chair opposite me. "I'll get us some drinks. What d'you want?"

"Apple juice, please. No alcohol for me these days."

I nodded without commenting and went to the bar to get the drinks. When I came back, she was looking at the menu, but she put it away again when I reached the table. Just as well. I very much doubted whether we'd be eating a meal together.

"So," she said, holding up her glass. "Cheers."

I picked up my glass to clink it against hers, thinking what a ridiculous gesture it was for such a strained, unnatural occasion, and saw her gaze narrow slightly at my fingers. Looking down at my hands, I saw there was still oil paint under my fingernails from my painting frenzy. And it occurred to me that Mum didn't even know I was an artist.

I took a sip of my wine and put the glass down on the table. But I didn't hide my dirty fingers from her disapproving gaze. She hadn't earned any explanations or consideration from me.

"I've been to Catterline a few times before," she said after a moment. "Joseph at the farm grew up here; he's full of tales about the artist painting the fishing nets on the beach. Joan something, she was called. Now, what was her other name?"

"Joan Eardley." I spoke the name reluctantly, unwilling to share Joan with her. My Joan.

"Yes, that's her. Joseph says he and the other kids used to go and talk to her when she was painting sometimes. She'd chat to them for a bit, then give them sweets to make them go away." She smiled. "He said, one time she'd gone off somewhere and left her painting on the easel—she was painting the row of cottages on the cliffs that day—and one of Joseph's friends picked up her paintbrush and painted in some smoke coming from one of the cottage chimneys. Can you imagine?"

Mum's face was animated as she spoke, almost as if she'd actually been there at the scene, witnessing the childish act of vandalism.

Almost as if we'd seen each other only last month, not what felt like a lifetime ago, when she abandoned me and Vi at our burning house.

"Still," she said. "I don't suppose she was cross, do you? It would only take a few sweeps of the paintbrush to reinstate the sky."

"Some things are easier to put right than others," I said, tired suddenly of superficial chit-chat. In other circumstances, we might have smiled together about her tale of Joseph and his friends vandalising Joan's painting. It might have led naturally to me talking about my own art. But the woman sitting in front of me hadn't even had the balls to admit to the people she lived with that she had two daughters, let alone that she'd abandoned them.

"What really happened that night, Mum?"

She looked down at the table. "That's what you've come for, is it? To ask me that? Not to get to know me or find out how I am?"

"What would be the point in getting to know you, even if I wanted to?" I asked bitterly. "When you've kept me and Vi a secret to everyone here. What did you tell your bloke you were doing tonight, anyway?"

She shrugged. "Meeting an old school friend who was visiting the area. Katie Meredith. He said it was a very pretty name and to pass on his compliments. I hated lying to him."

I laughed humourlessly. "And yet you've been lying to him ever since you came here. That's rich. Were me and Vi such a shameful secret?"

"Of course not." She pushed a stray strand of hair that hadn't caught into the ponytail back from her face. "Look, I ought never to have had children. I'm not mother material. No wonder, with the example my own parents set. They didn't give a shit about me, either of them. Either ignored me or screamed at me; nothing in between."

I shook my head. Didn't she realise she might have been talking about herself? The way she'd treated me and Vi?

"I got pregnant with you at sixteen, Lily. Far too young. I thought it might be my passport to freedom, but it wasn't. It was bleak. Lonely. You cried and cried, and I had no idea what to do to make you stop."

My friend was just the same, I could have said, because of course, her words made me immediately think of Inga. But I was too busy wondering whether she'd shut me in a room to cry for hours on end. Whether my deep-rooted fear of abandonment had started right back then.

Mum was still going on, saying something else about the fact that having a baby—me—so young had ruined her life, led her to drink—effectively blaming my existence for everything—but I'd had enough of it, so I cut in.

"Tell me," I said again. "Tell me what happened on the night of the fire."

She sloshed her apple juice around in its glass, avoiding my gaze. "I slipped out to meet a friend after you'd gone out. I didn't expect to be very long. But then she had a bottle of wine with her, so we had a drink. I was out longer than I meant to be." A haunted expression crossed her face. Good. She deserved to be haunted by the events of that night.

"Only when I got home, the house was an inferno." She looked up at me. "I couldn't believe it, Lily, I really couldn't."

"Why not?" I asked bitterly. "You'd left your eight-year-old daughter alone in a house with candles burning."

"They were tea lights, that's all. And I didn't know she was on her own. I thought you were home."

I felt sick. "I told you I was going out. I said goodbye to you."

"Well, I don't remember. Anyway, like I say, I couldn't believe it when I saw the house on fire. I was going to come and find you, make sure you were both okay, but then I saw you both—Violet held tight by a fireman, another fireman clutching you. And I thought . . . rightly or wrongly, *'They'd be better off without you, Sharon. You're a crap mother.'* So, I left."

I was back there, with smoke choking in my throat. Violet's screams ringing in my ears. "What did you feel, as you walked away and left us there, Mum?" I asked bitterly.

She shrugged. "I don't know, what you'd expect, I suppose. Panic. Shame. Fear that someone would spot me. It's a long time ago; I can't remember exactly." She took a sip of her apple juice, wincing at the taste, as if she wished it were something stronger. "But you needn't think I had an easy ride of it afterwards, Lily. I lived in squats. Hostels. On the street sometimes. I even had a brief spell in prison for breaking and entering. That's what finally helped me get free of the drink in the end, though. There was a counsellor in there. She helped me to turn my life around. I'll always be grateful to her."

It was what I'd wished for Vi, wasn't it? That she'd find a professional to help her. But I didn't want to find similarities between Mum and Vi, even though they were staring me in the face.

Suddenly I was exhausted; too exhausted to cling to my anger any longer. It was slipping away from me; I could feel it going. Leaving only a deep sadness in its wake.

"Did you never think of trying to find us?" I asked, without much hope.

Mum sighed. "Honestly? Even without the drink, I still thought you'd be better off without me. That the strain of looking after you both would set me off drinking again. I found the farm by accident after I'd hitchhiked up here to Scotland. They were very welcoming to me. Nonjudgemental. For the first time in . . . well, forever, I felt safe. Appreciated. So, I asked if I could stay with them for a while. I didn't mean to lie. Well, I didn't lie, really; I just didn't say anything about the two of you. I didn't expect to stay for that long, you see. Just long enough to get back on my feet. Only, somehow, it became my home, and by then, it was too late to tell them everything." She looked at me, frowning. "I don't suppose you've ever told a lie that's got out of control, so you wouldn't understand."

But I had, of course. I'd lied to Inga, to everybody, in exactly the same way about Mum. And that lie, when it had been exposed, had almost blown my friendship with Inga apart.

"You won't tell Callum about you and Violet, will you?" she said. "I couldn't bear to lose him. He's very important to me."

There was a sudden intensity in her gaze. This was the whole reason she'd come to meet me tonight. To exact this promise. Not to find out about me and Violet, about how our lives had been, since she'd left us so callously that night, but to make sure I wasn't a threat to her.

She'd been selfish and self-absorbed throughout my childhood, and she was still selfish and self-absorbed. She may not drink any longer, but her basic personality was exactly the same. She hadn't loved me and Vi then, and she didn't love us now.

And I didn't love her either.

I thought of little Noah suddenly, his gorgeous face as he smiled up at Inga. Demanding, yes. A lot of work, yes. But so brim-full of potential. Destined to fill his mother's life with joy and purpose.

What an utter waste to voluntarily give all that up.

"No," I said, feeling pity for the woman across the table from me. A woman who could only see as far as her own needs and desires. Poor Callum. He'd come across as a good man during our brief meeting. I hoped very much he wouldn't get hurt somewhere along the line.

"I won't tell him. You don't have to worry about that."

There wouldn't be any opportunity for me to tell Callum anything. Because I was never going to see Mum again, even if I returned to Catterline to paint every spring, summer, autumn, and winter for the rest of my life.

"What about your sister?"

Violet, I wanted to say. *Her name's Violet.*

"Violet's her own person; I can't tell her what to do. I'll make sure she's aware of the situation"—I would. Oh, I most definitely would. I'd tell her exactly what Mum was like. That she wasn't worth either of us ever thinking about her again—"but if Violet wants to come up here to meet you at some point, she will. If not now, then maybe in years to come."

A waitress stopped at our table. "Would you ladies care to order any food?" she asked.

I pushed my chair back, giving her a smile. "Not for me, thank you. I'll order something from my room."

Then I stretched my hand out towards Mum with the waitress still there, waiting to see if Mum wanted to order anything. "Goodbye, Mrs. Best. Have a safe journey home," I said.

Then I walked away.

My composure lasted until I was out of sight of the dining room. Then, halfway up the stairs, I had to pause to clutch at the handrail as reaction set in. I'd done it. I'd confronted Mum, and I'd found out the truth. I knew now that my depiction of her in *Phoenix* had been exactly right. And after my legs had stopped shaking and my breathing got back to normal, I'd be able to move on with my life. I would. I must. Because the woman I'd just left in the dining room wasn't worth spoiling my life for.

A text came through as I went into my room. Matt.

Thanks for your message and calls. Sorry not to get back before. I'm a bit churned up right now about everything. I hope you're okay? I'm back in the UK for Christmas. Talk then?

My heart swelled with hope. He couldn't hate me if he wanted to meet. Quickly, I typed a reply.

Sure, I'd like that. Let me know when you're back. Take care. X

Stupid to hesitate about adding the kiss. Stupid to put it in, delete it, then add it in again before I sent the message.

His reply came back.

Thanks, Lily. See you soon. X

It was something.

32

Before Matt returned to the UK, I heard from HMP Peterborough that Violet had added me to her visitor list, and I could now go to visit her. The hire car had gone back, so I caught a train to Peterborough and walked from the station. When I reached the prison, I lined up to show my ID, got searched, and was taken with the other visitors to my allocated seat in the visiting room.

As I sat and waited for Vi to appear, I did my best to tune out other people's conversations. It wasn't easy. To my left an anxious mother was trying desperately to communicate with her monosyllabic daughter. To my right a wife was staring miserably down at the table while her husband told her their son had learnt to walk. In front of me two sisters were both crying so hard they could barely speak a coherent word to each other.

What would Vi be like? We'd been so angry with each other the last time we'd met, and I had no idea how hard it had been in here for her these past few weeks.

Suddenly the door at the back of the room opened, and there she was, dressed in a drab grey tracksuit, her face turned towards the floor.

"Hi," I said when she took the seat opposite me, taking in the pallor of her skin and the dark circles beneath her eyes. "How are you, Vi?"

That got her looking up. "Absolutely peachy, thanks," she said sarcastically. "It's like a flipping spa break in here."

I sighed. "Don't be like that, Vi."

"Well, don't ask stupid questions then," she retorted. "What d'you think it's like in here?"

The old Vi. Bitter. Wanting to hurt me. I could have said she'd brought this on herself. That if she hadn't used and dealt drugs, she wouldn't be in here. But what would be the point? It would do nothing to bring us closer.

So instead, I told her about my visit to see Mum, because she had to know, didn't she? I described the farm, or what I'd seen of it. Told her about Callum. Mum's request that we keep our existence a secret from him. I said Mum was selfish. That she'd always been selfish. And that I didn't think it would be a good idea for Vi to ever try to see her, but that she must decide for herself whether or not she did.

Vi listened to all of it without interruption, picking at the skin at the side of her fingers. Then she said quietly, "It wasn't her fault."

I sighed. "I know. She told me about her difficult childhood. But even so . . ."

"No," Vi said. "I don't mean that." She broke off, looking suddenly emotional.

I leant towards her. "What is it, Vi? What d'you mean?"

Still that same quiet voice. "The fire. It wasn't her fault."

"Vi," I said, "Mum went out and left candles burning."

Vi shook her head. "Yes, but the candles would never have set the house ablaze if I hadn't picked one up and held it against the curtains." She looked at me, her eyes telling the truth. "I did it, Lil. I started the fire."

I gaped at her. "What?"

Tears suddenly started to spill down Vi's cheeks. She swiped them angrily away, starting to talk, the words flowing faster and faster as she went on. "I begged you not to go out that night, Lil. I begged you. But you wouldn't listen to me. You could see how upset I was, but you went out anyway. I didn't know Mum had gone out, but you know Mum; I'd have been alone even if she was there. You were walking up the hill to meet your friends. I could hardly see you anymore, you were so far away. But I knew you'd be able to see the lights in the house if you looked back. So I picked up one of the candles, and I . . . I didn't know curtains would go up so quickly. I thought you'd look back from the top of the hill. But . . . you didn't."

Oh, my God. Horrified, I saw myself, all those years ago, walking away from my sister. Hardening my heart against her pleas. *"Please don't go out, Lil! Please."* Doing my very best to focus on the pleasures of the evening ahead and not to give in to the impulse to look back and wave. Afraid that if I did, if I saw Vi's sad little face at the window, I'd be tempted to return home.

If I had looked back, Vi and I might never have been parted.

Now, in the bleak prison visitors' room, my sister's voice reached me as if from a long way away.

"I was so afraid, Lil. So fucking afraid."

I took Vi's hand across the table, heartbroken that she'd had to carry that guilt for all those years alone. How awful. How absolutely awful. No wonder she'd had to find a way to blot it out.

"It's all right, Vi," I said, as if she was eight years old all over again. "I promise you: everything will be all right."

"You don't hate me?" she asked, her eyes large and tear filled in her pale face.

"Of course not," I said. Because it was true. I could never hate my sister. Even after what she'd just told me. Even if she turned back to drugs as soon as she got out of this place. I would always love her. Unconditionally. The way our mother had never loved either of us.

You could love someone if you didn't agree with their choices, I knew that now. Loving someone unconditionally didn't mean you had to let them drag you down, or that you had to accept unkindness from them.

If necessary, you could love them from a distance. But you could still love them.

The way I loved Inga even though I'd always resented her for making me keep the abortion a secret. The way she loved me even though I'd meddled in her life. And, I hoped, the way Matt loved me even though I'd kept secrets from him for years.

33

Three days before Christmas, when the city was filled with sparkly people decked out in fake reindeer antlers like the ones Inga and I had been wearing the night we'd met Matt and Alex, Matt's text came through.

Home. Fancy meeting for a drink? X

I replied straightaway. Yes. Okay if I come to yours? X
I don't know if he was surprised by my suggestion or not, but his answer came back quickly.

Sure. Still a week until my tenants move in. 7pm? I'll cook something.

I might not be around to eat anything after the discussion I planned to have with him—a discussion that was going to severely test my newly founded resolution to be more open with the people I cared about. But I typed a cheery reply anyway.

Perfect! Thanks. See you then. X

Travelling to Matt's in a taxi, with the driver's Christmas music assaulting my ears, I thought how far I'd come since that long ago night with Matt and Alex when Inga and I had pretended to be fortune tellers.

Back then, this music would have made me want to scream, hide away, disappear into a dark hole of oblivion. Now, even though I would never like it, it was just a mild irritation. And this afternoon, at Inga's, I hadn't been able to help smiling at her over-the-top festive decorations. It was Inga's very first Christmas here, in her home, and to Noah's clear delight, she was making the absolute most of it. The little boy couldn't get enough of the lights, paper chains, and massive Christmas tree, smiling and kicking his little legs as he stared at them all. It was a joy to see, and I was supremely grateful that my friendship with Inga was back on track, and she'd invited me to join them on Christmas day.

Me, happy about an invitation to Christmas dinner.

The driver saw my smile in his rearview mirror. "Got some nice plans for this evening, have you, love?" he asked.

My smile grew shaky. "I hope so," I said. "It depends how things go."

I saw his eyebrows lift in the mirror. "Like that, is it?"

"Yes, it's like that."

"Good luck, love!" he called to me as he drove away, leaving me alone in front of Matt's house.

The outside light was on, illuminating my breath in the cold night air.

This was it. Very soon, I'd know what the future held for me. Without any crystal ball or tarot cards.

The door opened before I could press the doorbell.

"Lily, hi, come in."

Matt, wearing jeans and a Christmas jumper with a picture of a sheep on the front, the words above reading, *Fleece Navidad.*

As an icebreaker, it was pretty effective.

Despite my nerves, I couldn't help laughing at the pun on *Feliz*, the Spanish word for *happy*. "Good jumper."

Matt smiled down at himself. "Isn't it? Corny as hell, but 'tis the season to be corny. Here, let me take your coat."

"Thanks."

I shrugged it off. Gave it to him. He went to hang it up. I wished he'd just thrown it onto the back of a chair. It would have been much more relaxed.

"Can I get you a drink? There's all the usual Christmas suspects— advocaat, Baileys, sherry." He smiled. "My parents are here for Christmas Day, can you guess?"

Briefly, I pictured Mum, eating Christmas dinner with Callum, Diane, Tom, and all the others I hadn't met when I'd visited. I dismissed her from my mind.

"Or there's wine or beer, if you prefer?"

"A glass of white would be lovely, thank you."

"One glass of dry white coming up."

I followed him into the kitchen. It was filled with the fragrant smell of a casserole—warm, homely.

"Here." He handed me my wine. Picked up his own glass.

"Thank you. Cheers."

We clinked glasses, staying where we were in the warm, fragrant kitchen.

"I'm so sorry I haven't been in touch, Lily," he said, suddenly serious. "I should have been there for you after everything blew up at the gallery. How are you? How's Violet?"

But I didn't want to talk about Vi, not yet.

"I'm okay. You've been dealing with your own stuff. What Inga told you . . . it must have come as a shock."

He sighed. Put his wine glass down on the counter. "It did, I won't lie. That she kept it from me for all those years . . . It felt like a complete betrayal. To be honest, it made me question our entire relationship."

"I hated knowing and not being able to tell you," I said. "I'm so sorry."

He shook his head. "It did hurt at first, knowing you'd kept it from me. Then I realised that was daft. What else could you do? Inga should have told me."

"It was really hard," I said, wondering whether the strain of keeping Inga's secret had made it that much more difficult for me to keep quiet at other times—if that was partly why I'd dropped hints to Matt about her second pregnancy. Spoken to Harry about Noah the way I had.

"Inga should never have put you in that position," Matt said.

I shrugged. "She just needed a friend."

He sighed, picking up his wine glass again. "I suppose so. And she couldn't find a better one than you." He shook his head. "God, when I think of the night we met, me and Alex just back from our travels. Full of swagger. We grew up together, really, didn't we? Our friendship means the world to me. I'd hate to be without it." He smiled. "So you don't have to worry. This doesn't affect us at all. We're good."

My heart began to race. The stem of my wineglass was in danger of snapping, I was clutching it so tightly. This was it. What I'd come here for. The moment that might have me heading back out, the delicious-smelling casserole untasted. Could I do it? Yes, I had to.

"Aren't we?" he said, frowning at my obvious discomfort.

I looked up. Met his concerned gaze, everything I was about to say most probably already in my eyes. But I spoke the words, anyway. "That . . . isn't what I want."

Matt's frown deepened, his gaze sweeping over my face. "Lily, bloody hell. You don't mean that, do you? I was an idiot, I get that. I wasn't there when you needed me most. But—"

I interrupted quickly, hating to hear the hurt in his voice. "No, that's not what I meant. I meant . . . I don't want us to go back to the way things were." I took a deep breath. "Our friendship has always meant so much to me too. But . . . I don't want us to be friends any longer."

"You don't?"

"Well, yes," I stumbled, frustrated by my inability to express myself. "I do. Of course I do. But I . . . I don't want us to be only friends." I sighed. Closed my eyes. Opened them again. Met his gaze. "Isn't it obvious? I'm in love with you, Matt. I have been for a long time."

My chest was rising and falling as I snatched quick, panicked breaths. Every millisecond felt like an hour as I waited for him to respond. Then, magically, he began to smile.

"You can't imagine how long I've waited for you to say that," he said, and now my breath caught on a sob of relief, my cheeks suddenly wet.

"Oh, Lily," he said, "don't cry." And he reached out to pull me to him. But even though that was what I wanted most in the world, I moved away.

"I can't do anything behind Inga's back," I told him quickly. "She has to know. She has to be able to accept it."

Matt looked at me. Nodded. "Agreed."

Then he smiled again—a big, delighted smile that told me that, even if it took a while, everything was going to be all right.

34

Two Years Later

"Remember that time we drew a moustache on Grant's face while he was asleep?" Vi asked.

The prison visiting room was as stark as it had ever been, but it didn't impact me so much these days.

I frowned, thinking back. "Was it Grant? Or one of the others?"

Vi shrugged. "Not sure. It was fun, though, wasn't it?"

I laughed, remembering the shared triumph, both of us stifling our giggles as we backed away and made for our rooms. The consequences of our prank hadn't been fun, though. Not fun at all.

But these days I could shrug that kind of memory aside as quickly as it came. I wasn't traumatised by the past any longer, not since I'd talked it all out during my therapy sessions and moved on from it.

Vi was still talking about our troubled childhood to the prison counsellor, though, so even though I'd moved on from it, as far as I was concerned, she could talk about it all she liked.

"Did Matt drive you here today?" she asked.

I nodded. "Yes. We've got to get back quickly. Inga's baby's due any day. We're taking care of Noah while she's in hospital."

"Rather you than me."

"Noah's no trouble at all."

"Unlike me, when we were kids, then?"

Gradually, the old sarcasm and bitterness had left Vi's voice when she made these kinds of remarks. I'd like to hug the prison counsellor for that.

"You were all right most of the time," I said. "Except for when you were a pain in the arse."

"Once the big sister, always the big sister."

"Precisely. Speaking of which, have you made any plans for what you're going to do when you get out of here next month?"

The old Vi would probably have scowled and told me it was none of my business. The new Vi told me she was thinking about applying for an apprenticeship at a national park.

"The outdoor life, huh?" I said, thinking only very briefly about Mum and her prize-winning vegetables. "That sounds brilliant, Vi."

"Got your seal of approval, has it?"

"It has. Not that you need it. You're your own person, aren't you? You can do what you want."

She caught my eye. Smiled.

"Well," I said. "Within reason."

"How was she?" Matt asked when I joined him in the car.

I nodded, reaching over to kiss him. "She was good," I said. "Pretty positive."

"That's great," he said, and I smiled at him, noticing that his suntan was fading now that he was no longer travelling back and forth between the UK and Barcelona.

I was going to say something about liking his new pasty-white look, but my phone rang. Inga.

"Everything okay?"

"If you count being in utter agony being okay," she said with a groan. "How quickly can you get here? Harry's packing me a bag. This baby's coming early. We'll have to drop Noah off at Harry's mum's for you to collect him from there."

Beside me, Matt started the car.

"We'll be there before you know it," I said. "You can count on us."

"I bloody well hope so," she said.

I smiled. "See you soon, darling. Deep breaths. We're on our way."

Last time, with Noah, it had just been the two of us. Nowadays, Inga had a much bigger support network. We both did.

As Matt steered the car into traffic to head for home, Beryl's smiling face filled my mind. The words she'd written in her journal. *I'm so blessed.*

Me too, I thought. *Me too.*

Acknowledgements

Firstly, my thanks to you, my readers! It's such an honour that you've chosen to read my words.

As always, my heartfelt thanks to my agent, Carly Watters, for always having my best interests at the forefront of her mind.

To my editors, Alicia Clancy and Tiffany Yates Martin—thank you for "getting" this story, and for all you've done to help me to hone my early drafts into something I'm proud of. There was angst and denial along the way, and I appreciate your patience and gentle prodding. Carissa Bluestone and Nancy Holmes—thank you both so much for taking on the mantle of this novel so enthusiastically. It has been great to work with you. Thanks, too, to all the team at Lake Union, for your sterling efforts on my behalf. Also to Philip Pascuzzo for a fabulous book cover design.

To my writer friends, who are such a support, always ready to listen to my insecurities, to give me feedback, and to help me celebrate my achievements. I'll never take any of you for granted.

Thanks, too, to friends and family members who keep me afloat and are very much a part of everything I create. Love you all.

Book Club Questions

1. Choose three words to describe each of the four main characters in the book—Lily, Inga, Matt, and Alex.
2. Which of the four main characters did you find the most complex or intriguing and why?
3. Which of the four main characters did you like the most? Dislike the most? Why?
4. How did the secondary characters impact or influence the main characters and the story?
5. What would you say Lily's life goals are at the beginning of the book? How have they changed by the end of the book?
6. How would you describe the friendship between Lily and Inga? Between Matt and Alex? Between all four main characters? Did / how did these friendships evolve or change during the book?
7. Describe Lily's relationship with her sister, Violet.
8. Both Lily and Violet have been impacted by their rocky start in life. Do you think it affected both of them in the same way or differently? How does the past influence the decisions and actions they take?
9. To what extent do you think it's true that the book is about power struggles in relationships?
10. How did the author create conflict and tension in the

book? What was the main conflict or problem in the story and how was it resolved?

11. What were your favourite scenes in the book? Why?

12. Did you find any of the scenes shocking or surprising? If so, what shocked or surprised you about them?

13. How did the book make you feel? Which emotions did it evoke?

14. Did the book relate to anything in your own life?

15. Do you have any favourite passages or quotes from the book? If so, share which and why.

16. Do you like the book title? If yes, say why you think it works. If not, think of an alternative title.

17. If you were adapting this book for a movie, who would you cast in the main roles?

18. If you could ask the author one question about this book, what would it be?

About the Author

Photo © 2020 Graham James

Kitty Johnson is the author of *Prickly Company* and *Five Winters*. She has an MA in creative writing from the University of East Anglia and teaches occasional creative writing classes. A nature lover and artist, Kitty enjoys walking in woodland and on the coast with her dog and makes collages and paintings from the landscape. She loves a challenge and once performed stand-up comedy as research for a book—an experience she found very scary but hugely empowering. Kitty lives in Norwich, Norfolk, in the UK with her partner and teenage son. For more information, visit www.kittyjohnsonbooks.com.

Sign up for Kitty's newsletter via her website:
Website: www.kittyjohnsonbooks.com
Instagram: @kittyjohnsonbooks
Facebook: Kitty Johnson Books
Kitty is happy to attend online book clubs.

If you've enjoyed *Closest Kept*, please consider leaving a review!